M000077710

Au79

Other titles by Award-Winning Author
Anita Dickason

SENTINELS of the NIGHT

2017 Literary Titan Gold Book Award

Messengers of death, they ride the night wind and hear the cries of the dead. Can they stop a serial killer? FBI Tracker Cat Morgan is about to find out.

"Will have serial killer mystery fans and paranormal urban fantasy junkies alike getting excited over a new series which has something for just about everyone. A compelling debut novel." Readers' Favorite Review

"A riveting high stake read—Sentinels of the Night proves an edgy and notable debut for Dickason with the promise of more to come." Book Viral Review

GOING GONE!

2017 Book Viral Millennium Book Award/Longlisted Author
2017 Literary Titan Gold Book Award

A deadly game of political destruction that extends to the White House has drug cartels and terrorist cells lined up to cash in.

"The plot is expertly handled, and the writing is vivid and energetic with events unfolding in tightly focused chapters that take us to the crux of Dickason's narrative and here again, she excels at ratcheting up the tension and developing well-nuanced characters." Book Viral Review

"The shift in points of view is brilliant. "*Going Gone!* is a page-turner, a story with well-developed literary elements, but the suspense was biting -- all the time." Readers' Favorite Review

www.anitadickason.com

Au79

A Tracker Novel

Anita Dickason

This is a work of fiction. Names, characters, places, and incidents either are the product of the author's imagination or are used fictitiously, and any resemblance to actual persons living or dead, events, or locales is entirely coincidental.

Copyright © 2018 Anita Dickason

All rights reserved. No part of this book or cover may be used or reproduced, scanned, or distributed in any printed or electronic form without the written permission of the author except in the case of brief quotations in critical articles and reviews.

Publisher: Mystic Circle Books
Cover Design: Mystic Circle Books & Designs, LLC
Cover image courtesy of Pixabay

Editors
Susan Barton
Cheryl Pochert
Pat Pratt

ISBN:
978-0-9968385-6-6 (paperback)
978-0-9968385-7-3 (hardback)
978-0-9968385-8-0 (eBook)

Library of Congress Control Number: 2018904000

Acknowledgements

To my daughters,
Julie and Chris
Thank you for listening to the endless conversations
and all your helpful suggestions.
Julie, your military background was invaluable.
Chris, thank you for finding my plot.

To my sister,
Cheryl
What a joy it was to have your help in turning the
manuscript into a finished novel.

To my friend,
Pat
It is so nice having someone with your
ability in my corner.

List of Characters

Adrian Dillard, FBI Tracker
Andy Rodriguez, Laredo PD
Arthur Larkin, President--USA
Bill Goddard, FBI—Laredo
Bing Morris, Bar Owner
Blake Kenner, FBI Tracker
Cam Bardwell, Informant
Cat Morgan, FBI Tracker
Dale Kennedy, M.E.
David Parker, HSBC Bank
Donnie Martin, Corpse
Eddie Owens, Reporter
Frank Littleton, Federal Reserve
Gabriel Pearsall, Laredo PD
Jack Davis, Austin FBI
Jimmy Bishop, Editor
Joe Warden, Border Guards
Jonah Grigsby, Desert Rats
Karl Chambers, Laredo ATF
Kevin Hunter, FBI Tracker
Lance Brewster, TEDAC agent
Larry Henning, Texas Gold Depository
Linda Spencer, Laredo FBI
Matt Wilson, Laredo ATF
Nicki Allison, FBI Tracker
Norman Reynolds, Border Guards
Paul Daykin, FBI Director
Randy Atkins, Laredo ATF
Ryan Barr, FBI Tracker
Scott Fleming, FBI Tracker
Skip Thornton, Laredo PD
Stan Meyers, Border Guards
Stuart Dyson, Laredo ATF
Ted Phillips, Dallas PD Fusion Center
Tim Grimes, Laredo FBI
Todd Bracken, Texas Gold Depository
Tracy Harlowe—Laredo PD
Vance Whitaker, Homeland Security
Will Cooper, Austin FBI

One

He hated undercover assignments. Most could be defined with one word—sleazy. Despite its ominous purpose, this one wasn't any different. The bar stank. Smoke from the grills hung in the air, adding another layer of grime to the windows filled with flashing beer signs. Grease and dirt, and probably a good bit of blood mixed in, stained the wood floor. A rank odor of sweat rose from the bikers that edged the bar and grouped at the tables. Their attention was riveted on the action that flashed across the large TV screens mounted on the walls. An occasional cheer would resound when a touchdown was scored.

FBI Tracker Adrian Dillard leaned back in his chair, his long legs outstretched under a table tucked in a dark corner of the room. One arm rested on the scarred wood near a long-necked beer bottle. The other was on his leg within easy reach of the gun concealed by a grungy leather jacket.

He took a sip. His gaze wandered around the room, then back to the TV screen. While outwardly relaxed, his every instinct was alert. His neck tingled with a familiar sense of danger. Despite the rough stubble of whiskers and hair that brushed his collar, several of the bruisers in the place had already cast suspicious looks his way.

Would the informant show? He hoped the promise of the hundred-dollar bills in his pocket would be enough. An ATF agent, Stuart Dyson, was missing, and this might be his only shot at finding his whereabouts, or to learn if the agent was alive.

He glanced at the wall clock. Damn! The man should have been here by now. A whisper echoed in the tiny receiver in his ear. "Biker just pulled into the parking lot. He's wearing a red bandana. May be our guy."

Fellow Tracker Cat Morgan had the entrance covered from her position in a vehicle parked across the street. As he watched the door, Adrian shifted in his chair. His fingers inched closer to the gun.

When it opened, a burly man dressed in a black leather vest, t-shirt, jeans, and black motorcycle boots strode toward the bar. Tattoos covered his arms. A scraggly beard hung down his chest, and mousy-brown hair was tied in a ponytail. Wrapped around his neck was the red bandana.

With one foot propped on the rail, he leaned on the bar, and his eyes skimmed the tables until he spotted Adrian in the corner. His glance lingered on the black ball cap with the red and orange entwined circles before he turned to greet the bartender.

Adrian lifted the bottle to cover his lips, and whispered, "This is our man. He recognized my cap." When Adrian set up the meet, the recognition signals were the cap and bandana.

Cat said, "I got a picture of his face. I'm sending it to Nicki."

Adrian knew if anyone could do a fast turnaround on identifying the man, it was the unit's research guru, Nicki Allison.

The biker watched the TV while he waited for the bartender to hand him a beer, then crossed the room to Adrian's table. He turned a chair, straddled it, and laid his arms on top of the wooden back. After another quick look at Adrian's battered ball cap, he asked, "You the one looking for information?"

"Yeah."

"Where's the woman?"

After a sardonic flick of his eyes around the room, Adrian said, "I decided the atmosphere was unhealthy." Cat's snort echoed in his ear.

Au79

She was listening to the conversation through his open mic.

The biker's lips peeled back in a leer. "Too bad. I heard she was a real looker. You got the money? If you don't, I'm not saying anything."

"Tell me what I want to know, and you'll get it. Where's Dyson?"

"Dead." He grinned and took a swallow of beer.

Adrian's expression didn't change, though a sudden jab of anguish coiled in his gut. He pushed aside his bottle and leaned forward. "How do you know?"

"Ain't you a cool one? I just tell you the man's dead, and you don't even blink."

His gaze relentless, Adrian repeated the question.

The man answered, "I hear things. That's the scuttlebutt."

"Who killed him?"

The biker's eyes dropped to the bottle in his hand. "I don't know." He took another deep swig.

"Where's his body?"

"Can't tell you that either."

"So far, you haven't told me much. Why was he killed?"

With a shrug of his shoulders, the man said, "Word is that he was sticking his nose where it didn't belong."

"What was he investigating?"

The biker motioned with the bottle, pointing it at Adrian. "That's gonna cost you a lot more cash."

"How much?"

"Twenty-five grand."

"I'll need to set up another meeting. For that kind of money, I want to know who killed him, where's the body, and why he was killed. Is that clear?"

"You know where to leave a message when you get the dough. But I want my thousand bucks now. If you're not willing to fork it over, don't bother with another meet."

"Not here. Outside." Before Adrian pushed back his chair, he paused

3

to scan the room. Everyone, even the bartender, was watching the game. He stood and followed the biker out the door.

The man stepped to his bike, turned and held out his hand.

Adrian stopped in front of him and pulled the envelope from his jacket pocket. "Are you sure he's dead?"

When the man grabbed the envelope, Adrian's fingers brushed his hand.

"I said he was dead, and it's what I meant." He flipped through the bills before stuffing them in his pocket. Crumpling the envelope, he tossed it at Adrian's feet. Astraddle his bike, he sneered and revved the engine. With a roar, he pulled out of the parking lot.

From down the street a truck accelerated and passed the motorcycle. A shot rang out. The bike tilted and spun. The biker's body catapulted over the handlebars, struck the pavement, and rolled several times. With a squeal of tires, the truck skidded around a corner and was gone.

Adrian sprinted toward the twisted body. *Son of a bitch! There goes our chance to find Dyson.* He knew the man lied when he said the agent was dead.

Disgusted, he stared down. There was no point in checking for a pulse. The shattered face and head was unrecognizable, and his blood smeared the roadway. At the sound of footsteps, he glanced over his shoulder. Cat raced toward him.

"I called nine-one-one." She skidded to a stop alongside Adrian. "Hells bells, there went our lead."

The roar of engines echoed in the night air. Their heads swiveled to watch the exodus of bikers from the bar as they hauled ass in the opposite direction.

"Guess they didn't want to talk to the cops," Cat quipped. She stepped to the other side of the body. Bent over, her hand patted the pockets that weren't drenched in blood. "Did you get the license plate number?"

"No, too dark." His attention shifted to the police cars that screeched to a halt behind them. Flashing red lights and the glare of headlights lit up the street. He pulled out his badge case and held it up as an officer exited and ran toward him.

A controlled mayhem of people and cars soon filled the street. The medical examiner's van replaced the ambulance that didn't stick around once the medics confirmed the man was dead.

A woman, attired in plain clothes, stepped out of an unmarked car. She stopped to speak with one of the uniformed officers, then turned to stare at the federal agents standing on the sidewalk before striding toward them.

Tall, with a lanky build, her short dark hair curled around a thin face with deep-set eyes. With a look of suspicion, she held out her hand. "Homicide Detective Tracy Harlowe. My patrol officer says you are feds—out-of-town feds. What are you doing here?"

Adrian shook her hand. "FBI Tracker Adrian Dillard." He nodded toward Cat and introduced her. "We've been assigned to the investigation of the missing ATF agent."

"Stuart Dyson. I know him. So, who's the dead guy?"

"Someone we thought had information on Dyson's whereabouts." Adrian added the details of the shooting and motioned toward the body. "There's a thousand dollars in his pocket that I paid him."

"Hefty payment. What'd it buy you?"

Adrian hesitated as he assessed what he should say. "Not as much as I wanted. He claimed Dyson's dead."

In the glare of the harsh lights, her face paled, and lips tightened before she asked, "That's all you got?"

"He wanted more money before he'd say anything else."

"Do you know who he is?"

"No. I'd appreciate a call when you identify him." He handed her a business card. "Is there anything else you need from us?"

She looked over her shoulder at the body. "I guess not. Once I process the scene, I'll get the money back to you."

Adrian nodded, and they headed to their car. It was still parked in the lot across from the bar.

As Cat pulled onto the street, she said, "Did you notice her reaction when you said Dyson was dead?"

"Yes. I wondered about it myself." His phone rang. "It's Nicki." He tapped the speakerphone as he answered.

A chirpy voice said, "I identified the picture you sent. Your informant is Cam Bardwell. He has several priors for assault and drug possession. Did you learn anything about the agent?"

"He said Dyson is dead." Adrian relayed the details of the shooting.

"Damn!" Nicki exclaimed.

"Nicki, I'm not certain Dyson is dead. I think Bardwell lied."

Cat shot a questioning glance at him.

He shrugged, and then added, "Something about his body language didn't set right. Did you get a home address?"

Nicki rattled off the location.

He jotted it down. "See if you can find any associates. I'm not sure where we go from here, but we'll get back to you."

After he disconnected, Cat asked, "Is that why you asked Bardwell a second time if Dyson was dead?"

Adrian decided to stay with his original explanation. No point in muddying the waters any further with the real reason he knew the man lied. "Yes. Let's head to his house." He tapped Bardwell's address into the GPS system, then settled back into the seat. The events of the last few days spun through his thoughts.

****

Word had already spread through the federal agencies about the extraordinary ability of the new unit. The Trackers had gained a formidable reputation from an investigation of a serial killer, and a kidnapping case that involved children of influential politicians.

When the local investigation of Dyson's disappearance stalled, FBI Director Paul Daykin assigned the case to the Tracker Unit. Two hours later, he and Cat were on a plane headed to Laredo.

Despite the late hour when they landed at the airport, they were met by Dyson's supervisor, Karl Chambers. On the way to the ATF office, he filled them in on the details. "Stuart had asked for a few days off. He said he had personal business to take care of. There didn't seem to be anything out of the ordinary until a Laredo patrol officer found his car at an abandoned warehouse. Nothing indicated foul play, other than his laptop was missing. We've tried tracing his phone, but it's been turned off."

"What cases was he working?" Adrian asked.

"The latest was a theft of explosives from a local drilling company. Thieves used a stolen truck to ram a wall of the building where the explosives were stored. Once inside, they had easy access to whatever they wanted. The explosives were loaded into a second vehicle. By the time the cops reacted to the alarm, all that was left was the stolen truck."

"Do you think his disappearance is linked to this case?" Cat had asked, leaning forward to look at him from the backseat.

He tossed a quick glance over his shoulder at her. "It was our first supposition, but nothing's turned up in his notes. So far, there haven't been any leads on who was behind the theft, or what happened to the explosives. Since there hasn't been any chatter on the streets, we figured it's already in Mexico."

"What about his house, anything there?" Adrian asked.

"No. We searched it. Even his fiancée couldn't find anything missing or out of place."

When Cat asked about Dyson's office computer, she struck a nerve.

Karl's tone became abrupt and dismissive. "My agents searched his computer files. There was nothing suspicious. I've already set up an access link for your boss. You can look for yourself if you think it's necessary."

Despite the man's defensive attitude, Cat grinned. "Nicki Allison is our computer expert. Scott will have passed the link to her. If there's anything to be found, she'll be the one to do it."

Attempting to appease the irate supervisor, Adrian rephrased his next comment. "Even though you've already searched, I'd still like to look at his house. If nothing else, it'll let us get a feel for the agent."

Karl had given him a distinct what-the-hell look as he parked in front of the ATF building. "If you think it'll help, his fiancée gave me a key."

Inside, Karl directed them to a conference room before heading to his office. Seated at one end of the large table, an older man, middle to late fifties if the grey hair was any indicator, typed on a laptop. When they entered, he closed the cover and stood.

"You must be the Trackers. I'm Supervisory Special Agent Bill Goddard in charge of the Laredo FBI office."

Adrian knew Paul Daykin had contacted Goddard to inform him the Trackers would be taking over the case. From the disgruntled look on the man's face, it was obvious he resented their presence.

Cat stepped forward to shake his hand as she introduced herself and Adrian.

"My office is at your disposal, along with any assistance I, or my two agents, can provide." He motioned with his hand toward the table. "Car keys. One set is for the SUV parked in front, and the second is to a pickup truck parked in the garage next to my office." Goddard picked up his laptop, nodded to the two agents, and walked out the door.

Cat said, "He's definitely pissed. Between him and Karl, it's not an auspicious start to our investigation."

Adrian grunted and turned his attention to the table. Spread across the surface were the contents of Dyson's vehicle along with a stack of file folders. Most of the items, including pieces of trash, were in transparent plastic bags. He flipped through the folders. "These are the reports on the investigation."

Cat examined the bags. After rifling through them, she said, "Nothing here that seems suspicious."

Before they left the ATF office, Karl gave them the key to Dyson's house. When they searched the place, Adrian found a blank notepad lying under several magazines on the coffee table. When he tilted it toward the light, faint indentations were visible.

"I found something," he hollered. When Cat appeared in the living room doorway, he held up the pad. "Did you come across a pencil in your search?"

"I've got one in my bag." Cat picked up the backpack she'd dropped by the front door and pulled one from the side pocket.

With light strokes, he brushed the page, and read, "Bing's Watering Hole. There's a number—eleven. I bet that's the time."

The place was a local hangout for the bikers who roamed this part of Texas. Adrian devised a plan to go in undercover. He and Cat would pose as family members. The cover story was that Dyson had mentioned the meeting at the bar. They'd even printed up a few flyers to add authenticity to their story. He and Cat headed to the bar. After a hefty bribe, the bartender agreed to pass on a phone number to a man who might know something.

Now, the informant was dead, and they were back to square one.

****

Cat's voice broke into his thoughts. "Hey, did you fall asleep over there?"

Adrian straightened in the seat. "Nope, filtering what happened since we arrived."

With a smug tone, she said, "Well, I got something."

"What?"

"Bardwell's cell phone."

He looked at her in amazement. "How'd you get it?"

"I found it when I checked his pockets. You'd turned away to meet the officers. I decided to eliminate the red tape and grabbed it." Cat reached for the phone in her pocket and passed it to Adrian.

"Considering how his body bounced and rolled, I'm surprised it's not in pieces." He tapped the screen, and it lit up. "Hmm ... there are several numbers on here. I'll send them to Nicki."

After a quick glance at the GPS screen, she pulled to the side of the street. "Bardwell's house is the one on the right, and someone got here ahead of us. His front door is busted open."

They fanned out, guns drawn as they approached the house. Adrian was first through the doorway. He quickly scanned the living room before moving down a hall. Cat headed toward the kitchen. Once they determined the house was empty, they met back in the living room. Chairs and a sofa had been tipped over. The contents of drawers from the end tables were strewn across the floor, along with pictures that had been hanging on the wall.

Adrian stepped around the end of the overturned couch. "The entire house has been trashed."

"What a mess," Cat said. "They even dumped a container of flour in the kitchen. I wonder if they found what they were looking for?"

"Maybe not. Let's see what we can find. I'll start here, and you check the bedrooms."

As Cat walked out, he squatted and began to sort through the items on the floor.

A voice rang out. "Police! Hands in the air."

With a sigh of resignation, Adrian stood. His arms stretched over his head, he turned and stared at Detective Harlowe and a gun pointed at his chest.

Au79

Two

Washington D.C.

Scott Fleming, head of the Tracker Unit, strode through their new office. The last of the furniture had arrived the day before, and his agents were still getting settled. Though at the moment, that was only Nicki, his computer guru, Ryan Barr, the unit's profiler, and Blake Kenner. Adrian and Cat had been sent to Laredo. Kevin Hunter, the newest member of the team, was attending a forensics course at the FBI academy in Quantico.

Scott walked into Nicki's office and surveyed the extensive computer system. Her work area was larger than his. Computer tables with multiple monitors formed a half-circle, and Nicki sat in the center, much like a spider in the middle of its web.

Even though his unit was new, he'd quickly learned her computer skills were extraordinary. It was as if her brain was hard-wired to the system. Nicki had an uncanny ability to strategize the results she mined from the internet. For the last several weeks, she had concentrated on bringing their new software program, TRACE, online.

The program was intended to find elements of unsolved crimes that would link to a common criminal. When Scott first designed the software, the purpose was to identify peripatetic serial killers (PTC) that eluded detection. A PTC moved from location to location, and with no link between the killer and victim, their kills were never connected.

Once Nicki came on board as a Tracker, she began the process of setting up portals for local law enforcement agencies and connecting TRACE to the National and Regional Fusion Center network. The portals would be used to input details of unsolved cases into TRACE. The network would provide access to intelligence data that related to criminal and terrorist activity. Her enhancements to the algorithms used to research the internet would connect details that standard search perimeters missed.

"How's the new program working?" Scott asked.

Nicki spun her chair to face him, and grinned. "I'm loving it. I've been running tests, and it's amazing what's popped up."

"Anything more from Adrian or Cat?"

"Not since I updated them on Bardwell. It's interesting that Adrian doesn't believe the agent is dead. I hope he's right."

"I'm sure he is. Adrian has a way of knowing when someone lies to him."

Her phone beeped. "Text from Adrian. Hmm … phone numbers from Bardwell's phone. This should prove interesting." She rolled the chair back in front of her keyboard.

Scott grinned at her unending enthusiasm and left her to her devices.

Texas

"Son of a bitch! What the hell are you doing here?" Tracy Harlowe holstered her gun. "If I remember correctly, you said you didn't know your informant's name."

Cat appeared in the doorway.

Disgusted, she crossed her arms as she glared at Cat, then at Adrian. "Great, just great. I can't believe I fell for that '*I don't know*' line."

"If you'll calm down a minute, I'll be happy to explain," Adrian said.

"Why should I calm down? I've got a shooter running loose, a dead man, and federal agents that lied. Now you're tampering with my crime scene."

"We didn't lie. When you asked, we didn't know the identity of the victim. Cat sent a picture of him to our D.C. office. That's how we got his name and address. When we got here, the door was busted open, and the place was trashed."

"I suppose you think that's going to make me feel better. Well, it doesn't. You didn't even bother to call nine-one-one and report the burglary. I'd better not find your fingerprints splattered all over the place," Tracy growled, and pulled out her cell phone.

"Just wanted to set the record straight," Adrian said.

Anger glinted in her eyes as she requested a crime scene unit. She slid the phone back into her pocket. "Since you searched, did you find anything?"

"Not yet, but we just started. I don't suppose you have any extra rubber gloves with you?"

With a grunt of irritation, she stomped out of the room. Mutters about idiot agents echoed behind her. She was still mumbling when she walked back in and tossed a box of gloves on the coffee table. "Help yourself." She headed down the hallway to the bedrooms.

Cat grinned at Adrian, then picked up a pair and followed the detective.

When Adrian finished with the living room, he headed outside to a small detached garage at the back of the driveway. The side door had been kicked open. Inside, he quickly glanced around the small building. The structure was designed to hold a single car. Oil stained the concrete, probably from Bardwell's motorcycle. Several boxes had been upended and the contents scattered across the floor. It was the workbench against the back wall that grabbed his attention. Strewn across the top were tools and electrical equipment. They weren't intended for motorcycle repair.

Tracy stepped beside him and stared at the counter. "Good lord!

Is this what I think it is?"

"Yep. He was working on something other than his motorcycle engine." He snapped a few pictures with his phone and sent them to Nicki along with a brief note of explanation. Then he called Karl Chambers and told him what they had found.

Cat walked in and whistled when she spotted what lay on the counter. "That's not good." She tossed a quick glance at Tracy, and added, "Your crime scene unit just arrived."

"I'll be in the house."

Cat watched the detective as she walked out the door. Once Tracy was out of earshot, she said, "That woman has a lot of hostility. I wonder why?"

"Maybe she just doesn't like federal agents," Adrian responded.

Shrugging her shoulders, she eyed the bench. "Our biker boy was into some serious stuff. This looks like components for detonators."

"My thoughts exactly. I called Karl, and he's sending a team. Let's wait outside."

When a black van stopped in front of the house, Adrian was surprised to see Karl exit the vehicle. When he spotted Adrian and Cat, he strode toward them. His voice loud and abrasive, he demanded to know what happened.

Irritated, Adrian took a second. Getting riled wouldn't help. "This is the informant's house. His name was Cam Bardwell, and someone shot him outside the bar."

After hearing the details, Karl muttered, "I knew I should have had my agents in place."

"It wouldn't have made a difference. I suspect someone found out Bardwell agreed to meet me and took steps to silence him. He said Dyson was dead." Adrian wanted to add his doubts, but without solid evidence, it would open him up to questions he wasn't prepared to answer.

The man's jaw tightened. "Not what I wanted to hear." At the sound of footsteps, Karl turned. "What the devil are you doing here?"

Tracy glared at him. "My job, working a case."

"You were ordered to stay away from the investigation."

"I got a call about a shooting. How was I supposed to know it was connected to Stuart's disappearance? Now get off my back."

Adrian stared at the two, their faces bristled with hostility. "Would someone explain?"

Karl flicked a glance at him before saying, "This is Stuart's fiancée, and she's been ordered off the case."

Her voice vibrated with anger as she snapped back. "It's not going to happen. Whether or not it involves Stuart, I still have a homicide to investigate."

Jesus, and I told her he's dead, Adrian thought.

As if she read his mind, she scowled at him. "I don't believe he's dead."

"You know what will happen when your Captain finds out," Karl told her.

"This conversation is over!" She turned, her body rigid as she marched back to the house.

"Pig-headed woman," Karl exclaimed. "She may be an exceptional investigator, but she's going to get fired if she doesn't stay out of the investigation."

"In her defense, she did respond to a shooting. She didn't know until she talked to us."

"That's all well and good, but once she found out, she should have turned the case over to another detective." He followed Adrian and Cat into the garage. After perusing what was scattered on the table and floor, he looked at Adrian, and said, "You're right. He was building detonators wired to cell phones."

Two officers appeared in the doorway. Chains with gold badges hanging from their necks identified them as ATF.

Karl motioned to his men. "Matt Wilson and Randy Atkins. These are Agents Adrian Dillard and Cat Morgan," then added, "Check everything inside this building. Let's get out of their way. Did you get anything else from Bardwell?" he asked as they walked out.

Adrian said, "We have his cell phone, and I sent a list of numbers to Nicki."

"I'd appreciate it if you let me know what she finds," Karl said.

An angry voice erupted behind him. "You have Bardwell's phone?"

Hell, the woman moved like a cat. You didn't know she was there until she was ready to rake you with her claws. Turning, Adrian stared at the detective's outraged face. "Yes, I've got it."

"I really should cuff you and haul your ass to jail for interfering with an investigation," she snarled.

Karl said, "Tracy, this is a federal case. I've told you before that you need to back off."

"I have another suggestion." Cat held out her hand. "Let's start over. I'm Agent Cat Morgan. I'm sorry to hear about your fiancée, but we'd appreciate any help you can provide."

A look of suspicion crossed Harlowe's face as she glanced at the three individuals standing in front of her. With a sigh of frustration, she held out her hand. "I'll do whatever I can. Now, what did you find on his phone?"

Karl groaned. "I should have added pushy to my description."

"Hey, I can relate to pushy." Cat laughed and shook hands with the detective.

"Okay, what did you find?" Harlowe asked again.

Adrian pulled the phone from his pocket and handed it to her. "It's a burner. Nicki has the numbers and is running them."

She quickly scrolled through them. "Hmm ... who's Nicki, and what the hell is a Tracker?"

Another chuckle erupted from Cat. "It's a new unit set up a few months ago. Nicki's our resident research guru."

Karl added, "The Trackers were responsible for the rescue of the kidnapped children of several politicians a few weeks back."

Au 79

As her gaze darted between the two agents, Tracy whistled in astonishment, then said, "You were responsible for that operation? Wow. I'm friends with several officers in the El Paso PD. What I heard is the raid was a hell of an effort. Nothing but high praise."

Adrian nodded in acknowledgement, then wanting to change the subject, asked, "What did you find in the house?"

"Fingerprints, and the computer is missing. I wonder if they found whatever they were looking for. It wasn't your typical burglary. They didn't even mess with two TVs and other valuables. What about the garage?"

Karl answered, "My agents are inside. I'll know more once they're done. There are materials to assemble detonators as well as pieces of cell phones, but I didn't see a device."

A worried look crossed Tracy's face. "I don't like the sound of that. Stuart was investigating a theft of explosives."

"Tracy," Cat said, "If your techs are done, I'd like to go back through the house."

The detective stiffened. "They're packing up now. Do you think we missed something?"

"Hmm ... no, just want to look around." *God, the woman was as prickly as a cactus.*

Matt exited the garage and strode toward his boss. "We didn't find any explosive residue. Based on bits and pieces of circuit boards and wiring, I'd estimate at least ten timing devices were assembled and are missing. We need boxes to get this stuff back to the lab." He headed toward the ATF van.

Karl said, "I'll help them. Keep me posted."

"I need to get out of here as well," Tracy said. "As it is, I won't be done with the reports for several hours."

Adrian said, "I want to talk to you about Stuart."

"How about breakfast?"

"Name the time."

"Does six work for you?"

Adrian glanced at Cat who shrugged. He turned back to Tracy. "It'll have to."

"Red's Diner is near my office. I'll meet you there."

Once everyone left, Adrian followed Cat back into the house. "What are we looking for?"

"I'm not sure. Maybe nothing, but something tells me the burglars didn't find anything. Otherwise, why search the entire house?" She moved slowly around the living room, examining walls and baseboards. Then the kitchen, giving it the same scrutiny.

In one of the spare bedrooms Cat finally spotted something. The baseboard on the wall was discolored. She dropped to her knees and examined the section of wood, then ran her hand over it. "It has an oily feel." She tugged on the wood. A foot-long piece detached from the wall exposing a hole.

Lying flat, Cat looked inside. "There's something here." She pulled on the extra set of gloves she'd tucked into her pocket. Grasping the object, she slid it out.

Adrian whistled in surprise as he stared at a metal box. "What made you think of a hiding place like this?"

A mischievous grin crossed her face. "When my sister and I were kids, we had one just like it. It was our big secret. It wasn't until years later that we found out Mom knew about it." Her voice turned serious. "I bet this is the reason someone tossed the house." She stood and placed the box on the bed. "Well, hell. It's locked."

"I wonder if they found any keys on Bardwell's body?" Adrian asked.

"It would help to have the key, but I've got a tool in my backpack. Be right back."

Adrian muttered to himself. "Of course, she has a tool. What doesn't the woman carry in that damn bag?"

When she returned, she handed Adrian a bobby pin. He looked at her in disbelief. "This is what you call a tool?"

Grabbing the pin, she snorted. "Jeez, getting pretty technical here." She twisted one end, then shoved it into the lock, and gently rocked it until she heard a click. Opening the lid, she shot a smug look at Adrian. "Guess you can call it a tool when it does the job."

"Where'd you learn that trick?"

"Hmm ... here and there," she said as they gazed at the contents. "What did the ATF agent say, maybe ten detonators?"

"Uh-huh," he said, and snapped several pictures of the two devices with his phone.

"So, where's the rest of them?"

"The answer to that scares the hell out of me," Adrian said.

Three

Washington D.C.

His briefcase in one hand, Scott reached for the light switch. When the phone vibrated against his chest, followed by chimes, he turned and headed back to his office. At the sight of Adrian's icon, a sinking sensation settled in his gut. Dropping the briefcase on the desk, he answered.

Adrian said, "Scott, we've got a major development."

After listening to Adrian's explanation, Scott asked, "How certain are you about the detonators."

"I'm certain. Whoever killed Bardwell didn't waste any time getting to his house to grab the devices. When they didn't find them all, they searched the house. When you add a missing agent, theft of explosives, and a dead informant who claimed Dyson was killed because of his investigation—one alone is cause for concern, but together; I'd say we've got a problem."

Scott asked, "How soon can you send me a report?"

"It'll be to you within the hour. I'm sending pictures of the detonators."

Disconnecting, he dropped into his chair and tilted back. With his feet on his desk, he stared at the ceiling. His phone beeped. It was the pictures. He slowly scanned each one, then settled back into his contemplation of the ceiling as he pondered Adrian's information. He rearranged the details for any other conclusions, and after several minutes conceded his agent's instincts were right. Since he had handpicked each of the team, not only for their investigative skills, but their unique talents, he had confidence in their judgement. Bottom line, they had a problem. He sent a text to his agents to report back to the office. The next call was to inform his boss, Director Paul Daykin.

When he answered, Scott said, "Paul, we have a situation," and relayed the details.

Paul asked the same question. "How sure is your agent that devices are missing?"

"He's certain. I'll send you a copy of his report as soon as I get it."

After a short pause, Paul said, "I'll inform the Secretary of Homeland Security Vance Whitaker and get back to you."

Texas

While Adrian talked to Scott, Cat rummaged through the house looking for a cardboard box. Finding one, she set the metal box inside and headed out the front door. Their truck was still parked at the end of the block. After turning off the lights and attaching the crime scene tape across the front of the doorway, Adrian followed her.

As she pulled away from the curb, Cat asked, "What did the boss man have to say?"

"Not much. Wants a report as soon as I can get it to him. We need to head back to the ATF office." He tapped a number on his phone. "Karl, it's Adrian. Are you still at the office?"

"Just left. Why?"

"You need to see something we found."

"I'm turning around and will meet you there."

Karl drove into the parking lot as Cat and Adrian exited their vehicle. When he walked up, she handed him the cardboard box.

Adrian explained its contents, then added, "If your agent was correct, eight detonators are missing."

"Let's go inside."

Karl set the box on his desk, then made a call. Cat and Adrian settled into the chairs. A few minutes later, Matt walked in. He looked at his boss with a raised eyebrow.

Motioning to the cardboard box, Karl said, "Inside is a metal box with two devices they found in the house."

Matt looked inside before he picked it up. "Who handled it?"

Cat replied, "I did, and I had on gloves."

He nodded and walked out the door.

"Karl, do you mind if I use an office? I need to send Scott a report," Adrian asked.

"You can use mine. Nothing I can do until morning, so I'm headed home."

Washington D.C.

His computer screen flashed an alert for an incoming message. It was Adrian's report. After reviewing it, Scott knew he'd been right to alert his boss. The investigation was now a matter of national security. It was possible someone else would take over the case. He didn't like the uncertainty. Still, his team would continue to work the problem until told otherwise.

The outer door opened. Voices sounded in the main conference room. Nicki and Blake had arrived. When they appeared in the doorway, Nicki said, "Ryan's on his way up. What's going on, boss man?"

Scott frowned at the nickname, which prompted Nicki's mischievous smile to light up her face.

"Humph," he grunted, then said, "Roundtable discussion on Laredo. There's a pot of fresh coffee. We might need it," His tone was grim.

Once everyone was seated around the conference table, he passed out copies of Adrian's report. As his team perused the documents, he said, "Adrian's certain several detonators are missing, and are linked to the missing ATF agent and stolen explosives. I agree. I've already notified Paul who's contacting Vance Whitaker."

With a pensive stare at the papers in front of him, Ryan asked, "Are we still in charge of the investigation?"

"I don't know. For right now, we work the case. We need all the intel we can find on disgruntled factions. Ryan, you work that angle. If you could develop a profile, it might help narrow our focus. Blake, examine the pictures from the garage and the two devices. You might spot a detail ATF missed."

"It's been several years since I worked with the explosives unit at TEDAC. My knowledge will be rusty."

Scott said, "I know, but right now you're the only one with any expertise in explosives."

Surprised, Ryan shot a quick glance across the table at Blake. "I didn't know you had been assigned to TEDAC." Mentally, he ran through what he knew of the Terrorist Explosives Device Analytical Center. It was part of the Bureau's Laboratory Division and analyzed the materials in terrorist improvised explosive devices, better known as IEDs.

"First assignment, right out of the gate."

Ryan whistled. "That's unusual. You must have had some impressive credentials."

"I guess that's one way of looking at it. I was assigned to an explosive's unit when I was stationed in Afghanistan," Blake said.

The gruff tone and bleak look that flashed across Blake's face dialed back Ryan's curiosity. Blake had always been reticent about his military background, and now, Ryan knew why.

Scott glanced at Nicki who was examining the photos from inside the garage. "Nicki, set up a new set of parameters in TRACE. Look for any type of activity that deals with missing explosives or suspicious explosions. Did you come up with anything on the phone numbers from Bardwell's phone?"

"Not yet. The search program is still running."

Blake asked, "What about the company that had the explosives stolen? Did the ATF run a background on their personnel?"

"Good point," Scott said. "Let's find out. Nicki, contact Karl Chambers, see what he's got, then run another search. Take it deep, what you call your dungeon quest. Maybe something will pop up." He paused, then added, "Add the missing ATF agent. Any questions? We've got a starting point, let's see where it takes us."

As he stepped into his office, his phone rang. It was his boss.

"Scott, Vance is in my office. Putting you on the speakerphone."

Scott greeted the Secretary of Homeland Security Vance Whitaker and then said, "Paul, I take it you've read Agent Dillard's report."

"Yes, and Vance has a copy. We agree with your assessment. Since you already have boots on the ground in Laredo, you're still in charge of the investigation. What do you need?"

Scott felt a surge of relief. "Files on terrorist factions and the active threat file," he answered.

Vance said, "Scott, I'll assign an agent to interface with your unit. Who's the liaison?"

"Ryan Barr."

Paul asked, "Do you need any additional personnel?"

"No. If necessary, I'll pull Agent Hunter from the academy."

Vance said, "I've advised the President of a potential threat. I'm to keep him informed. Translated, that means you need to be prepared to provide the briefings."

Scott detected a slight note of humor in his voice. Vance probably remembered his previous dealings with President Arthur Larkin and Scott's idle comment about the hot seat.

As he hung up, a familiar tingle coursed through him. The threat was real. A target had been selected, though he wasn't going to argue terminology with Whitaker. At least, not until he had evidence to back up his gut instincts. He shot a short text to Adrian and Cat to set up a conference call the next morning, then headed out the door to inform his team the Trackers were still in charge.

Texas

Adrian entered the hotel's small dining room. Cat was already seated at a table with a cup of coffee and a file folder in front of her. After receiving his boss's text, he had called and set up the early morning meet. He figured they'd have the place to themselves, and he was right.

He dropped his briefcase alongside Cat's backpack and her briefcase, then walked to the coffee pot. With a glance over his shoulder, he asked, "Find anything we missed?"

"Not really." She closed the folder and slid it into the briefcase. "Any theories about Scott's call?"

His phone rang. He said, "No, but we're about to find out," and hit the answer button. "Morning, boss."

"Is Cat there?" Scott asked.

"Yep, got you on the speakerphone."

"The rest of the team is here." A rumble of greetings echoed in the background. Scott continued. "Per Director Daykin, this is still our case. On this end, Ryan is running down leads on terroristic threats and working on a profile. I had Blake examine the pictures you sent."

Blake interjected, and said, "The ATF's estimate of the devices might be low."

Adrian murmured, "Well, hell," then added, "Any idea how many we might be talking about?"

Blake answered, "Maybe two more."

"Instead of eight that are missing, we're looking at ten," Adrian said.

"That's a real possibility," Blake said. "Get all the evidence from the garage, and the devices you found to TEDAC in Huntsville, Alabama. They might be able to be more precise."

"I'll get everything shipped out. What else?"

Scott answered, "At this point, the only solid information we have is two men who are linked to Bardwell. I'll let Nicki explain."

Nicki's voice echoed. "I found a news article that included the names of two men who were arrested with Bardwell five years ago for drug possession. I'm sending you a file on each. I ran the numbers from Bardwell's phone. They're all burners and have been disabled."

Cat said, "Does anyone else feel that someone is one step ahead of us? They knew Bardwell was going to meet with us, so they kill him, burglarize his house, and now destroy phones that were used."

"Could be. What's your next step?" Scott asked.

"A meeting with the Laredo homicide detective, Tracy Harlowe. Turns out she's Dyson's fiancée. After that, it's the ATF office. Karl should have his reports. Then it's onward to Bill Goddard's office. What about the personnel at the drilling company? Has anyone checked them?"

"Nicki is working on that as well as Stuart Dyson."

Adrian said, "I'll add one more to the list as soon as I have his name. It's the bartender at the bar where I met Bardwell."

Before ending the call, Scott asked, "Any questions?"

Adrian glanced at Cat who shook her head no. "That's it for us."

Cat reached for her backpack and case. "I hate to think Dyson might be part of this, but it's happened before."

"Well, let's see what our feisty detective has to say," Adrian said.

****

Red's Diner, weathered and run-down, had long passed its heyday. Judging by the number of police cars in the parking lot, it still had a strong clientele. Inside, a long counter with red-topped stools extended almost the entire length of the building. Behind the counter was an open kitchen. Booths lined the front windows and scattered in the middle were several tables.

When they walked in, Tracy was seated in a corner booth. Her hands cradled a cup, and she had a distraught look on her face as she stared at the table. When Cat greeted her, her eyes shot up. The distress vanished, replaced by a guarded expression.

A waitress walked up. The agents slid onto the seat and ordered coffee for starters, then looked at the breakfast menu.

Cat asked, "What's good?"

"Pancakes, the best in Laredo."

Adrian's gaze skimmed her. Her eyes, while alert, had slight smudges under them. She'd obviously made it home as her attire was different, but Adrian doubted she got much sleep.

When her gaze met his, he said with a sympathetic tone, "Short night for us too."

She nodded as the waitress appeared with mugs of coffee and refreshed Tracy's cup.

Cat took the detective's advice and ordered the pancakes, but Adrian went with the biscuits and sausage gravy. He took a sip of coffee, then said, "Tell us about Stuart."

Tracy's face softened for a few seconds. "As good a person as you'd find anywhere. He's been with the ATF for almost ten years and most of it here in Laredo." Her expression changed, the wary look returned, as she asked, "What specifically are you looking for?"

Why the caution, he wondered, before he said, "We need to get a better feel about his personal life, his habits, how he conducted his investigations, and any problems he had."

"He's a first-rate agent with an obsession for the minutia in an investigation. Stuart believes the smallest detail can be the key that breaks open a case. He's been responsible for shutting down two rings dealing in stolen guns. He'll go wherever the case takes him, anytime, day or night. As for problems, as far as I know, there aren't any, at least not any more significant than any person has."

The waitress dropped plates of food on the table. When nothing was set in front of Tracy, Cat raised her eyebrows.

"I ate a couple of hours ago. As your partner said, short night."

"Did he mention any details about the explosives theft from the drilling company?" Adrian asked.

"I knew about the break-in. Using a stolen truck to ram a building is more common than you might realize, though it's usually a gun store or pawn shop."

"Karl told us Stuart had taken time off. Any idea what he was doing?"

"He said he'd be out of town, and not to worry if I didn't hear from him. I suspected it was another case he was working on, but I'm not in the loop, don't have a security clearance." She leaned back and took a deep breath. "I can't believe he's dead."

Adrian wondered whether he should tell her. He glanced at Cat, who was seated beside him. Her head turned, and her gaze met his. She slightly inclined her head as if to say yes.

"I don't think he's dead," Adrian said.

Tracy's body tensed, and she leaned forward. "How do you know?"

"I didn't like how Bardwell responded to a couple of my questions. I think he was lying. Why, I don't know, at least not yet."

A sheen of tears brightened her eyes as she turned her head to stare through the window. "Is it possible?" she muttered to herself.

"What about his family? Does he have any here?" Cat asked.

Her head snapped around. "Uh ... no, he doesn't. His parents and one sister live in Ohio."

Adrian asked, "Do the names Joe Warden or Donnie Martin ring a bell?" He tapped the screen on his phone and accessed the mug shots Nicki had sent, then turned it toward Tracy.

Her fingers brushed his as she repositioned the phone before saying, "I know them, small time hoods. What's the connection?"

"They were arrested with Bardwell on a drug charge a few years back."

"I'll check them out when I get to the office. Anything else you need?"

"The identity of the bartender at Bing's Watering Hole. Whoever killed Bardwell knew about the meet. The bartender is the one who set it up."

"I don't know him, but I'll find out. By the way, just how did you connect with Bardwell?"

Adrian explained finding the embossed notepad, how he and Cat had posed as family members, and their offer of a reward.

"That's strange. Karl and I searched the house. I didn't spot a notepad. Hmm ..." A troubled look crossed her face, and her fingers drummed the table. "Just where again did you find it?"

"Under a stack of magazines on the coffee table," Adrian said.

Tracy asked, "If I need to find you later, where do I look?"

"We're headed to the ATF office to pick up their reports, then a meeting with Bill Goddard. From there, I'm not certain, but you've got our numbers." He scooped up the last piece of biscuit smothered with gravy.

After asking if they needed a refill on their coffee, the waitress dropped a ticket on the table.

Cat picked it up and slid out of the booth. With a nod of goodbye to Tracy, Adrian followed.

Tracy watched the two agents as they strode across the room. Her gut tightened from a sense of foreboding mixed with fear. *Stuart, what have you done?*

Four

Cat parked near the front door of the ATF building and glanced at Adrian. A frown furrowed his face, and he'd been uncharacteristically silent since leaving the diner. "What's got you in deep thought? Is it Tracy? I felt there was something she wasn't telling us."

"Hmm … you might be right," he murmured. The emotions he sensed during that brief contact with the detective filtered in his mind. It wasn't grief over losing a loved one. Yes, the detective had secrets.

"Any ideas?"

"Not a clue." He missed Cat's look of disbelief as he stepped out of the car.

Karl's two agents were seated in his office when Adrian and Cat entered. After they settled in a chair, Karl said, "Matt and Randy finished processing the materials from the garage. The only prints are Bardwell's. There are the copies of the reports." He motioned to a stack of documents on the corner of his desk.

"Do you still think we're looking at ten detonators?" Adrian asked.

Karl glanced at his two men, then said, "No, the count may be higher, possibly two more."

Adrian didn't want to create hard feelings by telling them Blake had already upped the count. Nodding, he said, "Please ship everything to TEDAC."

Matt spoke up. "Already done. The boxes are on a plane, and I spoke to the intake agent. Our request has been labeled urgent. I have a bad feeling about this one."

"That seems to be the consensus," Cat said. "Scott told us this morning that Homeland Security has been notified."

His tone edgy, Karl shot a look of displeasure at Adrian and Cat. "That's probably why I got two calls. One from your boss and one from the ATF Director. They wanted to make sure I knew the Tracker Unit was in charge. What else do you need from us?"

Adrian said, "Start with your contacts or informants on both sides of the border. Is there any chatter or rumors floating? We need a list of any radical groups in the area known to hold a grudge. Go back over your case files, check for common threads. You know this area, we don't." He hoped Karl got the message. This was not about who was in control.

Adrian added, "Interview the drivers who deliver for FedEx, UPS and the post office. They might remember something. Nicki is running a background check on Bardwell's financials."

"We do have two known associates—Joe Warden and Donnie Martin. Nicki found they'd been arrested with Bardwell," Cat said.

Karl had been scratching notes. "Matt. Check our files for information."

"Detective Harlowe's also running down that lead. We met with her this morning," Adrian said.

"That could be a problem. Her Captain ordered her off the case."

"That's what you mentioned last night," Cat said. "Why? It would seem she's in the perfect position."

"A reporter, Eddie Owens, insinuated Stuart engineered his disappearance. Tracy marched into the newspaper office and confronted him. According to several eyewitnesses, if another reporter hadn't grabbed her, she would have decked him." He chuckled. "I'd liked to have seen that. Owens is a real pain in the ass. Her supervisor, Captain Rodriguez, and I discussed the incident. We believe Tracy is a loose cannon. She's emotionally involved. It would be a conflict of interest and could jeopardize the investigation."

Knowing he was about to add another layer of irritation, Adrian said,

"As far as the task force is concerned, she's back on the case. She knows Dyson, and we can use her insight. Do I need to talk to Rodriguez?"

A glint of anger sparked in Karl's eyes. "No, I'll handle it. Just keep her under control, if that's even possible. She's the type of officer who doesn't hesitate to bend the rules."

"Sounds to me it's just what we need," Cat said, and earned another glare of resentment from Karl.

"Do you have an office we can use?" Adrian asked.

"After my early morning phone calls, I figured you'd be here for a while and set one up. Bill and I flipped for the privilege."

Adrian grinned. "Did you win or lose?"

He smirked, then said, "I lost."

Cat and Adrian chuckled as they gathered up their reports and followed Karl to an office across the hallway. Inside were two desks and a small conference table. Cat dropped her backpack and briefcase on a desk. "This will be perfect."

Karl nodded and headed back to his office.

"How do you want to handle this? If we split up, we can cover more ground," Cat said.

"I'll swing by the FBI office. Then, I want to talk to the bartender. I think I'll stay in my role of the brother still snooping around."

"If you don't need me, I'll stay here and work with Matt and Randy. I want to examine their case files."

"That sounds like a game plan," he said. He reached for his cell phone and tapped the screen. When Nicki answered, he quipped, "How's the digital witch this morning?"

Since joining the unit, Adrian had acquired a healthy respect for Nicki's uncanny ability with computers. When she took over the design and implementation of TRACE, the system had taken on an almost surreal power as it sifted through millions of bits of information.

"Have you come up with a new name?"

A laugh rang out, then Nicki said, "Inspiration hasn't hit, but it will."

Adrian had activated the speakerphone, and Cat chuckled. Nicki was an avid game player and had started to use code names for her research. The team had a betting pool on how long it would take her to change the name TRACE.

Nicki added, "I'm sending you a picture of Bing Morris. He's the owner of Bing's Watering Hole. So far, his financials are clean. He's been arrested for drunk driving and a couple of assaults."

Adrian tapped his screen. "Now, isn't this interesting. The bartender is the owner, and he's the one who set up the meet with Bardwell. I'm headed out to talk to him. Let Scott know the evidence from Bardwell's garage is already at TEDAC. The ATF agents have upped the estimate on the number of detonators, which agrees with Blake's assessment."

"Did you know Blake was in a military ordinance unit and assigned to TEDAC when he got out of the academy?" Nicki asked.

"No, I didn't." The Tracker Unit was new, and there hadn't been much of an opportunity for the team members to get to know each other. Plus, Blake was the most reticent of the group. "That's going to be helpful," Adrian added before ending the call.

"You sure you don't need me to watch your backside at Bing's?" Cat asked.

Adrian just grinned and headed out the door. His thoughts shifted to the dilemma named Tracy Harlowe.

****

She parked near the front door. The place looked even worse in broad daylight. The surface of the lot was pitted with potholes. Most of the paint had worn off the wooden structure. A vehicle was parked on the side.

Tracy picked up the dash-mounted mike and relayed the license plate to the dispatcher. It was registered to Bing Morris, the owner of the bar.

Shoving the door open, she stepped into a dimly lit room. The grime on the windows blocked most of the sunlight, though a few beams managed to find a clean spot, which only highlighted the filth on the floor. The wall-mounted TV was tuned to a morning sports show, and a man stood behind the bar with a notepad in his hand. At the click of Tracy's boots on the floor, his head swiveled. His eyes flicked to the badge on her belt. "What brings you here?" His voice reflected the look of hostility on his face.

"You Morris?"

"Yeah, what's it to you?"

"I'm investigating the shooting outside your bar last night."

"I heard a shot. That's all I know."

"I seriously doubt that, considering the victim had just left this place." Leaning on the edge of the bar, her eyes skimmed the room in disdain, then refocused on Morris. He was a big man, thick-chested, with beefy arms and hands. Long hair, streaked with white was tied back in a ponytail that hung down his back.

"Lots of people come in here, doesn't mean I know anything about them," he snarled, and tossed the notepad on the counter.

"Well, tell me about this one," she said, and described Bardwell.

Morris shrugged, his eyes darted away from her steady gaze. "Saw him in here a couple of times, but like I said, I don't know anything about him."

Lying bag of shit, Tracy thought. "If I don't hear something other than a fricking lie, I'm sending the fire department and code enforcement to inspect this rat trap you call a bar. I bet there are enough code violations that I can shut you down for months."

Rage flashed in his eyes, and his hands curled into fists. Tracy felt his urge to reach across the bar and drag her across it. She never moved, and her eyes remained locked on his face. Backing down was not in her vocabulary.

A u 7 9

Five

Adrian parked alongside a black SUV. He eyed the vehicle and silently cursed. His plan to continue his undercover persona may have just gone in the dung heap. He'd bet his next paycheck Tracy was inside. Would she remember he'd posed as a family member? Hell, what a mess. Only one way to find out.

Shoving the door open, he strode inside. His gut tightened at the sight of the bartender's thickset body leaning over the bar. Morris' eyes gleamed with hatred as he stared at Tracy. At the sound of the door, his gaze shifted toward Adrian. He straightened and stepped back. Tracy spun, her hand sweeping downward to her gun.

"Whoa," he said, and extended his hands upward. "I'm just looking for information about my missing brother."

Tracy stepped to one side keeping both men in view and said, "I'm a Laredo PD detective. Who are you?"

"Robert Dyson. The family put up a reward for information that leads to his whereabouts."

"I'm investigating the shooting. So far, Bing here hasn't been very cooperative."

Morris crossed his arms over his chest. His eyes still gleamed with anger. "You can send all the damn enforcement cops you want, but I can't tell you what I don't know."

Adrian said, "You set up the meeting with a man I met in here last night, the one who was shot. I was hoping you might know his name, and how he knew my brother."

"I seen this guy, a biker, the one that was killed, in here a few times. When you showed me a picture, I remembered seeing the two of them talking a couple of times. When the biker showed up, I passed on a phone number, like you asked me to do."

Adrian said, "If you recall, you were paid. Who else did you tell about the meet?"

"Uh … no one. Just passed on the number."

Adrian reached over and picked up the notepad.

"That's none of your damn business," Bing growled, and snatched the pad from Adrian's hand.

"Just curious what you'd be doing this early in the morning."

"I'm done answering questions. Told you all I know. Now get the hell out of my bar." He turned his eyes toward Tracy. "That includes you. Unless you got a warrant, don't set foot in here again."

A hard look settled on Tracy's face. "I've got news for you. You can't keep me out, warrant or no warrant, and I'd love for you to try. I'll have you on your ass so fast, you won't have time to blink. That's not a threat, it's a promise."

Looking at Adrian, she said, "Mr. Dyson, unless you have more questions, I think we've drained this shallow well dry," and turned toward the door.

"The family is still offering a reward, and it's been increased to ten grand. You've got my number if there are any takers," Adrian said.

In the parking lot, Tracy leaned against the side of the car as she waited for Adrian.

"Drained the shallow well dry?" Adrian said, and grinned as he walked toward her.

Tracy chuckled. "Seemed appropriate for the place and person." The laughter quickly faded as her demeanor turned serious. "Only problem, we didn't get very far. He knows more than he's saying."

The brief contact with the bartender's hand when he grabbed the notepad flashed in Adrian's mind. "I think you're right. Let's get out of

Au 79

here before we discuss this any further. Bing's just a little too curious."
Adrian had spotted the man at one of the windows.

"There's a coffee shop a few blocks away, or we can go back to my office. I have a copy of the medical examiner's report. I'd planned to stop by the ATF office and drop it off."

"Your office. Go on ahead, and I'll catch up with you."

Tracy nodded and gave him the directions.

Adrian settled behind the wheel and called Cat. "Anything new?"

"Not so far, but I'm still slowly working my way through the case files. How about on your end? What happened with Bill Goddard?"

"I gave him what information we had. His agents were out of the office, so I didn't get a chance to meet them. Ran into Tracy at the bar. She was having a tête-à-tête with our bartender."

"Did she blow your cover?"

"No, I managed to send a signal, and she picked up on it. Bing clammed up though, claims he doesn't know anything. I raised the reward, and he didn't even blink. He's involved."

"Are you headed back here?"

"No, I'm meeting Tracy at her office." He disconnected. Adrian hoped once Bing realized Tracy had left, he'd want to talk. Instead, he'd stared at Adrian for several minutes before moving away from the window.

****

Tracy strode into the bullpen of the homicide division, her backpack hooked over her shoulder. Sliding the sunglasses from her nose, she scanned the room as she crossed to her desk. Pete and Art were on the phone and Skip, her partner, who manned the desk across from her, was busy on the computer.

His head jerked up at the thud of her backpack hitting the floor. "Jeez, you look like something the cat dragged home."

"Humph!" She settled in her chair. "Some people would say if you can't say something nice, don't say anything."

He grinned. "I hate to be the bearer of bad news, but your day is about to get worse. The Captain wants to see you—pronto."

Tracy groaned and ran her fingers through her hair. What she didn't need was another session with Rodriguez. The sting of the last one still hadn't receded.

"Any idea what he wants?"

"No, but he's been on a tear for the last thirty minutes, wanting to know where the hell you were. Is there some reason you aren't answering your phone?"

"Jeez. I put it on mute and forgot to turn it back on."

A voice erupted from an office at the back of the room. "Harlowe, get your ass in here."

With a grimace on her face that had Skip grinning again, she headed to the Captain's office.

"Have a seat," he told her.

The order increased her trepidation, since sitting wasn't usually required when he barked out orders. Rodriguez was an old-school cop and ran his division by the book. Despite being over fifty, his just under six-foot frame was compact and lean. His hair was always neatly trimmed, the uniform pressed, and his shoes glistened. Fair, but tough, it was his attention to detail that at times drove his subordinates a bit nuts.

"What do you need?" She felt a faint tingle of pride when her voice didn't reflect her inner turmoil.

"How about an explanation why you don't answer your damn phone," he growled.

"Um … an oversight on my part. Won't happen again," she said, not wanting to set off questions why she had it on mute.

"Better not. Why the hell are you involved with the investigation into Stuart's disappearance. I ordered you to stay out of it."

Not surprised he'd found out, she said, "I didn't exactly plan on getting involved. I caught a shooting and ran into a couple of FBI agents assigned to the investigation."

"You should have handed it off to another detective the moment you knew it was connected. Disobeying a direct order is grounds for suspension."

She gulped, then said, "Yes sir. I know. But it wasn't intentional."

He glared at her for a few seconds, long enough to make her want to squirm in the chair. "This time, I'll let it slide. What saved your hide is the call I got from Karl Chambers over at the ATF. Those two FBI agents you mentioned asked that you be reassigned to the case."

Caught by surprise, she stammered. "Um … uh, does this mean you approved the request?"

"Against my better judgment, I did. But I'm giving you fair warning. If you even think about stepping out of line again, you'll find yourself on deep nights at the auto pound. Now, get out of my office and go find out what they want."

Tracy stood and as she headed to the door, said, "Uh, yes sir, thank you."

His voice stopped her in the doorway. "Keep me in the loop. I know how hard this must be for you."

Nodding, she left his office. As she dropped into her chair, Skip looked at her, his eyes sympathetic.

"What happened?"

"I'm back on the case. Can you believe it?" Tracy explained the phone call Rodriguez had received.

"Considering he doesn't usually backtrack on a decision, I would have to agree. Who are these two feds?"

"Trackers. Ever hear of them?"

Skip shook his head no. "What new wrinkle has the FBI come up with now?"

"It's some specialty unit. They handled the kidnapping case out in El Paso a few weeks back." Her head swiveled toward the door. "And you're about to meet one."

Skip watched the tall, lanky man stride across the office. He never would have guessed he was a federal agent. From the long hair, black leather jacket, black jeans, to the cowboy boots, he didn't fit the mold of the polished wingtip shoes and black suits he was accustomed to seeing.

"Adrian Dillard," the agent said, as he stopped and held out his hand.

Rising, Skip shook hands. "Skip Thornton. Pleased to meet you."

"What kind of strings did you just pull?" Tracy asked, a suspicious tone in her voice.

Adrian's eyebrows twitched upward as he looked at her. "Strings?"

"Yeah, strings. I'm back on the case."

"Merely suggested your knowledge of Agent Dyson and this case could be invaluable."

"Hmm … whatever it took, I appreciate it," she grudgingly added.

Adrian got the feeling this was a woman who didn't readily accept favors.

"I've got court this morning, have a case going to trial. You're welcome to use my desk." Skip stood and grabbed his suit coat. Turning to Tracy, he gave her a hard stare before saying, "Keep me posted," and headed to the door.

Adrian dropped into the still warm chair, and asked, "Anything on Warden or Martin?"

Tracy tossed an envelope across the desk. "That has Bardwell's autopsy report, no surprises there, and the criminal history for the two men. A couple of arrests for drugs and assault. Nothing that's significant."

Adrian removed the documents from the envelope and briefly scanned each page. "Is there a last known address? I want to check the locations."

Damn, Tracy was hoping he wouldn't ask. Since she planned to check the residences, she didn't want any company.

When he didn't get a response, Adrian shifted his gaze from the report to her face.

"Uh ... they should be in the report."

Adrian flipped the pages. "Nope, not here."

"Must have forgotten to add that page," she muttered, and sorted through a mound of paperwork on her desk. "Here it is." Heat spread across her face as he looked at her with raised eyebrows.

"Planning on going solo?"

She snorted in disdain. "Nothing I can't handle."

"I've heard the term loose cannon in connection with your investigations."

"Sometimes shit happens," she said.

"Well, I would appreciate your keeping it to a minimum in this case."

A grin split her face. "Deal."

"Your car or mine."

"I'll drive since I know the town and you don't."

Adrian grabbed the envelope and followed her out the door. His phone rang as he slid into the car. It was Cat.

"Adrian, I found something in an old case Stuart handled last year. Joe Warden was listed as a suspect in an investigation on a weapons shipment into Mexico. Stuart set up surveillance but was never able to connect Warden to the shipment the ATF confiscated."

"This might be our first break. How'd he come up with Warden as a suspect?"

"The file only indicates an anonymous tip. Evidently, he never identified the informant," Cat answered.

"Tracy and I are headed to his house. Anything else?" He listened for a few seconds, then disconnected.

"Did Stuart ever discuss an arms shipment he investigated last year?"

A thoughtful look on her face, Tracy turned the key in the ignition. "Yes, there was a case, but I don't recall he said much about it. Just that his team was on the track of a big arms deal. He was never forthcoming on his cases, and I understood it. As I mentioned earlier, as a lowly

Laredo detective, I don't have a security clearance." A trace of bitterness bit through the words.

Once again, Adrian pondered what was behind the detective's comments. "Joe Warden was a suspect in the case."

"Well, it answers where we go first," Tracy said.

****

A pickup truck was parked in the dirt driveway leading to a run-down frame house on the west side of Laredo. As Tracy pulled to a stop, an elderly man in bib overalls stepped out of the house and stood on the front porch. Hands in his pockets, he rocked on his feet.

Tracy's call to dispatch identified the registered owner was Bufford Taylor with a nearby address.

As she exited the vehicle and walked toward the porch, she held up her detective shield and identified herself, then said, "This is FBI Tracker Adrian Dillard. What's your name?"

"Bufford Taylor." He examined her badge, then turned his rheumy eyes to stare at Adrian. "Hells bells. Knew it was too much to expect you might be interested in renting the house."

Tracy choked back a laugh and heard Adrian clear his throat behind her. "How long has the house been for rent?" she asked.

"As of today. I came out to collect the overdue rent. Found it empty. The sorry bastard—oh, sorry, ma'am, the uh … tenant had cleared out."

Adrian asked, "Who was renting the house?"

"Joe Warden. Been here for over a year, and there was always a problem with the rent. Can't say I'm sorry to see the last of him."

"Do you mind if we look inside the house?" Tracy asked.

"No, go ahead. What'd he do?"

"Just a person of interest in a case we're investigating. Any idea when he left?" Adrian asked, as he followed Tracy inside.

"No."

In the living room, the few pieces of furniture were covered with dust. Trash littered a dirty and stained carpet. Empty beer bottles sat on the coffee table.

Behind him, Taylor muttered a soft curse, then said, "Gonna cost some money to get this place cleaned up. Might even have to replace some of the furniture. The rest of the house is the same. My pigs are cleaner than this muttonhead." More curses erupted as he eyed Tracy across the room.

Tracy asked, "Mr. Taylor, I'm requesting your permission to have a team of officers examine what's left in the house."

"Yeah, sure. I don't mind."

Adrian asked Taylor to wait outside, then walked into the kitchen.

Tracy followed him. She snickered and handed him a set of gloves. "I'm assuming once again you're not prepared. I'll start on the bedrooms."

Slipping on the gloves, he grinned. The woman didn't cut anyone any slack. In the corner, a trash bag was upended, spilling bottles, cans, and coffee grounds. Dirty dishes and pans were piled on the counter and in the sink. He turned and followed Tracy down the hallway.

He stopped in the doorway of a small room. While it was as dirty as the rest of the house, at least there wasn't trash covering the floor. The bed was unmade, and the sheets may never have seen the inside of a washing machine.

Several of the dresser drawers were open. It appeared Warden had left in a hurry. A few socks and dingy underwear were all that was left behind. Nothing in the closet except an old pair of tennis shoes.

Adrian met Tracy in the hallway. "Anything in the other bedroom?"

"No. It's empty. From the dust marks on the floor, it looks like it was used to store several large boxes."

Outside, Taylor leaned against the front of his truck. When the two officers appeared, he straightened. "Find anything to help you?"

"Not yet. I have a permission form I need you to sign," she said, before striding to her car.

"Did you ever see anyone other than Warden?" Adrian asked.

"No, he seemed to be a loner."

"What kind of vehicle did he drive?"

"Chevy pickup, black, had a fifth wheel in the bed. Looked fairly new."

"Do you know where he worked?"

"When he rented the place, said he was in construction, and occasionally drove a big rig. It was one of his excuses when the rent was late. He'd gone out of town."

"When was the last time you saw him?"

"Oh, I guess it's been at least two, maybe three months. I try to check on the place at least once a week. His truck was never here." Taylor rubbed his chin, a thoughtful look on his face. "Come to think of it, it might be longer than that. My memory's not so good these days. I did ask one time when I called about the rent. He said he was out-of-town working a job."

Tracy walked up, laid a form on the hood of the truck, and handed Taylor a pen as she explained, "This form gives the Laredo Police Department permission to search your house and remove any items pertinent to a criminal investigation."

Taylor signed his name, and Tracy tore off the back copy and handed it to him.

When Adrian's phone rang, he stepped back from the two to answer it. Nicki was on the other end.

"We got a preliminary report from TEDAC," she said, her voice somber. "It's not good. They found a partial fingerprint on a broken circuit board. It belongs to Stuart Dyson."

Adrian's gut twisted into a knot, and he turned away, his voice low to keep Tracy from hearing his comments. "They find any other prints?"

"Bardwell's. This is going to muck up what's already a bad deal. I'm waiting for the results of my search on Dyson. Maybe something will provide a clue. Blake is in the boss man's office breaking the bad news to him."

Au 79

Adrian said, "Cat found a link to one of the two men arrested with Bardwell in Dyson's case files. Joe Warden was a suspect in a confiscated weapons shipment. Tracy and I are at Warden's house. He's gone, and it looks like he left in a hurry. We need a license plate number for Warden's vehicle," and added the details Taylor had provided.

"Plugging in the data as we speak," Nicki said.

As an afterthought, he added, "While you're at it, search for a vehicle for Martin. I bet he's gone too."

Adrian slid the phone into his pocket. He looked at Tracy as she talked to Taylor. How the hell was he going to tell her?

Six

Washington D.C.

Blake tapped on Scott's open door. When his boss looked up, he stepped into the room.

Scott laid aside the document he'd been reading. He eyed his agent's grim face, and the documents in his hand. "What have you got?"

"A preliminary report from TEDAC. They didn't find any explosive residue but did come up with something the Laredo ATF agents missed. It's not a slam against Chamber's outfit, just that TEDAC has better equipment."

Scott knew he wasn't going to like what he was about to hear.

"There's a partial print on one of the broken circuit boards. It belongs to Stuart Dyson."

"Damn." For a few seconds, there was silence as the information filtered through Scott's mind. "How about Karl Chambers or Bill Goddard? Do they know?"

"Not yet. Nicki is calling Adrian. We figured you might want to make the other two calls."

"Not really." His mind raced over the possible ramifications. Was it possible the agent was involved? Or was there another explanation? Then he added, "But, I don't have any choice."

Blake dropped the report on Scott's desk. "Your copy."

With a grimace, Scott picked up the phone.

Au 79

Texas

Tracy met the crime scene personnel and quickly covered the details of the search. As the two techs, each lugging a large case, strode inside the house, Tracy turned to Adrian. "Ready to head to the next location."

He nodded and thanked Mr. Taylor for his cooperation before walking to Tracy's car. As he slid inside, he shot a quick glance at her. This was going to be a difficult conversation. As she turned the key in the ignition, he said, "We got the report from the Terrorist Explosive Device Analytical Center, better known as TEDAC."

Mystified, she glanced at him. "What report?"

Adrian covered the background on the agency, before explaining the evidence confiscated from Bardwell's garage had been sent to them for evaluation.

"You got a lead, that's what the phone call was about. What is it?" Her voice was eager with anticipation as she turned onto the highway.

When he didn't answer, she shot a sharp look his way. "What's wrong?"

With a neutral tone in his voice, he said, "They found a partial fingerprint, and it belongs to Stuart. Any idea how it got there?"

If not for the seatbelt, the abrupt swerve to the shoulder and the stomp of her foot on the brakes would have propelled him through the windshield.

Jamming the gearshift into park, she shifted toward him. Her voice, husky with anger, she said, "What do you mean they found his fingerprint. It's impossible."

"Whether it's impossible or not, the fact remains it's Stuart's fingerprint. We need to figure out how and why it was on a circuit board. So, don't kill the messenger."

Her body slumped against the seat, the anger replaced by disbelief and even a hint of fear in her eyes.

What's she not telling me? Adrian wondered.

"I don't know. Maybe he was using Bardwell as an informant and met him in the garage."

"That's a far stretch. Stuart would have known what was on the table and how it would be used."

"Of course, you're right, but he's not involved. I know the man."

"Okay, I can accept that for now, but it still doesn't answer how his fingerprint got onto a piece of evidence."

"Sitting here isn't going to find any answers," she said. Shifting gears, she punched the accelerator.

Adjusting the seatbelt again, Adrian asked, "Are you certain Stuart never mentioned any names?"

Irritated, she said, "No. I've already told you that. It was one of ..." she stopped abruptly, then added, "Maybe someone at the ATF knows, but I don't."

Hmm, one of what? Adrian thought, but only said, "Cat's working on it." His phone rang. "Speak of the devil ..."

When he answered, Cat said, "Blake called about the fingerprint. Any idea how it got there, and have you told Tracy?"

"We're just discussing it, and she doesn't have a clue. How about Karl?"

"He got a call from Scott. Stuck his head in my office to find out if I knew. He's flipping out, but it's to be expected. What are you doing with Tracy?"

"We just left Warden's house, and he's flown the coop. She has a team processing the place. We're on our way to Martin's location. He's probably gone. Did you get the files on the informants?"

"Not yet. I'll follow up with Karl."

Washington D.C.

Leaning back, Nicki's gaze scanned her office, and she sighed with delight. Before they moved in, Scott had a wall removed to enlarge the room to accommodate her computer equipment. She never expected to have carte blanche to design her ideal system. The final addition was the wall-mounted monitor the technician had just finished installing. It covered half the wall. With one tap on the keyboard, she could change the picture from a single screen to a split-screen, one for each of her systems. With the installation of the equipment complete, her next challenge was to finish setting up the links to agency databases.

A beep and a message flashed up. The last link to the Fusion network was complete. Fusion Centers were national, state, and local agency databases that maintained details on any individual who had interacted with law enforcement. Her phone buzzed.

"Agent Allison."

"Nicki, this is Ted with the Dallas Fusion Center. Check your incoming messages. I just completed the throughput test of the link, and you're good to go."

"Just saw it. Thanks for the help."

"Anytime. And when you get a chance, I'd be interested in learning more about TRACE."

Over the last two weeks, Nicki had been coordinating the installation of the link with Lieutenant Ted Phillips at the Dallas Police Department. They'd become good friends as they shared network horror stories.

"Once the expansion is complete, I'll give you a shout."

"I hear you, it takes time. Enjoyed working with you," he said.

As she hung up the phone, her head swiveled at the sound of a tap on the door. Ryan stood in the doorway with a cup in each hand. The aroma of freshly brewed coffee wafted in the air.

"Scott's called a conference session. I just made a fresh pot."

Standing, she stuck a pen in the ball of black hair piled on top of her head, then grabbed a notepad. "I hope one of those is for me."

Ryan grinned. Nicki's addiction for coffee was only rivaled by Cat's. "I figured the fastest way to pull you out of your den was to offer a bribe," he said, passing her a cup.

Scott and Blake were seated at the large conference table. As she and Ryan sat, Scott said, "Finding Dyson's fingerprint changes the investigation. Whether we like it or not, we have to consider the agent as a possible suspect."

He glanced around the table at the grim look on his agents' faces. "All we can do is work the problem. Blake, any leads?"

"Two groups in the Laredo area have been on Homeland Security's watch list for the last couple of years. So far, their activity has been more noise than action. I haven't found any links between the groups to either Bardwell, Warden, or Martin. I'm still running down members."

"Has the info been sent to Adrian and Cat?"

"I sent it off a few minutes ago. Cat's working on Dyson's case files at the ATF office. She's been updating me with summaries. Nothing so far."

Scott glanced at Ryan. "Anything on a profile yet."

A look of frustration crossed Ryan's face. "No. Since we don't know who we're dealing with, it's difficult to make any predictions at this stage of the investigation. If it's a homegrown terrorist, the profile has changed over the last few years. International and local influences, lone-wolf syndrome, and multiple other factors can easily be the trigger. Until we narrow down the possibilities, my theories won't have much relevancy."

Scott nodded his head in agreement. "I'm not surprised. Nicki?"

"The links to the Fusion Centers are complete. Having that access will open up additional sources of information." She passed on Adrian's latest intel about Warden.

Scott asked, "Anything on Dyson's background?"

"So far, he's clean. Financials are consistent with his salary. He's been an exemplary agent. Hard to imagine he would go rogue. I established a link to his office computer, and Blake is working on it."

Scott looked at Blake who said, "Nothing yet."

"An agent out of the Cincinnati office is on the way to interview his

A u 7 9

family. Ryan, expect a call." Scott paused and looked at his team. "Anything else any of you need?"

As his agents headed back to their office, Scott leaned an arm on the table. His pen tap-danced on the surface, a sure sign he was deep in thought. He had an exceptional ability to find patterns where others saw chaos. The first time he picked up a Rubik's Cube, he had solved the riddle of the colored panels within minutes. As a student, the ability earned him national honors in chess. After graduating the FBI Academy, he had quickly learned he could apply his strange gift to human behavior and netted several serial killers who had gone undetected for years.

A familiar twinge sent a surge of adrenaline through his body. He knew. A target had been selected, and there was a pattern. He had the first piece of the puzzle, the detonators. His fear was the lack of time.

Seven

Texas

The car bounced as another tire dropped into a pothole. They were impossible to miss as Tracy steered around several on the dirt road. Up ahead was a ramshackle, white frame house surrounded by a yard littered with old appliances and cast-off furniture. "Any bets the inside is as bad as the outside?" she said.

Adrian chuckled. "No, don't want any part of that action."

Tracy stopped near the edge of the roadway, and they surveyed the house. An old Ford pickup was in the driveway. She ran the plate through the dispatcher, and it came back registered to Donnie Martin. "Maybe we lucked out, and he's still here."

Loud barks erupted, and two dogs raced around the corner of the house. As they reached the fence that bordered the driveway, they went into a frenzy, spinning and jumping as they collided with the wire.

"The barks should bring someone to the door," Adrian said.

When he stepped out of the car, the barks turned to growls.

"Glad they're on that side," Tracy said.

When there was no response from inside the house, Adrian slid his jacket back and pulled his gun from the holster. He stepped onto the porch and eased toward one of the windows. "Can't see in."

Tracy stepped to the other side of the door. Her pistol in one hand, the other pounded on the wood. "Police, open up." The clamor of the dogs increased, their growls and barks frantic. She glanced over her shoulder to be certain they were still on the other side of the fence.

Adrian reached for the door knob. It turned. He shoved it open. A metallic odor filled the air. It was a smell a cop instantly recognized.

"Hell!" Adrian said, before he stepped inside.

A man, face up, was sprawled across the living room floor. Blood pooled around the head and body. One bullet had hit the face and another to the chest.

Tracy moved to the open door of the kitchen, then followed Adrian down the hallway. They checked the rest of the house, holstered their weapons, and walked back to the living room.

"No forced entry. He probably knew his killer," Tracy said.

Careful to avoid stepping in the blood, Adrian squatted near the body, his gaze surveying it from head to toe. Behind him, Tracy was on the phone talking to the dispatcher.

When she hung up, she stepped closer. "How long do you figure he's been dead?"

"Not long, this blood's fresh. Damn, if we had come here first."

"No point in second guessing ourselves. It doesn't make a bit of difference now," Tracy said.

Adrian rose and glanced around the room. Empty beer cans, a couple of magazines, and a large ashtray filled with marijuana butts sat on the coffee table. "I thought I caught an aroma of weed." He motioned toward the table.

Tracy had stepped to a small desk in front of the window. "Look at the dust marks. He had a computer, and it's gone."

"We've got to do something with those dogs," Adrian said. Their sharp barks echoed in the room.

"I told the dispatcher to notify animal control."

Adrian stepped into the kitchen. Empty pizza boxes and beer cans cluttered the table. "We need to check the pizza joint. Do they deliver?"

"Raz's pizzeria is a couple of miles from here. And, yes, they do.

We'll swing by there once we're done here. I want to take a closer look at the bedrooms."

"Hmm … okay," Adrian said, as he examined a newspaper lying on the table. It was the Laredo Observer. What caught his attention was the paper had been folded to an inside page with a column by Eddie Owens. The title read "Missing ATF Agent." As he read the article, the reporter alluded to an unnamed source that indicated the agent had intentionally disappeared. So, this is what started the run-in with Tracy. *An unnamed source, now what is this all about?* His senses had started to tingle when Bardwell was shot, and with each step they took, his uneasiness increased. Someone was yanking their chains and staying just ahead of them.

He snapped a picture with his cell phone and sent it to Nicki.

****

Frustrated, Eddie Owens tossed his pen on the desk. Seemed nothing ever turned out right. Now his editor was on his back over the incident with the Laredo PD detective. Told him next time he'd better have facts, something more than an anonymous caller.

He remembered the surge of exhilaration when he got the call. Eddie believed he'd finally gotten a break, his name would be the byline on a story that would hit the major news networks. Ever since he'd been the editor of the high school paper, he'd dreamed of making it big, and becoming a hotshot reporter. He'd show all those kids who bullied him for his thick glasses and pimply face. Instead, when his old man died of a heart attack, any hope of college and a degree in journalism vanished.

The only reason he was working at the newspaper was because the editor, Jimmy, was his second or third cousin. His mother had begged and badgered until he agreed to give Eddie a job. It didn't take long for his excitement to dwindle away. Jimmy wasn't interested in news stories. They weren't the focus of the paper.

Eddie stared at the partially typed article on his computer. Who cared about the winner of a bake off at a local church or the homecoming king and queen? Eddie sure as hell didn't, but he had to keep his mouth shut. If he got fired, it was back to sacking groceries at the B&B market.

His phone rang. Hell, let it ring, no reason to answer it now. Probably some soccer mom wanting to promote her kid. It stopped, then started again. Irritated, he grabbed the receiver, "Owens."

"I've another item for your column."

It was the same voice, the one from the first call that said Dyson had arranged to disappear. Eddie had printed the tip, and the next thing he knew Detective Harlowe had stormed into his office demanding a retraction and to know his source. When he refused, she started to take a swing at him. Too bad Bernie, another reporter, had stopped her. Otherwise, he could have had her arrested for assault.

"Are you listening?" the man asked.

"Not interested. Your last tip didn't pan out so well."

"This one will. Dyson's fingerprint was found in the evidence the ATF removed from Cam Bardwell's garage."

"What! Fingerprint. Uh, hold ... hold on, don't hang up." Eddie shoved papers aside looking for the pen. His voice sputtered with excitement. "Who's Bardwell? What evidence?"

"Bardwell was shot outside a bar, and the federal agents are investigating. They hauled several boxes of materials out of his garage."

"Holy crap, how do you know?"

The only sound was the buzz of the phone line. Owens looked at the receiver in disbelief. Maybe his dream wasn't dead.

He tapped in Bardwell's name on his computer. A local news channel had reported a biker, Cam Bardwell, had been shot outside a bar. Damn Jimmy. Why hadn't he called to send him out to cover the story? Disgusted, he knew the answer. It wasn't the stupid-ass focus of the newspaper.

The dispatcher's voice came over the police scanner that set on the corner of his desk. Crime scene personnel were being dispatched. The answering voice was Detective Harlowe. Owens wrote down the address and ran a search. She was at a house in the county. That was out of her jurisdiction. What the hell was she doing there? Only one way to find out. Screw the bakeoff. He grabbed his camera bag, and the police scanner, and headed for the door.

Washington D.C.

Blake stopped in the doorway of Nicki's office. The petite agent's fingers flashed over the keyboard. Long black hair, which normally hung to her waist, was piled on top of her head. Jeans and a sweatshirt rounded out her attire. One of the rules Scott had eliminated was the Bureau's dress code. While the others had readily shifted to casual clothing, with Blake's military background, it wasn't a comfortable change. He frowned as he viewed his shiny wingtip shoes and the cuff of black pants that topped the shoes at a precise length. There were times he felt he didn't fit in with the atmosphere of the new unit.

He tapped on the doorjamb. Nicki was notorious for her innate ability to tune out everything around her. When he didn't get a response, the second try was a loud rap. That got her attention, and she swiveled her chair to face him.

"Nicki, this setup is really amazing." His gaze swept the computer equipment and the large wall monitor.

Her voice bubbly with enthusiasm, she said, "Isn't it great? And the best news is agencies are starting to access the TRACE portal to upload their files."

Shaking his head in amazement, he switched to the reason for the interruption. "I came across a comment on Dyson's computer. Two days before he disappeared, he logged a reference about a new informant. One who had information on a cartel dealing arms. Can you check his calls for that day?"

Nicki spun back to her keyboard. "Sure can, both on his office phone and cell phone." A few clicks and a list of calls popped up on the monitor. "Cross referencing the numbers." She highlighted the entries.

"Isn't this interesting. There's a match to a call he received on his office phone. The good news is that it's one of the numbers on Bardwell's phone. The bad news is the number belongs to a burner phone, and it's kaput." She jotted the number, date and time on a notepad, ripped off the sheet, and handed it to Blake.

Waving it in the air, he said, "Better than nothing. Thanks, Nicki."

Her phone beeped. "Wait a minute, Blake. This is an incoming text from Adrian."

He stopped in the doorway as Nicki read Adrian's message and examined the photo. "You'll want to read this." She tapped the phone, and the image appeared on the wall monitor.

Blake stepped closer to read the article, then whistled in surprise. "An anonymous tip. What's the date of the article?"

Nicki shifted the image to see the top of the paper. "The day after Stuart Dyson disappeared."

"It adds another layer of complications. I'll let Scott know."

"Tell him it's on his computer."

His boss was on the phone and motioned to a chair in front of his desk. Listening to Scott's side of the call, he realized the caller was Vance Whitaker, the Secretary of Homeland Security.

When Scott hung up, he leaned back in his chair and rubbed the back of his neck. "Whitaker isn't happy, and that means the President's also not happy. Just a matter of time before I'll be headed to the White House for a briefing."

Blake said, "Maybe this will help. I came across a new lead." He explained what he'd found on Stuart's computer along with Nicki's info.

"Puts us back in the cartels. Maybe this isn't tied to any terrorist cells."

"Could be, but for now, I'm not eliminating anyone."

Scott nodded. "I agree."

"That's not all," Blake added. "Adrian sent an article. Nicki just kicked it over to you. It came out the day after the agent disappeared."

Scott tapped his keyboard, and the image appeared on his screen. As he read, his senses tingled. "We need to find out more about this anonymous caller."

"On it," Blake said before striding out the door.

Scott picked up his pen. Tap, tap, the rhythmic beat echoed. An emerging pattern filled his thoughts as he pondered the significance of the article.

Eight

Texas

Adrian leaned against the side of Tracy's car and watched personnel from the county sheriff's office haul out boxes of possible evidence. The homicide was in the county's jurisdiction and sheriff deputies had taken over the investigation. Tracy was still inside waiting for the M.E. to bag and load the remains of Donnie Martin.

A pickup truck pulled behind one of the squad cars parked alongside the road. When a man climbed out and reached inside to pull out a camera case, Adrian groaned. Dealing with a reporter was not his favorite pastime.

The man snapped pictures of the house, the squad cars, and the medical examiner's van before he turned the camera toward Adrian.

He sighed in resignation when the reporter headed toward him with determination in every stride. "This is as far as you go."

"Who are you?"

"FBI, Adrian Dillard. What's your name, and who do you represent?"

"Eddie Owens, and I work the news beat for the Laredo Observer."

That got his attention. Adrian had researched the newspaper on his laptop as he waited for Tracy. The articles were more attuned to community events than the news. Owens was on his list of individuals to contact.

In his early twenties, the reporter was younger than Adrian had expected. Tall and gangly, he was attired in jeans and a sweatshirt. Unkept strands of hair that stuck out from under a ball cap framed a thin face. Eyes that nervously blinked behind wire-rimmed glasses added to the geek look.

Owen's gaze darted to the activity of the officers, then back to Adrian. "What's going on? Why's the M.E. here?"

"No comment. I do have a couple of questions for you. You wrote an article about the missing ATF agent."

"Yeah, so what? What's that got to do with you?"

"I'm interested in the tip you got. Who contacted you."

Owens snorted in derision before he said, "I don't have to tell you."

"Maybe and maybe not. Depends on whether I connect you to the crime. If you're involved, protecting your source might not be in your best interest."

"That sounds like a threat, Agent Dillard."

Adrian hooked his thumbs in his jean pockets. "When I make a threat, there won't be any doubt. Let's just say it's a friendly piece of advice. Cooperation trumps stupidity any day of the week."

For a few seconds, Owens hesitated, then decided Dillard was running a bluff, trying to get information. His backbone stiffened. He had a second call. He wasn't backing down. "You're FBI, not ATF. Why the interest in Dyson?"

"Time for you to leave."

Fear and excitement rolled together, and his voice rose to a squeal. "You can't do that. I have a right to report what the police are doing out here. Is Dyson inside?"

"I can order you off this property." Adrian straightened, took his hands out of his pockets and rested them on his hips. "Unless you want to be arrested for obstruction, move back to your truck."

Owens began to back up. He had one last shot. What kind of reaction would he get?

"Did the ATF find Dyson's fingerprints at Cam Bardwell's house?"

Au 79

Despite the hard glint in Adrian's eyes, his facial expression didn't change. He took another step toward the reporter.

A look of glee appeared on Owens' face. His instincts told him the caller was right. "I'm going, I'm going." Turning, he headed to the road.

Son of a bitch! How'd he find out? Since Owens had stopped in front of his truck and continued to take pictures, Adrian leaned against the car. Not wanting the reporter to see any reaction, he couldn't risk using his phone. His mind raced over the possibilities, and he kept coming back to one answer. Someone on the inside had to provide the information.

Tracy stepped out the door and held it open. A gurney appeared with a bagged body. Two attendants eased it down the porch steps and rolled it to the back of the waiting van. The M.E., who Adrian had met when he arrived, followed.

On the porch, Tracy hesitated, her face hardened. Adrian suspected she had spotted Owens. With a short jump, she bypassed the steps, and with a long stride, crossed the yard and jerked open the car door. Nodding her head towards Owens, she said, "What's that sorry bastard doing here?"

Adrian slid into the passenger seat. "According to him, covering the news," he replied, and hooked his seat belt.

Turning the key to start the engine, she added, "Next time he gets in my face, he'll find more than news."

"Good thing you were inside then. All that blood would not have been a pretty sight."

"What the hell are you talking about?" She glowered at Owens as she passed the truck.

"Let's not stomp the brakes again when I tell you."

"If you don't stop yammering and tell me what happened, I may be tempted to take that swing at you."

"Yes, ma'am." His tone turned somber. "Owens asked about Stuart's fingerprint."

"He did what! How the hell did he find out? We just found out."

"I've been pondering the same question myself, and I don't like the answer that keeps coming up."

Tracy's foot stomped the accelerator as she darted a glance at her rearview mirror. The reporter's truck was still visible. "Hells bells. We've got a snitch somewhere."

Adrian sighed and adjusted his seatbelt. "Yes, we do."

"Are you hungry?"

With his mind still on Owens, it took a few seconds for the shift in topics to register. When it did, the distant memory of biscuits and gravy flashed in his thoughts. "Famished."

"Any interest in pizza? Thought we might stop at Raz's Pizzeria on the way back, see what we can find out about those boxes sitting on Martin's table."

"Good idea." The setting sun reminded him it would soon be dark, and he needed to catch up with Cat. He tapped the speed dial.

"Adrian, where are you?"

"Long story. Are you still at the ATF office?"

"Yes. I'll be here for another hour or so. I have a couple of files I want to finish before I call it a night."

"Tracy has suggested pizza. Are you interested?"

"You bet."

"Any preference?"

"None. Do you want me to wait here?"

"Yes. As I recall, I saw a breakroom."

Disconnecting, he glanced at Tracy. "When we're done, we'll take a couple with us and head to the ATF office."

****

The pizza shop was a small building next to a strip mall on the outskirts of town. Tracy pushed open the glass door, and the aroma of tomatoes, garlic, and pepperoni filled the air. Adrian's mouth watered.

A man wearing a red and white checkered apron presided over a cash register. Behind him, a large round oven filled the middle of the open kitchen. At the sound of the door, he glanced their way, and a broad grin split his face. He strode around the end of the counter. "Damn, Tracy, if you ain't a sight for sore eyes. You're looking good, even for a cop," he said, before grabbing the detective in a huge bear hug.

A chuckle erupted as Tracy hugged his thick neck before stepping back. "Buzby, good to see you." Turning toward Adrian, she motioned with her hand. "Meet a new cop in town. He's a fed, so tread lightly. Adrian Dillard, this is Buzby Cortland, the owner. His son and I went to the same high school, even hung out together our senior year. How's Jake doing?"

He nodded to Adrian, then said, "He's still in the military. He's teaching new recruits how to jump out of planes."

"Hmm ... he always was a bit of a dare devil."

His gaze shifted back to Adrian. "I hope you're here for a pizza and not because I'm in trouble."

Tracy smiled to reassure him. "We do want to order a couple of pizzas, but we also have a few questions we'd like to ask you."

His face turned somber. "Let's get the pizzas going, and we'll sit and talk. What do you want?"

Tracy looked at Adrian. "Your choice?"

"I like them loaded."

"Give us two of your specialties then, extra-large."

Buzby let out a roar. "Michael, two extra-large, all the way."

A man's head popped around the corner of the oven. "Okay, boss. Be ready in about twenty minutes."

"You want something to drink, iced tea, soda?"

When they said no, Buzby motioned to a large corner table.

Once seated, he said, "What can I help you with?"

"Do you know a Donnie Martin or Joe Warden?" Tracy asked. "Martin lives a couple of miles from here."

A disgusted look crossed Buzby's face. "Warden doesn't ring a bell, but Martin does. Been selling pizzas to him ever since he moved into the old Watkins house." His head tilted back as he thought. "Guess that would be about one, maybe two years ago. What's he done?"

Tracy replied, "Someone put a couple of bullet holes in him."

"Can't say I'm sorry. Didn't have much use for the man."

"What can you tell us about him," Adrian asked.

"I'm pretty sure he was dealing dope." He flicked a glance at Adrian. "You know how it is when you run a place like this. You hear rumors. I know the county raided his house a couple of times, but don't know if he was ever arrested."

"Did you ever deliver to his place?" Tracy asked.

"I did at first, but he had those damn dogs. I kept telling him if he expected me to deliver he'd better have them penned up. When one of my drivers came close to getting bit, I said, that's it. If you want a pizza, you come pick it up. Haven't been back to his house."

Tracy leaned forward, resting her arms on the table. "There were two of your boxes on his kitchen table."

"Yeah, he stopped by around noon yesterday."

"Anyone with him?" she asked.

"Hmm … he came in alone, but he was with someone. Martin always parked in the handicapped spot by the front door. Another reason the man pissed me off. There wasn't anything wrong with him. Yesterday, I didn't see the heap of a truck he drove."

A surge of adrenaline shot through Adrian. "Did you see who he was with?"

"When he left, I was cleaning tables." His hand motioned to one in front of the window. "He headed to a truck parked near the street. I couldn't see the driver, but it was a black truck."

Adrian glanced at Tracy and caught the glint that sparked in her eyes. He was certain they had the same thought. Was it Warden?

He shifted his attention back to Buzby. "Do you know if he was employed anywhere?"

"He did odd jobs for some of the contractors in town. I heard he was good with his hands, carpentry, stuff like that. It's about all I know."

"Did he make any comments while he was here?" Tracy asked.

"Oh, he whined and moaned about why I wouldn't deliver. He said he had a fence for the dogs. But he did that every time he came in."

Tracy asked, "Buzby, do you have a telephone number for him?"

Surprised, his gaze darted from Adrian to Tracy. "There should be one on file." He pushed his massive body out of the chair and headed to a door at the back of the room.

At the questioning look on Adrian's face, Tracy said, "We didn't find a cell phone or computer."

He nodded. "Good thinking."

When Buzby returned, he slid a paper with a phone number across the table. "This should be a good number. He used it to call in the pizzas yesterday."

Adrian reached across the table, grabbed the paper and slid it into his pocket. A voice rang out from the kitchen. "Pizzas up."

Adrian and Tracy both reached for their wallet. Buzby held up his hand. "No charge, it's on me."

A scowl crossed Tracy's face. "Buzby, you know how I feel about free meals. I appreciate your offer, but I'll pay."

Buzby grinned, and then said, "You might as well keep your money, cause I'm not taking it. This has nothing to do with you being a cop but about being an old friend."

With a sigh of resignation, Tracy pushed her wallet back into her hip pocket. "Well, how can I argue with that."

The bell over the door tinkled. Tracy glanced over her shoulder. "Damn," she muttered under her breath.

In strolled Eddie Owens. His gaze swept over the three at the table. "Hello again, Detective Harlowe, Agent Dillard."

Her voice rough with anger, she said, "What the hell are you doing here?"

Eddie's eyes slid around the rest of the dining area, before he said,

"It's a public place. I have as much right to be here as you do." His gaze shifted to her face. "What are you doing here? Is this part of what you're investigating, or pretending to investigate?"

Her eyes flashed, and her lips twisted in a sneer. "Guess you've wasted your time. I'm here to pick up a couple of pizzas."

Standing, she nodded to Buzby. "Thanks for the fast service. The next time you talk to Jake, tell him I said hi." She strode to the counter to pick up a large plastic bag.

"Nice to have met you," Adrian said before he followed Tracy out the door. His last glimpse of Owens caught the glare of hostility the reporter directed toward Tracy's back.

Tossing the bag on the back seat, she climbed behind the wheel. Adrian reached back, picked it up and set it on the floor. "Admirable restraint, Detective."

"What a prick."

"Well, he doesn't like you any better. Until we figure out what's going on, you need to watch your back."

Nine

When they walked into the breakroom, Cat was pushing two tables together. Tracy dropped the pizza bag on the table, saying she needed to make a pit stop.

As she stomped out of the room, Cat raised her eyebrows. "What's got her in a snit?"

"A run-in with a reporter. Part of today's happenings," he said. He removed the paper plates, plastic silverware, and the two pizza boxes from the sack.

"Oh, my, gosh, that smells good. Until you called, I didn't realize I was starved." Flipping open the box, she surveyed the large pie piled high with meats and vegetables. "Where did you find this? It looks delicious."

"Another part of the story."

"Your day must have been a lot more productive than mine." Sliding a large section on a plate, she bit into the hot crust. Strands of cheese trailed over the edge. She chewed and then moaned in ecstasy. "I think I've died and gone to heaven. This is unbelievable."

"You want a soda?" Adrian asked, eyeing the machine in the corner.

Cat mumbled and held up a finger as she swallowed. "Karl said there are cans in the refrigerator. I'll take whatever's there."

He set three cans on the table, slid one in front of Cat, and popped the lid on another. After taking a swig, he asked, "Where is everyone? The place seems deserted."

"When I told Karl, you didn't know when you'd be back, he sent everyone home. They were here all night. Matt had everything boxed up and on a two a.m. flight to TEDAC. That's why we got a fast turnaround on the report, though they're still running some tests."

Walking in, Tracy heard Cat's comment, and said, "I heard about the fingerprint," her voice tight with emotion.

A sympathetic look crossed Cat's face as she glanced up and saw the fear in Tracy's eyes. "There's got to be a logical reason why Stuart's fingerprint was there. We just don't know what it is yet. Any ideas?"

She dropped into a chair and reached for a piece of pizza. "I wish to hell I did."

Adrian reached for a slice at the same time. His fingers brushed the top of her hand. It was a light touch, but the shock of the emotion he detected resonated through him. Tracy was terrified, but of what?

"I'll start with the update," Cat said, sliding another piece onto her plate. "Matt and Randy talked to UPS, FedEx, and the mailman. None of them remember any deliveries to Bardwell's house. It's one lead we can cross off the list." She took a sip of soda. "What happened today?"

Adrian quickly filled her in on Martin and Warden.

"So, one's dead, and the other is in the wind," Cat said.

"Yeah, that about sums it up," he said, before taking a large bite.

Disgusted, Cat tossed her empty can in a nearby trash bin. "And someone is still ahead of us. What's the deal with the reporter?"

Before he could answer, Tracy spoke up. "That jackass showed up at Martin's house, then followed us to the pizza joint. Adrian thinks he's dangerous. I think he's a bag of empty wind."

Adrian slid another slice on his plate. His tone grim, he said, "Eddie Owens knew about the fingerprint. We've got a leak. Someone is yanking this guy's chains. Why? I don't know, but that's what makes him dangerous."

Cat glanced at her watch. "Wonder if anyone's still in the office?"

He slid the plate aside and reached for his phone. "I'd bet money on it."

Au 79

Washington D.C.

Scott stood in Nicki's doorway. "Let's call it a night." His gut told him the investigation was about to turn south on them, and when it did, they'd be working around the clock.

Nicki tapped a key before swiveling her chair to face her boss. "I need to get this last portal up and running. Are Blake and Ryan still here?"

Scott had already learned Nicki was addicted to her computers, and he'd likely find her asleep on the couch when he arrived the next morning. "No, they've already left. Nicki, whatever you're working on can wait until tomorrow. Go home."

"What about Adrian and Cat. Don't we need to talk to them?"

Scott grinned. He was familiar with her stalling tactics. "I sent them a text asking for a conference call in the morning. Go ... home."

With a sigh of frustration, she nodded.

When Scott's phone rang, Nicki's eyes lit up with expectation. "Don't even think about staying," he said, before he answered.

Adrian's voice was on the other end. "Scott, are you still at the office?"

"Yeah, why?"

"I'm with Cat and Detective Harlowe. I got your text about the call, but since Tracy was here, I hoped we'd catch you before you left."

Scott tapped the speakerphone key and dropped into the spare chair next to Nicki's. "I'm in Nicki's office."

Cat's voice echoed in the background. "Oh, good, I wanted to talk to her. First, say hi to Tracy Harlowe."

Once greetings had been exchanged, Cat continued, "Nicki, I loaded all the pertinent details from Stuart Dyson's cases into TRACE."

"I'll check the incoming data, see if anything pops," Nicki said.

Adrian took over the conversation and covered the day's events.

Scott pursed his lips as he listened. The issue with the reporter was troublesome. "Do you think there's a leak in the investigation?"

"It's one possibility. The problem is the timing. The reporter's comments came on the heels of us receiving the report. Just a little too close for the leak to be internal. I'll talk to Karl in the morning, find out who he told," Adrian said.

"One other note," Scott said. "Blake found a reference to a new informant on Dyson's computer two days before he disappeared." After covering the details, he asked, "Tracy, did Stuart ever talk about his informants?"

Her voice echoed in the background. "No, he didn't."

"Hmm … I was hoping he might have told someone who it was. Blake has added cartels to his search. Anything else?"

Adrian said, "Nicki, I'm sending you the number of Martin's cell phone. Plug it into the Obi-Wan system."

Laughing, Nicki said, "Will do. Obi-Wan, I like that."

Scott groaned. "Don't encourage her. She's coming up with enough nicknames on her own."

Another laugh erupted from Nicki, and she was still chuckling when Scott disconnected the call. "Scott, I do need to check Cat's data and the phone number. I won't stay late."

"I'd better not find you asleep on the couch in the morning." The harsh voice was offset by the twinkle in his eyes as he walked out the door.

Nicki typed in the phone number, followed by the data Cat had input, and hit enter. A goblin danced across the screen instead of the usual signal, a rotating circle as the system processed the information. The number only took a few seconds to locate. It was one of the defunct burner phones.

Grabbing her backpack, she slung it over her shoulders and turned toward the door. A whistle and several beeps sent her spinning toward the wall monitor. In large red letters, ALERT flashed on the screen.

A surge of excitement shot through her. This had to be a return on one of her searches. Despite the order from her boss, she couldn't leave now. The backpack thudded as it hit the floor, and she reached to tap a key. A newspaper article popped up on the screen.

Au 79

Enlarging it, she dropped into her chair and read. A bridge on a remote county road in Oklahoma had collapsed. A rancher on his way to a stock show had just crossed it. When interviewed, the man said a few seconds were the difference between his escape and being killed. Local authorities claimed the collapse was due to age and poor maintenance.

Nicki eased back in her chair and stared at the article. It seemed straightforward and innocuous. It was widely known many of the bridges across the country were old and in disrepair. So, why did this set off a tingle? She glanced at the date, two days ago. Tapping in a new command, she set up a search for bridges that had collapsed in the last year.

The goblin danced.

Texas

"A couple of pieces left," Tracy said, motioning toward the open box.

Cat groaned. "I couldn't eat another bite, though that has to be the best pizza I've ever eaten."

Adrian was fiddling with his computer but looked up to nod his head in agreement.

"Okay, what has you so occupied over there?" Cat asked.

"The info Blake sent on a couple of factions on Homeland's hit list. I found several news articles about them."

"Hmm ... who are they?" Tracy asked.

"Desert Rats and Border Guards. Both have headquarters not far from here," Adrian said.

"I've heard of them but never had any dealings with them. They talk a lot, but it never amounts to anything serious. I'll check around the PD, see if anyone knows them."

"That's what one of our agents said, a lot of hot air. Still, something could have triggered a change. If you come across any names, let me know," he said, closing the laptop.

Tracy picked up the two boxes and tossed them into the trash. "What's on your agenda for tomorrow?"

"Cat, are you finished with the files?" Adrian asked.

"Yes. What's on your mind?"

"In the morning, I want a meeting with Karl Chambers and Bill Goddard. After that, let's take a road trip."

"Ah ... going visiting, are we?"

Adrian glanced at Tracy. "You're welcome to join us."

"Can't. I want to follow up with the M.E. He knows his stuff, but sometimes he needs a nudge." She picked up her Laredo PD ball cap and put on her jacket. "As soon as I know something, I'll call."

Cat listened to the sound of receding footsteps echoing in the hall. "She is one disturbed individual. I keep getting these strange vibes."

Adrian said, "Something's churning inside her. It centers around Stuart."

****

Tracy leaned against the car seat and closed her eyes. Taking deep breaths, she tried to slow the racing heartbeats that pounded against her chest. Since Stuart had disappeared, she felt as if she stood on a precipice overlooking a bottomless abyss. One wrong step and she would plunge into the depths.

With a sigh, she started the engine. Working with the agents had proven to be more difficult than she expected. When Adrian's gaze met hers, he seemed to be able to see into her soul and know her innermost secrets. Cat was cut from the same cloth. Her eyes held a look that was older than time itself, as if she was of another world.

Jeez. She was getting morose. What the hell was wrong with her, attributing mysterious qualities to the two agents. With a shake of her head, she thrust away the thoughts. What she needed was a good night's sleep, not some psychic babble floating in her mind. Tomorrow was another day, and she'd figure a way out of this mess.

Au79

Ten

Washington D.C.

Scott unlocked the door and flipped on the lights. The bright glare pushed back the gloom of the rainy day that filtered through the wide windows.

He dropped his briefcase in his office and strolled to the breakroom. A pot of coffee was the first item on his agenda. After a restless night, he needed a strong jolt of caffeine. A soft snore was his first signal. Mumbling a few curses, he hit the light switch.

Stretched out on the couch, his research guru was sound asleep. Several more curses rolled in his thoughts as he tapped her shoulder.

Eyes shot open, and her head snapped upward. A guilty look crossed her face as she swung her legs to sit up. "Hey, boss man, what time is it?"

Irked, he said, "Too damn early for you to be here and asleep on the couch—again."

Her gaze shot to the clock on the wall. "My program!" She jumped up and raced out the door, her words echoing behind her. "Be back in a minute."

Shaking his head in amazement, he added coffee to the state-of-the-art appliance. It was one of his contributions to the new office along with the extra-long couch snugged up against the wall.

As he waited for the coffee to percolate, he pondered the reason Nicki was here. Since she still had on the same clothes from the last time he saw her, he knew she hadn't left the office. Despite the fact he was her boss, she always seemed to finagle a way around his orders. He wasn't concerned about her machinations. Nicki was one of the most dedicated and talented agents he'd ever encountered. He was fortunate to have snagged her for his team before some other Dudley-Do-Right found out about her amazing skills.

With a cup in each hand, he headed to her office. Time to find out what had pushed her hot button.

Her fingers flew over the keyboard, as multiple images flashed on her new toy, the monitor. He had to pull a few strings to get it. Lucky for him he had the backing of not only his boss and Vance Whitaker but also the President.

Setting her cup on the desk, he asked, "Okay, what's going on? What's so important you ignored a direct order to go home and not spend another night on the couch?"

Nicki shot him a smirky grin. Two taps and she motioned toward the screen. "Here's why."

Scott stepped closer to scrutinize the images, three newspaper articles about the collapse of a bridge.

"Give me the condensed version," he said.

"Three bridges within an eight hundred-mile radius of Laredo, one in Oklahoma and two in Texas, have collapsed in the last three weeks. All were attributed to old age and disrepair. They're in remote areas with little traffic that wouldn't generate any major news media attention." She sat back and watched him, waiting for him to make the same connection she'd made.

His mind raced over the possibilities, connecting seemingly random dots. He didn't like the picture they painted, but it was too early to rush to any conclusions.

He glanced at her. The eager anticipation in her eyes sparked a corresponding excitement. "It's possible, Nicki, but before we get ahead of ourselves, we have to make sure."

She grinned. Scott's quick perception was one of the perks of her job.

Nicki didn't have to explain in excruciating detail.

"Pull up a map of the three locations." He pulled his phone from the pocket of the jacket he hadn't had time to remove. Tapping his speed dial, he waited for Blake to answer.

A sleepy voice answered, "Yes, sir."

"Blake, pack a bag. You're going on a road trip to Oklahoma and Texas. You need to be at the airport in an hour. Call me as soon as you're ready to leave, and I'll give you the details."

"Uh ... okay," Blake replied, as Scott disconnected the call.

After surveying the map, he punched in another number to the flight headquarters for the Bureau. "Roger, this is Scott Fleming in the Tracker Unit. I need a plane on standby to transport one of my agents to Oklahoma and Texas. I'll text the locations to you. Agent Kenner will be at the airport in an hour."

As he disconnected, Nicki asked, "Do you think he can find any evidence?"

"If anyone can, it'll be Blake. I'll be in my office." He turned toward the door, then stopped and glanced back over his shoulder. Nicki was already back at her keyboard.

"Hey," he said. When she looked up, Scott continued, "You're off the hook about the couch, but don't think I've forgotten it. Good work on finding those articles."

A mischievous grin crossed her face, and he shook his head at the glint in her eyes. The woman was impossible.

He entered his passcode on his computer and began a search of the three locations. Since the one in Oklahoma was the latest incident, he'd have Blake inspect that one first. He sent the coordinates to Roger, then made a call to arrange for a rental car to be waiting at each of the airports.

Rising, he picked up his coffee cup, then set it back down when his phone rang. It was Blake.

"Headed out the door. What's going on?" Blake asked.

Scott explained the articles Nicki had found and where the bridges were located. "This may just be a coincidence, but it's one I don't like. I want you to inspect the bridges for explosives. A plane is waiting at the airport. I've also arranged for local transportation. Anything else you need?"

"Scott, even if your supposition is correct, it may be next to impossible to find any evidence now."

"I know. No pun intended, but we'll cross that bridge when we get to it."

"Call TEDAC and arrange for Lance Brewster to meet me in Oklahoma. He's been working on a new handheld chemical detection device to identify explosive residue. I'll call him. I need to make sure he brings all his equipment."

"Consider it done. What else?"

"I finished the research on the membership of Texas factions late last night. There are several scattered across the state, but no red flags on any of them. Two are near Laredo. I've already sent the information to Adrian. All that's on file is the head guy, no members. Other than an occasional protest to the local news media, they're low-key."

"I'll have Ryan start a trace on their movements. See if they made a trip to Oklahoma or the two Texas sites."

"Good idea. I'll call later today. This could get a bit dicey."

Texas

Adrian's hand swatted the air around his ear. How the hell did a pesky mosquito get into his room? Then he realized the sound was his phone. Shifting his head toward the nightstand, he squinted at the clock radio. Who would call at four a.m., and where'd he put the damn phone?

Across the room, a light glowed. His hand groped for the switch on the lamp. The ringing stopped. Tossing the bed covers aside, he swung out of bed and crossed to the small desk.

A u 7 9

The persistent sound started again. With a sinking feeling, he looked at the caller ID. With a tap, he answered, "Morning, boss."

"Sorry for the early morning call, but there've been developments."

He dropped into the chair as Scott detailed the information on the bridges and Blake's trip. "I'd like to see those articles."

"Check your emails, you should have them. Once Blake and his TEDAC buddy get a chance to examine the Oklahoma bridge, we should know if this is a wild goose chase."

Adrian's sense of uneasiness told him Scott wasn't wrong. He wasn't high on coincidences either.

"Blake said he sent you the results of his research on militant groups."

"Cat and I are headed to the headquarter locations today. Karl Chambers wants a meeting. It's first on the agenda."

"Any reason I should be concerned?" Scott asked.

"No, we've got it covered." After a couple of follow-up comments, he disconnected. Adrian opened the email with the attachments and perused each article. The time span, three weeks with the last three days ago, was disquieting. His anxiety increased.

Picking up the phone, he tapped the screen. A sleepy voice answered, "This had better be good."

"Since my wake-up call had our boss on the other end, this one's not going to be any better."

"Damn, was afraid of that. What happened?"

Adrian gave her a condensed version of Scott's call, then added, "Karl Chambers and Bill Goddard are my next calls."

"I'll meet you downstairs in about thirty minutes," Cat said.

****

Karl was walking across the lot when Cat parked. With a briefcase in one hand and a coffee cup in the other, he waited for them on the sidewalk. As they exited their car, he said, "When I get a call this early in the morning, I figure my day will be as crappy as yesterday."

Adrian hadn't given Karl any details. "You might be right. I called Bill, and he's on his way."

"I was afraid you would agree with me. Matt and Randy should be here in a few minutes," he said, as he led the way inside the building. "Let's set up in the conference room."

Cat sniffed. The aroma of Karl's coffee wafted in the air. Adrian had rushed her out of the hotel before she had a chance to grab a cup. "I need coffee," she said, and headed toward the breakroom.

Adrian chuckled, then said, "If you haven't noticed, she has a severe coffee addiction."

"She fits right in with this crew of mine. We have a coffee pot in the conference room. I'll get it started."

Adrian dropped his briefcase on the large table as Randy stepped into the room followed by Matt, who said, "Can't be good to get pulled out of bed this early."

Karl glanced over his shoulder and grunted, then hit the button to start the coffee maker.

Bill walked in and set a briefcase next to the chair. He glanced around the room. "Morning, everyone."

"I need to connect to a printer to run off a few copies," Adrian said, opening his laptop.

"There's one across the hall. I'll get the access code," Randy said. He passed Cat as she was coming in the door.

Dropping her backpack on the floor, she set her cup on the table. "Access code?"

"Need a printer."

"Oh." She took a sip of the hot brew and sighed in contentment.

Randy reappeared and slid a piece of paper across the table to Adrian.

Once everyone had a copy and was seated at the table, Adrian said, "One of our agents, Blake Kenner, is on his way to Oklahoma. Three bridges have collapsed over the last three weeks. One in Oklahoma and two in Texas. You have a copy of the locations and the newspaper articles."

While they examined the documents, he got a cup of coffee.

Karl looked up, his face puzzled. "I'm not following. These articles say the collapse was due to age and lack of repair. What does this have to do with our investigation?"

"We're not certain there is a connection." He sat back down. "That's what Blake is going to find out. An agent with TEDAC is meeting him there. They'll test for explosive residue or any other sign of an explosion."

Bill tossed the documents on the table. His face reflected the disparaging tone in his voice. "It all seems a bit farfetched. What makes you think it was deliberate?"

"Timing and proximity," Adrian answered. "Three bridges in three weeks, all within a day's drive from Laredo. When you factor in the missing devices, it's too coincidental. We believe it's enough to warrant an investigation."

Karl's elbows rested on the table, his fingers steepled, as his eyes flicked over the documents spread out in front of him. "Okay, I get your reasoning, but why blow up a bridge in the middle of nowhere?"

"Can't answer that one."

A snort erupted from Bill. Adrian glanced at him and bit back the sharp retort that would only exacerbate the man's attitude. Instead, he calmly looked around the table. "If anyone has any ideas, I'm open to any opinions."

Matt had been studying the articles. "I agree with the timing. It does look suspicious. Is it possible this is a dry run, a test of some kind?"

"It could be one answer, but for what purpose?" Cat said.

Randy dropped the articles on the table. "I guess to find out what it takes to bring a bridge down."

"What happens if your team finds something?" Karl asked.

"The investigation will be turned over to TEDAC. A team is on standby, ready to head to Oklahoma, and Blake will be on a plane to the next location. All we can do is wait for their results."

Another snort of contempt erupted from Bill. "What a waste of time. Even if you do find evidence of explosives, there's nothing to connect it to our investigation."

With a thoughtful look on his face, Adrian stared at Bill before he slid another set of documents to each of the group. "That's not all. These are the reports on a homicide that happened yesterday." He described the events at Warden and Martin's house. "We need to locate Warden. It's likely he was with Martin the day before he was killed. Tracy Harlowe has put out an All-Points Bulletin. You should have received the APB."

Karl nodded. "I saw it, though I wasn't sure of the connection."

"He's involved in whatever is going down," Adrian responded.

"When did Harlowe get put back on this case?" Bill asked.

"Yesterday," Karl said.

His voice harsh with hostility, Bill asked, "How the hell did it happen?"

"At Adrian's request, I contacted Rodriquez and requested she be reassigned," Karl said.

Hoping to ease the tension with a shift in the conversation, Cat interjected and said, "Every detail of Dyson's cases has been uploaded to TRACE along with the list of informants you've used over the last five years. I'm hoping we find another connection." She glanced at Bill, who sat across the table from her. "Bill, we need the same from you, a list of informants."

A scowl crossed his face. "Agent Allison already has access to our database."

"Please check with your agents. They might have names that aren't in the case files."

Though it was obvious he was unhappy over the request, he nodded in agreement.

"We had one other surprising incident yesterday." Adrian rose and walked to the coffee pot. "It dealt with a reporter, Eddie Owens."

"Where did you encounter that slime-ball?" Karl asked.

He filled his cup. "Showed up at Martin's house."

"Probably heard the call come out on the scanner," Randy said.

"Hmm ... that's not the problem." Turning, he had a view of everyone seated at the table. "I'm trying to figure out how he knew about Dyson's fingerprint. Any ideas?"

Eleven

When Tracy's feet hit the floor, she felt as tired as when she went to bed. Tossing and turning seemed to be the norm rather than the exception.

A shower helped. As she dressed, her mind circled around everything that had happened with the investigation. Uncertainty waged a constant war in her thoughts. Should she tell the agents? No, she couldn't, not yet.

Sighing in frustration, she buttoned her black Laredo PD shirt and tucked it into the black tactical pants. Picking up the gun belt hanging on the bedpost, she headed to the kitchen. As she passed the living room, she looked at the disorder and the fine film of dust that covered the wood floor and furniture. Housekeeping wasn't high on her list of priorities, but she'd never let it get this bad.

Her eyes skimmed the contents of the refrigerator. The last trip to the grocery store was a distant memory. Seemed her life had gone on hold the night they found Stuart's car.

Thank god for yogurt and its lengthy expiration dates. She grabbed one and leaned against the counter. While she ate, she pondered the day's agenda. Tracy was glad Adrian and Cat were off on their own. She didn't need them interfering in the visits she had planned. The first on the list was the morgue.

She parked in the section reserved for official vehicles, grabbed her backpack and headed inside. Her nose crinkled at the smell. There was always a sickening, underlying odor no amount of cleaning materials or air freshener could eradicate.

Doris was behind the reception desk and greeted her as she walked in. "Tracy, you're here early, even for you."

"Hoping the doc has finished with the Martin autopsy. How are you doing?"

"Hmm … not bad. Got a new litter. You sure I can't interest you in a dog?"

Tracy grinned. Back when she was a rookie, she answered a call at Doris' house. The woman raised show dogs, and someone stole her prize poodle. It took her a couple of days to track down the animal. A local fraternity decided the new member's initiation included stealing the dog. Once Doris had the dog back, she wanted to drop the charges. Tracy wasn't about to let the boys off the hook and came up with an alternative solution, one that was a fitting punishment. The fraternity members had to clean Doris' kennels every week for a year. Ever since then, Doris had been trying to give Tracy a pup.

"Not today," she said, as she thought about dust. "Poor thing would probably die of neglect and starvation at my place."

"Well, young lady, when you're ready, you just let me know. Doc Kennedy's in his office."

The door to the M.E.'s office was open. Soft, persistent mutters echoed in the hallway. Tracy paused in the doorway. Dale Kennedy was slumped in his chair, his gaze fixed on a desk cluttered with stacks of documents and file folders. Fingers slid through his gray hair, pushing strands into spikes as he growled, "Where the hell is it?"

Tracy chuckled to herself before she said, "Lose something?" Kennedy's habitual habit of misplacing glasses, documents, and even his coffee cup, was the gist of many jokes among his personnel. The only area where he was meticulous was the autopsy. Defense attorneys hated him. He was the proverbial immovable rock on the witness stand. Kennedy never forgot a detail.

At the sound of her voice, he looked up, and a sheepish grin crossed his face. "Yeah, my dang calendar. But what the hell, it's here somewhere. Come in." He motioned with his hand. "Come on in."

"Just checking to see if the Martin report was done," Tracy said, sinking into a chair in front of the desk.

"I finished it up early this morning. I'm missing two test results but should have them in a couple of days."

"What did you find?" she asked.

"It was rather straight forward. I recovered three rounds. Two in the chest and one to the head. It was the kill shot. He might have survived the other two."

"Caliber?"

"Oh, uh ... nine mil."

"Anything else I should know?"

Kennedy's chair creaked as he leaned back and crossed his hands over his generous belly. "No."

Images of a body lying on the street flicked through her thoughts. "Has the bullet from the Bardwell homicide been compared to the ones from Martin?"

"Yes. It's one of the results I haven't received. I emailed the report. Do you need a hard copy?"

"I do. I'm meeting the feds later, and they want one."

He turned to his computer, and with a couple of light touches on the keyboard, paper spewed from the printer in the corner behind him. With a quick swivel of the chair, he grabbed the stack of sheets and stapled them before handing the report across the desk.

"Has anyone come forward to claim Bardwell's body? We haven't located any relatives," Tracy said.

"I did. When I plugged his name into my system, I found he'd been admitted to the emergency room. A sister in Houston was listed as the emergency contact. She's supposed to arrive sometime this afternoon."

"I'd like to talk to her. Call me when she gets here. Thanks for the quick report," she said, and rose from the chair.

Au 79

"Tracy."

She turned at the door.

"Anything new on Stuart?"

At the look of sympathy in his eyes, tears caught in her throat. Her voice husky with emotion, she said, "No. Nothing."

Doris was on the phone, so she only nodded as she passed the desk.

Outside, she took a deep breath of fresh air to get the smell out of her nose. She closed her eyes and allowed a few seconds of emotion before pushing back the sense of foreboding that seemed to be ever-present. Her plans needed her concentration and focus.

****

Adrian's gaze skimmed the faces of the four men for any reaction. Cat settled back in her chair with an intent look on her face as she surveyed the group at the table.

Karl was the first to recover. "Wait a minute. This doesn't make sense. Do we have a leak?" Agitated, his fingers drummed the table. "When your boss called to tell me about the report, he said one of his agents had just notified you. When was that?"

Adrian said, "I was still at Warden's place."

Karl glanced at Bill. "When did you find out?"

"Right after you did. Or at least it's what Scott indicated when he called."

"Then there can't be a leak," Karl said. Catching the glare from Bill, he added, "Don't get in another uproar. I didn't mean to imply it came from your office. The timing's all wrong."

Bill eased back, hesitated, then said, "You're right." His gaze shifted to Adrian. "You said he showed up at Martin's place. Owens must have known before he headed there, which means he knew before we did."

Adrian moved to his chair. "I don't like the timing either, and I damn well don't like the idea of a reporter stirring the pot."

Matt asked, "What'd you tell him?"

"No comment, and for now I'd like to keep it that way. Was there

85

any follow upon the article in the Laredo Observer? Did anyone talk to the reporter?"

Karl said, "No. At the time, Bill and I didn't believe it was relevant."

Adrian looked at the two men. "It is now."

Karl frowned, and Bill shot an angry glare at Adrian, but neither made a comment.

Cat said, "The real problem is we have to treat Stuart Dyson as a suspect."

A deep sigh arose from Karl. "I know, and the thought sits like a chunk of lead in my gut. It's difficult to reconcile the possibility he's involved in whatever's going on."

"As my boss would say, let's work the problem. What do either of you know about two groups, Desert Rats and Border Guards?" Adrian asked.

Karl said, "We've been monitoring them for years. They occasionally run a protest, but that's about all."

Bill added, "We've done the same. They're low-key. Hard to imagine they'd be involved."

"The two groups popped up on the radar when our profiler, Ryan Barr, started a search. Their headquarters are our next stop. We'll be in touch later." Stuffing his folders into his case, Adrian looked at Cat. "Ready?"

Walking across the parking lot, Cat said, "Want to flip to see who drives?"

"If you don't mind, you drive," Adrian replied.

"Bill Goddard has a lot of latent hostility," Cat said.

"He's probably still ticked over losing control of the investigation."

"Okay … maybe." Still, she wondered if there was another reason. She tapped in the coordinates for their first stop, and they headed out of town. Occasionally the voice on the GPS would break the silence with a change in directions.

Adrian had opened his computer and was focused intently on the screen. Cat glanced his way, wondering what he was up to and was about to ask when he said, "The bridges are all the same style of construction. A beam bridge, the type held up by piers."

"Hmm ... and this helps us how?"

"Not sure, but any insignificant detail can be critical. Wish we'd hear something from Blake."

Washington D.C.

The same thought rolled in Scott's mind as he paced, a habit he'd never been able to break. He'd made two trips to the breakroom, then stopped in the doorway to Nicki's office. Engrossed in reading a document that scrolled across her wall-mounted monitor, he didn't want to disturb her. His next stop was Ryan's office, but he was on the phone. Then it was back to the breakroom to get another cup of coffee. On the return trip to his office, he stopped in the conference area. Despite the presence of his two agents, the place seemed empty.

Scott turned to stare out a window. The view did little to allay his anxieties. Overcast, a heavy fog had rolled in, obscuring the nearby buildings, and added to his sense of isolation. He had no family. His parents died in a car crash when he was ten. Raised by an elderly aunt, she passed away several years ago. He was a man who was alone, but seldom did he feel lonely. Today was an exception. He missed the interaction of being in the field and running the investigation. Instead, he was confined to an office and had to wait for others to do the work.

Shaking off the strange mood, he glanced at the wall clock. Blake and Lance Brewster, the TEDAC agent, should be on site. In the last phone call, Blake indicated he didn't expect it would take long. That was three hours ago. Settling into his chair, he raised the cup to take a sip. When the phone rang, in his haste to set it down, the hot brew sloshed on his hand. Well, hell, he thought and grabbed a tissue from a nearby box as he glanced at the screen. It was Blake. "What'd you find?"

"Lance found traces of explosive residue. He's calling it in to his boss."

"Any idea how this was missed?"

"I spoke to the local state transportation personnel. It never occurred to them it could be intentional. I can understand their reasoning. It's in a remote section of the county, with little traffic, so why would anyone want to blow it up. They chalked it up to old age and lack of maintenance. Hold on," Blake said.

In the background, Scott could hear a distant voice.

Blake's voice came back on the line. "Sorry about that. The state inspector just arrived, and he's upset."

"Did you have any trouble?"

"Not really, but we got damn lucky. The state had already started to repair the bridge. Another day and our evidence would have been hauled off. Lance has already called the highway department in Texas to stop any repairs on the other two bridges."

"When do you plan to leave?"

"Another hour should wrap it up here. I'm sending you a preliminary report of our findings. Once we're in the air, I'll get a more detailed report to you."

Scott signed off, and when his computer beeped, he pulled up Blake's report. Though the jargon was a bit technical, it provided confirmation a bomb had been used to destroy the bridge. He forwarded the report to his agents along with a text to Adrian and Cat about Blake's findings, then hit the speed dial for his boss.

Twelve

Texas

Cat swerved to avoid another large pot hole. "This road needs some serious repair."

Adrian looked up from his computer screen. The dry desert, flat and barren on each side of the remote road, was broken only by clumps of cacti, low brush, and a railroad track—not a house in sight. "Are you sure you're on the right road?"

"According to the GPS we are."

A ping echoed over the sound of the engine. Adrian's phone was on the console. He picked it up and tapped the screen. "Message from Scott," he said, and read the text.

Cat said, "I'm not surprised. I expected that's what they'd find."

In the hazy mirage that rippled across the roadway, several buildings appeared.

"Not much here. I wonder what keeps the town going? I still haven't seen a house." Adrian closed the laptop and laid it on the backseat.

They passed the city limit sign. Ahead was a service station with a single, old style pump.

Cat pulled in and parked in front of the building. "This is the address for the Desert Rats."

Exiting, she stood for a minute beside the car and stretched, working the kinks out of her neck and shoulders as she scanned the small town. Several buildings, most with boarded up windows, lined the roadway.

A grocery store next to a hardware store appeared to be the only active businesses.

Adrian stepped around the back of the car, and his gaze swept the structure in front of them. "This was a train depot that's been converted into a service station."

The long structure was old and weathered with entrances on each end. Over one door, the sign, faded and peeling, read: Grigsby's Service. A poster in the window warned to pay first, then pump. A dust devil swirled around one end, rattling the screen door that covered the open doorway.

"Let's see if our man, Jonah Grigsby, is here," Adrian said, and strode toward the door.

A bell tinkled overhead as they entered. A thin layer of dust covered the food, drug, and household products that filled two rows of metal racks. A wall-mounted cooler held an assortment of cold drinks and beer.

Motioning toward a living room visible through an arched doorway that divided the building into two sections, Adrian said, "This answers my question of where at least one person resides."

As he spoke, a man stepped through the doorway. "Can I help you folks?" In his early sixties, he stood well over six-foot, with a broad chest and beer belly. A rough stubble covered his cheeks and chin, but it was the sunken eyes that drew Adrian's attention. They held a hard and hostile glint.

Out of the corner of his eye, Adrian caught Cat's movements as she eased further into the store and leaned against a counter. She had the open doorway covered.

"We're looking for Jonah Grigsby," Adrian responded.

"What for?"

Adrian pulled out his badge case and flipped it open. "Agent Dillard, FBI. We have a few questions."

The man snorted. "You think that's gonna impress anyone around here? She a fed, too?" His gaze darted toward Cat with a look of disdain before moving back to Adrian.

"Yeah, she is. Are you Grigsby?" he asked, as he slid the case back into his pocket.

The man's feet shifted to widen his stance as his thumbs hooked in his pants pockets. "I am. Unless you got a warrant, I suggest you get the hell out of my store and out of town. Folks around here don't take kindly to strangers, especially the cop kind."

Adrian never moved, his gaze locked on Grigsby's face. "Oh, believe me, I can get one. I'll haul your ass to Laredo and then ask my questions. Your choice."

"Fucking feds, think you can run roughshod over everyone."

"No. Not everyone, unless we have a reason. Now, what's it going to be? Here or Laredo?"

"Bastard. I've got nothing to hide."

"Then you shouldn't mind a few questions. I'm interested in the Desert Rats. Are you the head of the group?"

"Hell, everyone knows that."

"What does your club do?"

"Nothing. We're just a bunch of guys who like to shoot the bull together."

"And what is it you shoot the bull about?"

Grigsby's jaw tightened. "We're not breaking any laws, and you can't prove otherwise."

"Didn't say you were. How many members do you have?"

"None of your goddamned business. And the answer will be the same in Laredo."

Adrian pulled out his phone, tapped the screen and brought up a mugshot of Warden. "Is this one of them?" He turned the screen toward Grigsby.

The man stared at Adrian.

His tone hardened. "I asked you a question. Do you know this man?"

Grigsby's gaze shifted to the phone. A spark flashed in his eyes. "Never met him. Who is he?"

"How about this one?" This time it was Martin's face on the screen.

"Don't know him either. What's the deal?"

"They're persons of interest in a case we're investigating. If I find out you lied, I'll be back with a warrant."

Adrian glanced at Cat. "Ready?"

"Yes." She moved toward the door.

Adrian stared at the man until he heard the rattle of the screen door, then turned. Cat held the door open and watched Grigsby until Adrian cleared the doorway, then followed.

As she exited the parking lot, she said, "Someone was watching from the living room. I caught a glimpse of movement. A man, but I couldn't see his face."

"Did you notice the change in attitude when he looked at the pictures?" Adrian asked. "He lied about knowing the two men, but he wanted to know why we were asking."

"How do you know he lied?"

It didn't take a touch to tell him. "There was a brief spark in his eyes when he looked at their pictures. We need to dig deeper into his background. How far is it to the Border Guards?"

"About ten miles from here."

"Good. I've got time to call Nicki."

"Hey, witchy woman," he said, when Nicki answered.

"Not me. That's the woman you're roaming Texas with," Nicki responded, and chuckled.

"Don't remind me. No owls, so that's good." Cat's mysterious link to owls had become common knowledge within the team. Whenever they showed up, a dead body wasn't far off. Adrian wondered how it felt not to hide behind vague explanations. Still, habits of a lifetime were hard to overcome, and he had no desire to be the focus of speculation, even within the team.

Cat piped up. "Don't be talking bad about me. Adrian has the speakerphone on."

"Any news on the missing agent?" Nicki asked.

Adrian answered, "No, still running down leads, which is why I called. We've been visiting with the head of one of the factions Blake found, the Desert Rats. I need a complete rundown on the leader, Jonah Grigsby. He knows more than he's willing to admit. We need to find out what it is."

"I'm one step ahead of you. I've already plugged his name and the leader of the Border Guards, Norman Reynolds, into TRACE." Nicki tapped a key to check, and the goblin danced across the screen. "Nothing yet, but I'll call if I get something."

"Any more info on the bridges?" Adrian asked.

"Blake and the guy from TEDAC are on the move, headed to the next one in Texas. Scott has been holed up in his office since he got the phone call. Knowing our boss, I bet his brain has kicked into high gear along with the damn tapping of his pen. We've threatened to take it away from him."

Adrian and Cat laughed. "Good luck on that one," he said. "We're coming up on our next visit. Call you later."

Adrian disconnected as Cat stopped in front of a locked metal gate connected to a ten-foot high wire fence. In the distance, several buildings were visible.

"Hmm ... big change from the last place. Do you see any way to get inside?"

"Got a feeling we've already been spotted." Adrian motioned to a rising cloud of dust behind a truck headed to the gate.

Exiting, they walked to the front of the car. Cat leaned against the front fender, arms crossed her chest as she watched Adrian examine the lock on the gate.

"Bolt cutters won't work on this one." He turned his attention to the fence. "It looks new, and this type of fence doesn't come cheap. They sure don't want anyone to get inside. It's electrified."

The truck came to a screeching halt, and two men, attired in military-style camouflage gear, jumped out and slung rifles over their shoulders.

"Didn't you see the no trespassing signs? Turn around and get the hell out of here," the driver shouted.

"FBI. We're here to talk to Norm Reynolds."

"Let's see some identification."

Cat slid her arms down and rested her hands on the hood of the car. One was inches from the pistol on her hip. While she seemed at ease, her eyes never left the two men who stood in front of the gate.

Adrian held up his badge case, the sunlight gleamed on the gold badge. The passenger moved closer to the gate, then stepped back. He nodded to his buddy.

"What if the Commander doesn't want to talk to you?" the driver asked.

"It would be in his best interest to meet with us," Adrian said.

The driver stepped to the side of the truck and made a phone call. After a short conversation, he turned back to the gate.

"He's not interested, and unless you have a warrant, you're trespassing on private property." They straightened and swung the rifles off their shoulders.

Cat moved away from the car and stood a few feet from Adrian. After several seconds, the two men stepped back to their truck. With a squeal of tires that churned up another dust cloud, they headed back to the compound.

"I'd sure like to get a look at what's inside those buildings," Cat said.

Adrian nodded, his attention on the gate as he examined the construction. Lifting his head, his eyes moved along the fence line, noting the spacing of the metal t-posts. He searched for cameras in the mesquite trees on each side of the entrance. He took a last look at the location of the buildings before walking back to the car. His intuition told him he'd need to know every detail before this was over.

Au 79

After leaving the medical examiner's office, Tracy swung by the station. For what she had in mind, she needed a different car, one that didn't scream cop. She also needed to check her message board.

Walking in, she spotted Art, Skip, and Pete huddled around Art's desk. So much for getting in and out of the office without her co-workers seeing her.

At the sound of her footsteps, Art looked up. He tapped Skip on the shoulder, and when he glanced up, Art nodded toward the door.

"Uh-oh ..." Skip said.

"Okay guys, what's going on?" she asked, striding across the room to see what had their attention.

"Now, Tracy. Take it easy." Skip shifted his body to hide what was on the desk.

She stopped, her hands rested on her hips as she eyed the three men and the nervous expression on their faces.

"And just why should I take it easy?" she asked, a grim note in her voice.

Art and Pete shrugged their shoulders and looked at Skip.

"Uh ... the latest issue of the Laredo Observer is out," he said.

"Crap, what did that scumbag write now?" She pushed her way through the group to stare at the newspaper spread across the surface. Grabbing it, she read the article. "This is fricking unbelievable. He makes it sound as if Stuart is responsible for Bardwell's death. That rat-bastard!"

"Tracy, you can't go off the deep end with this. If you read it closely, he's worded his story so he's not liable, unless the fingerprint is a fabrication," Skip said.

A bleak look crossed her face, and she tossed the paper back on the desk. "No, it's not."

"What!" the three men said in accord.

"The feds discovered a partial print that's Stuart's on a piece of evidence taken out of Bardwell's garage."

"How'd you find out?" Skip asked.

"Adrian Dillard, the FBI agent, got a call yesterday while we were at Joe Warden's place. Skip, do you remember Warden?"

"Yeah, I do. We got him on an assault charge last year."

"He cleaned out his house and is gone."

Skip asked, "What's the connection to Bardwell?"

"An agent who works with Dillard found an old newspaper article about an arrest of Bardwell, Joe Warden, and Donnie Martin."

Art said, "I never ran across Warden, but I did Martin. He was a suspect in a series of burglaries last year. Find out anything about him?"

"Dead end, literally. Yesterday, someone put three slugs in him. After finishing up at Warden's house, we headed to Martin's place. He was dead when we got there. That's when Owens showed up and asked Dillard about the fingerprint. He must have known before we did."

"What did they pull out of the garage that's got everyone in a tailspin?" Pete asked.

Tracy glanced around the office to be sure someone hadn't walked in before she said, "Materials to make detonators."

Stunned, the three detectives stared at her. Skip was the first to break the silence. "Does Owens know this?" Then he answered his own question. "No. If he did, it would be plastered across the front page of that rag. What can we do to help?"

"Right now, I don't know. The two D.C. agents have taken over the investigation. They're out checking on the Desert Rats and Border Guards."

"Those are two groups I'd put at the head of my list of suspects," Pete said. "A few days ago, Sanchez in the gang unit mentioned he'd seen an uptick in activity by the Guards. He happened to be in the area and drove by to check out their compound. A new security fence has been installed. Said it looked high dollar."

"Now, isn't this interesting. Why, all of a sudden, are they concerned about security?" Tracy asked. "Skip, would you do me a favor? Run a background on Warden and Martin. See if there's anything new. I also need to find out if we've got any information on file about the membership for the two groups. Adrian asked for a list. I'm headed out to check on a lead."

"I'll take care of it. Are you sure you don't need me to go with you?" Skip asked.

Tracy didn't want him bird-dogging her steps and wasn't about to tell him why. Low-keying what she planned to do, she shrugged, and said, "Nah, this is just a surveillance for a couple of hours. No need to tie both of us up."

Skip knew his partner, and when she got that innocent, wide-eyed stare, he knew she was up to something. A grim note crept into his voice. "Don't do anything rash. Let the feds handle this."

She patted him on the shoulder. "Don't worry. I just got back into the investigation, and I'm not giving Rodriguez any reason to pull me again."

Turning, she headed to the corkboard that had vehicle keys hanging from hooks. Grabbing one, she walked out the door.

Skip grumbled, "Who does she think she's kidding. She's off on some wild stunt. I've a good mind to follow her."

Art said, "It might not be a bad idea. I'll run those backgrounds and get the list Tracy requested."

Skip passed by the key board and grabbed a set.

Tracy stopped at her locker and changed into her undercover attire—scuffed boots, ripped jeans, t-shirt, hooded sweatshirt, and a ball cap. She stuck her pistol in the waistband in the small of her back. Grabbing her backpack, she went out the back door of the station to the employee parking lot. Her vehicle, a beat-up pickup, was parked against the back fence. Bing Morris was at the top of her suspect list. His bar was only about twenty minutes away. She'd have plenty of time to watch who went in and out.

Thirteen

Washington D.C.

Ryan hung up the phone and grabbed the notes he'd made. Tapping on the doorframe to get Scott's attention, he stepped inside.

"I just got off the phone with the agent who interviewed Dyson's parents and sister." He dropped into a chair. "All he came up with was a comment from his mother. She said Stuart seemed to be distracted the last two times she talked to him. But when she asked what was wrong, he said it was just a problem with a case. Nothing for her to worry about."

"I didn't expect we'd get anything out of the contact, but it had to be checked off the list. Anything else?"

"You asked Blake to check into the reporter's article. I got a text from him, asking if I'd handle it. The Laredo Observer is a small newspaper that runs to social and local events. It's not the type of publication for exposés or controversial issues, which makes it even more puzzling why Eddie Owens has reported on two issues with the Dyson investigation."

"There's been a second!" Scott exclaimed.

"One came out this morning about Dyson's fingerprint."

Scott said, "Since he asked Adrian if it was true, we should have expected it. Was there any mention of the explosive devices?"

"Not a word. I sent you a copy of the article."

"Hmm ...." He leaned back in his chair as the pen in his hand tap danced on the desk. After a few seconds, he laid it down and looked at Ryan. "Someone knew about the fingerprint and calls Owens but says nothing about the devices. Any theories?"

"Not yet, at least not any I'm ready to discuss."

Scott nodded. "What about Owens' background?"

"Born and raised in Laredo. He's twenty. Father died when he was a senior in high school, mom works in a real estate office. Has a younger sister, eighteen. He worked odd jobs after graduation. The one before the newspaper was at a grocery store. He's related to the editor, which is probably why he got the job. No criminal history, I couldn't even locate a traffic ticket."

"Would you say he was gullible and ambitious?"

"It's exactly how I would describe him. He was the editor of the school newspaper. And it's why I believe he may have been targeted in whatever is going on in Laredo. Besides lacking in experience, he's the type whose buttons could easily be pushed."

"So, someone is using him," Scott mused.

"That would be my take."

Another knock on the doorframe and Nicki stuck her head in.

"Is this a private conversation or can anyone join in?"

Scott waved a hand toward a chair. "We were discussing the reporter in Laredo."

"Ryan sent me the second article. It's odd that it's about the fingerprint but not the devices. I have more bad news. It's the ballistics report." She laid a document on the desk. "After the Martin shooting, I contacted the medical examiner to ask that any reports be sent to me before he released them. He ran a comparison of the bullets removed from Bardwell and Martin. They came from the same gun. It belongs to Dyson."

"Holy hell!" Ryan exclaimed.

"How does he know?" Scott asked.

"Stuart was involved in a shooting a couple of years ago, and the ballistics on the rounds he fired were on file. When the M.E. ran the tests, the match popped up."

Scott's hand rubbed his neck as a look of frustration settled on his face. "Contact the M.E. and tell him to put a lid on the report. I don't want anyone other than Adrian and Cat to know about it. That includes Detective Harlowe. We're not going to give someone an opportunity to drop that tidbit into Owens' ear."

"Already done. I called him as soon as I read the report. He said he hasn't mentioned his findings to anyone in his office or Harlowe."

"Let's hope we can keep it that way. If this gets out, it'll create a firestorm of adverse publicity."

Texas

When Tracy passed the bar, the parking lot was empty. At the sight of the closed sign hanging on the front door, she changed her game plan. A boarded-up thrift store was at the end of the block. She pulled behind the building, parked and surveyed the deserted alley. Before she stepped out of the truck, she grabbed a small, zippered bag from the console.

She moved with a fast pace until she reached the back of the bar. Stepping to a window, she peered in. The kitchen was dark and empty. At the door, Tracy examined the lock before pulling rubber gloves and a locksmith tool from the bag. A couple of twists and she heard a click. After another glance that swept the alley, she opened the door and stepped inside.

She stopped, listening for any sounds as she surveyed the room. A large opening led to the bar. She spotted another open door alongside a commercial-sized refrigerator. It was an office. Once she was satisfied she was alone in the building, she walked into the small room. A desk with a computer and printer, two file cabinets, and a chair left little space.

Au79

Seated in front of the computer, she tapped the keyboard. A login screen appeared. She didn't dare take the time to guess at a password. The desk drawers were a catchall for odds and ends. She turned her attention to the file cabinets. Folders were labeled for invoices, utilities, and employment activities. She quickly scanned each one, before moving onto another drawer. It wasn't until she reached the bottom one that she found something—a locked metal box.

Picking it up, she set it on the desk. A few twists with a smaller lockpick, and she lifted the lid. It was filled with papers. She thumbed through the stack. Most were legal contracts, property deeds, and loan documents. Tracy eyed the printer, debating whether she could get away with making copies when she heard the honk of a horn and then angry voices. She stuffed the documents back into the box and replaced it in the drawer.

****

When Skip walked out the back door, he saw Tracy pull out of the parking lot. He ran to his vehicle. When he turned onto the street, her pickup was already several blocks ahead. He sped up, but the light turned red as he reached the intersection. All he could do was watch her brake lights flicker as she turned onto another street.

His fingers drummed the steering wheel in frustration. She was obviously headed to the west side of town. But where? At least it wasn't the Observer's office, which was in the opposite direction. Then it dawned on him, it might be the bar where the biker was killed. All Skip could do was hope he'd made the right guess.

When he reached the street where the bar was located, he spotted her truck at the end of the block as she turned into a vacant parking lot. What the hell was she up to? He drove past the bar. It was closed, and another light went off. *She's going to search the place.* When he passed the empty building and saw her walking in the alley, he was certain. Damn! The woman's putting her career on the line, to say nothing about ending up in jail.

101

Skip circled the block and parked on the opposite end of the street. As the minutes passed, his nervousness increased. *Come on Tracy, get the hell out of there.* A pickup drove in and parked in front of the bar. *Christ! I bet that's the owner.* He pulled behind the truck and honked his horn. Hopping out, he hollered and flashed his badge at the man who stood at the front door.

****

She stepped to the side of the doorway that led to the bar and peeped around the edge. At the sight of Morris' truck parked in front of the window, a jolt of fear energized her. She had to get out. As she passed the open door to the office, she glanced inside to be certain she hadn't left any signs of her presence, then headed to the back door. She flipped the lock on the inside before pulling it shut and trotted back to her truck.

Before she drove out of the parking lot, she looked down the street at the bar. Morris stood on the front step and facing him was Skip. What the hell was he doing here? She couldn't drive off and leave him. Tracy pushed her hair under her ballcap and put on a pair of sunglasses. As she passed the bar, she revved the engine to get Skip's attention. When he glanced her way, she sped up and turned the corner, then pulled to the side. A few minutes later, Skip passed her, and she followed him back to the station.

He waited alongside his car as she backed into the parking space. Fisted hands rested on his hips, and an angry scowl crossed his face. She sighed. In some respects, an ass-chewing from her partner was worse than one from the captain. She turned off the engine and slid out of the truck. Hoping to head him off, she said, "Why'd you follow me?"

"Don't you turn this back on me. If I hadn't, you'd probably be on your way to the county jail. I know you broke into his bar. What the hell were you thinking? You're so damn hardheaded, you won't listen to anyone."

They'd been partners for the last seven years. She'd seen him angry on many occasions, but never quite like this. "Skip, I know Morris is involved with what's happened to Stuart. I can't let it go. I've got to do something. I hoped to find a lead, anything more than what we've got now."

He slumped against the side of the car, his anger faded. "Tracy, I know. This has to be eating at you. Next time, let me know, so I don't have to chase you all over the goddamn town just to watch your backside. Okay?"

She grinned. "Deal. So, how'd you end up in Morris' parking lot?"

"I caught up with you when you parked behind the thrift store. It didn't take a rocket scientist to figure out what you were up to. I set up across the street to keep an eye on the place. When Morris drove up, I knew you had to still be inside. I stopped him just as he got to the door. He doesn't like cops. It was easy to provoke him. I hoped you'd hear us."

"I did. Thanks."

"Did you find anything?"

"No. His computer screen was locked. There wasn't anything in his files. The only oddity was a metal box with a bunch of legal documents. I'd just started looking at them when I heard your voices. I wish I would've had a few more minutes."

"Don't even think about trying that stunt again," Skip warned her.

"If I do, I'll let you know."

He turned to walk into the PD, and grumbled, "Like I said, hardheaded."

"Hey, thanks to you, I didn't get caught." Her phone rang. "I'll catch up with you. This is Doc Kennedy."

"Tracy, you wanted me to call when Bardwell's sister arrived. She's here now. I told her you wanted to talk to her. How soon can you get here? The quicker, the better, she wants to leave."

"Be there in ten." She looked down at her attire. Well, it couldn't be helped, there was no time to change. "Did you ever get the ballistics results?"

There was a hesitation before he answered. "No. Um … still waiting for it."

When she walked into the medical examiner's office, Doris gave her a long stare before raising her eyebrows. "Is this the new attire for homicide detectives?" she quipped.

"Just for today." Tracy grinned, then added, "Doc called."

"He's started an autopsy, but said to tell you the sister, Nancy Gibbons, is in the conference room."

An overweight woman, with bleached hair and heavy makeup, had a phone to her ear when she opened the door. Seeing Tracy, she said, "I'll have to call you back. Someone's here."

"Ms. Gibbons, I'm Detective Harlowe."

The woman eyed her with a look of suspicion. "You're a cop? You don't look like one."

Tracy pulled out her badge case and flipped it open. "I can assure you I am. I'm the detective in charge of the investigation of your brother's death. I'm sorry for your loss."

The woman sniffed. "Not much of one. Cam always was a deadbeat. I'm just surprised it didn't happen sooner."

"Please, have a seat. I'd like to ask you a few questions."

"Don't know what I can tell you," she said, and settled in a chair. "I haven't seen Cam for over a year, though we talked on the phone a few times."

"What did you talk about?"

"Money, mostly. He was always hitting me up for a loan, except the last time. Said he was about to make a big score. Bragged about how he'd finally be on easy street."

"Did he say how?"

"No. Told me to mind my own business when I asked. The less I knew, the better off I'd be. I figured he was up to no good. Is that why he was killed?" She looked around. "I don't suppose you can smoke in here?"

"No, I'm sorry, you can't."

Au 79

She grunted in disgust.

"How long ago was the last call?"

"Hmm … about a week ago. One minute he's bragging about hitting the big time, the next he's on a slab in the morgue."

"Do you know any of his friends or anyone he worked with?"

"Just those damn biker gangs. It's why he liked living here."

"Did he ever talk about them, mention any names?"

"Uh, no. I don't remember any names. Wait a minute, he did tell me about one a few months back. At the time, I told him it was a funny name for a bunch of bikers, and he just laughed. What was it?" Long red fingernails tapped the table. "Oh, yeah, that's it. Guards, the Border Guards."

"What'd he say?"

"Oh, just that he'd linked up with a group of guys who thought like he did."

"Nothing else?"

"No, that's all he said. I went by his house, and it's covered with crime scene tape. What's going on?"

"Someone burglarized it, and we're still investigating."

"When can I get in?"

"It'll be a couple of days before I can release it. What's your phone number and address? I'll call you."

"Didn't believe he'd have anything worth stealing."

After jotting the information in her notepad, Tracy handed her a business card. "If you happen to think of anything else, please call me."

Tracy nodded to Doris as she passed the desk, though her thoughts were on the connection she'd just found. Were the Border Guards involved in whatever Stuart was into? *Are you still alive?* In her gut, she didn't have a sense he was dead. *So, where the hell are you?*

Fourteen

The phone, lying on the console, rang. He looked at the screen. "It's Scott." He tapped the answer button, then the speakerphone.

"Adrian, where are you?"

"Cat and I are headed back to the ATF office. We finished our visits to the Desert Rats and Border Guards."

"Anyone else in the car?"

Adrian sent a quick glance of puzzlement toward Cat, as he said, "No. Just the two of us."

"We've got more bad news, and I don't want anyone else to know." He explained the results of the ballistic test.

"Christ, it puts Stuart Dyson at the top of the suspect list," Cat exclaimed.

"It does," Scott said.

"What about Tracy Harlowe?" Adrian asked.

"She doesn't know. We've told the M.E. not to release the report or discuss the results with anyone. Until we can figure out what's going on, I don't want this to get out. The media will have a field day over an agent who's gone rogue. Do you know about the latest article in the Observer?"

With a note of disgust in his voice, Adrian said, "No, but I bet it was about the fingerprint, right?"

"Yes."

"When we get back to town, I'll pick up a copy," he said.

"What happened with the two groups?"

Adrian explained the results of their visits, then added, "If we can find a link connecting our victims and Dyson to either faction, it would give us a starting point."

"Scott, any news from Blake?" Cat asked.

"He's landed at the airport and has a two-hour drive to get to the location. We won't know anything until tomorrow. What's your next move?"

"Not sure, seems we're at a standstill. I may have another go at Morris, the bar owner. See if I can shake something loose there."

After Adrian disconnected, Cat said, "What about the reporter? It's time we had a meeting with that young man, see what he knows."

Adrian agreed, saying, "Let's swing by the newspaper office and find out."

Located in a small office complex, a sign adhered to the glass door identified the Laredo Observer. As they stepped out of the car, Cat studied the rundown building. "Not much overhead in this place."

Inside, a counter extended the width of the room with a narrow opening on one end. Behind it, a cluster of desks faced each other. *Editor* was printed on a closed door at the back.

A woman seated behind the counter looked up. "Can I help you?"

"We'd like to talk to Eddie Owens," Adrian said.

"He's not here. Do you want to leave a message?"

"How about the editor, is he in?"

"Yes. What's your name? I'll tell him you are here."

Adrian flipped open his badge case. "FBI Agent Adrian Dillard, and this is Agent Morgan."

Her eyes widened, and she abruptly stood. The chair rolled backwards. "Uh, yes, just a minute." She rushed to the back office.

Cat grinned. "Guess they don't get many federal agents popping in on them."

A man in his early forties stepped out of the office and strode toward the counter. His face held an expression of wariness and distrust.

"I'm Jimmy Bishop, the editor. How may I help you?"

"We'd like to talk to you about two articles that have appeared in your newspaper."

Bishop glanced at the woman next to him, who was listening with a look of avid interest.

"Let's go back to my office."

Inside, there was barely enough room to shut the door without hitting the two chairs in front of the desk. Bishop leaned back in his chair and crossed his hands over his stomach.

He eyed each agent, before he asked, "What do you want to know?"

"Where did Eddie Owens get his information about Stuart Dyson?"

"It was an anonymous call."

"Are you certain? Is it possible Owens knew and didn't tell you?" Adrian asked.

"I don't like your inference he lied. When I say we don't know, that's exactly what I mean."

"When did he get the calls?"

"You'd have to ask him."

"Can you tell us anything about the caller?"

A sly look of interest gleamed in the editor's eyes. "No. Why are you so concerned?"

Adrian leaned forward, his gaze locked on Bishop's face, which paled as the man stared back. "A federal agent is missing, and anything that connects to our investigation is our concern, including phone calls to your newspaper."

"Sounds as if your agent may not be missing but has gone AWOL. As an editor, it's a concern to this newspaper."

"I wouldn't recommend a rush to judgment on that idea, Mr. Bishop."

"Agent Dillard, I hope that isn't a threat!"

"A piece of advice. One you should heed." He pulled out a business card and reached across the desk to hand it to the editor. "Have Owens call me. I want a meeting with him."

Bishop looked at the card, opened a drawer, and tossed it inside. "I'll tell him, but it's up to Eddie whether he wants to talk to you."

Adrian stood, turned and reached for the doorknob. As he followed Cat out the door, he looked over his shoulder at the editor. "It's not a request. If he doesn't call me, I'll have him picked up as a material witness."

As they left the parking lot, Cat glanced at Adrian who appeared to be lost in thought. "You were a bit heavy-handed back there. How come?"

"I wanted to see what type of reaction I would get."

"What did you learn when you touched him?" Cat asked.

"Uh, what?"

"Oh, come on, Adrian. Everybody in our team has some peculiarity they're hiding. You think I didn't pick up on the fact yours is touching someone."

He eyed her with a cautious look and made a small, noncommittal noise.

"Got you flustered, have I?" Though she chuckled, she shot him a look of sympathy. "I felt the same way when Ryan pinned me to the wall several months back with a similar observation. You might as well give it up, it's not something you can hide. At least, not with us."

"I guess I should have seen this coming, but it's a topic I'm not comfortable discussing."

"I know. Still, sharing my gift saved my life. Don't you think it's about time to bring yours into the light of day?"

"It's not anything strange or mysterious, but it tends to make people nervous. My mother explained it as an enlightened sense. Something that's been passed down from our early Irish ancestors. In Gaelic, the name is *aireachtáil eischéadfach*."

After several attempts to repeat what he said failed, Cat's laughter erupted.

Adrian chuckled. "Does sound like a mouth full of mush, doesn't it? The closest English translation would be ESP."

"So, how does it work?"

"The simplest answer is that it's like an animal who can hear sounds and detect odors a human can't. You might say I'm a human lie detector. I know when a person has lied."

"Hell of an asset for a cop."

He laughed. "It doesn't always work. Most of the time, my insight requires a strong emotion in another person. I've learned fear, anger, grief, or even stress are the triggers."

"It's why you pushed Bishop's buttons. You were trying to provoke a negative reaction."

"You got it," he said, as Cat drove into the parking lot of Bing's Watering Hole. "Let's see what happens with our bartender."

Inside, about half the stools and tables were occupied. Morris stood behind the bar wiping a glass with a towel. His gaze hardened into a hostile stare when they came through the door.

Cat moved to a table near the wall. Seated, her eyes scanned the room as Adrian approached the bar.

"What the hell are you doing back here?" Morris growled. His voice carried over the din of the TV, and several customers turned to glare at Adrian.

His gaze flicked over the other men, then shifted to Morris. "Looking for information," Adrian replied, as he leaned on the bar.

"Unless you've got a warrant, I don't have to talk to you."

Adrian's stare never wavered. He waited.

Morris cleared his throat, and said, "I know who you are. Coming in here, bullshitting me about being the brother of a missing agent. Typical cop. Lying to get what you want." He set the glass down with a bang and picked up another.

Now, isn't this interesting, Adrian thought. *I wonder how you found out I'm an agent.* "Who told you?"

"Don't remember and wouldn't tell you if I did. Get the hell out of my place."

"Now, Bing. That's not a very nice attitude when I paid you all that money. I guess you forgot that part of the deal."

"I said, get out!"

A rumble erupted from several men.

"It's not going to happen. And I don't think you or your buddies here want to take on two federal agents."

Morris looked at Cat and grunted. "Her? She's not likely to be a problem."

Adrian glanced at Cat. She grinned and brought her hand out from under the table and laid her pistol on top.

"You really don't want to mess with her," Adrian said. "She can put a bullet in your eyeball without even thinking about it."

The other men eased back in their chairs. Cat looked at them, and said, "Wise move, boys."

Adrian smirked at Morris. "Now, where were we? Oh, yes, the missing agent. I'm still looking for information and will pay for it. Since you were so cooperative before, I wanted to give you the first option at the extra cash."

"I've got nothing else to say, and I don't know anything. You're wasting your time."

"Well then …" He raised his voice. "If any of you gents are interested in earning ten grand, I'm paying for information about a missing agent, Stuart Dyson. I'll leave my card. Give me a call." He pulled out two cards, one he flipped toward the end of the bar.

Morris' fisted hands rested on the wood surface. Adrian reached across and slid the other card under his hand. "Offer's still open for you." He eased back from the bar. "Ready, Cat?"

"Yep," she said, and stood. With the pistol in her hand, and keeping an eye on the occupants, she stepped to the door. Adrian strode across the room, and she followed him out.

"That was enlightening," Cat said, as she exited the parking lot.

"He's lying through his teeth. Whatever's going on, he knows."

"I wonder how he found out we're agents."

"I had the same thought. It's time to move him up on the suspect list."

"Where are we headed now?"

"ATF. We still need to meet with Karl, and I want Bill Goddard there. We can arrange for the surveillance and wiretaps on Morris. Then, we need to get a bite to eat."

"We should also check in with Tracy," Cat said.

He picked up his phone and tapped the speed dial for Bill.

****

"Morris, you've been told not to call me, so this had better be urgent," Reynolds said.

"Those damn agents were back at my bar, snooping around again. And earlier today, I had a visit from another Laredo PD detective."

"Which agents?"

"The ones who posed as family members."

"What'd they want this time?"

"Still offering money for information. Said I didn't know anything and not to come back unless they had a warrant."

"You told them you knew they were agents!" Reynolds exclaimed.

"Yeah."

Muttered curses sounded before Reynolds said, "Morris, you've got shit for brains. Now they'll wonder how you found out. Goddamn it! When will you learn to keep your mouth shut? What'd they do?"

His voice defensive, Morris said, "Nothing. They up and left."

"Who was the Laredo detective?"

"Some guy I'd never seen. Thornton."

"What'd he want?"

"More questions about Bardwell. I think there was …"

Reynolds interrupted, "I'm not paying you to think. Just shut up and don't talk to anyone, I don't care what they threaten. Do you understand?"

Disgusted, Reynolds tossed the phone on the desk and stared out his window. Morris had served his purpose. Now, he'd become a liability.

Fifteen

Tracy stared at an aerial map of the Border Guards' compound on her computer. When did they add new buildings? The last time she'd seen the place, there were two small storage sheds and an old farmhouse. Now, three metal barns formed a half-circle behind the house.

Skip stepped beside her. She looked up at him. "Did you know they'd added buildings?"

He studied the screen before he said, "No. It's been several years since I've been there. Wonder what they're up to? Pete mentioned a new fence."

Her phone rang. She tapped the answer button and said, "Adrian. You're one step ahead of me. I was getting ready to call you."

"Where are you?"

"At the PD. I wanted to follow up on your request for the list of members. Much to my surprise, we don't have any on file. And that's straight from the head of the gang unit who said the group has always been low-key. We've never had a reason to monitor them. Also, nothing more on Martin and Warden than what we've already found."

"I was hoping you'd have names. All we've been able to locate are Reynolds and Grigsby. Appreciate the effort. Nothing ever comes easy. We're leaving the ATF office. Do you want to join us for dinner?"

Tracy glanced at the computer screen. "Thanks for the invite, but I'll pass. How about breakfast?"

"Okay. Same place and time?"

"That's good for me. See you then."

Skip had grabbed his briefcase and waited to leave until she hung up. "Are you going to tell them about your little escapade today?"

"Probably not, since I didn't find anything that will help."

"Go home, get some rest," Skip told her.

"Um ... I will, just want to finish some paperwork before I leave. See you tomorrow."

Tracy watched him walk out the door, then turned back to her screen. She had another stop to make before she headed home. She glanced down at her attire. Time to change clothes again.

****

Adrian pushed back his plate. Not a scrap of food was left. He'd been so focused throughout the day, he hadn't given a thought to eating. He glanced at Cat's plate, and it was almost as bare. "Looks like this place was a good choice for both of us."

Cat said, "It was. I've always been partial to Italian cuisine."

He swallowed the last of the beer, looked at the bottle and debated whether to have another. One was his limit when he was on a case. This probably wasn't the time to change his habits. "What's your opinion of the meeting?"

Earlier, they had stopped at the ATF office to set up the Morris surveillance. Not only were Bill and Karl there, but also their agents. It turned into a lengthy discussion as there was considerable dissension about who would do what, and when. It was finally decided that Karl's two agents would take the first shift.

Cat sighed and swirled the remaining wine in her glass. "Something seemed a bit off, some uneasy vibes."

"Is that why you've been distracted?"

"Uh-huh. I've been rolling the reasons in my mind, but I can't pin it down."

"I got the same impression but kept thinking it was just tension, a rivalry between two local agencies."

"I'm not certain, but I don't believe that's it," Cat said.

He pulled out his phone and hit the speed dial for Nicki.

"Hey there," she answered.

"How's the new office working out?"

"Adrian, this new monitor is amazing. And I'm getting more links set up for TRACE. All in all, it's coming along rather nicely."

Adrian laughed. "You and your toys."

Nicki quipped back. "Don't forget, buddy, these toys may end up pulling your butt out of the fire one of these days. You need to be a bit more respectful."

Another chuckle erupted from Adrian. "Yes, ma'am. I hear you, loud and clear. I have a question for you."

"Shoot," she said.

"Did you find any connections between the personnel in the ATF and FBI office that might link to any of the victims or possible suspects."

"No, but I didn't specifically target a relationship."

"It may be a dead end, but one I'd like explored."

"You got it. What else?"

"Cat and I had a couple of interesting conversations with …"

Nicki interrupted, saying, "Hold that thought, the boss man just walked in."

The next voice he heard was Scott's, who asked, "What happened?"

Adrian covered the details of their confrontation with the editor and Morris, then added, "We've got a team of local agents following him. Scott, have you ever met Karl Chambers, Bill Goddard or any of their personnel?"

"No. Did something pique your interest?"

"Nothing that I can pin down. I asked Nicki to dig deeper into their backgrounds. Anything from Blake?"

"No. I don't expect a call until tomorrow."

"Okay, we're calling it a night."

Adrian looked at Cat. "I've a hunch tomorrow might prove interesting."

A u 7 9

****

Before leaving the office, Tracy had studied the layout of the roads leading to the compound on the aerial map. She spotted an abandoned house near the Guards' location that might be a good place to stash the truck.

After turning onto the road that led to the compound, she slowed, searching for the entrance to the house. When she spotted it, she backed in, just in case she needed to make a fast exit. With the truck parked next to the ramshackle building it wouldn't be noticeable to any cars on the road.

Stepping out the truck, she paused. She could see the glow of lights from the compound. She hung a pair of binoculars around her neck. Dressed in black attire from head to foot, she should be near invisible in the deep shadows cast by the rising moon.

With an easy pace, Tracy strode along the edge of the road until she reached a curve adjacent to the corner of the fence line. She crossed the bar ditch and realized she had a major problem. No crawling through, or over this one, the damn thing was electrified.

Pissed, she hesitated. Was it worth her time to go any further? She could see the glow of lights from the compound. *What the hell, I'm here. I might as well look at the place.* As she neared the entrance, she stopped next to a row of mesquite trees that bordered the inside of the fence. Flood lights lit up the buildings and a half-dozen pickups.

After adjusting the focus on the binoculars, she homed in on the vehicles, but none of the license plates were visible. Several men, dressed in military-style camouflage clothing, milled around the buildings. Some carried large boxes from a metal barn that were added to a stack near the house.

The sound of an engine grew in intensity. Headlights of an approaching vehicle flashed across the roadway. The driver would certainly be able to see her as he passed. She had to hide, but where? It was too late to cross the road and take cover in the heavy brush on the other side. The ditch was her only option. Despite the trash and weeds, it was deep enough. With a fervent prayer that nothing alive awaited, she scrambled down the side. She grunted in pain as large rocks dug into her back. She rolled onto her stomach and pulled the remnants of a trash bag over her.

The squeal of brakes sent a sharp thrust of fear through her. Had the driver seen her? A door opened, and a man's voice said, "Once you're inside, stop." The creak of the gate opening echoed.

She didn't dare lift her head to find out what was going on, but the damn weeds tickled her nose. She cautiously moved her hand to push them away from her face. All she needed was to have a sneezing fit.

The truck moved, and the lights shifted away from where she huddled. When she heard the slam of the gate, she got to her knees and looked over the culvert. An eighteen-wheeler with a box trailer was headed toward one of the metal buildings.

She crawled out of the ditch and moved back to her position by the fence. The truck had parked, and two men exited. A third man approached them, and after a few seconds, they turned to gaze at the gate. Her hackles kicked into high gear. When a pickup roared into view, she knew. She jumped over the ditch. As soon as her feet hit the road, she ran.

Behind her, the truck screeched to a stop. A shot hit the ground ahead of her, kicking up dust and rocks. Fear added speed as she raced along the road. Another shot and dirt flew. A few more yards and she rounded the curve and was out of sight.

Gasping for air, her lungs burned as she slid behind the wheel. Tires spun as she shot out of the driveway. She punched the accelerator. Behind her, the truck rounded the curve. Thankful for the inspiration that made her study the aerial map, she turned at the first intersection and weaved her way through the backroads.

She didn't relax until she saw the lights in her rearview mirror disappear. As her breathing eased and the adrenaline rush faded, the questions circled in her mind. Why the elaborate security system? What did they need to protect? Why did they need a big rig truck? And why the hell did they try to kill her?

****

He hit the speed dial on the burner phone. When Reynolds answered, the caller said, "Reynolds, you've got a problem with Morris. It's time to get rid of him."

Reynolds said, "I already figured that out. I got a call from Morris. He said two agents and another detective showed up at his bar. Morris doesn't know when to shut up. I'll take care of it."

"Don't wait. Do it now. Those D.C. agents are having Morris followed."

Reynolds said, "Dammit, I told you I'd take care of it, and I will. If anyone gets in the way, well it's their bad luck. I had visitors today, probably those same agents. And ...." The caller interrupted.

"I know. They're on a fishing expedition, that's all. There shouldn't be any reason for them to return."

"Shut up and listen," Reynolds said. "Another visitor showed up tonight, and saw the truck arrive. We tried to stop him, but he got away. Find out who it was!"

"What did you do?" Anger vibrated in the caller's voice.

"Let's just say that one of my men rarely misses. This time he did."

"You idiot. Don't you ever stop to think before you act? So what if someone saw the truck? It wouldn't have been a big, fucking deal until you started shooting. It's raised another red flag, just like the damn detonators."

"I'm sick of hearing you harp about them. We've got more than enough. Just handle your end, and I'll take care of the rest, but I want a name. Get it."

A click echoed in his ear, and Reynolds was gone. Aggravated, he shoved the phone back into his pocket. The man was unpredictable, something he hadn't anticipated. It was starting to cause problems.

Sixteen

When the alarm sounded, Tracy rolled on her back. Her face scrunched at the sudden stab of pain. *Where'd that come from?* Then, the memory of her trek the night before, and rolling into a ditch filled with unknown objects and rocks, flooded her mind.

For a few seconds, she relived the terror she'd felt as bullets zinged by her. *Whatever is going on out there, those guys were playing for keeps.* This time, she wouldn't be able to keep quiet about her adventure.

When she walked into the diner, Adrian and Cat were seated in a booth by the window. Cat slid over to make room for her as she greeted the two agents.

The waitress stepped up with a cup in one hand and the coffee pot in the other. She sipped the hot brew and sighed. "Okay. I can face the rest of the day."

Cat laughed. "I felt the same way. Nothing beats the first taste of coffee in the morning."

A smirk crossed Adrian's face as he stared at his partner. "Or at noon, or in the afternoon or evening." He looked at Tracy. "Cat's addicted to the stuff."

Tracy's brief bout of enjoyment died as she brought her thoughts back to the reason for the meeting. After the waitress took their orders and topped off the cups, she said, "Yesterday, I interviewed Bardwell's sister. She was at the morgue to claim her brother's body. We've got a link to the Border Guards."

Adrian shot a keen glance at her. "And?"

"She talked to him a week before he was shot." She continued with the rest of the details.

Cat nodded. "We were at the Guards' compound yesterday. They have a high-dollar electrified fence and cameras."

"I found that out the hard way. I stopped by last night to check out the place."

Surprised, Cat turned her head and stared at Tracy. "By yourself?"

"Yeah."

A frown crossed Adrian's face. "That was a bit fool-hardy." He explained the unfriendly reception they received.

"You fared better than I did. Someone took a couple of shots at me."

"What!" Adrian and Cat exclaimed in unison.

As the waitress approached with their plates, Tracy's eyes flashed a warning. A look of pain crossed her face as she leaned back. Adrian's gaze had never left her face. His eyebrows lifted in a silent question.

Once the waitress had moved to another table, Tracy said, "Just a few bruises. A reminder of last night."

"You'd better explain," Cat said, as she picked up a piece of bacon.

Between bites of the pancakes she ordered, Tracy told them what happened, then added, "I don't believe the truck driver could've seen me in the ditch, which means they have motion detectors. It's the only way I could have been spotted."

"What do you remember about the truck?"

"It looked new. The truck was a dark color, and the box trailer was white. The side I could see was plain, no names. I didn't have time to get any license plate numbers."

"We need to make another pass by there," Adrian said.

"I'd offer to go with you, but I've got a meeting." She reached into the backpack sitting on the floor next to the bench seat and grabbed her wallet. Dropping a few dollars on the table, she said, "I'll try to catch up with you later."

"One other item before you leave," Adrian said. "We put Morris under surveillance. Matt and Randy from Karl's office have the first rotation and will switch out with Bill Goddard's agents."

For an instant Tracy froze, then pushed the money to the center of the table. "Oh? When did you get that set up?" she asked, her tone casual.

"Last night. We stopped by for another visit. Someone had clued our friendly barkeep in on the fact we were agents."

Tracy hoped the relief she felt didn't show on her face. Informing a federal agent that she burglarized a building was not a smart career move. If she'd found something, it would have been different, but since she didn't, no point in advertising her crime spree.

Cat waited until Tracy was out the door before she said, "Did you notice her reaction to the surveillance?"

"Sure did. Wonder what she's been up to that she doesn't want us to know? I'd better call Scott and tell him the Guards just got more aggressive, and we've got Bardwell linked to the Guards."

Washington D.C.

Scott yawned as he stepped inside the dark office. It had been a short night. It had taken hours to review all the results from Nicki's background search of the extensive list of people connected to the investigation. They found nothing. Still his instincts told him they'd missed a link, a connection that would unravel the maze surrounding the agent's disappearance.

His phone buzzed as he strode down the hallway to the breakroom. It was Blake.

After greeting his agent, he asked, "Any news?"

"Not yet. We're at the bridge and waiting for enough light to run the tests. What I can see is it'll be worse than the Oklahoma bridge. The new bridge is under construction, and we don't know if there's any debris left to test."

"Do you have any conclusions?" He hit the button to start the coffee brewing.

"I wish I did. I got a call from the supervisor of the TEDAC team in Oklahoma. They confirmed what we already knew. It was blown. They decided not to wait for our test results. Teams are on the way to the Texas sites."

"Smart move," Scott said.

"Where are we in the investigation?"

Once Scott had filled him in on the Laredo events, Blake asked, "When I finish, am I headed back to Washington or to Laredo?"

"Hmm …. I'm not certain."

Blake signed off. Scott poured a cup of coffee and headed to his office. His next call was from Adrian. The news about Harlowe's brush with the Guards, the truck, and Bardwell's connection to the Guards added pieces to the puzzle. He was beginning to find his way through the maze.

Texas

Irritable and tired, Eddie pushed open the door to the newspaper office. His plan to follow the detective and find out what she was up to hadn't quite worked out. He didn't find Tracy until after she was home, and he'd wasted the night in his car watching her house. When she left this morning, he followed her to the diner, then to the police department. Hoping she'd stay put, he swung by his apartment for a quick shower before heading to his office. He'd check his messages, and then go back to the police station.

His bag hit the floor with a thud. He picked up a stack of mail waiting on the desk. After sorting through the envelopes, he tossed them in a tray. Wasn't worth his time to open them. He checked his messages, then pulled his file on the investigation from a desk drawer.

"Eddie." His boss's voice boomed from the doorway of his office. "Get in here. We need to talk."

Damn. What was Jimmy in a stew about now?

When he stepped into the office, his boss motioned to the chair. "Close the door and have a seat."

Slouched in the chair, Eddie eyed Jimmy's grim face. "Uh ... something happen?"

"I had a visit yesterday from two federal agents."

An uneasy tingle trickled down his back. "What'd they want?"

"You and your anonymous caller. I told them we didn't know who had called. That's the truth, right?"

Eddie gulped, his tension increased as Jimmy's gaze hardened. "Yes."

"It damn well better be. I'm not going to jeopardize this paper or protect your butt by lying to a federal agent."

"I swear, Jimmy. I don't have a clue who called."

"Okay, but if you find out, I better be the first to know, or you'll be back sacking groceries. And if he calls again, you tell me. Now, get back to work."

"Uh, okay. Thanks. I, uh, I promise to let you know." Eddie pushed himself out of the chair.

"Oh, one more thing," Jimmy said, and tossed a business card on the desk. "The agent wants to talk to you. Call him today. No excuses. He threatened to have you arrested if you don't."

Eddie reached over and picked it up. "I will."

Back at his desk, curses rumbled in his head. Because they were related, Jimmy believed he could push him around. He looked at the card, tempted to tear it up and toss it in the trash. His eyes darted to Jimmy's office. No, he'd better give the damn agent a call.

Au79

When Cat and Adrian walked into the ATF office, they were surprised to see Bill Goddard sitting in front of Karl's desk.

After greeting them, Adrian moved a chair to the side to let him watch both men. Cat leaned against the wall, her hands tucked in her pockets.

"Bill, we had planned on stopping at your office today. You saved us a trip."

"I'm checking the surveillance schedules," the man replied.

Karl said, "After you left last night, Bill and I changed the assignments. Instead of Matt, Randy is teamed with Bill's agent, Tim Grimes. We felt it would be better if we used an agent from each office, instead of losing both our agents at the same time."

Bill nodded. "Linda Spencer, from my office, and Matt, will take over at noon. The last time I talked to Tim, he said Morris was still at home."

Adrian said, "The Border Guards have moved up on our list of suspects."

Bill's eyes darted from Karl to Adrian. "Is there a reason?"

"Last night, Detective Harlowe stopped to look at the place, and someone took a couple of shots at her."

"She okay?" Karl asked.

"Yes."

A grunt of disgust erupted from Bill. "I don't know why the Laredo Police Chief hasn't fired her. Over the years, she's been involved in several questionable events. I wouldn't put it past her to have made up the incident. I still say it was a mistake to put her on the task force."

"Now, Bill, we both know she's a damn good detective. She digs until she gets results," Karl said.

Adrian eyed Bill's angry face before he glanced at Karl. "In this case, Karl, you're right. Before her hasty exit, she spotted an eighteen-wheeler pull into the compound. Any idea why they would need a big rig truck?"

Leaning back in his chair, Karl let out a short whistle. "I can't think of a single reason. Bill, how about you? Any ideas?"

Still fuming, Bill said, "I don't have a clue, and I'm not convinced it's even relevant. I have an appointment." He stood and picked up his briefcase. He glanced at Cat, then Adrian. "I don't like the direction this investigation has taken." He walked out.

Cat studied the empty doorway, a thoughtful look on her face. "He doesn't like Tracy. Why the animosity?"

A frown crossed Karl's face. "They had a run-in a couple of years back. He filed a complaint with the department. They ruled in her favor. He hasn't forgotten."

Adrian's phone rang. Not recognizing the number, he let it roll to his voice mail. He stood, and said, "Karl, we'll be in touch later."

As they strode out of the building, he listened to the message, then hit the callback number. He glanced at Cat. "Eddie Owens called."

When the reporter answered, Adrian said, "This is Agent Dillard."

"My editor told me to call you."

"Where are you now?"

"At the office."

"I'll be there in a few minutes."

"You're wasting your time. I can't tell you anything."

"I need to be the judge of that. Wait there."

Once Cat exited the parking lot, he said, "You know those vibes we talked about last night?"

Cat nodded.

"They've gotten more intense," Adrian said.

"I figured that was why you didn't mention our return visit to the compound, or those boxes Tracy spotted?"

He nodded. "Until we get a better sense of what's going on, any information we pass on needs to be after the fact, not before." He paused, collected his thoughts, and added, "And, maybe, not even then."

****

When the door opened, Eddie looked at the two people who entered.

A u 7 9

He recognized the man, the agent he'd met at the Martin homicide. He still had a steely, grim-eyed expression. His eyes shifted to the woman. Dazzled, he gaped. Her hair, a bright cloud of red with golden highlights, curled around an elegant heart-shaped face with high cheekbones and green eyes. He couldn't take his eyes off her. She was beautiful. She couldn't be an agent.

Her eyes scanned the room, then settled on him. The hard stare, like her partner's, sent shivers down his back. He hastily revised his opinion. Nervous, he stacked the newspapers spread across his desk. Two slid onto the floor, and he bent over to pick them up.

Adrian settled in the chair, and Cat propped her hip on the adjacent desk.

When Eddie straightened, Adrian said, "We met before. I'm Agent Dillard, and this is Agent Morgan."

Clutching the newspapers, he nodded.

"We want to talk about your caller."

"Uh, … I don't know who called. That's the truth."

Adrian stared at him for a long minute.

The penetrating scrutiny intensified Eddie's jittery nerves. He laid the papers on the desk, knocking more to the floor. A blush stained his face, and he tucked his hands into his lap.

Despite a spark of sympathy, Adrian wasn't about to ease up on the pressure, not with what was at stake. "How many calls have you received?"

"Just … just two."

"When did you receive the first one and what time?"

Eddie reached across the desk to pick up a calendar, careful not to hit the remaining stack of papers. He opened it, laid it on the corner and pointed to an entry.

Cat slid off the desk and looked over Adrian's shoulder. She said, "It's the day after Stuart Dyson disappeared."

Adrian pulled out his phone and shot a picture of the calendar.

127

"What about the second call."

Eddie flipped the page and pointed to another entry.

After snapping a second picture, Adrian said, "Tell me what the caller said on the first call."

"He said Dyson deliberately disappeared. He hadn't been kidnapped."

"What else?"

"Nothing. That was it."

"That's all you had?" Adrian stared at him in disbelief. "You wrote an article filled with accusations against a federal agent based on that?"

Eddie sunk back in his seat, his voice defensive. "I thought it was news. Something was going on, and I reported it."

"Did you even ask who was calling, or for any kind of proof?"

"Uh ... no. He hung up before I could."

Disgusted, Cat snorted, and when Eddie glanced up at her, her eyes flashed with anger.

"Hey, I was just doing my job!" he exclaimed.

Rapping the desk with his fingers, Adrian brought Eddie's attention back to him. "What about the second call. Was it the same caller?"

"Same voice." He looked at Cat. "At first, I told him I wasn't interested. His first tip hadn't done so well."

She nodded, and asked, "What did he say?"

"This one would, and then said a fingerprint belonging to Dyson was found in some evidence in the garage."

Adrian asked, "Did he mention the location, or is it something you decided to add?"

"No, I didn't add it. He said the garage. Even told me the ATF had removed a lot of boxes."

"Anything else?"

"He hung up before I could ask any questions."

Adrian leaned back, a thoughtful expression on his face.

Eddie watched Cat out of the corner of his eye. He wondered if she was married. He didn't see a wedding ring. Lost in his fantasies, he flinched when Adrian tapped the back of his hand that lay on the desk.

"Tell me about the voice. What did it sound like?"

"I don't know. It was just a voice."

Cat stepped to the side of Eddie's chair. A fragrance, like fresh rain, floated in the air. He looked up. He couldn't take his eyes off her face. He'd never met anyone like her.

She said, "Let's try this. Eddie, I want you to lean back in your chair and close your eyes."

"Huh! What!" he squeaked.

"Humor me." When Eddie's eyes closed, she said, "Concentrate on my voice." Her tone shifted, becoming low and melodic. "Replay the conversations in your mind. Think about the tone and the words used."

After a few seconds, Cat asked, "Tell me about the tone."

"It was low, almost a whisper."

"You're sure it was a man's voice?"

"Yes."

"Listen to the words. Was there an accent? Did he sound like a Texas home boy?"

"No, they were more precise. Emphatic like your partner's."

"If you heard it again, would you recognize it?"

"I don't know."

Cat looked at Adrian and nodded her head toward the door.

Adrian stood. At the rattle of the chair, Eddie's eyes popped open.

"You have my number if you think of anything else," Adrian said. "And if this guy calls again, I don't care what time of day or night, you call me. If you don't, you'll find yourself sitting in jail on a charge of obstruction."

Eddie nodded. Watching them walk out the door, his nervous tension twisted into a sense of exhilaration. Whatever was going on, he was in the middle of it, and if he played this right, it could be his big break. He picked up the agent's card and tapped it on the desk. He might call and then again, he might not.

Outside, Adrian said, "That was an intriguing interview technique."

"I found out several years ago I could alter my voice to create a hypnotic effect. It's a useful tool to get someone to remember details, though we didn't get much on this one."

"A lot of the locals have a distinct Texas accent, which eliminates a few we've talked to."

"You're right. Did you get anything from your contact?"

Adrian thought about the light tap on Eddie's hand. "He wasn't lying about the caller. He doesn't know. Let's drive by the compound. I'd like to look at that eighteen-wheeler. Oh, by the way. I think you've got an admirer."

Au79

Seventeen

Washington D.C.

Scott hung up the receiver. He closed his eyes, and his fingers stroked his temples to ease the increasing pain of a headache as he thought about the phone call. At the sound of a light cough, his eyes popped open. Nicki stood in the doorway, a concerned expression on her face. Ryan was behind her.

"Good timing, have a seat," Scott said. "Blake called and confirmed what we suspected. The bridge was blown. He's on his way to the third site, but it's just a formality. We're both certain it'll be the same."

She settled into the chair in front of his desk. "I haven't found any more news articles. They probably have what they need, and there isn't a reason for another trial run."

Nodding toward Nicki, Ryan said, "Whatever the plan, we think it's been set into motion."

Scott said, "It's pretty much my opinion and that of our boss and Vance Whitaker. I just got off a conference call with them. Neither are happy. The subtext is the President is annoyed. They want answers, and we have none."

He picked up his pen. "Adrian also called this morning. Tracy Harlowe was watching the Border Guards last night, and one of them took a shot at her, but not before she saw an eighteen-wheeler arrive."

The pen started it's tap dance. Nicki grinned at Ryan and raised her eyebrows in a silent question. Ryan chuckled as he remembered his threat to take the pen away, but shook his head no.

At the sound, Scott stopped and glanced at his two agents. "What?"

Ryan, with an innocent look on his face, said, "Oh, nothing."

"Humph," Scott grunted. "We need to go at this from a different direction. What would they gain by blowing up a bridge, and why do they need a big rig?"

"A diversion?" Ryan said. "So far, the bridges have been in remote locations, and no one was harmed. But on a busy highway, it could have massive consequences."

"Hmm …" Scott mused. "A disaster affecting people's lives would pull all the local first responders. Cops and medics would be there in full force."

"Whatever they're after, then, would have to be located close to the site," Ryan added.

"Maybe it's just to stop traffic. To kidnap someone or steal something in a vehicle. A good reason to have a big rig," Nicki said.

"Another good possibility. The problem is where? It could be any place in the country. Ryan, any thoughts?"

"Based on all the intel and the events to date, I believe whatever is going down is in Texas. Even the Oklahoma bridge wasn't that far away. The incident with Tracy Harlowe increases my conviction."

"I agree. Nicki, start TRACE on a search for major events scheduled in Texas. Ryan, check with other agencies, see if they know about anything of significance that's scheduled to happen in the next few weeks, though my gut tells me we're down to a few days."

"Are you scheduled for a meeting with the President?" Nicki asked.

"Not yet, but it's only a matter of time."

Texas

He stared out the window as he pondered the identity of the Guards' night visitor. Should he tell Reynolds? Everything was in place, and he

132

didn't need any more controversy. The problem was that he couldn't rely on Reynolds not finding out from another source. He really didn't have a choice.

When Reynolds answered, he said, "Your he ... is a she, Detective Harlowe. Leave it alone. If the woman gets to be a problem, I'll handle it. That's an order!"

Reynolds slid the phone into his pocket. This was one order he'd ignore. Besides, it would give Stan a chance to redeem himself.

****

Tracy stared at her computer screen and stewed. Not wanting to get tied up all day with the two feds, she'd lied about the meeting. Morris was who she wanted to go after.

"You're too quiet. What's rolling in your head?" Skip asked her.

She shot him a quick glance. "Just thinking about Stuart."

"Oh. I know it's tough. Anything I can do?"

A surge of guilt struck for using her feelings as a distraction. She had to keep Skip from getting any further involved.

She shook her head. "Are you still headed to court?"

He glanced at his watch. "I'd better get a move on. What're your plans?"

"I'll be here most of the day. I've gotten behind on my reports and need to get caught up."

A look of disbelief crossed his face, but all he said was he'd see her later.

She gave him a few minutes to get clear of the building before picking up her backpack. It was early, and she figured Morris was probably at his house.

What happened at the Guards' compound dominated her thoughts as she drove out of the parking lot. She missed seeing the pickup that pulled away from the curb.

The street where Morris lived was deserted. Since his truck was parked in the driveway of a house on the corner, he must still be at home. Wondering where the surveillance team was hiding, she turned onto the side street and parked. A fence surrounded the sides and back. A dog howled, and the sound came from the backyard. Striding to the front, she noticed the blinds were drawn.

Tracy pushed the doorbell and heard the chimes inside. After a few seconds, she punched the doorbell again. Nothing. Her apprehension built as she pounded the door with her fist. The only sound was the wail of the dog.

She reached for her pistol and stepped to the fence gate. Easing it open, she looked into the yard. Not seeing a dog, she moved to the back corner of the house. Her back against the wall, she leaned forward. Damn!

Morris lay face down on grass that was stained by a substantial pool of blood. A large Labrador was curled against his legs. The dog stared at her, then whimpered.

Tracy slid around the corner and stepped onto the back porch. The door to the kitchen stood open. Inside, she quickly scanned the room before moving through the rest of the house. It was empty, but someone had torn the place apart.

Outside, uncertain what the dog might do, she slowly approached the body. The dog pushed at Morris' leg with its nose. A footstep sounded behind her. She whirled, her gun coming up toward the threat.

"Don't shoot, don't shoot," Eddie cried out.

"What are you doing here?" She holstered the weapon.

"I saw you going through the gate and wondered what you were up to."

"Eddie, get out of here now. If you don't, I'll throw your ass in jail."

He held up his hands. "I'm going."

She watched him step through the gate before turning back to the body. Tracy stepped around the pool of blood before she dropped to one knee. She laid two fingers on Morris' neck.

A click sounded, and her head shot up. Eddie stood at the corner with a camera. He turned and ran.

Nothing she could do. She wasn't about to chase him down the street. She tapped the speed dial and called dispatch to request a crime scene unit, the medical examiner, and animal control.

The dog whimpered again. Large, sorrowful eyes watched her. She reached across the body, and the animal nuzzled her hand. "You may be the only friend this guy had," she muttered.

****

Eddie was ecstatic. Once he was out of view of the house, he pulled to the side of the road to look at the pictures on his camera. The detective knelt by the body with her hand on his neck, the dog curled next to the man. In the next, she looked direct at the camera. Yes! He high-fived in his mind, then glanced at his watch. He had enough time to get it into tomorrow's edition.

****

Cat tapped the brakes to slow the car as they approached the Border Guards' compound. When the gate came into view, she stopped on the side of the road. Two pickups were parked in front of a metal building. The eighteen-wheeler was gone.

"No place to hide it," Adrian said.

"Tracy mentioned boxes. Is that why it was here?" Cat asked.

"Could be. I wonder what time Tracy was out here." Adrian reached for his phone, but before he could call, it rang.

"Tracy, I was just about to call you. What?" Adrian listened, then said, "We're on our way. What's the address?"

Cat had already turned the car around by the time he hung up.

Adrian tapped an address into the GPS. "Someone killed Morris."

"Where the hell was the surveillance team?"

His voice bitter, he said, "Good question, and one I want an answer to." He punched another number. "Karl, have you had a call from the team on Morris?"

"Randy just called. Morris is dead."

"I know. I got a call from Tracy."

Karl said, "Not sure what happened yet. I'm on my way there."

"So are we." He disconnected.

****

Tracy stood near the wall of the house and watched the medical attendants load Morris' body onto a gurney. Doc Kennedy strode over to her.

"Any idea of the time of death, Doc?"

"Probably somewhere between midnight and three. One bullet to the chest."

"I need you to compare the bullet to the other two. Did you ever get the other report?"

"Uh … not yet."

This was the second time he hesitated when she asked. "Doc, is there something you're not telling me?"

"No, not at all."

Karl Chambers rounded the corner of the building. A look of relief crossed the doctor's face as he turned away from Tracy to follow the gurney.

As soon as she was done here, her next stop was Kennedy's office. She wasn't buying his answer.

"Tracy, what happened?" Karl asked.

"I came out to talk to Morris and found him in the backyard. Randy and Tim are inside."

Tracy stepped through the kitchen into the living room with Karl behind her. At the sight of the destruction, he let out a short whistle. "Trashed is an understatement. I wonder what they were looking for."

"I don't know." What she didn't tell him was she'd searched the place before anyone arrived.

"Tracy, where are you?" Adrian's voice echoed outside the back door.

"Inside," she hollered.

Randy walked down the stairs that led to the bedrooms as Cat and Adrian stopped alongside Tracy.

"Good lord, what a mess." Cat's eyes skimmed the room.

Adrian looked at Tracy. "Any idea what happened?"

"No. This is what I found when I came out here to talk to him." She added the details of finding Morris' body in the backyard.

Adrian asked, "Do we have a time frame for when he was killed?"

"Doc Kennedy said between midnight and three," Tracy answered.

"Randy, did you find anything upstairs?" Karl asked.

Motioning to the destruction in the living room, Randy said, "The upstairs is even worse. Tim is still searching."

Adrian stepped closer to look at the upended couch and chairs, the bottoms ripped out, the broken drawers from the end tables and a bookcase that had its contents dumped on the floor. "Randy, what time did you start your stakeout?"

"Around one this morning."

Surprised, Adrian said, "Why were you late? You should have been here earlier than that."

Stuffing his hands in his pockets, Randy shrugged. "The last-minute change to replace Matt with Tim from Bill's office took a while to get organized."

"Was Morris here when you arrived?" Adrian asked.

"His truck was in front, and the light was on in the kitchen."

Persistent, Adrian asked, "Did you see him?"

An embarrassed look crossed Randy's face. His eyes flicked to his boss, and then he looked away. "No, we didn't." He knew they had screwed up, and spent the night and morning guarding a dead man.

Adrian stepped into the kitchen and looked up at the ceiling light. "It's still on. Do you know when he left the bar?"

"No. We swung by there before heading here. It was closed."

Tracy had followed him into the kitchen.

"Tracy, what made you suspicious?" Adrian asked.

"A dog howling in the backyard. He was curled next to the body."

Adrian looked around. "Where's the dog?"

"Animal control has already picked him up." The thought of the animal at the dog pound was troublesome.

"Did the dog stay in the house?"

"Yes. There's a bed in the utility room," Tracy replied.

Adrian paced back to the living room. "I bet he got home, opened the door to let the dog out, and the killer was waiting for him."

Tracy interrupted, "His bar. We need to check it." She turned and rushed outside.

"Karl, we'll talk to you later," Adrian said, as he followed Cat who was already behind Tracy.

Eighteen

Tracy's gaze scanned the front of the building as she parked. The front door appeared to be secure. Cat parked alongside Tracy's car. When the two agents exited, she said, "I'll check the back." Footsteps crunched on the gravel as they followed her.

"We're too late." She stopped as she viewed the broken door.

Adrian and Cat walked past her.

"Let's see how bad the damage is," Adrian said.

Pulling her phone, Tracy called the crime scene unit's sergeant. Once the team finished with Morris' house, they'd head to the bar.

Tracy stepped over broken pieces of the door and walked into the kitchen. Cat was checking out the bar area, and Adrian stood in the doorway of the office.

When he heard her footsteps, he turned. "No way to tell if anything's missing."

Tracy stopped beside him, her eyes skimmed the small room. The desk and file cabinet drawers were open. Folders and papers were scattered across the floor. She cleared her throat. "Maybe not."

At the wary tone in her voice, Adrian's head swiveled, his gaze suspicious as he looked at her. "You might want to explain that comment?"

"Yesterday, I was in this office." She stepped into the room, careful not to disturb any of the papers that littered the floor.

He leaned against the doorjamb, his arms crossed over his chest. "A detail you haven't bothered to mention."

She shrugged her shoulders as she stared at the file cabinet.

"Was Morris here?"

"No."

"Then how did you—happen—to be in his office?"

She looked up with a guarded glint in her eyes. "It's something you don't want to know."

"Tracy, what the hell did you do?"

"Let's just say I know the computer is missing." She motioned toward the file cabinet. "There was a locked metal box in the bottom drawer, and it's gone."

Cat walked up. "The file cabinet under the bar has been rifled." Sensing the tension, she glanced at her partner, then at Tracy. "What's going on?"

A scowl crossed Adrian's face. "Tracy is making me play twenty questions, but I'm not getting all the answers."

Tracy rolled her eyes. "Oh, for Christ's sake. Yesterday, I saw a computer on the desk and a metal box in the file drawer. They're gone. That's all there is to it."

"What were you doing here?" Cat asked.

"It's really better if we don't discuss it."

"See what I mean," Adrian said.

Despite her partner's obvious irritation, Cat grinned. "Okay, I'll play. How did you know about the box?"

"I opened it."

"The box or the drawer?" Cat asked.

"Uh … both."

Adrian straightened. "Wait a minute. You said the box was locked."

A mulish look crossed Tracy's face. "Did I?"

Adrian threw up his hands in a defensive gesture. "Dammit. Just tell us what you found, and we won't draw any suspicious conclusions."

"It was full of legal documents, deeds, contracts, stuff like that. I didn't get a chance to get a close look at them. There was an interruption."

Adrian muttered, "I just bet there was. Morris probably showed up."

Her good humor restored, Tracy smirked.

Adrian's phone rang. "It's Scott. I'll be outside."

He answered, and said, "Hold on a minute," and stepped over the debris in front of the door. "It's been a busy morning."

After listening to Adrian's details of the latest homicide and burglary, Scott asked, "Any idea why Morris was killed?"

"Not yet. Did you hear from Blake?"

"Yes. He confirmed the second bridge was blown and is headed to the third. We're taking a different tactic, exploring reasons to target a bridge."

After Scott explained the theory about a major event being the target, Adrian said, "That makes sense. I can add another piece to the puzzle — the eighteen-wheeler. Cat and I drove by the compound, and it's gone."

"I don't like that."

"Neither did we. There's something else." He hesitated, thinking about how to phrase what he needed to say.

"Yes," Scott prompted.

"Cat and I are picking up vibes we don't understand. I'm also disturbed about how the surveillance on Morris was handled. We're censoring the details we provide to Karl Chambers and Bill Goddard."

"Are you getting a sense one of them is involved?"

"I hate to go that far without more evidence. Let's just say it could be one of them or their agents."

"That's good enough for me. Since I told them you and Cat are in charge, I don't expect to have any contact with either one."

"We talked to Eddie Owens today. He doesn't know who the caller is, but the fact he got the calls is enough to create suspicion."

As he disconnected, Cat stepped beside him, followed by Tracy. At a warning look from Adrian, Cat didn't ask the question that hovered on her tongue.

"Tracy, are you staying here?" Adrian asked.

"Only until the crime scene unit arrives. Why?"

"I want to talk to you, but not here. Where can we meet?"

"Back at the PD, if you like."

Adrian nodded, then turned to head to their vehicle.

Alarmed at Adrian's tone, Tracy's stomach rolled with trepidation and anxiety. She had a feeling she wasn't going to be able to dodge their questions any longer.

****

Pulling onto the street, Cat asked, "What was that all about?"

Adrian covered the details of his discussion with Scott.

When he finished, she said, "I had the same suspicions about the delay on the surveillance. Seems a bit convenient."

"There may be nothing to it, but it's another coincidence, and this case has just too many of them to my liking."

"Are we running out of time?"

"I think the clock is ticking. The truck is a red flag."

He tapped a number on his phone. "This is Agent Adrian Dillard. I'd like to speak with Doctor Kennedy." When a deep voice answered, he identified himself, and added, "I'm calling about the autopsy on Bing Morris. If possible, I'd like the bullet compared to the other two, the Bardwell and Martin homicides."

"I've already received a request from Detective Harlowe. She also asked about the first results and is getting impatient over not getting an answer. Agent Dillard, am I still to keep it under wraps?"

"Yes. If she contacts you again, refer her to me. I'll handle it. How soon do you think you'll have an answer?"

"I'm getting ready to start the autopsy. Barring any unforeseen problems, it should be later today."

"Please call me as soon as you have the results," Adrian said, and disconnected.

"What's the deal with Tracy?" Cat asked.

"Despite her hardheaded reticence, I think she broke into the bar yesterday and searched Morris' office."

Cat chuckled. "That accounts for her reaction to the mention of surveillance this morning at the diner. She was wondering if she'd been caught. The woman sure doesn't hesitate to take risks."

****

Tracy glanced at her watch as she exited the bar's parking lot. She had time to swing by the M.E.'s office before heading back to the PD. Her phone rang. It was Skip.

"Okay, where the hell are you? I thought you were staying at the office. What's this I hear about Morris?"

"I took a trip to his house and found him dead. I'm on my way back, with a stop at Kennedy's office. I need a favor."

"Sure, what?"

"The crime scene techs are going to drop off several boxes of evidence. Would you put them into the conference room, then lock it?"

"I guess you'll explain when you get back, right?"

She chuckled. "Yes. You'll get all the down and dirty."

Tracy greeted Doris as she passed by the desk, but spotting Kennedy in the hallway, she didn't stop.

"Doc, hold up a minute."

He turned. "Tracy, didn't expect to see you this soon. I'm getting ready to start the autopsy on Morris."

"I wanted to ask again about the ballistics report. What's going on you're not telling me?"

"I was ordered to not discuss the results. If you want to know anything, you need to ask Agent Dillard."

Her face paled. "It's about Stuart, isn't it?"

A kindly expression crossed his face. "I'm sorry, but I can't say anything. I need to get the autopsy started."

Tracy watched him walk away. A feeling of desperation and hopelessness rushed over her. What was she going to do?

When she strode into her office, the room was abuzz with activity. Skip and Art were on the phone, and Pete held court at his desk with a group of schoolchildren and two adults. She grinned at the sight. Occasionally, a nearby school would use the PD for a field trip, and the detectives took turns in a show and tell about their jobs. Pete must have drawn the short straw today.

Dumping her backpack on the floor, Skip greeted her as he hung up his phone.

"Maybe I ought to chain you to your desk. You can't seem to step foot out of this office without landing in the middle of another debacle."

She grunted as she eased back into the chair, mindful of the bruises on her back. "You don't know the half of it."

A commotion at the door caught her attention. It was a crime scene officer with boxes stacked in his arms.

Skip glanced around. "I meant to mention your evidence wasn't here yet. Does the Captain know you're going to commandeer his conference room?"

"Crap, no. I guess I'd better go talk to him."

"While you're talking to him, I'll take care of the boxes."

As she directed a glance at Captain Rodriguez's office, she sighed. She hated the thought of another go-round with him. How much should she tell him?

When she tapped on the side of the door, he glanced up. "Tracy, come in." He laid the document he'd been reading on the desk.

"We had another shooting that's connected to Stuart's disappearance," she said, and sat on the edge of the chair. "It's Bing Morris, the owner of the bar who set up the meet with Bardwell. I found him dead in his backyard."

"What were you doing there?"

"Just following up on a lead in the investigation. I wanted to interview him again."

"Hmm ..." he mused, with a hard glint in his eyes.

"One shot to the chest. It happened sometime early this morning. His house was ransacked. And we also found someone had tossed his bar."

Au 7 9

"We?"

"I was with Adrian Dillard and Cat Morgan. They're the FBI agents heading up the investigation." Dropping their names might allay the suspicion she saw in his expression. It worked.

"Any problems working with them?"

"No, none. Matter of fact, they're on their way here for a meeting. Several boxes of evidence were removed from the two crime scenes. I need to use the conference room for a few hours to go through it all."

"I don't have a problem with that."

"Thanks, just wanted to let you know. One other item, Eddie Owens, that reporter with the Laredo Observer, followed me today. He snapped a picture of the crime scene before I could stop him. It'll probably be in tomorrow's paper."

"I don't like the idea he followed you."

"Neither do I, but I'll be watching for him now." Standing, she turned toward the door.

"Tracy, is there something you're not telling me?"

She glanced over her shoulder. "No, sir. That was it," she said, and escaped out the door, hoping the lie didn't show on her face.

Inside the conference room, large taped boxes were strewn across the table and more were piled against a wall.

"Jeez, what's in these?" Skip asked.

"Every scrap of paper from Morris' house and bar."

As Skip looked around the room, he said, "When you said several, I thought it would be five or six. This'll take hours. Do you want help?"

She hesitated, then said, "No, but thanks. I'm not sure what I'm even looking for."

He stepped to the door and closed it. "What's going on?"

Tracy filled him in on the details. When she reached the part about the encounter with the Border Guards, she waved her hands in the air at the look of anger on his face.

"Tracy, you can't keep going out on a limb like this. One of these times, someone will saw it off behind you."

"I know. I took a risk, but it paid off. We gained valuable intel out of it."

"Does the Captain know about one of the Guards taking potshots at you?"

"No, I didn't tell him."

Skip sighed in frustration.

"Skip, if I say anything, he's likely to pull me off the investigation. I can't take a chance. You know I can't."

He nodded.

A tap sounded on the door, and Tracy opened it. Adrian and Cat were in the hallway. They stepped inside, and Tracy closed the door, then introduced Cat to Skip.

After greeting the agents, Skip said, "I've got to leave. I have a witness I need to interview. Tracy, if you need ..." He stopped and made a calling motion with his hand.

"Thanks, Skip. I will."

After he left the room, Cat and Adrian eyed the boxes while Tracy explained.

"Since we're here, we can help while we talk," Cat said.

Tracy picked up a box from Morris' house, set it on the table and cut the tape. Inside were stacks of paper. Cat and Adrian did the same.

Tracy laid aside a utility bill and reached inside for another one. "I stopped by Doc Kennedy's office. He said he couldn't give me the results of a ballistics test he ran on Bardwell and Martin. I had to talk to you. Why?" She didn't miss the look that shot between Cat and Adrian. So, there was something. The tension built inside her.

Adrian's eyes turned toward her, a look of compassion on his face.

Tracy braced herself, her body rigid.

"The bullets came from Stuart's gun," Adrian said.

A jolt of trepidation shot through her. "What! No! That can't be. How ..." She took a deep breath. "How does he know?"

"Stuart was involved in a shooting a year or so ago."

Comprehension dawned on her face. "He was, and the test results on his gun would be on file. Oh, my god. I asked Kennedy to compare the bullet from Morris to the other two."

"I know," Adrian said. "I made the same request."

"You think it's Stuart's gun, don't you?"

"I can't be certain, but I believe it's likely. Tracy, Stuart is our prime suspect."

"There's got to be some explanation. Stuart wouldn't do this."

He hesitated, then said, "It's time you came clean with us. We've known from the onset of this case you've been hiding something. We need to know."

Tracy leaned forward, her elbows on the table and her head in her hands. Her mind raced. This wasn't how all of this was supposed to have happened. An image of the last time she saw Stuart floated in her thoughts. She really didn't have any choice.

Nineteen

The only sound was the rustle of paper as the two agents scanned document after document. A sigh broke the silence as Tracy looked up.

"Stuart went undercover."

Adrian cocked an eyebrow, his gaze steady as he waited.

"The day before he left, we had lunch. Stuart said he had an informant who knew about a big arms deal. It involved a lot of money. The ringleader wanted details on the ATF, how it operated, and was willing to pay big bucks. If Stuart was interested, the informant would set up the meeting, but it meant he would be gone for several days. When Stuart said he'd agreed, we argued."

She leaned back, her hand rubbed the back of her neck as she remembered that day. He had been so confident he had everything under control. "Stuart had already covered his absence at work by asking for a few days off. He planned to go in, get what he needed, and then get out. I was the only one who knew, and he swore me to secrecy. I didn't like he was going solo, with no backup from anyone."

When she stopped, Adrian asked, "Why by himself?"

"Said he felt safer if no one knew. When I asked why, he just said he was uneasy over the way the last couple of operations had gone down. I was the only one he trusted."

"Have you heard from him?" Cat asked.

"No, but he said he wouldn't call until he was in the clear, and not to panic if he was gone longer than he anticipated. If it got out what he was up to it could endanger him. He didn't expect any trouble. I wanted a way to contact him, but he said it wouldn't do any good. His phone would be turned off." Her lips twisted into a wry grin that didn't change the bleak look in her eyes. "Stuart's hardheaded and as stubborn as an old mule when it comes to his job."

The thought crossed Adrian's mind that Tracy and Stuart had a lot in common. "What was the deal with the reporter, Eddie Owens?"

"When Stuart's car was found, everything started to spiral out of control. Karl and Bill treated it as a kidnapping case. If Stuart's suspicions were correct, I couldn't say anything without putting him at risk. When I saw the newspaper article, it scared the hell out of me. Until then, the investigation hadn't made the news, but then it did and in the worst way. I had no choice but to confront Owens, hoping to shut him down."

"What about Bardwell?" he asked.

"When he told you Stuart was dead, I thought it was likely that he was Stuart's informant. That was a bad moment."

Cat reached across and touched Tracy's tightly clasped hands. "When you showed up at the crime scene, we didn't know you were Stuart's fiancée. Karl Chambers never identified you by name."

"That doesn't surprise me. Karl and I butted heads over the investigation. I suspect he was responsible for getting me kicked off the case."

While Adrian agreed with her, he didn't want to add to the bad feelings that already existed between her and Karl. Instead, he asked, "Any ideas on the fingerprint?"

"It was a possibility Stuart had been in the garage. It seemed to be the only plausible explanation. But now his gun is involved, and that's even more terrifying. Someone else fired those shots, not Stuart. He's either dead or a prisoner, which means his fingerprint might have been planted."

"Tracy, what time did you see the truck last night?" Cat asked.

"Around ten. Why?"

Adrian responded. "It was gone this morning. We need to get into the compound, and what happened to you last night gives us an in."

"I want to go with you."

"No. It's not a good idea. We don't need you ruffling their feathers. I'd like to search the place, but I don't have grounds yet for a warrant. Maybe we'll see or hear something we can use."

Tracy grunted, disgusted at his response, though she understood his reasoning.

Cat closed the lid on a box, saying, "This one's done. If you haven't finished by the time we get back, we'll pitch in."

As the door closed behind the two agents, Tracy jerked the tape from another box. She hated that she wasn't going to get a look inside the compound.

****

Cat stopped in front of the gate. Nothing had changed from their earlier drive-by. Two pickups were still parked in front of a metal building. "Looks pretty quiet."

Adrian slid his phone into his pocket. During the drive, he had called Scott and passed on the latest developments. "Well, let's see if we can rattle their cage. I want to take another look at that lock."

Stepping out of the car, he strode to the front gate and dropped to one knee to examine the locking mechanism. Cat stopped beside him.

"This is state-of-the-art security," he said. "Makes you wonder what they're trying to protect."

At the sound of an engine, Adrian stood. One of the trucks was headed their way. "Here come the troops."

The same two men from their first visit erupted from the truck, rifles slung over their shoulders and strode toward them. "Nothing's changed from your first visit. Get the hell out of here," the driver said.

"Get on your phone and call your boss. We want to talk to him. It's his choice, here, or I get a warrant," Adrian said.

A u 7 9

The two men eyed the agents. Adrian had taken a wide stance, his jacket pushed back for easy access to the gun on his waistband. Cat had stepped to the side of the driveway, her hand rested on the butt of her gun.

The driver pulled a portable radio from his pocket. After a short conversation, he said, "Commander Reynolds will talk to you."

"Smart decision," Adrian said.

The gate swung open. The two men piled back into their vehicle. The driver pulled to the side of the driveway and waited until Cat and Adrian's vehicle cleared the gate. The pickup pulled behind them.

The driveway ended in a large gravel parking lot. In front of them, three metal buildings formed a semi-circle. The front of the house faced the driveway. Cat pulled to a stop in front of the porch.

As Adrian exited the car, his eyes scanned the area until he heard a door bang. His attention shifted to a man in his mid-forties who stepped onto the porch. Adrian recognized him from an old newspaper article he'd found. Dressed in a crisp camouflage uniform with a gun belt strapped around his waist, he was the quintessential picture of a soldier. Adrian knew it was nothing but a façade. The man had never served a single day in the military. Norman Reynolds was a typical blowhard who hated the federal government, or at least claimed he did. Either way, he made money from the memberships he sold.

His fingers hooked in his belt, he eyed Adrian, then his gaze flicked to Cat and lingered as his stare raked her from head to toe. With a grunt of contempt, he looked back at Adrian.

"You Dillard?"

Adrian nodded his head.

"I'm here, what do you want to discuss?"

"It would be easier inside," Adrian said.

"Whatever you have to say can be said out here."

Adrian leaned against the side of the car, his arms crossed over his chest. He stared at the man for several seconds. "We're investigating the disappearance of ATF agent Stuart Dyson. Do you know him?"

"Heard the name on the news. Never met the man."

"That's odd, because Bing Morris said he talked to you about the missing agent." It was a bluff, but Adrian wanted to see if he got a reaction by tossing out Morris' name.

Reynolds' only reaction was a slight stiffening of his body. If Adrian hadn't been watching, he'd have missed it.

"Who?" Reynolds asked.

"The owner of Bing's Watering Hole."

"Don't know him. I'd say someone handed you a line of bull."

"Morris was killed last night."

As if it was unimportant, Reynolds shrugged his shoulders. "Hadn't heard."

"What about Donnie Martin?"

"What about him?"

"Another associate of yours that's dead."

A chuckle erupted. "Dillard, someone is sure doing a number on you. Just how did you connect me with Martin?"

Ignoring the question, Adrian said, "There's another, Cam Bardwell. He's dead too. Seems like knowing you is downright unhealthy."

"I don't know what you're talking about. Those men have nothing to do with me. Now, if that's all you wanted to ask, get the hell off my property."

"No. I'm not done. We're investigating an incident that happened here last night. We'd like to hear your version."

A sneer crossed the man's face. "You're just the typical fucking federal agent, making up shit to justify your actions. We've had a problem with coyotes getting hung up on the fence. One of my men fired a couple of rounds to scare one away."

Adrian smiled, though the humor never reached his eyes. "Now, isn't this interesting? I didn't mention it was a shooting. How'd you know that's what I was talking about?"

Anger flashed across Reynolds' face. "Any more questions, talk to my lawyer." His heels clicked as he spun and marched into the house.

The two Guards who had taken up a position near the front porch slid the rifles off their shoulders.

Adrian cast a contemptuous look at them. "Any threatening moves and I'll have a reason to arrest the lot of you." The two men glanced at each other, before they got back into the pickup.

Cat glanced in the rearview mirror as she drove off the property. The truck that followed them stopped at the gate. "That could've gotten a bit dicey."

"They're sure itching for a fight." He tapped the speed dial, and when his boss answered, said, "Put the Border Guards at the top of the suspect list. We just left their compound, and they're up to their eyebrows in whatever is going down."

Washington D.C.

Scott hung up the phone. Thoughts twisted and turned as he contemplated Adrian's comments. He could see an emerging pattern. Time for a team meeting.

Frustrated, Nicki typed in another keyword. She was batting zero on any leads from the background searches. Now she was searching for connections between the three dead men and the local FBI and ATF agents.

Engrossed in building the search perimeters, the tap on the door didn't even register. She was in what she laughingly referred to as her zone. When a hand touched her shoulder, she jerked. Her head shot up to see Scott's eyes gleaming with laughter.

"Not funny, boss man," she said, as she viewed the mistyped words on her screen. She fixed the problem, then spun her chair to face him as he propped a hip on the corner of her desk.

"Probably not, but sometimes it's hard to resist. I don't believe I've ever met anyone with such total focus as you."

Ryan stepped into the office.

"Grab a chair for a quick confab," Scott said. His phone rang. Answering, he tapped the speakerphone. "Blake, what're the results?"

His tone grim, Blake answered, "Positive. Same as the other two. The TEDAC team is on site, gathering what they can to ship back to their labs. They're putting a rush on the tests, though it doesn't look promising it'll help us."

"Are you done there?" Scott asked.

"We're finished. What's the next step?"

"Head to Laredo. I have a hunch Adrian and Cat will need your expertise and the backup." Scott caught the look of surprise that flashed between Nicki and Ryan.

Blake said, "Okay. I mentioned to Lance that's where I might be headed. He'll be with me."

"Good idea. I'll let Adrian fill you in when you get there."

After disconnecting, Scott said, "The Border Guards are our primary suspects," and added the details of Adrian's call.

"Sounds like it's getting tense in Laredo," Ryan said.

"One of the reasons I wanted Blake there. With a possibility a local agent is involved, it puts Cat and Adrian at risk."

Nicki's phone rang. At Scott's nod, she answered it.

"Nicki, Ted from the Dallas Police Department. I've got bad news."

"Don't like the sound of that. Is it the link between the Fusion Center and TRACE?"

"No. The throughput test was a hundred percent successful. In our last conversation, you mentioned the theft of explosives in Laredo. The method used to break into the building caught my attention."

"Using a truck to ram the building can be pretty effective," she said.

"We've had a similar string of burglaries in the Dallas area. Only the targets have been pawn shops and gun stores. I ran a search for thefts that involved explosives. I found three within the last month. One near

Au 79

San Angelo in West Texas, another in El Paso, and one in Carthage. That's in East Texas. Stolen pickups were used to ram the side of the buildings."

"Do you have access to the reports?"

"I uploaded the details into TRACE but also emailed you a copy of the reports."

Nicki quickly tapped the keyboard and opened her emails. Clicking on the attachment, she hit the print key. "Got em'. Appreciate the heads-up thinking."

"Sure thing. If you need any help, let me know."

"Thanks, Ted." Reaching for the papers in the printer tray, she handed them to Scott. "That was Lieutenant Ted Phillips in the Dallas PD's Fusion Center. He found three more thefts of explosives."

Scott and Ryan passed the reports to each other until all three had been read.

Ryan said, "This is one hell of a lot of missing explosives. What are they planning on destroying?"

A grim tone in his voice, Scott said, "That's what we have to figure out—and fast." He picked up his phone to call Adrian.

Texas

He glanced at the screen. It was bad timing, but he couldn't ignore the call. "Hold on." He pushed back his chair and headed out of his office. Outside, he asked, "What's wrong now?"

Reynolds said, "Those agents showed up again."

"They don't know anything. They won't unless you screwed up and made a stupid remark."

Reynolds said, "I don't like your fucking attitude. You're in this deeper than we are, and if we go down, you'll be right with us. Make a call. Find out if the schedule has changed," and disconnected.

He seethed with anger, hating the fact that Reynolds was right. He couldn't afford to get rid of him. Not yet.

****

When Scott disconnected, Adrian laid the phone on the console and leaned his head against the seat.

Cat, who had been listening as she drove, said, "Four thefts. How bad can that be?"

"I don't know. I'm not an expert. Since Blake will be here in a couple of hours with a guy from TEDAC in tow, they can tell us. For right now, let's keep it to ourselves."

"We've got to find a way to search that compound," she said.

"Yes, we do, but it's not possible. We don't have enough to justify a search warrant."

"I know, but by the time we get the evidence, it may be too late," she grumbled.

"I sure didn't get a lot from Reynolds. He reacted to the mention of Morris, and then there was the slip about the shooting. While it confirms our suspicions, it's still not enough. I was hoping to at least get inside the house."

"Something you said to him was interesting. It was about the three dead men. Why were they killed? What reason would Reynolds have?"

"Hmm ... good question."

Cat mused. "I've been thinking about Tracy's comment that the fingerprint was planted. What if there was a plan to point the finger at Dyson? If Bardwell hadn't been shot, we wouldn't have found the fingerprint."

Adrian stiffened, his mind raced over the possibilities. "It makes sense. And if he was the informant, eliminating him got rid of the connection to Stuart. A dead man can tell no tales."

"Only problem is the detonators. The way Bardwell's house was torn apart, I bet Reynolds didn't plan on losing a couple." Cat paused as she swung into the oncoming lane to pass a car, then added, "Killing him might have been premature. Still, it hasn't done us much good. We aren't

Au79

any closer to finding out their plan than the night we found them."

Adrian said, "The Martin shooting was also suspect. Until he was shot, nothing had been done on a ballistics test. No one knew the bullet that killed Bardwell came from Stuart's gun. Was it the reason Martin was killed? With two victims, the bullets would be compared. At the time, I thought three shots at such close range were an overkill. Were three fired to make sure we had a good one for comparison? Someone had to know Stuart's gun was in the system. Reynolds wouldn't, which brings us back to our suspicions a law enforcement officer is mixed up in this."

"But how does Morris fit into this picture of complicity?" Cat asked.

"I bet Morris screwed up when he let on he knew we were agents. I don't think Reynolds tolerates mistakes. He gets rid of Morris and puts another nail in Dyson's coffin. His plan worked. Stuart has gone from victim to suspect. Except he didn't count on Tracy," Adrian replied.

Cat mused. "I wonder what prompted the search of Morris' house and bar?"

Twenty

Tracy leaned back in the chair. She twisted and rolled her head to ease the tension in her neck and shoulder muscles. It seemed she had sat for hours in one position as she sifted through bills, invoices, sales receipts, and other miscellaneous scraps of paper. Nothing, and only two boxes remained. She sighed, straightened and ripped the tape from the nearest one.

Her hand reached inside to pick up a stack of papers. Thumbing through them, she quickly scanned each one before she laid it aside. When she grabbed another stack, a small sticky note fell onto the table. Scribbled on it was *27.43 lbs how many*, followed by several question marks.

How odd. She studied it for a few seconds before dropping it on the table. She continued to skim the other papers, but her thoughts kept circling around what the weight meant. Was it important or just someone doodling? Once she reached the bottom of the box, she replaced all the documents except for the note.

Halfway through the contents of the last box, she found another note. This one had a telephone number scribbled on it along with a time, eight o'clock. Once she'd examined what was left, she picked up the two notes, and made several copies of each, then returned the originals to the boxes where she found them.

She called the night supervisor in the crime scene office to request an officer pick up the boxes and take them to the evidence room. While she waited, she studied the copy of the note. She couldn't think of anything that weighed 27.43 pounds, especially in connection with the operation of a bar.

When the officer arrived, she signed the evidence log and slid the copies of the two notes into her backpack. Walking out the door, her phone rang.

It was Cat. "Are you still at the PD?"

"Just leaving, headed home."

"We need to talk to you. Give me your address, and we'll meet you there."

"What's up?" Tracy asked, not exactly thrilled at the thought of the two agents in her house.

"We'll explain when we get there."

"We can meet somewhere if it would be more convenient."

"No, we need total privacy."

That doesn't sound good. She rattled off her address, then wondered whether she should pick up a six-pack and maybe some snacks. Since she'd pass a convenience store on her way home, the delay wouldn't amount to much. She should still be there before the agents arrived.

When she turned into her drive, she sat in the car for a few seconds and stared at her house. The fear and anxiety that started when Stuart went undercover had become a living entity inside her. At times, it threatened to overwhelm her. Something had happened to Stuart, or he would have contacted her by now. Was he dead? Sitting in the car getting morbid wasn't going to find the answers. Maybe the feds had come up with something on their visit to the Border Guards. She could only hope.

With a moan of dejection, she opened the door and slid out of the car. Reaching into the backseat, she picked up her backpack and slung it over her shoulder, then grabbed the six-pack of beer and a bag containing an assortment of cheese and crackers.

When she closed the door, the deep shadows surrounded her. Preoccupied, she hadn't noticed her front yard was unusually dark, then realized why. The street light on the corner was out. Another task for her to-do-list, call the city and get it fixed.

On the front porch, she juggled the beer and bag with one hand while she reached to unlock the door. The thud of a footstep sent her spinning. A man, his face and body a black mass, rushed up the steps. She threw the beer and bag at him and shifted to the side. Grabbing the strap of the backpack, she swung it like a baseball bat. The computer packed inside made a very satisfying crack as it struck the side of his face.

A voice roared, "You bitch. I'm gonna enjoy killing you." Grabbing her, he slammed her against the porch rail and his legs straddled her. Hands circled her throat. Pinned against the wood slats, she couldn't reach the gun under her jacket. The other hand was entangled in the strap of the backpack. The weight dragged her arm down, and she couldn't shake it loose.

Even though her position didn't provide any leverage, she thrust upward with her knee. She connected, and he grunted in pain. The pressure eased. Her free hand came up, fingers extended to jab him in the eyes. His head jerked back. Curling her fingers into a fist, she struck him in the face. His grip slipped.

A car horn blared, and lights flashed across the front of the house. A harsh voice echoed in her ear. "Until next time, bitch." The hands were gone. Footsteps pounded, and a shot rang out.

Her lungs heaved as she sucked in air with deep gasps. Propped against the railing, she untangled her hand and dropped the backpack. Her hands rubbed her throat as her thoughts cleared.

"Tracy," a voice shouted. "Tracy? Are you all right?" Cat ran up the steps.

"I think so." Her voice cracked.

Cat stepped in front of her. "Look at me." When Tracy lifted her head, Cat's eyes skimmed her face and the vicious red blotches on her throat.

"Let's get you inside and get ice on those bruises."

Au 79

Adrian stepped onto the porch. Glass tinkled as he stumbled. He muttered and looked down at the beer bottles and other items strewn across the wood. He picked up the keys lying in front of the door. Unlocking it, he stepped inside and flipped the porch light on, then headed back to the car to turn off the lights.

Cat grabbed Tracy's arm and steered her through the doorway. Coughing, Tracy stumbled into the living room and dropped onto the couch. Cat disappeared through an open doorway that led to the kitchen.

Adrian walked in and looked down at her.

Her voice raspy, she asked, "What happened to the man?"

"When we pulled into the driveway, Cat hit the horn. He took off running. I got off a shot but missed. He was around the corner and in a car before I could catch up with him."

"He was waiting for me. Got to me as I was trying to unlock the door." The image of the dark yard flashed in her mind. "The street light was out. I wonder …"

Cat walked up with a bag of frozen peas in her hand and interrupted. "Put it against your throat. It'll help ease the pain."

A weak grin crossed Tracy's face. "I thought they only did this in the movies."

"Not knowing where you kept plastic bags, I couldn't make an ice pack."

Adrian walked outside and picked up the groceries and the backpack. As he headed to the kitchen, he said, "Not sure we want to open any of these bottles yet. We're likely to have beer spewing onto the ceiling."

"I stopped on my way home. Seemed like a good idea at the time."

"It was. Any thoughts on the identity of your assailant?" Cat asked.

It dawned on Tracy just how well-timed the stop had been. "No, he had on a face mask, and I didn't recognize the voice."

"What did he say?" Adrian asked

Tracy hesitated and considered the man's last threat—*until next time*. If she mentioned it, she'd have someone continually looking over her shoulder. It wasn't how she operated. No, it would be better if no one knew that tidbit. "Just that he'd enjoy killing me. That was after I hit him in the head with my backpack."

She slid the peas around to the other side of her throat. She had to admit it helped, though she didn't want to think about how bad the bruises would look in the morning. "Did the crackers and cheese survive?"

Adrian said, "Yes, but let's wait on them for now. I can't imagine swallowing would be a pleasant experience." He settled in a chair across from her, and Cat sat on the end of the couch.

"Any idea why someone attacked you?" he asked.

Tracy had already been rolling the question in her head. "No. None."

"Could it be connected to what happened last night at the compound?"

"I don't see how. The only people I told are you two and Skip. I didn't even tell my Captain. How would they know it was me?"

Occupied with holding the bag on her throat, she missed Adrian and Cat's reaction to her comment.

Adrian said, "You might want to rectify that when you get to the office tomorrow morning. Bill Goddard and Karl Chambers know, and they might just mention it to your boss."

"Oh, hell. You're right. I'll be in deep do-do because I didn't tell him, but it'll be a lot worse if he finds out from someone else. Why did you want to talk to me?"

Adrian recapped what happened at the Guards' compound, then said, "Tracy, we need you to think back to everything you can remember about what Stuart said."

"Hmm … I already did."

"Is there some detail you might have missed?"

She looked at them with suspicion. *What was going on here?*

Hoping to placate Tracy's distrust, Cat said, "We believe Stuart's been set up to take the fall."

With a sigh of relief, Tracy said, "Thank you. I was beginning to wonder if I could ever convince you he's innocent."

Adrian added, "The shootings and evidence left behind are too coincidental for our liking."

"I've never doubted Stuart." Tears misted in her eyes. "I told you that in our first meeting at the diner. He's a damn good cop." She sniffed. "Or maybe it should be—was."

"Tracy, I don't believe he's dead." Adrian leaned forward as if to emphasize his words. "If this is a plot to implicate him, I think they'll keep him alive until they're finished."

She stared into his eyes and saw the conviction. A twinge of hope built.

"Think back to what he said." His voice was intense. "Did he give you any clue about the informant, or the location where they'd meet?"

"No, he didn't, but there was something. That note."

"What about it?" Cat asked.

"I didn't understand how you found it. I searched his place before you did, and the note wasn't there."

"Are you certain?" he asked.

"Absolutely, I'm telling you it wasn't there. Someone planted it."

"One of your earlier comments has me puzzled," Cat said. "It was about the car, how it started the investigation." She glanced at Adrian. "Remember when Karl Chambers met us at the airport, he said there wasn't any sign of foul play, so was it the location that triggered all of this?" She looked back at Tracy. "Why did Stuart leave it at an abandoned warehouse?"

A thoughtful look crossed Tracy's face. "I didn't think it was odd at the time, just figured he didn't have a choice. Informants are paranoid, and it doesn't take much to spook them, especially a meet in a public place."

Adrian said, "It's a reasonable explanation. You said you butted heads with Karl. Why?"

A note of bitterness crept into her voice. "When I questioned why the rush to a full-blown investigation, he said it was a federal case. Told me to stay out of it, that I didn't have the necessary security clearance to be in the know."

"Do you know who decided to go ahead with the investigation?"

"Since Bill Goddard was in charge, I assumed he made the decision. Is it possible Stuart is a prisoner at the compound?"

Adrian answered. "I doubt it. Even if he had been, they'd have moved him by now. We've threatened them with a search warrant. Our problem is all of this is supposition, no evidence to back up a warrant,"

"Jeez, I almost forgot. I found something in all those boxes. Where's my backpack?"

"On the floor behind you. I'll get it." Reaching over the back of the couch, Cat grabbed a strap. "Damn, what do you have in here?"

"My computer. I hope I didn't damage it when I clobbered the guy."

"It's a wonder it didn't knock him out."

"It would have if I'd had enough room to take a good swing."

Tracy laid the partially thawed pack of peas on the table, unzipped a compartment in the bag and pulled out a file folder. She handed two sheets of paper to Cat, who looked at them and then passed them to Adrian.

"You can find out who the phone number belongs to faster than I can. But the weight thing has me stumped. What would weigh 27.43 pounds?"

"I don't have a clue," Adrian said, as he reached for his phone to text the phone number to Nicki. "Which box?"

"The phone number was in the stuff from his bar, but the note with the weight was from his home."

Adrian's phone rang. Answering, he said, "Blake, where are you?" He listened, then said, "We'll be there in about thirty minutes."

Cat asked, "Blake's here?"

"Yes, he's checking into the hotel."

At Tracy's questioning glance, he said, "Blake Kenner is another Tracker," then realized Tracy didn't know about the bridges.

"Nicki found newspaper articles about several bridges that have collapsed within the last month. One in Oklahoma and two in Texas. The timing seemed suspicious. Blake and a TEDAC agent flew to the locations to check for explosives. All three bridges were blown."

Shocked, Tracy leaned back. The bag of peas, forgotten, sat in a puddle of water on her table. "The missing detonators. Were they used?"

"We don't know."

"Wait a minute, why didn't anyone know someone took those bridges down?"

"They were old, in a remote area, and there were no injuries. Nothing to make the local officials suspicious," Adrian explained.

"Why is Blake and that other agent here?"

"They have a background in explosives that neither Cat nor I have."

"Is something or someone here the target?" Tracy asked.

Adrian shrugged. "We're not sure, but we've located three more thefts of stolen explosives, all in Texas, and just like the one here. We've got to go. Are you going to be okay by yourself? I don't like you being alone."

"I'll be fine. I won't get blindsided again. Besides, I have an excellent security system, and I'll have my pistol next to me."

As Tracy escorted them to the door, Cat said, "There's another bag in the freezer. Use it, it'll help."

"Thanks for your timely intervention tonight."

Watching Cat back out of the drive, she thought, *they have no idea what a close call she just had.* Then her mind shifted to Stuart. There must be a way she could get into the compound, and what the hell weighed 27.43 pounds?

Twenty-one

Walking into the hotel, they heard a shout from across the lobby. It was Blake, who stood in the doorway to the lounge. As they approached, he said, "I've been waiting for you to get here."

They followed him to a table in the corner where a tall, lanky man rose to greet them. "Lance, meet Adrian Dillard and Cat Morgan. This is Lance Brewster," Blake said.

Adrian stared at a man who was the antithesis of an agent. His hair curled over his shirt collar. A band of freckles across his nose, and wire frame glasses added to a nerdy, disheveled appearance. But then, he probably looked the same to the TEDAC agent. Another benefit of being a Tracker, they didn't have to conform to the Bureau's dress code.

A waitress walked up and set two baskets of chips and bowls of salsa on the table before taking their order. Cat and Adrian ordered a sandwich. When Blake and Lance passed on the food, Adrian gave them a questioning look.

"We ate before we got on the plane. Scott said you'd fill us in on what's happened here."

For Lance's benefit, Adrian started at the beginning, with Bardwell's murder. His recital was interrupted when the waitress brought their drinks, beers for the men and a glass of wine for Cat.

When he reached the part about the theft of explosives, Lance interrupted. "I'd like a copy of the reports. How much was stolen?" His gaze turned grim as he listened to Adrian's answer, then said, "Combined it's enough to ..." he stopped as the waitress

Au79

reappeared with two plates of food.

Cat waited for her to walk away, then asked, "To do what?"

"Bring down the damn Golden Gate Bridge."

Adrian grunted. "That bad?"

"Oh, hell, yes, and more," Lance said.

Cat leaned forward. "Lance, would the detonators have been used on the bridges?"

"Highly likely, and it would only take one. Knock out one of the support pillars, and it could cause the entire bridge to collapse. If not, there's at least a gaping hole."

She said, "Okay, let's assume worst case scenario. They had twelve, we found two, three would have been used, that makes seven that are left?"

Lance nodded his head in agreement. "With those detonators and the missing explosives, there is a potential for a massive amount of destruction."

"What about the weight? Any ideas there? What about something related to explosives?" Adrian glanced at the two men. "You're the experts." He took a bite of his sandwich.

"I've been running that question in my mind since you mentioned it, but I'm not coming up with anything," Blake said, then added, "Lance. How about you?"

He shook his head. "Nada, nothing."

"Then what else could it be?" Cat chewed while her fingers tapped the screen of her phone. "Here's one, a man caught five fish in a fishing competition that weighed 27.43 pounds, another about a cow and butter. Hmm ... don't think this will solve our problem."

Blake asked, "How certain are you this group, the Border Guards, is involved?"

"It wasn't until Tracy saw the eighteen-wheeler, and someone took a shot at her. Then Reynolds came up with a fishy story about taking potshots at coyotes." Adrian took a sip of his beer. "One other item I hadn't mentioned. She was attacked on her front porch earlier this evening. We got there just in time. When you called, we were at her house."

"How bad is she hurt?" Blake asked.

"Some bruising on her throat, but she'll be fine," Cat said.

Blake's glance darted between Cat and Adrian. "Any idea why?"

"Cat and I bounced that question around on our way over here. Since she's Stuart's fiancée, maybe they think she knows something, or she's getting too close, or it could be because she saw the truck. She's a loose cannon."

Blake shook his head. "An attitude like that won't help us."

"I don't like it either, but she's put the Guards square in the middle of this." Adrian took another bite.

"Does Scott know all of this?"

He swallowed, and said, "I called him after we left Tracy's house."

"Any ideas on a target?" Lance asked.

"We don't have a clue. Ryan and Nicki are searching for some type of activity over the next few days. So far, they haven't found any," Adrian said.

"Considering our primary suspects, it could only be one of two possibilities, make a statement, or money." Blake set his bottle on the table. "Given their history, making a statement doesn't seem to be in their wheelhouse. So that leaves money. Drugs or weapons would be the likely options, something that would require a truck."

Lance said, "Here's another possibility. They've stolen a lot of explosives. If they want to haul all of it around, they'd need an eighteen-wheeler or a whole lot of pickups."

Cat said, "You might be right. Remember Tracy mentioned seeing stacks of boxes at the compound the night they took a shot at her. Was that some of the stolen explosives?"

Adrian pushed his plate aside and settled back in the chair. "Without a better description, it won't do any good to put out an APB."

"Where would they get one?" Lance dipped a chip in the salsa. "Lease, buy it, steal it?"

"Good point, an eighteen-wheeler is not a vehicle you can acquire at your local dealership," Blake said. "They don't seem to range far from home, judging by the bridge locations."

"I'll get a list of leasing companies in Texas. If we don't get anywhere, we can expand the search. There's something I saw. What was it?" Cat paused. "Warden, Joe Warden has a commercial license."

"I bet he was driving that truck," Adrian said. "When Tracy and I spoke with the man who owned the house Warden rented, he said Warden was a part-time truck driver."

Blake said, "The truck could have come from Mexico. I did find a comment on Dyson's computer. It was about an informant he was going to meet on a cartel arms deal. Nicki ran a trace on his calls on the day he logged the entry. It was two days before he disappeared. He got a call from a number that showed up on Bardwell's phone. The number was one of those burner phones we couldn't locate."

"That matches what Tracy told us, except we thought the informant was Bardwell," Cat said.

At the questioning look on Blake and Lance's face, he said, "There's more we haven't had a chance to tell you. According to Tracy, Dyson went undercover to get a lead on an arms deal, and to get the name of the ringleader. Tracy was the only one he told. He said that he was uneasy over a couple of investigations and felt safer if no one knew." He added their suspicions over the trail of evidence to implicate Dyson.

Blake stared at Adrian. "Hell! They've set him up as the patsy."

"That's what Cat and I believe. Proving it is something else. Right now, all the evidence points to Stuart. We've also got another problem, and it's in line with Stuart's misgivings. Someone in either the local FBI or ATF office may be involved, which is why I'm not telling either of them any more than is absolutely necessary. I think Stuart is still alive, but that could change if they get wind of what we're up to."

"So, where the hell is he?" Lance asked.

"Do we know if the Guards own any other property?" Adrian asked.

"Not sure. I know Nicki was running every possible connection before I left."

Cat picked up her cell phone. "I'll send her a text about the property search and one for a registration."

His voice harsh, Adrian said, "We need to figure out a way to get onto that property."

Washington D.C.

Scott hung up the phone. Despite the fact he expected the call, it was still disconcerting to be on the receiving end of a request. No, who was he kidding? A meeting with the President wasn't a request, it was an order.

Nicki's tap on the door broke his concentration. His gaze shifted from staring at the phone to her face. "Ryan made a pot of coffee, want a cup?"

"Hmm ... yes. We need a meeting. Stop by Ryan's office and let him know."

Dropping his notepad on the conference table, he turned to look out the darkened window and the reflection of his face that stared back at him. His hand massaged the tense muscles in his neck as he thought about the phone call, and what the hell he could tell Larkin tomorrow morning.

Sighing, he turned back to the table and pulled out a chair. A hand slid a cup in front of him. He looked up into the sympathetic gaze of his research guru.

"You heard?" he asked.

Nicki settled into a chair and took a sip from her cup. "Yep. This is a great new office, but as far as being soundproof, it leaves a lot to be desired. So, you're headed to the White House tomorrow."

He nodded. "The man is going to want answers. I don't have them."

Ryan sat next to Nicki. "Maybe some good ole' fashioned brainstorming will help."

"I got a text from Cat," Nicki said. "Wants to know if the Guards own any other properties. She also wants a search on who owns a big rig truck. She mentioned Warden has a commercial driver's license."

"It ties into what Adrian told me earlier on the phone."

After listening to the details of the call, Ryan exclaimed, "Dyson's the scapegoat, and Tracy got in their way. Do they have any idea who the inside person is?"

"No, but they've cut Karl Chambers and Bill Goddard out of the loop. Are we any closer to finding the target?"

Nicki said, "We were comparing notes earlier. Ryan hasn't located any shipments that would garner the attention of a group of radicals. I haven't found anything more than the usual … football games, concerts, weddings, business meetings, that type of activity."

A look of frustration crossed Ryan's face. "We're looking for the proverbial needle in a haystack."

Scott took a sip of his coffee before saying, "What weighs 27.43 pounds?"

"Huh? Boss man, what hat did you pull that out of?"

Scott flicked a quick glance at her. Her eyes sparked with mischief.

Shaking his head, he continued, "Tracy found a note in a box of evidence from Morris' house." He scrolled to the image on his phone Adrian had sent and handed it to Nicki. "There's also a phone number we need to run down."

She made a note of it before passing the phone to Ryan.

"The weight and how many?" Ryan stared at the screen as he mentally added the details to the profile he'd created. "If this note has any bearing on the Guards intentions, I don't think it's drugs. Boxes of manufactured drugs could be a specific weight, but not street drugs. It might refer to a type of weapon or ammunition."

"Hmm ... that could fit," Scott said. "We know Stuart Dyson had an informant about a weapons deal for a cartel. It's why he went undercover, to find out who was the ringleader."

"Until we figure out what weighs 27.43 pounds, we're back to the needle," Ryan said.

"Nicki, plug a new search into TRACE, see what you come up with. Ryan, start making calls, military, weapons manufacturers, anyone who would be shipping weapons. Even an eighteen-wheeler loaded with ammunition would bring a pretty penny on the black market."

Walking back to his office, Scott felt marginally better. Maybe he could tell the President a high fatality explosion wasn't imminent.

A u 7 9

Twenty-two

Texas

Exhilaration surged through him as he hung up the phone. It was another anonymous tip. This time, the caller told Eddie to investigate the bullets that killed Bardwell, Morris, and Martin. He'd find a link to Stuart Dyson. Visions of the accolades that would be heaped on him for his investigative reporting skills swarmed in his mind. Even Jimmy was happy. When Eddie showed him the picture he'd taken of Harlowe bending over Morris' dead body, the man had stuttered in his excitement. Eddie's article and the picture were the headline on the front page in tomorrow's paper.

Now he had the beginnings of the next article. He just had to find out what the hell the caller was talking about. Then he remembered the visit from the agents. A wave of doubt and uncertainty put a damper on his elation. If he called and told them, he'd lose the chance at the story. No, he'd take his chances.

He needed information on testing a bullet. Eddie tapped his keyboard and watched the articles scroll across his screen. After a few minutes of research, he learned how a bullet could be matched to the gun that fired it. Tomorrow he'd start with a visit to the Laredo Police Department. If he didn't get any answers, then he'd head to the M.E.'s office.

****

After a shower and another cold compress on her neck, Tracy began to feel half-way human. The questions she mulled while letting the hot water ease the tension in her muscles coalesced into a plan.

Tracy grew up hiking the desert around Laredo with her dad before he passed away. She knew the terrain and how to dress for the rough conditions.

In the spare bedroom closet, she grabbed her heavy canvas pants, a long-sleeved shirt, hiking boots, and a down-filled jacket. Opening her gun safe, she picked up two extra magazines for her duty weapon, then eyed her scoped rifle. Should she take it? No, it would get in the way.

The magazines fit in an interior pocket of her coat along with a small flashlight and a small bag containing her locksmith tools. On her way out of town, she'd stop at the PD to pick up an NVG, night vision googles.

Once she was dressed and her gear assembled, she still had a couple of hours to kill before leaving. She pulled up an aerial map of the compound on her computer. The rear property line butted up against a ranch with several buildings and a large stock tank. A fence separated the two properties. The aerial image of the fence was outdated. She had no way of knowing if it had been replaced. She zoomed in, looking for a likely spot to cross. She found one. Near the fence was a dirt road that circled behind the stock tank.

Before exiting, she zoomed out for a wider view of the terrain. An image clicked in her mind—the metal box in Morris' office. It contained a county map. She'd given it a quick glance before moving it aside to look at the other documents.

Why did he have a map tucked inside? What county? She closed her eyes and pictured her fingers reaching to pick it up. The name on the front, what was it? "Burnet!"

Her hand reached for her phone, then stopped. If she called, they might show up at her front door again. A text would work if she worded it right. The short message read, "Remembered a Burnet County map was in metal box. Throat too sore to talk, see you tomorrow." That should suffice.

A u 7 9

Whistling, Eddie glanced at the time as he shut down the computer. Even though it was late, he'd swing by Harlowe's house before he went home. So far, following her had been a smart move.

Her house was at the end of the block. As he drove past, he didn't see her vehicle. Was she there? The truck could be in the garage.

Parked on the side street, his fingers drummed the steering wheel. He should go home and come back in the morning. But he'd be awake the rest of the night wondering if he'd missed another opportunity. Only one way to find out. He grabbed the small flashlight stuck in the door panel and slid out, then gently closed the door. Just be his luck some nosy neighbor would hear and call the cops.

Nervous, his eyes darted from side to side, from the houses to the street and back as he strode along the sidewalk. The pounding of his heart seemed to echo in his head.

Eddie walked up the driveway to the garage door. Even with his face pressed tight against the glass, it was too dark to see inside. Damn, should he use the flashlight? If anyone was watching, they'd see the beam, even if it was only for an instant. He glanced around again. It should be okay.

In the quick flash, he viewed an empty garage. Where was she? He rushed back to his truck. At this time of night, the only place he could look was the police department.

A block from the PD, Eddie slowed for a red light. A vehicle shot through the intersection. It was Harlowe's pickup, and she wasn't on her way home. The light turned green. He sped up and made a fast turn to follow. Eddie could see the tail lights ahead, but he wasn't gaining any ground. He managed to keep her in sight until she turned onto another street. By the time he got there, she was gone. Where was she headed? Mystified, he had no choice but to go home.

Tracy was in and out of the PD in minutes. A couple of officers on the late shift had spoken to her, but no one seemed curious she was at the station this time of night. As a homicide detective, her hours were erratic.

As she sped out of town, her nerves ramped up, and her chest tightened at the thought of what lay ahead. Though she'd never admit it to anyone, she was afraid. No one knew where she was going, or why. She thought about sending another text message to the agents, then decided it was a bad idea. They'd try to stop her, or worse confront the Guards. If Stuart was there, it could get him killed. She couldn't risk it.

After turning onto the road that ran along the backside of the Guards' property, she slowed. The moon had yet to pop over the horizon, and the illumination from the headlights faded into the murky darkness. She passed the ranch house and dirt road that led to the stock tank. The barn she'd spotted on the aerial map should be a few hundred yards ahead. It might be a good place to stash the truck. She tapped the brakes again. Her eyes scanned the edge of the road. In the pitch-black of the night, it would be easy to miss the driveway.

She parked behind the dilapidated structure. Turning off the engine, she sat for a few minutes and tried to settle her nerves. Her mouth was dry. A few sips from the water bottle in the console did nothing to help. Sitting here wasn't going to accomplish anything. She was either going to do this or turn around and go back home.

Tracy checked her phone. It was on mute, and she slid it back into her coat pocket. Picking up the NVG, she opened her door. The cold rush of night air sent a chill down her back.

Locking the doors with the remote, she started to put the keys in her pocket, then stopped. If by chance this didn't go right, she didn't want to give Reynolds or any of his cronies a set of keys to her truck and home. She laid the keys on top of the back tire. It wasn't a surefire hiding place, but better than her pocket.

With her head tipped back, Tracy stared at a night sky filled with twinkling lights. An eerie silence surrounded her. She took a deep breath, then let the memories of such nights with her father flow through her. For a moment, it seemed he was next to her.

With a sigh, she pulled on the NVG, pushing her hair back when strands caught on one of the straps. The night turned green. She headed to the road, staying on the asphalt until she reached the dirt road. Following it, she moved at an easy pace until she reached the stock tank, then veered off into the brush and mesquite trees.

When she spotted the fence, she stopped and studied it. It hadn't been replaced. This was old barbed wire, overgrown with weeds and brush. She found it odd they weren't paranoid about the back, though she was relieved.

The fence crossed a dry creek bed, making it a good spot to crawl under the wire. Once she was on the other side, she eased her way over the rocks and ruts. The creek ran along the edge of the property and would be easier to follow than sidestepping the heavy brush and clumps of cacti. From her study of the map, it was a two-mile hike to reach the buildings.

When the creek turned to meander off the property, she pushed through the brush that bordered the bank, thankful for the heavy canvas pants. Still, she occasionally felt the bite of a sharp barb.

She rounded the end of a pile of dirt and stopped. A jolt of fear raced through her. Men stood in the clearing in front of her. *You idiot. Get a grip on yourself*, she thought, realizing they were targets. Wooden frames cut to the size of a human being were nailed to posts stuck in the ground. Stepping in front, she eyed the holes punched in the head and chest. Guess this is where these guys hone their shooting skills.

Ahead was the compound. She stopped and scrutinized the buildings. There were the three large metal ones, the farmhouse, and two small wooden structures that were the closest. She decided to start with those and eased her way to the nearest one. Hugging the side, she peeped around the corner before moving to the door. Opening it, she quickly stepped inside. Nothing but tools and farm equipment.

The second building was the same. It was filled with rolls of barbed wire, hand tools, and a large stump grinder.

Stepping back outside, her gaze darted from the farmhouse to the nearest metal building. Which one first? While she didn't believe Stuart would be inside the house, it would be better to start there and find out if anyone was still awake. Tracy crept toward the side, then worked her way to the back of the house. She peeped around the corner. A porch extended along the rear. She stepped up and edged her way to the back door.

All seemed quiet. She retraced her steps, then headed to the first of the large metal buildings. There were no windows on the side and none on the back. After a quick peek around the corner at the opposite side, she leaned against the back of the building. Damn, not a single window. She'd have to try the door at the front. If it was locked, she was screwed. She couldn't risk exposing herself for the time it would take to pick a lock. Stepping along the side, she glanced at the adjacent building. Well, hallelujah, it had windows.

Before she stepped in front of the building, she scanned the yard for any movement. Slipping along the front, her hand reached for the doorknob.

The flood lights flashed on, and the override on the NVG kicked in, the green vanished. Before she could react, a voice that was unnervingly familiar said, "Move, and I'll blow your fucking head off."

A hand grabbed her wrist, twisted her arm behind her back and shoved her face forward against the side of the building. A foot kicked her legs apart. A hand searched her pockets. The gun was yanked from her holster, and the knife clipped to her pants pocket ripped off.

The arm that held her locked against the building jerked her back and spun her around. The NVG was stripped from her head and tossed on the ground. Fear ripped through her as she stared at two men. One she recognized as Reynolds, who stood with his legs spread, fists resting on his hips. A sneer crossed his face as recognition blazed in his eyes.

The other, his face rough-hewn, stared at her with an expressionless look. His eyes didn't seem to blink. She didn't recognize him, but she knew who he was by his voice. He was her assailant from earlier in the evening, and he held a pistol aimed at her face.

His voice contemptuous, Reynolds said, "Well, Stan, guess the third time's the charm. You don't have to track her down after all."

A laugh erupted from Stan. Despite the debilitating terror that threatened to drop her to her knees, Tracy straightened. Unconsciously, her chin lifted. She'd be damned if she'd let them know she was petrified. Her voice was steady, as she said, "You won't get away with this. Cops will be crawling all over the place if I'm not back on time."

Another laugh, this time from Reynolds. "Stupid bitch. You really think that bluff will work? I'm betting no one knows you're here. If they did, you'd have backup. It's how cops work."

"I'll handle this," Stan told his boss. His gun never wavered as his cold hard gaze raked her body. "I'd like to have some fun before I put a bullet between her eyes."

"No, we're not going to kill her. Since she's here, I've got a better use for little miss priss who believes she's a badass cop."

Before she could dodge out of the way, his fist connected with the side of her face. Her head rocked as pain exploded. Her knees crumpled. A black mist pushed aside all her thoughts and fears. *Is this what it feels like to die?*

Twenty-three

When his phone chirped, signaling an incoming text, Adrian groaned. He'd just drifted off to sleep. In an endless rehash of the investigation that produced nothing new, they'd sat in the hotel bar until it closed. Then Ryan called, and it was another conversation that went nowhere.

Exhausted, he wanted to ignore it. Surely, a text could wait for another few hours. Hell, better find out. The curiosity, if nothing else, would continue to jab at him. But he was going to be royally pissed if it wasn't important.

Swinging his feet out of bed, he walked to the desk and picked up the phone. It was a text from Tracy. She remembered seeing a map in that missing metal box. Where was Burnet County? His interest piqued, all thoughts of sleep vanished. Dropping into the chair, he opened his computer. Burnet County was located northwest of Austin, the capitol of Texas.

Leaning back, he contemplated the map on the computer screen.

Why would Morris have a county map in a locked metal box, and why did someone steal the box in the first place? Didn't Tracy mention it contained several legal documents, even a deed? Christ, had they missed a critical detail?

As he mulled over the possibility, a comment from Cat popped into his mind. She'd questioned why Morris' house and bar had been searched? Was the box the reason?

He glanced at the clock. He hated to call, but this was too important.

There was no choice.

A sleepy voice answered, "Agent Nicki Allison."

"Sorry to wake you."

"Oh, Adrian. No, it's all right. I'm still at the office."

"You were sleeping on the couch again."

"Uh, yeah."

"Does Scott know?" Everyone in the office knew about the tug of war between Scott and Nicki over her sleeping on the couch. The bets were on Nicki winning as she always seemed to find a way to get around one of his edicts.

Ignoring his question, she said, "Give me a minute to get going. Be right back."

In the background, he heard the clink of glass. He chuckled, knowing it was the coffee pot.

"What's up?" Her voice was more alert. He figured she'd gulped down at least half a cup.

"I got a text from Tracy." He read the message, then said, "When we discovered the break-in at the bar, Tracy said a metal box from a file cabinet was missing. She also said it contained a deed and legal documents. Did you run Morris to see what property he owned?"

"No, I didn't, but I will. Where is Burnet County?"

"Northwest of Austin."

Nicki mused. "Hmm …the map's in a box that was stolen, must have some significance. Did you ever figure out why Tracy was at the bar?"

"Burglarized the place, though she won't admit it. Not only did she break into the bar, but also the box. She can be very tight-lipped. I'll find out more when I get to the PD."

"Have you come up with any ideas on the weight?" she asked.

"Not yet, though our best guess is something to do with weapons."

"That's the theory we're going with. Ryan's running down possibilities, and I've got a search running in TRACE."

"I know. Ryan called earlier. Here's a bit of unpleasant news. Lance said the stolen explosives could bring down the Golden Gate Bridge. He also brought up the idea the semi might be used to haul all the stolen explosives."

"Interesting theory. We hadn't thought of that. I'll pass it on to Scott. He's got a meeting with the President later today."

"Jeez, glad it's not me."

"Can't disagree. You were in Austin when he had to walk the gauntlet at the White House over the kidnapped kids. It was rough, but at least he had answers going in. This time, we're still in the dark."

"Now that I'm thoroughly depressed, I'm going back to bed," Adrian said.

"Thanks, a whole lot. Looks like I'll be staying awake," she quipped.

"You love it. Trying to keep you off the computer is a near impossibility. And there's always the couch."

She chuckled. "Get some sleep. I promise I won't call unless I find something. Good night."

Laying the phone on the table, his thoughts shifted to the mystery of 27.43 pounds. Was it the key they needed to break open the case or were they wasting valuable time? The doubts built, and his sense of foreboding and anxiety deepened. Thinking about the contents of the damn metal box didn't help. Nothing he could do now. His first stop would be the PD, and he'd get answers, even if Tracy had to write them.

Washington D.C.

It had been a long night. Thoughts of what he'd say, how to say it, what not to say, in the upcoming meeting with the President had him dozing in spurts. He'd finally given up.

The sun wasn't even a glimmer in the sky when he arrived. The office was dark, except for a glow down the hallway. Damn, he'd bet money she'd stayed the night.

Au79

Stopping in the doorway, he knew he was right. Despite the change in clothes, her hair gave her away. When he leased the office, he'd arranged for the use of the fitness center on the first floor. His team, including himself, made full use of the facility and even kept spare clothes on hand. The thick, coal black hair that reached her waist hung loose and was still damp.

Tapping the door to get her attention, he walked in and settled in a chair. She spun to look at him with a sheepish grin and, without hesitation, threw Adrian under the bus.

"I know. I was supposed to go home, but Adrian called."

Scott leaned back in the chair, an arm rested on the desk. "One of these days ... oh, hell, what did Adrian need?"

Grinning, she swiveled back to her computer. "Burnet County."

"Okay, I'll bite. What's so important about Burnet County?"

"It's near Austin, and Tracy saw a map in Morris' office when she broke into the place."

"When she did what?"

"Hmm ... don't think you were supposed to know about the break-in. Disregard it. She found a metal box in Morris' office. Whoever tossed the bar stole it. Tracy remembered seeing the map and sent Adrian a text. He called me." She stopped and took a deep breath.

"Just tell me about Burnet."

"Well, that's the problem, I can't. If it's tied to what's going on in Laredo, I haven't got it figured out. I've been working on it since Adrian called. He also wanted me to check into any property Morris owned. I'm running the program now. The phone number Tracy found on the note was Bardwell's phone. Since Morris set up the meet with Bardwell, it doesn't help."

Scott groaned in frustration. "There's nothing, then, that puts us any further into this equation."

"There's a couple of other items, not what I'd call good. Lance said the stolen explosives could bring down the Golden Gate Bridge and suggested the eighteen-wheeler might be hauling all the stolen explosives."

"That's a possibility. Nothing on the weight?" He glanced at the goblin dancing on her screen.

"Not yet,"

"After I get a shot of caffeine, I'll be in my office trying to figure out what to say to the President."

Ryan came through the front door as Scott headed to the breakroom. After greeting his boss, he dropped his case in his office, then followed Scott.

"I see Nicki got here early."

"Ryan, you don't need to cover for her. I already know she didn't leave." He jabbed the start button.

Ryan grinned before saying, "Didn't really think I'd be putting one over on you. Did she come up with anything new?"

"Adrian called her. Did you know Tracy broke into Morris' bar?"

"I did. I talked to Adrian last night. How'd you find out?"

"Nicki let the cat out of the bag. Tracy sent Adrian a text she remembered seeing a Burnet County map. It's near Austin."

The coffee maker dinged. Ryan picked up the pot, poured a cup for Scott, one for himself, and a third for Nicki. "Why would Morris have a map?"

"Same question I had. I was going to pull it up when I got back to my office."

"Let's look at it on the monster screen in Nicki's office."

Ryan set Nicki's cup on the corner of her desk, careful to keep it away from any of her electronic equipment. When the map popped up on the screen, the two men sipped their coffee and studied the image.

"Not much there," Nicki said. "Just a little over forty-two thousand people in the entire county."

"Until we can figure out the target, none of this makes sense," Ryan said.

Scott turned. "I'll be in my office."

Once he was out of earshot, Nicki said, "The boss man's worried about the meeting."

Ryan nodded. "I know."

Texas

The call woke him out of a sound sleep. A surge of anger shot through him at the sight of the number on the screen. His wife groaned and rolled over. "Who is it?"

"Just work, go back to sleep."

Answering, he said, "Hold on." It didn't stop Reynold's voice on the other end.

"Find out if anyone is in an uproar today."

Downstairs, he closed the door to his office before saying, "Dammit Reynolds. Whatever problem you've got, you handle."

"How many times do I have to remind you? If I have a problem, then you've got one. Find out what they're doing."

"What are you talking about?"

"We had an early morning visitor snooping around the buildings."

"Who was it?"

"The one you assured me you'd handle if she got in the way."

"Jesus, what the hell have you done?"

"What I had to. Unless you want this to blow up in your face, you'd better damn well keep me in the loop."

"Is she dead? No, don't answer that. I don't want to know."

A sadistic chuckle echoed on the other end. "I don't suppose you do. What's the status of the shipment?"

"It's on schedule."

The line went dead. Sinking into a chair, he ran his hand over his face. What had been a foolproof plan was about to go down the crapper. He knew it in his gut.

****

Adrian strolled into the hotel dining room, a newspaper under one arm. Cat, Blake, and Lance were already seated at a table. After greeting them, he dropped the newspaper in front of them. "The latest issue of the Laredo Observer. Take a gander at the front page." While they read the article, he filled a plate with bacon and eggs, grabbed a cup of coffee, and set the items in front of the remaining chair.

"She won't like this," Cat said, as she studied the picture of Tracy kneeling beside the dead body. "Eddie Owens is getting to be quite an annoyance."

Adrian grunted. "He's a royal pain in the ass. Got a text from Tracy last night." He relayed the details before he scooped up eggs on a fork.

Blake asked, "What's so important about Burnet County?"

Adrian swallowed. "Don't know yet. I handed off the information to Nicki when I got the text. I think that box is the reason Morris' house and bar were searched."

"That makes sense." Cat slid her plate to the side and leaned her elbows on the table. She pulled up a map on her phone. "Wow. There's not much there, just a few small towns." She handed the phone to Blake, who looked at it, then passed it to Lance.

"Maybe she'll remember some other detail on what was in the box. Have you talked to her this morning?" Cat asked as Lance passed the phone back to her.

"Not yet, but we need to meet her at the PD."

"I'll call her." She tapped a number on her phone. It rang, then rolled to Tracy's voicemail. After leaving a message, she said, "Hmm … that's odd. She usually answers. Wonder if her throat is giving her problems. If we don't hear from her, let's swing by her house and check on her."

Adrian's phone rang. "Dillard," he answered.

"Agent Dillard, this is Detective Skip Thornton. Have you talked to Tracy this morning?"

Au 79

A trickle of uneasiness built. "No, we tried to call, but it went to her voice mail."

"Same here when I tried to call. I'm worried. A clerk from our equipment room stopped by my desk looking for her. Seems Tracy checked out an NVG in the wee hours of the morning. Do you know anything about that?"

Curses floated in Adrian's mind as the uneasiness morphed to a full-blown sense of trepidation. His voice grim, he said, "No, I don't. Cat and I are getting ready to leave the hotel and will go by her house. Don't do anything until I call you."

Disconnecting, he said, "The damn woman picked up an NVG early this morning. Skip hasn't been able to contact her."

"Hell!" Blake muttered. "Does this mean what I think it does?"

"Yes. She searched the Guards' compound looking for Stuart. Blake, call Scott. Fill him in on what's happened. Then meet us at the ATF office. Don't say anything about Tracy until we get there. If she's missing, we need to get a search warrant. Right now, I'm not sure what's the best way to approach the problem we've got with Chambers and Goddard. If she's there and the Guards get wind we're coming ..." He couldn't finish the thought. Pushing back his chair, he said, "Let's go."

In the car, he tried her phone again. The call rolled to voice mail. "They've got her. I know it. Like an idiot, I fell for that line—her throat too sore to talk."

Anxious, Cat's hands gripped the wheel. "Don't beat yourself up over it. Tracy's one cagey woman. If she's at the compound, we might find her truck. If she's not home, I'll make a pass by the place."

Cat turned onto Tracy's street. The driveway was empty. Still, there was one other chance. She stopped in front of the house. "Check the garage to be sure."

Adrian hopped out, ran to the door and peered through the window. Shaking his head, he raced back to the car.

Once she cleared the city limits, Cat hit the accelerator. As they turned onto the road that led to the compound, she slowed to look at every driveway and possible hiding place for a vehicle. They spotted the abandoned house Tracy said she had used. She stopped in the road, and Adrian ran to the rear of the house. "Not there," he said, as he got into the car.

As they drove by the compound, it appeared to be deserted.

Cat went on down the road and turned around. Still nothing on the second pass. Any hope they had, died.

"Let's head for the PD." He grabbed his phone and called Blake.

"Where are you?"

"In the ATF parking lot."

"Change of plan. Meet us at the PD, homicide section. Tracy's not at her house, and we checked out the compound. Nothing."

When he disconnected, he caught the questioning glance Cat cast at him.

"I don't want to use the ATF or FBI personnel. But we can use the PD's. I'm going to talk to Rodriguez."

Twenty-four

Folded to the lead story, the newspaper covered the console. Giddy with excitement, Eddie's eyes darted between the road and the paper. That was his article and his name on the front page. He'd already received several phone calls from acquaintances. He couldn't call them friends. Most of the time, they wouldn't bother to say hi if he passed them on the street. But now, they wanted to know how he got mixed up in a major federal investigation.

With every glance, his determination hardened. If there was to be another article, he had to get those test results. He'd changed his mind about who to contact first. The medical examiner might be better. Detective Harlowe would probably kick him out the door.

Entering the building, he approached the receptionist and asked to speak to Doctor Kennedy. When asked for his name, his back stiffened, and he tried to infuse a note of authority in his voice. "I'm Eddie Owens, the news reporter for the Laredo Observer, and would like to ask Doctor Kennedy a few questions about a recent case."

The woman eyed him with suspicion until he pulled out the business card he'd printed at the newspaper office. She tapped a button on the phone, informing whoever answered that a reporter, Eddie Owens, was in the lobby.

After hanging up, she directed him down the hallway to the doctor's office. He reached for the notebook in his pocket and tapped on the door.

A voice said, "Come in."

When he stepped inside, a large man in blue scrubs looked up. "You Owens?"

"Yes, sir, I am."

"I'm Doc Kennedy. Have a seat and tell me what you want."

He perched on the chair. Now that he was here, his nerves hummed with anxiety. He cleared his throat, then said, "I'm investigating the deaths of three men, Cam Bardwell, Bing Morris, and Donnie Martin."

The friendly smile on the doctor's face vanished, though he didn't say anything.

Eddie rushed to fill the silence. "I'd like to know about the bullets."

"What is it you want to know?"

"Were ballistic tests done?"

"Yes."

"Uh ... well, what were the results?" In his eagerness to hear the answer, he scooted closer to the edge of the chair. It tilted, and he almost fell off. The notebook landed on the floor. Embarrassed, he felt the heat rise in his face as he picked it up and slid back on the seat.

"I can't comment on any test results. I suggest you contact the lead detective, Tracy Harlowe."

"Since you conducted the tests, I would prefer to hear an explanation from you. I'd also like a copy of the results. Doctor, I'm sure you realize I'm just reporting a story."

Hostility sparked in the man's eyes. "Time for you to leave."

Eddie panicked. He hadn't expected the angry response. Desperate, he tried another tactic. "If there's anything hinky about the results, the public has a right to know. Was there something that might implicate Stuart Dyson as the shooter."

The doctor's voice rose to a roar. "Get out of my office before I call security, and have you thrown out."

"Okay, okay, I'm going. But I know Dyson's involved, and I'm going to find out."

Muttering curses, he rushed down the hallway. When the

Au 79

receptionist smirked as he passed, he shot a nasty look her way.

He seethed with resentment as he got behind the wheel. How was he going to get the test results? As much as he hated the thought, he'd have to try at the PD. Still it might not be all bad. There was a chance he'd find out where Harlowe went last night.

****

The doctor sat in his chair, pondering Owens' visit. The anger eased, leaving him uneasy as he thought about the man's questions. How did he find out Dyson was involved?

He opened a drawer and picked up his appointment calendar. He'd jotted down Agent Dillard's number when he called about the ballistic tests.

"Dillard," the agent answered.

"Agent Dillard, this is Doctor Kennedy, the medical examiner."

After exchanging greetings, Adrian asked, "Did you get the tests back on Morris?"

"I did, and the bullet came from Dyson's gun."

"We expected it. I appreciate your call."

"That's not the only reason I called. Not sure if this means anything, but I had a strange visit from an Eddie Owens. Claims to be a news reporter for the Laredo Observer."

With a grim note in his voice, Adrian said, "I know him. What'd he want?"

"The test results on the bullets that killed Bardwell, Martin, and Morris."

There was a short silence before Adrian asked, "Did he mention the men by name?"

"Yes, he did. But that's not all. He alluded to the possibility Dyson was the shooter."

"What did you tell him?"

"That I couldn't comment on the test results. He would need to talk to Detective Harlowe. Then I kicked him out of my office."

A wry chuckle erupted. "Well done, Doc. I'll take it from here. And those test results are still to be kept under wraps. Tracy knows, but no one else other than my team. I'd appreciate it if we could keep it that way."

"You don't need to worry, I will."

"Thanks for the heads up."

****

Jabbing the disconnect button, Adrian exclaimed, "That damn idiot!"

Cat turned off the ignition. "I take it you mean Eddie Owens."

Adrian relayed the gist of the conversation.

Shaking her head in amazement, she said, "Owens got another phone call, and didn't call us. I guess, I shouldn't be surprised."

"It's exactly what happened. We'll have to deal with it later." He tapped the speed dial for his boss.

"Scott, we believe Detective Harlowe attempted to search the compound early this morning and has disappeared. I need to expedite a search warrant, but don't want to involve Karl Chambers or Bill Goddard."

"You'll have it within the hour. How are you going to handle the search? I don't like the idea of the four of you going in without backup."

"I'm going to use Laredo PD personnel."

"If you need any help with the Police Chief, let me know."

"Will do."

Inside, they turned down the hallway that led to the homicide division. As they entered, Blake was seated in Tracy's chair across from Skip, and Lance leaned against a nearby desk. They were in deep conversation. At the sound of the door, they looked up.

"No sign of her at the house, and we didn't locate her car at the compound. Have you heard anything?" Adrian asked, directing his gaze at Skip.

The man shook his head. "Nothing. I tried her cell phone several times. I set up a trace, but it's been turned off."

Au 79

Blake asked, "What's the game plan?"

"I'll let you know in a minute. Skip, is your Captain in his office, and does he know she's missing?"

"He's upstairs in a meeting, and he doesn't know. I was waiting to hear from you. I hoped you'd find her at her house. It's not the first time she's turned off her phone."

"If the conference room is available, I'd like to meet there. And I need someone to print off an aerial map of the entire compound. Can you get Rodriquez down here?"

Skip nodded. "Not a problem. I'll get the map."

"We'll wait in the conference room. I'd like to have you sit in."

Adrian headed for the door, followed by the other agents.

Inside the conference room, Blake settled into a chair. "Do you think we can pull this off before Karl Chambers or Bill Goddard get wind of what's going on? They'll be pissed when they find out."

"We're going to try. I don't like it any more than you do. Until we know who is leaking information, I can't take a chance on someone alerting Reynolds we're coming."

His phone rang. "Speaking of which, this is Karl." Answering, he said, "Morning, Karl."

"Bill is in my office. Can you swing by and bring us up-to-date on the investigation?"

"Karl, I'll get back to you later today. Cat and I are running down a couple of leads."

With a note of eager anticipation in his voice, Karl asked, "Do you have something new?"

"No, there's nothing, just tying up loose ends. I'll tell you about it when I see you."

Disconnecting, a grim look crossed his face. "Under the circumstances, a bit of misdirection seemed appropriate." The idea a fellow officer was involved had eaten at his gut and having to lie added another level of aggravation.

193

The door opened. A man in a neatly pressed uniform, with the insignia of a captain, walked in followed by Skip.

"I'm Captain Andy Rodriguez." He extended his hand as Adrian stepped toward him.

After introducing himself, Adrian did the same with the three agents. Rodriguez nodded to each one, then asked, "How may I help you?"

"Please sit down. This'll take a few minutes. Skip, close the door."

A guarded look crossed Rodriguez's face as he sat.

"Before I get into any explanations, this conversation cannot leave this room."

The scowl on Rodriguez's face deepened, but he nodded in agreement.

"Detective Harlowe is missing."

Rodriguez's body tensed, and a look of disbelief crossed his face. "How do you know? And then someone," his head swiveled toward the detective seated next to him, "needs to explain why I'm just finding out I have a missing detective."

"Until we walked in a few minutes ago, Skip wasn't certain she was missing. He told us that Tracy had checked out an NVG. We suspect she attempted to search the Border Guards' compound early this morning. When we were unable to contact her by phone, we checked her house. She's not there, and her cell phone is turned off."

Rodriguez eased back. "That's all the proof you have?"

"You may or may not be aware the Dyson investigation has been assigned to the Tracker Unit. We're convinced the Border Guards are involved. Not even Karl Chambers or Bill Goddard are fully aware of certain events that have transpired. There's a reason I'm not at liberty to discuss, but it's why I'm requesting your help."

Skip's phone rang. He excused himself and left the room.

Adrian picked up where he'd left off. "I'm waiting for a search warrant for the Border Guards' compound. I need additional officers to assist in the execution of the warrant."

Rodriguez stared at him for several seconds before he asked, "How many do you need?"

"I'd like a SWAT team and Skip."

Rodriguez pulled a phone from his pocket and hit the key pad. After a short conversation, he disconnected and said, "Lieutenant Gabriel Pearsall is on his way. He's in charge of the tactical division. I'd appreciate it if you'd keep me informed of any details you're able to share."

He stood and turned to walk out. Skip entered carrying a paper tube. As Rodriguez passed him, he said, "Skip, keep me posted, and I mean before the fact, not after."

"Yes, sir," the detective responded, then turned toward Adrian. "Here's the map. Eddie Owens is in the lobby."

A glint sparked in Adrian's eyes. "I want to talk to him."

Turning to Blake and Cat, he said, "When Pearsall gets here, get the raid set up. I want to move as soon as we have the warrant in hand. Lance, any issues from your side on being involved in this?"

Lance grinned, then said, "Not a damn one."

"Skip, let's find out what Mr. Owens has to say."

Twenty-five

When Adrian and Skip entered the reception area, Owens leaned against the wall near the front door, his thumbs tapped the screen of his phone. At the sound of footsteps, he looked up, and his face paled. Shoving the phone into his pocket, he straightened.

"Eddie." Adrian's calm tone was belied by the frown on his face. "I planned on tracking you down today."

"Uh, why?" Eddie eased toward the door.

"I think you know the reason, and we're going to talk about it for a few minutes."

Eddie's face turned pasty white. "I … uh … I got nothing to say," the man stuttered, and took several steps backward.

Skip grabbed his arm. "You're not going anywhere, and don't think otherwise."

Eddie swallowed. Panic gleamed in his eyes. "You don't have any call to treat me like this. I haven't done anything wrong."

Adrian said, "That's what we're going to find out."

Skip hauled him down the hallway to a small interview room. Inside was a desk with several chairs. After shoving Eddie into one, he leaned against the wall behind him.

Adrian sat in a chair across the table. He waited, his gaze steady as he studied the man.

As the silence continued, Eddie's nervousness increased. He fidgeted. Fingers drummed the table, his body shifted in the chair, and eyes flicked around the room to avoid looking at Adrian. When he blurted out, "I haven't done anything wrong, you can't keep me here. I have rights," his voice squeaked.

"There's a small detail you seem to have forgotten. The last time we talked, I mentioned an obstruction charge."

"I'm not admitting anything."

"We know you got another call."

He groaned. "That damn doctor called, didn't he?"

"Did you really believe he wouldn't?"

Owens shrugged, crossed his legs, then uncrossed them.

"Eddie, I want to know what the caller said. You haven't broken any laws—yet. But if you don't tell me the truth, I'll have you arrested. You'll go from here to a jail cell."

Eddie shifted. Adrian waited.

"Last night. Guy called last night," Eddie muttered.

"And?" Adrian asked.

"Said I should ask about the bullets."

"That was all, just ask about the bullets?"

"Um...no. He mentioned the three guys who were killed. Told me that I'd find the ATF agent was involved."

Adrian asked, "What else?"

"That was it, I swear, that's all he said."

"You're certain?"

"Yeah, nothing else."

Adrian leaned forward. "What did you do?"

Eddie scooted back. "I don't know anything about bullets. I researched and found out about the M.E. It's why I went to Kennedy's office. When that didn't work, I thought I might get something from Detective Harlowe." A sly look appeared. "She's not here, is she?"

"How do you know she's not here?"

His shoulders hunched forward, and he stared at the table.

"Eddie, did you follow her again?"

He mumbled, "Maybe."

It was difficult to ignore the jolt of anticipation. "When?" Adrian hoped Eddie hadn't picked up on the importance of the question.

"After I left the newspaper office, I went by her house. She wasn't there, so I came here. I saw her truck and followed her, but I couldn't catch up."

"Where'd you lose her?"

"She was headed out of town, going west on FM 477."

"What time?"

"Hmm ... I guess around two this morning."

The memory of the incoming text sparked in his mind. He bet she sent it, then left the house. "Why were you up at that hour of the morning?"

A defensive note in his voice, Eddie said, "I wasn't doing anything wrong. Like I said, I was at the office researching."

Adrian stood. "You're free to go, but this is your last warning. If you do anything that hampers my investigation, I will have a warrant issued for your arrest. An officer will find you, handcuff you, and haul your sorry ass to jail. Do you understand?"

His eyes downcast, Eddie nodded.

Skip opened the door, and said, "Let's go."

Dejected, Eddie strode across the parking lot. His story was gone, and it wasn't fair. The bitterness was a lead weight in his gut. He'd never get answers as long as that agent was here. Wait a minute. A surge of his innate sense of curiosity struck. Why was the agent at the PD? And why the question about where he'd last seen the detective? Had something happened to her? He got the brush off when he asked to speak to her, and then the other detective showed up. Hell, yes! Something had happened, and maybe he wasn't going to miss a chance to hit the big time with the story. He'd just have to figure out how to steer clear of the feds.

He looked at his truck. By now, they'd probably recognize it a mile away. He needed another vehicle. Bet he could talk his sister out of the clunker she drove. She was always on him about wanting to borrow his truck.

****

Inside the conference room, several new officers had arrived. Hunched over the table, Blake, Cat, and another officer studied the aerial map. Cat looked up. "Adrian, meet Lieutenant Gabriel Pearsall, and his team. This is Adrian Dillard."

He nodded to the officers who lined the wall and shook hands with the lieutenant, who said, "It's Gabe."

"Adrian, I've got the search warrant," Cat said. "Gabe is getting copies made."

Blake slid the map toward Adrian. "We're set and ready to go. We kept the plan simple. The four of us will pull up to the gate. We're going to take two cars, extra cover if this goes to shit. Skip will hold back along with Gabe and his team. If we get inside, they'll follow. If we don't, then Gabe's team will move up and force open the gate. They know the fence is electrified."

Adrian glanced around the room as his thoughts circled the pros and cons of the plan. "I like it. It keeps this to a low profile. I just learned Eddie Owens, the reporter for the Laredo Observer, spotted Tracy leaving the PD. He followed but lost her on FM 477. I'm certain she was headed to the compound."

Gabe pointed to the backside of the property. "Since you've already checked the road in front of the compound for her vehicle, I sent two officers to check the back road."

Adrian glanced around the room. "Let's get this done."

Outside, the SWAT team assembled around their van, suiting up in their specialized equipment. Blake and Lance each carried a vest they'd borrowed from the PD. Instead of the rental from the airport, they would use an unmarked police car. Vests for Cat and Adrian were in the trunk of the vehicle Karl provided when they first arrived.

As Cat exited the parking lot, Adrian's phone rang. He recognized the number he had programmed for Gabe.

"Adrian, my men just found Tracy's truck. It was parked behind an old building near the backside of the compound."

The hope Tracy wasn't there died. Now, his only hope was that she was alive.

Cat stopped in the driveway leading to the compound. Blake pulled alongside. The other vehicles in the convoy stopped on the edge of the road.

"Looks deserted," Cat said, as she got out of the car.

"Only one way to find out." Exiting, Adrian stared at the camera trained on the front gate and waited. He'd give them a few minutes before they busted the gate open. Blake and Lance moved alongside him.

When a pickup drove around a building, he stepped back to the side of the car. The driver screeched to a halt and jumped out. His hands on his hip, he surveyed the four agents with a look of contempt. "Commander Reynolds has nothing to say. You're not setting foot on this property."

Adrian said, "He doesn't have a choice. I've got a search warrant. Open the gate."

The man reached inside and picked up a radio lying on the dash. His voice was a low murmur. He tossed it back into the truck and slid behind the wheel. The tires spun as he headed back to the house.

Adrian tensed, not liking what just happened.

Gabe stepped next to him. "How long are you going to give them?"

"Not long."

A few seconds later, the gate swung open. The agents piled into their cars, and Gabe ran back to his. Cat lead the way as the vehicles drove onto the property. Once the tactical van was near the house, it stopped. Officers climbed out and swarmed the area. Cat pulled to a stop behind the pickup that had parked near the front steps to the house.

Reynolds stood on the porch. He viewed the activity with a smirk on his face. As Adrian walked up the steps, he said, "We haven't broken any laws. There's no justification for your actions. If you do have a search warrant, I demand to see it."

Adrian handed the document to him.

Reynolds unfolded it. After reading the warrant, he looked at Adrian. Anger sparked in his eyes. He stepped back and gestured toward the open door.

"Are the buildings unlocked?" Adrian asked.

"No. I'll have them opened." He turned and barked an order to the driver of the truck.

They'd already decided that Skip and Lance would search the outer buildings, and Adrian, Cat, and Blake would take the house.

The foyer led to a large living room with two small rooms on one side. A doorway leading to the kitchen and dining room was on the other side. A long hallway led to the bedrooms. Blake broke off and headed to the kitchen, and Cat started down the hallway. Adrian started with the living room.

With the ease in which they gained entry, he knew Dyson and Harlowe weren't here. What he hoped to find was evidence they had been. His eyes surveyed the room. Other than a closet, the possibilities were limited. The office might prove more productive. At the sight of the computer on the desk, he itched to have a go at it. But for now, he'd have to pass.

Reynolds leaned against the doorjamb with his hands tucked in his pockets. "If I knew what you were searching for, I might be able to help," he quipped.

Despite the surge of irritation at the sight of Reynolds' self-satisfied smirk, Adrian's face was impassive as he calmly brushed past the man.

The second room held two large safes and another desk. Reynolds opened the safes. Adrian eyed the rifles, shotguns, and pistols.

"They're all legal."

Ignoring him, Adrian walked back to the living room. Blake walked out of the kitchen shaking his head.

Cat stepped into the living room and shook her head no.

Adrian said, "Let's check with Skip."

Outside, Gabe's officers ringed the compound. The driver of the truck leaned against the hood. Dressed in a t-shirt and camouflage pants, the man was well over six-foot and solidly built. His muscular arms crossed his chest. Despite the loose fit of the pants, his legs, crossed at the ankles, stretched the material tight over his thick thighs. His face had the same self-satisfied smirk his boss had.

Reynolds had followed the agents out the door. Grinning, he propped a hip on the porch rail.

Motioning to Gabe, Adrian asked, "Did you get this guy's ID?"

Gabe pulled a small notebook from his shirt pocket. Flipping it open, he tore out the page and handed it to Adrian. "Stan Meyers, thirty-two. Home address on his driver's license is about ten miles from here."

Adrian folded it and stuck it in his pocket. As he passed Meyers, he glimpsed a shadow on the side of the head. He turned and stepped closer. Meyers never moved, though his jaw tightened.

Adrian examined the injury to his face, and said, "That's some bruise. How'd you get it?"

Meyers snorted, "None of your damn business."

Adrian said, "Everything, and I mean everything you do is my business. Don't forget it."

As he walked off, a mutter echoed behind him. "Fuckin' cop."

Skip walked out of the end barn, followed by Lance.

Adrian motioned toward the three metal buildings. "Anything?"

"No," Skip replied. "They've been cleaned out. Even the concrete floors have been scrubbed clean."

"Damn. I was hoping we'd find something. What about those two small buildings?" He looked at the wooden structures. A tactical officer stood by the door.

"Storage for farm equipment. But ..." He hesitated until Adrian glanced back at him. "All's not lost."

Leading the way to the building, he explained, "We found several small footprints. I've taken pictures with my phone, but I need better ones. I've called our crime scene techs. They should be arriving shortly."

Opening the door, he pointed to a large oil stain on the floor near a stump grinder. "Those are fresh prints."

Adrian leaned inside the doorway to get a better look. They were either a woman's or maybe a child. Since he hadn't seen any evidence of children, he'd opt for the fact it was probably Tracy's.

"That's not all," Skip added. "There are several faint prints on the back porch. I'd bet she went from this building to the house. You can see the tracks going to the door, and then back to the steps."

Adrian headed to the back of the house. Another tactical officer stood by the porch. Walking alongside the porch rail, Adrian could see the footprints appeared to match the ones in the building.

Turning, he strode back to the front and motioned for Gabe to join them. "Arrest both men. Keep them separated. I don't want any discussion between the two."

He glanced at the other agents. "Inside is a computer. Load it up along with all the files in the office."

Gabe signaled to several of his officers. After a short discussion, two headed toward Meyers, who straightened and curled his hands into fists. Before he could take a swing, the officers grabbed his arms, spun him around and handcuffed him. One read him his rights.

He looked over his shoulder at Adrian. The hate spewed as he cursed, and then added, "You're a dead man."

"That sounds like a threat to a law enforcement officer. Ka-ching, let's add a charge."

As two other officers arrested Reynolds, he glared at Adrian. As his rights were read, he ignored the officer. Instead, he shouted at Adrian. "You've got no grounds to arrest me. I'll sue your ass for false arrest and police harassment. You can kiss your career goodbye."

Adrian glanced at him and walked away.

Gabe put Meyers in his car and assigned one of his officers to drive Skip's car with Reynolds. Skip would stay behind to meet the crime scene unit and ride back with them.

Adrian called Scott. The call rolled to his voice mail. He left a message. Glancing at his watch, he said, "He's probably in his meeting at the White House." He sent a text — *Reynolds arrested, have computer and files, agent and detective still missing.*

Au79

Twenty-six

Eddie had switched vehicles with his sister, who was ecstatic over getting to drive his new truck. He threatened her with every dire warning he could imagine if it came back with even one scratch. After eyeing her dirty, dinged up car, he almost changed his mind. Was the story worth it? Then the vision of his name as the byline flashed in his thoughts. Eddie turned the key in the ignition and backed out of her driveway.

He arrived at the PD in time to see a convoy of vehicles leaving, all headed in the same direction as Harlowe had the night before. What was going on? Only one way to find out. He followed.

When they turned onto a county backroad, he slowed, hoping he could stay far enough back they wouldn't spot him. As they rounded a bend, brake lights flashed on the rear vehicle. Were they stopping?

Up ahead was an old farmhouse. He pulled into the rut-filled, weed-infested driveway, and was glad he was driving his sister's car.

Stepping out, he eased the door shut. Eddie ran until he reached the curve. He scrambled over the bar ditch and crept forward. Ahead the SWAT van had stopped, and officers climbed out the back. Two of the cars were parked in the entrance, and Agent Dillard stood in front of a gate.

"Oh, my, god!" he whispered. Pictures, he needed pictures, then remembered he'd left the damn camera in the car. He raced back wondering if he should move the car behind the farmhouse. Would a passing car see it? He vacillated between moving it, or not moving it.

Would they hear the engine and investigate? No, better to leave it where it was.

He grabbed the camera, slipped the strap over his head, and dashed back. All four agents stood in front of the gate. A pickup was parked on the other side.

His hands trembled as he removed the lens cap. Calm down, he told himself. If the pictures were blurred, they wouldn't be worth a plug nickel. He clicked several times, shifting to get the van and other vehicles.

The gate swung open. Once everyone was back in the vehicles, they drove in.

Could he take a chance and get closer to the gate? If he did, they'd probably see him. He might have to be satisfied with what he had — unless? Maybe there was a way.

He crossed the road. Crawling through the barbed wire fence, he worked his way through the brush until he was several hundred yards from the road. Several times he cursed at the sharp barbs that stabbed his legs. He changed direction and followed the fence line until he was in front of the gate.

The vehicles were parked near the house. He dropped to one knee and his finger hit the button, click, after click, after click.

When most of the officers disappeared inside the buildings, he sat and watched. He wasn't leaving until this was over. It must be a search warrant, but who owned the property? He didn't recognize the two men. One leaned against the truck, and the other stood on the front porch.

When the agents came out, he snapped shots until they all walked behind the house. When they reappeared, two officers grabbed the driver and then the guy on the porch. Holy crap! It was getting better and better. Agent Morgan carried a computer out of the house, and other agents hauled out boxes. He got it all on film.

When the tactical van and other cars left, they passed an SUV emblazoned with Laredo PD Crime Scene. It parked in front, and an officer appeared from behind the house. It was the detective who confronted him in the lobby. Two men exited, and one grabbed a case before they followed the detective to the back of the house.

Jeez, what did they find? Despite the curiosity that churned inside him, there was nothing he could do. Sensing he had all he could get, he stood. Then another car arrived. Eddie repositioned the camera. A man, dressed in a suit, got out. He looked around, then walked toward the house.

The detective came around the corner. The man ignored him and kept walking. The detective moved in front of the steps to block him. The camera lens magnified the look of rage on the man's face and the tense expression on the detective's. When the detective shook his head and gestured toward the gate, the man turned and stomped to his car.

Wheels spun, tossing up dirt and gravel, as he tore out of the driveway and hit the accelerator.

Eddie ran. The rush of adrenaline blocked the pain of the jabs from needles on the cactus and dry brush. He had to get to the PD and find out what was happening there.

****

"Tracy. Tracy. Wake up."

The voice was persistent, over and over, the same words repeated. She didn't want to hear, there was too much pain. It was easier to slide back into the black pit.

"Tracy. Tracy. Wake up."

Her eyes slowly opened. She was lying on her side, jammed against a wall. Her body ached, and the bright sunlight pushed the pain in her head to new heights. She groaned and closed her eyes.

"Tracy, open your eyes. Come on, listen to me. You've got to wake up."

Her voice hoarse, she said, "Stuart?"

"Oh, thank god. You've been lying there for hours. Yes, baby. Look at me. You can do it."

Her head shifted toward the sound, and she reopened her eyes. Bile rose in her throat from the sharp spasms in her head and neck.

"That's it. Good. I've been so afraid you wouldn't wake up," he said.

Several feet from her, Stuart was propped against a wall, his wrist handcuffed to an eye bolt embedded in the leg of a large work bench. Oh, god, his face. What wasn't hidden by a stubble of whiskers was marbled with black, purple, and red. One eye was swollen shut, and his upper lip was split. He looked like hell, but he was alive. The fear she had lived with ebbed.

"How bad are you hurt?" His voice was thin and thready. "You've got a hell of a bruise on your cheekbone and more on your throat, and a black eye. The bastards hauled you in here and tossed you on the floor. Is anything broken?"

"Uh ... give me a minute." She took several deep breaths. The nausea and vertigo eased. Despite the sharp pains that radiated in her head with each movement, she struggled to push herself up, only to discover one hand was handcuffed the same as Stuart's, except the eye bolt was in the wall. Tracy scooted, wiggling and twisting, pushing with her feet until she was sitting somewhat upright. Motionless, she waited for the pain to recede before she said, "It looks like everything's working."

"What happened?"

Her mind still fuzzy, she had to think for a minute. "I searched the Border Guards' compound for you. Reynolds, the head guy, and one of his pet apes caught me. Reynolds slammed his fist into my face."

"Don't tell me you went in without backup?"

"Um ... well, yeah, I did. We didn't have enough to get a search warrant. I had it all planned. If I found you, I was going to call in the troops."

"I should have known. You've always rushed in where anyone else wouldn't even take a step."

"Hey, you should talk. Look what you did!"

"So, where did you pick up the bruises on the throat?"

"The pet ape attacked me on my front porch. Where are we?" Her eyes scanned a room filled with workbenches, a desk, several chairs and file cabinets. She was near the corner on the wall opposite the door. Stuart was on the adjacent wall.

"I'm not sure. I've been in and out. One of Reynolds' men, probably your pet ape, likes to use me for his daily exercise."

"How bad are you hurt?" She didn't like the sound of his breathing.

He shifted, angling his body toward her. His face grimaced in pain. "Feels like a couple of broken ribs along with the injuries to my face. They unlock me just long enough to use the bathroom twice a day. So far, I haven't passed any blood. I don't believe my internal injuries are severe. What I haven't been able to figure out is why I'm still alive."

She leaned her head back and took several deep breaths.

"You okay?" he asked.

"Yeah, just have to let the pain recede."

"Fill me in on what's going on."

"A team of FBI agents, Trackers, is here from Washington and took over the investigation."

"I've heard of them."

"Stuart, it's a hell of a mess. Everyone thinks you're the culprit. Your fingerprint was found in evidence taken from Cam Bardwell's garage."

"Bardwell was my informant. What did he tell the agents?"

"Nothing. He's dead, along with two other men, Donnie Martin and Bing Morris, the guy who owned the Watering Hole. All were shot with your gun."

For several seconds, the only sound was Stuart's labored breathing and Tracy's deep breaths.

"They've set me up to take the fall for all of this."

"We finally figured it out."

"We?"

"I'm part of the task force. Now, tell me what happened to you."

"Everything went according to plan. I met Bardwell at a warehouse on the edge of town. We left in his car and headed west. He had brought along a thermos of coffee. The damn stuff was drugged, and it's all I remember until I woke up in here with Reynolds in the chair watching me."

"And you don't have any idea where here is?"

"None. Reynolds questioned me several times, which is why I was used as a punching bag. Always the same questions, mostly about who I had talked to."

"He's making sure he's got all his loose ends tied up. Do you know what's going on?" Tracy asked.

"I might. Tell me everything that's happened on your end."

Tracy started from when she was called out to Bardwell's murder. When she finished she hesitated, then added, "I did find an oddity in the stuff we took out of Morris' house. It was a note that had a weight, 27.43 pounds followed by a question—how many."

Stuart leaned his head against the wall. His lungs wheezed. "How many detonators are missing?"

"Matt and Randy removed the evidence from Bardwell's garage. Matt said it looked like there were ten. Do you know what they're after? The theory is drugs or weapons."

"Tracy, it's not."

When he fell silent, Tracy prompted him. "So, what *is* their target?" Listening to his answer, disbelief and shock flashed through her.

The door opened, and a man stepped inside.

Stuart muttered, "I'll be damned. Reynolds isn't the ringleader after all."

The man chuckled. "How are our lovebirds doing? Having fun yet?" he said, followed by another sadistic laugh. "Enjoy it while it lasts. You're going on a road trip. Unfortunately for you, it's one-way. Matter of fact, you won't ever be going anywhere again." As he walked out the door, his laughter erupted. The lock clicked.

Twenty-seven

Washington D.C.

Scott gathered his files and stuffed them into his briefcase. He glanced at his watch. His team was probably on their way to the Border Guards' compound. Over the last several months, he had learned the wait was one of the most difficult tasks for a supervisor.

Since he had a few minutes before the limo would arrive, he wandered out into the bullpen, then to Ryan's office. He could hear the agent's voice. Stopping in the doorway, he waited for Ryan to finish the call, before stepping inside.

At the sound of the footsteps, Ryan glanced up and dropped his pen on the desk. "This is slow going. I've been in contact with all the major arms manufacturers. They don't want to release any information on their shipping schedules, and understandably so. I wouldn't pass information over the phone even if it was the President calling. I've contacted the local FBI offices to send an agent to their headquarters. It's taking time. You ready for the meeting?"

"No, but I don't have a choice. The man will want answers, and I don't have them. How about military shipments?"

"I made multiple calls and there's nothing in the immediate future that would raise a red flag. And I still haven't had any luck deciphering the riddle of the weight."

Nicki's shout echoed in the background. "Scott! Ryan!"

Scott hollered, "Ryan's office."

She skidded to a stop in the doorway, her face triumphant. "I found it. I know what weighs 27.43 pounds."

When Nicki stopped talking, the two men eyed her. Whenever she unraveled a knotty puzzle, she'd find a way to dramatize her answer.

A glint of humor in his eyes, Scott accommodated her. "Well, what is it? We're waiting with bated breath."

"A u 7 9."

"What the hell is that?" Ryan said.

With hands on her hips, an expression of superiority crossed her face. "Jeez, I can't believe two highly intelligent agents don't know the chemical elements or the periodic chart."

Mystified, Ryan and Scott looked at each other. Each shrugged their shoulders.

Scott groaned in frustration. "Okay, we give up. Explain."

"Gold! *Au* is the chemical element symbol and comes from the Latin word *aurum*. 79 is the atomic number on the periodic chart."

His face still puzzled, Ryan said, "That doesn't tell us much."

Nicki sighed. "Okay. It's a gold bar, and to be more precise, a 400-Troy-ounce Good Delivery gold bar. It weighs 12.4 kilograms or 438.9 ounces which is …" her fingers rapped the door, "27.43 pounds. The physical characteristics for a Good Delivery bar is set to precise measurements. It's used for international trade between governments, central banks, and other investors."

In disbelief, Ryan said, "That can't be right. Why in hell would a man who owns a biker bar in Laredo be interested in gold bars?"

Scott glanced at his watch. "I have to leave. Both of you, start digging. Find out why."

Downstairs, he pushed open the front door. The limousine stopped beside the curb. A young man hopped out of the front seat and opened the rear door.

Scott thanked him as he slid inside. Seated on the opposite seat was his boss, Paul Daykin. Memories of his first meeting with President

Larkin flicked in his thoughts. Paul had been in the car waiting for him then. On that trip, he wondered if he'd still have a job after delivering some very bad news to the President.

As the driver wove his way through the heavy D.C. traffic, Scott and Paul discussed the upcoming meeting.

"I expect Larkin's not going to be satisfied with our progress, not when explosives are involved," Paul warned him.

"I know. A missing ATF agent, and now we've got a missing homicide detective, along with enough explosives to take down any bridge in the country. It's enough to scare the living hell out of anyone. I think we're close to a breakthrough."

"Hmm ... I hope you're right. Though I'm not the one you'll have to convince."

Inside the White House, they followed a Secret Service agent to the Oval Office. When the door opened, two men stood inside. As Scott entered, he gave himself a few seconds to absorb the power and grandeur of the room. He didn't believe he'd ever lose his sense of awe.

His thoughts were broken by the President's voice. "Scott, good to see you again, even under these circumstances."

"Mr. President, you're looking well," Scott said, as they shook hands.

Six-foot, with a slim build, the President had just turned sixty. Despite the gray streaks in his dark hair, he looked years younger.

Larkin smiled and patted his stomach. "The wife put me on a low-cal diet. Don't like some of the food, but I do feel better."

Scott smiled and turned to greet Vance Whitaker, the Secretary of Homeland Security.

Larkin waved Paul and Scott to one of the two sofas that faced each other. Surprised, Scott maintained his calm demeanor. He'd just been upgraded. In previous visits, he'd sat in a chair facing the two couches, what he had referred to as the hot seat.

"Vance has been providing details of your investigation, but I'd like to hear a complete analysis."

"Yes, sir. As you're aware, this started when a Laredo ATF Agent, Stuart Dyson, disappeared. Director Daykin assigned the case to the Tracker Unit. Agents Adrian Dillard and Cat Morgan were sent to Laredo."

Scott proceeded to outline the events as they occurred and the conclusions of his team. He ended by adding, "This is a broad overview."

"I'm curious about a few items. How did you initially locate the bridges?"

"TRACE, the software program I designed to track criminals who elude traditional methods of investigation, has been upgraded. Agent Nicki Allison has added a number of enhancements and was responsible for finding the news articles."

"Still, what made you suspicious?" President Larkin asked.

"The timing and locations were just a bit coincidental, and going on a hunch, Blake and an agent from TEDAC were sent to investigate."

Relaxed, his arm resting on the arm of the couch, the President grinned. "I sincerely doubt hunch is even a word in your vocabulary. Your unit has an uncanny ability to link pieces of random information that seem to have no connection."

Paul chuckled, then said, "It's exactly what they do."

"Despite the evidence against the ATF agent, you're certain that he has been framed?" Larkin asked.

"Yes. The evidence is another series of suspicious coincidences."

"How solid is the connection to the Border Guards?" Vance asked.

"They're our prime suspects. We've narrowed their motivation to two options. The first was to make a statement. Since the group is not known for protests, we eliminated it. The second was money. Until earlier today, we believed the intent was to steal a shipment of weapons, which could be sold on the black market."

His phone vibrated, indicating a text message. "Excuse me a minute. I need to check this." He glanced at the President, who nodded his head in acquiescence. Scott read the message, and said, "It's an update on the search warrant. Per Agent Dillard, Norman Reynolds, head of the Border Guards, has been arrested, and a computer and other documents seized." He pocketed the phone.

Vance leaned forward. "You mentioned arms shipments. What's the status?"

"Agent Barr is coordinating the contact to major weapons manufacturers as well as the military. I won't use the word hunch," and smiled at the President before he added, "It's my belief that whatever is planned will happen within the next two to three days. So far, we haven't identified a target within that time frame."

"Scott, what changed this morning?" President Larkin asked.

"We're fairly certain that we've found out what weighs 27.43 pounds."

The President said, "You just lost me."

"Before Detective Harlowe disappeared, she found a note in the files of one of the murdered men that referenced the weight followed by the question—how many. Our first theory was ammunition or a type of weapon. This morning, Agent Allison discovered the answer. A 400-Troy-ounce Good Delivery gold bar weighs 27.43 pounds."

The President said, "Gold? How could it possibly connect to a group of radicals in Laredo?"

"I don't know yet, but I hope to have answers by the time I get back to my office."

Vance said, "Good lord. Is it possible?" When all eyes turned to him, he added, "I may know? I need to make a call."

Vance strode to the desk and lifted the receiver. "This is Secretary Whitaker. I need to speak to Frank Littleton, the Federal Reserve Chairman. If he's not in his office track him down." While he waited, he drummed his fingers on the desk.

A jolt of anticipation shot through Scott. His senses tingled. Whatever Whitaker was after would connect the dots.

"Frank, it's Vance." He listened, then said, "What's the status of the gold shipment we discussed two weeks ago?"

After several seconds, he said, "When is it scheduled to leave, and do you know the security arrangements?" He picked up a pen and jotted notes on a pad lying on the President's desk, then said, "Not certain. I'll get back to you." After thanking Littleton, he hung up.

He looked at Scott. "Remind me to never bet with you. I'd be a sure loser. A shipment of gold bullion bars is scheduled to leave New York City tomorrow and is headed to the Texas Gold Depository."

His relaxed demeanor vanished. "Vance, we need to stop the shipment," the President said.

"I agree, but we need to hear from Scott before I call Frank back."

"I'm not familiar with the details of the depository, but is it by any chance, in Burnet County?" Scott said.

Surprise registered on Vance's face as he answered, "Yes. It's near Burnet, which is northwest of Austin. How did you make the connection?"

Another link clicked into place in Scott's mind. "Detective Harlowe spotted a map of Burnet County in a biker bar in Laredo." He hoped no one would ask how. When Vance's only comment was about the detective being in the right place at the right time, he felt a twinge of relief.

Vance continued by saying, "About three years ago, a push was made by the University of Texas and Texas A&M University to move their gold reserves from New York City to Texas. Two years ago, the Governor of Texas signed a bill to create the depository. Construction of the facility was completed two months ago. Close to one billion dollars in gold bullion owned by the universities is set to be transferred."

"How's it being shipped?" President Larkin asked.

"It's being trucked from New York City to a military base, then by plane to Fort Hood, Texas, where it will be transferred to another truck for transport to the new facility." Vance glanced at his notes, then said, "The plane leaves at eleven tomorrow night."

"What are the security arrangements?" Scott asked.

"Frank said the details have been a closely guarded secret, which raises an interesting question. If the gold is the target, how in hell did the Border Guards find out?"

Scott's mind raced, pondering the possibilities and consequences. They still had two people missing. If they weren't dead already, they would be if the Guards found out the shipment was cancelled.

"I'd like to know the answer to that question myself," Scott said. "There's something else I didn't mention. I hesitated to raise the subject until I had confirmation. Secretary Whitaker has just provided it. My agents in Laredo have suspected someone, either in the local ATF or FBI office is involved. I would like to speak with Chairman Littleton."

The President looked at Vance. "I'd like to hear what he has to say. Call him and ask if it would be convenient for him to attend this meeting."

"Mr. Secretary. Please request that he not mention the purpose of the meeting to anyone," Scott said.

Vance looked at him and after a couple of seconds nodded his head in agreement.

After a short second call, Vance said, "Chairman Littleton is on his way."

"Anything else, Scott?" the President asked.

Scott gathered his thoughts. A plan had started to formulate. Still the President might not be willing to go along with it. "Yes. That plane has to leave on time."

"What!" Larkin exclaimed. "I thought we agreed to stop the shipment."

"Yes, we did, but not the plane. If Agent Dyson and Detective Harlowe are still alive, stopping the convoy will sign their death warrant. And there are still missing explosives, enough to take down any bridge in this country, or thousands of other targets. It's a threat that will rise in another direction if we don't stop it now. We know the why, now we must find the where. That plane needs to arrive in Fort Hood, and we'll use the trucks as a decoy."

Larkin stared at the floor for several seconds, a look of concentration on his face. When his eyes lifted, and his gaze met Scott's, he nodded his head. "I'll approve it, but if any innocent bystanders are killed or injured, we'll all be crucified."

He rose and walked to his desk. He pushed a button, and a voice came on the line. "Yes, Mr. President."

"Henry, I'd like a pot of coffee and assorted cold drinks."

"Yes, Sir."

"If you'll excuse me for a minute, I'll step out for a moment to make a phone call," Scott said.

Scott nodded to the men and walked out of the room.

The President glanced at Paul and Vance. "Opinion gentlemen?"

Vance said, "Scott's right. We either stop the threat now or face it in the future. I'm beginning to place a great deal of trust in that man's ability and that of his team."

Au79

Twenty-eight

He leaned against the wall in the hallway and tapped the speed dial for Adrian. "Where are you?"

"Standing in the parking lot at the PD. Did you get my text?" Adrian asked.

"Yes. What did you find at the compound?" He listened to his agent's explanation and then said, "We've identified the weight. It's a gold bar. Tomorrow, a plane loaded with close to one billion dollars in gold bars is headed to Texas."

Adrian muttered, "Holy Hell! I bet it's somewhere in Burnet County."

"You're right. The destination is the Texas Gold Depository located near Burnet, which is the county seat. I'm still at the White House. The meeting has been delayed. We're waiting for the Federal Reserve Chairman, Frank Littleton, to arrive to discuss a change in plans."

His tone grim, Adrian said, "Scott, if you stop that shipment, any chance of finding Stuart or Tracy still alive is gone."

"I know, and that's why I'm not stopping it. The plane's just not going to have the gold on board."

"This should be interesting. What's your idea?"

"I'm still working on that. Plan on a conference call this evening."

Adrian's comment of good luck echoed as he disconnected. He'd need it. The lives of two people, and possibly countless others, was riding on the decisions that would be made over the next few hours.

219

Despite the President's assurance, if Scott couldn't provide a cohesive plan, the approval could easily be reversed.

Texas

Cat had waited while Adrian talked to Scott. Once he hung up, she said, "From your end of the conversation, it sounds like our investigation is on the move."

As they strode to the front door of the police station, he filled her in on the details. Blake and Lance had already arrived and were moving boxes from the lobby to the conference room. "Cat, tell them about Scott's call and start searching the computer and files. I'll talk to Rodriguez and then interview our two guests."

Rodriguez was on the phone. When he saw Adrian in the doorway, he quickly ended the call. His face and tone anxious, he asked, "Did you find anything?"

"I'm certain she was there." Adrian explained the evidence they'd found. "We've arrested Reynolds and one of his tag-alongs, Meyers. They're both screaming for a lawyer, so I doubt we'll be able to hold them long. I confiscated their computer and files."

"Are you interviewing them?"

"Yes, did you want to sit in?"

"No, but I'll watch from the outer room."

As Rodriguez escorted him to another part of the building, Adrian said, "Let's start with Meyers."

At the end of a hallway was a large metal door. Rodriquez tapped a code into the security pad, and a buzzer sounded. The door swung open. Inside, six holding cells were on one side and three interview rooms on the other. Gabe stood in the hallway. At the sound of the door, he turned and greeted them.

"Did they call an attorney?" Adrian asked.

"No. We just arrived, and there hasn't been an opportunity to let them have access to a phone. Meyers is in the first room, and Reynolds is in the second."

Adrian nodded his head and opened the first door. A small anteroom had a one-way mirror. Adrian could see the man seated at the desk facing the door in the next room.

When he opened the inner door, Meyers' eyes flicked upward and filled with rage. A sneer crossed his face.

"Well, if it isn't the hot shot federale. I got nothing to say and demand that I be allowed to call my attorney."

"You'll get a chance." Adrian sat in a chair on the opposite side, his back to the mirror. Unperturbed, he crossed one leg over the other and stared at Meyers. His gaze never wavered.

After several seconds of silence, Meyers shifted in his chair. "Didn't you hear me, I said I want an attorney. I know my rights."

"Hmm … I'm sure you do."

Adrian continued to stare at the man.

Meyers' cuffed hands rested on the table. The clink of the metal links broke the silence as his fingers drummed. "What the hell's going on here? Just get me a goddamn phone."

"Oh, one's coming. I just thought I'd keep you company until it arrives."

"I don't want your fucking company. I told you I'm not answering any questions."

"I don't recall I've asked any. Maybe we can have a nice chat while we wait."

Meyers snorted, and glanced at the mirror, then back at Adrian who lounged in the chair. "What is this, a freaking sideshow? How many people are watching?"

"Don't know. Don't care. Does it bother you?"

He shrugged his shoulders and turned his gaze from the mirror.

"We've got a missing detective."

Meyers chuckled. "Like I give a rat's ass."

"Interesting bruise on the side of your face. Wouldn't think someone could get the better of you, but just goes to show, brute strength doesn't count for much."

The man's face grew red, and his body stiffened. The handcuffs clinked.

Adrian tilted his chair back, his hands rested on his thighs as he mused. "A gung-ho guy like you. Seems to be a strange injury, almost like someone hit you in the head with a heavy object. I wonder what it could have been."

"You're just another fucking cop, making a big deal out of nothing."

"You should be worried. Anything happens to our detective, you could end up on a one-way trip to Huntsville. You do know about Huntsville? It's where they house prisoners on their way to be executed."

Meyers sneered. "You've got shit for brains if you think I had anything to do with her disappearance."

He waited, his gaze locked on Meyers' face until there was another uneasy shift of the man's body. Adrian's chair dropped to all four legs when he leaned forward, his arms rested on the table. With a menacing tone, he said, "I never said the detective was a woman."

Enraged, Meyers started to rise, then sank back down.

"Smart move." Adrian's lips curved up in a sneer. "Where were we? Oh, yes—the missing detective. How'd you know she was a woman?"

Meyers flicked a glance over Adrian's shoulder at the mirror, then stared at the table, his lips tightly compressed.

"Guess you don't want to talk about that. Let's try explosives. That might be of interest to you. There was a theft of those not long ago."

The only reaction was a slight stiffening of Meyers' shoulders.

"Your buddy, Cam, liked to build detonators. Must have been what got him killed. Where were you when he was shot?"

Meyers' eyes never looked up, but his lips curled in a smug smile.

Au79

Adrian stood, his hand reached across the table, his finger tapped the back of Meyers' hand.

When the man looked up, Adrian said, "You think about the missing detective, three dead men, and missing explosives while I talk to your boss. Don't forget the threat you made, because I haven't."

Rodriguez and Pearsall, who had been watching in the anteroom, followed him out the door into the hallway.

"I'm certain he's the one who attacked Tracy last night."

"What the hell are you talking about?" Rodriguez said. "What attack?"

"My mistake, I should have mentioned it earlier." Adrian went over the details of the assault, then added, "She hit her assailant in the head with her backpack that contained her computer. That's how Meyers got the bruise."

A cynical expression settled over Rodriguez's face. "I have a feeling that's not the only thing you haven't told us."

"I need to talk to Reynolds. He's going to be more difficult to trip up."

Adrian stepped to the second door. The configuration of the room was the same as the first. Reynolds was seated in the same style chair that faced the mirror. Unlike the aggression displayed by his associate, his demeanor was relaxed, and his face composed. His cuffed hands rested in his lap.

"This illegal search will never hold up in court," he said, as Adrian entered the room.

Closing the door, he leaned against it. "I don't mind letting a judge decide."

"I demand I be allowed to make a phone call."

"A phone will be here in a few minutes."

Reynolds' eyes flicked to the mirror. "Whoever is watching, I hope this is being recorded. My rights have been violated. Multiple requests to contact my attorney have been ignored, and I've been denied due process." His eyes flicked back to Adrian. "I have nothing to say."

"Guess I'll have to do the talking. I had an interesting chat with your colleague. Maybe we'll have the same." Adrian strolled to the table and pulled out the chair. Like Reynolds, he leaned back, his manner casual, his gaze steady on the man's face. Reynolds stared back, his face impassive.

"An ATF agent is missing, and now a Laredo detective has disappeared." He waited, giving the man a chance to respond. When he didn't, Adrian added, "We believe you were involved in their disappearances."

Reynolds continued to stare at Adrian. His body language never changed. His facial expression altered to one of boredom.

"And … we found evidence the detective disappeared while on your property."

Reynolds' body tensed ever so slightly. "You're lying. You didn't find anything. And, if you did, it was probably planted."

Adrian smiled. "It would be difficult to plant this type of evidence. I'm sure you don't want to be bored by the details. But, that's not all. There are also three dead men and stolen explosives. I'd bet those will be more difficult to explain."

"I don't know what you're talking about, so there'll be no need for any explanations."

"Figured you'd say that. It will all come out in court, your role in three murders, the thefts." He stopped, his head cocked to one side as he studied the face of the man across the table. "Yes, you're the type, the righteous fanatic who'll protest all the way to the death chamber."

Reynolds sneered. "Being a cop doesn't make you the arbitrator on how another person chooses to live their life. You'll find out before long."

"It does when that person steps across the line and destroys lives." Adrian leaned forward. "I'm curious. What will I find out?"

Reynolds' eyes shifted to the mirror. "When do I get my damn phone call?"

Seeing the anger build, if he kept pushing the right buttons, the man might slip up. He stood and walked around the table. Grabbing Reynolds' shoulder, he shoved him back. "Where are Agent Dyson and Detective Harlowe?"

"Fuck you. I don't have a clue."

The door opened. Adrian glanced up at Rodriguez, who signaled for him to step outside. He nodded and straightened, his gaze locked back on Reynolds' face. "If they're dead, I'll see that you fry in hell. We're not done here."

In the hallway, Rodriguez said, "Bad news. I got a call from Skip. Just as they were leaving the compound, an attorney arrived. Reynolds called him when you showed up with the search warrant."

"Damn, I was hoping for a little more time. I need to find out if my team has had any luck with Reynolds' computer."

He called Cat. "Any progress on the computer?" He listened, then said, "An attorney is probably on the way to get these two clowns released."

Disconnecting, he looked at Rodriguez and Gabe. "Nothing yet. Cat's working on bypassing his security codes. Any thoughts on what you've heard?"

Rodriguez shook his head.

Gabe said, "Just a gut instinct, but I'd say these two are knee-deep in whatever you've got going."

Adrian turned and stepped back into the interrogation room.

Reynolds had resumed his calm demeanor, though Adrian wasn't fooled. The slight changes in body language and what he felt when he touched the man said otherwise. He'd lied about knowing the whereabouts of Dyson and Harlowe. Hidden under the man's calm demeanor was elation and anticipation. The man enjoyed the interaction, thinking he had the upper hand. Adrian wasn't sure he didn't. Since Scott's call, he knew they were running out of time.

Twenty-nine

Washington D.C.

When Scott stepped back into the Oval Office, the aroma of freshly brewed coffee wafted in the air.

"Help yourself," the President said.

Scott poured the coffee into an elegant mug embossed with the presidential seal. Picking it up, he eyed the cup before taking a sip.

Behind him, a chuckle erupted. Scott turned to face the President.

"When I took office, the coffee cups were those dainty, tea style with small handles. After dropping one, I told my staff to get me mugs, something with a handle I could hold."

A tap sounded on the door, and when it opened the man who walked in was, in Scott's opinion, the second most powerful man in the country. As the Federal Reserve Chairman, Frank Littleton controlled the central banking system in the U.S.

While Scott had seen numerous pictures, he'd never met him. As Littleton greeted the President, he assessed the man's plump face and short, pudgy body. Despite the expensive suit, his unassuming appearance didn't immediately convey a sense of authority, until the man turned and was introduced to Scott. Intelligence sparked in his dark eyes, a look that weighed and evaluated in an instant. For a moment, as their hands gripped, Scott felt an unfamiliar like-mindedness. As he withdrew his hand, Littleton smiled, as if aware of his thoughts.

Au79

"Gentlemen, please be seated. Frank, refreshments if you are of a mind." President Larkin's hand motioned toward the table.

"Don't mind if I do," Littleton said. As he poured coffee into a mug, he asked, "Now, what's going on with the gold shipment?"

The President laughed. "Always direct and straight to the point. I'm going to defer to Scott and let him explain."

Scott provided a condensed version of the events that led to the meeting, then added, "We have every reason to believe an attempt will be made to hijack the gold shipment."

"If that's indeed the case, the shipment must be cancelled. It's not worth the risk," Littleton said, before taking a sip of his coffee.

Scott said, "The trucks need to leave New York on time tomorrow, just without the gold."

"What? Why?"

Scott explained the concern for the missing officers and explosives.

Littleton settled back on the couch, a look of intense concentration on his face. "You want a decoy convoy."

"Yes, that's exactly what I want. How to set it up will depend on the answers to several questions I have."

"Fire away," the Chairman said.

"How are the bars shipped?"

"Large shipments are loaded onto wooden pallets constructed to hold a maximum of one ton of bars, then covered and strapped with bands of metal."

"How heavy is this shipment?"

"Hmm ...." Littleton paused, then said, "Fifteen hundred bars would weigh between twenty and twenty-one tons. Value, which fluctuates based on the market, would be around eight-hundred million."

"Who knows about the shipment?"

"To the best of my knowledge, there's the personnel with the Texas Gold Depository, David Parker, CEO of the HSBC Bank where the gold is stored, the commandants at Fort Hood and McGuire Air Force Base,

Secretary Whitaker, and my office. There has been tight security and a need to know before anyone was told."

"Do you have a list of the names?"

"No, I don't."

"Who else in your office is aware of the shipment?"

"My administrative assistant, John Eberly. Since the gold is not owned by the federal government, there was no need to involve anyone else. That's why it's in a New York bank and not in the Federal Reserve vaults. Even my role is basically a courtesy."

"Who's coordinating the shipment on this end?"

"David Parker."

Scott turned to Vance Whitaker. "Anyone in your office involved?"

"No. This is in the private sector and doesn't fall under Homeland Security. Like Frank, the notification I received was also a courtesy."

"That leaves the bank, the army and air force base, and the depository?"

"How do you plan to make the shipment look real?" Littleton asked.

"Tough question, and I don't have an answer yet. I need to speak with David Parker to get the specifics on the transfer."

The President stood. "I'll call him." Stepping to his desk, he tapped a button. "Henry, please get David Parker at HSBC Bank in New York City on the phone."

Scott had an idea but needed to confirm its feasibility. He pulled his laptop from his briefcase. When several options scrolled across the screen, a smile crossed his face.

The desk phone chirped, and Henry's voice said Parker was on the line. Larkin tapped a button and said, "Mr. Parker, this is Arthur Larkin. Thank you for taking my call. You are on the speakerphone." He identified the individuals listening, then asked, "Can anyone hear your end of the conversation?"

"No. I'm alone in my office. Mr. President, how may I help you?"

"This deals with the gold shipment from your facility tomorrow. Our conversation is not to be shared with anyone in your organization."

"I understand."

"Agent Fleming has a few questions."

Scott stepped to the front of the desk. "Mr. Parker, would you please explain the procedures for the gold shipment?"

"Certainly. Gold bars are stacked on wooden pallets that can support up to one ton of bars. Tomorrow the pallets will be loaded into numerous armored vehicles and depart via a convoy to McGuire Air Force Base where the gold will be transferred to a transport plane. The plane is scheduled to leave at eleven p.m. and fly to Fort Hood, Texas. From there, the gold will be trucked to the Texas Gold Depository."

"What are the security arrangements?"

"Vans with armed security officers will escort the trucks from the bank to the base. It's my understanding the arrangements are the same in Texas, with one difference, a single truck, an eighteen-wheeler will be used."

At the mention of the truck, Scott's instincts tingled at the confirmation of another link. "Why multiple trucks on your end instead of a single eighteen-wheeler?"

"It's easier for small trucks to negotiate New York City traffic."

"That makes sense. Why Fort Hood instead of the Austin airport?"

"Todd Bracken, the Director of the Depository, believed using the airport in Austin was too great a risk. Setting up the transfer at Fort Hood was less complicated. It's also why the gold is being shipped at night, less risk."

"How many individuals know about the shipment?"

"My staff, comprised of three people, the commandants at both military bases, and the personnel at the depository. We've restricted the dissemination of information on a need to know basis."

"What about the trucking company and its personnel?"

"The company that provides the trucks and guards is one we've used before. Still, we've held off sending a request until today. Once the plane lands in Texas, the depository is in charge, so I can't answer for them. Is there a problem?"

"We believe an attempt will be made to hijack the gold shipment after it arrives in Texas."

"It won't be difficult to stop the shipment."

"No, that won't work. There are extenuating circumstances. The trucks must leave on time, but not with the gold. Instead, they will be loaded with lead ingots." Scott caught the flash of surprise that crossed Larkin's face followed by a grin.

"Lead ingots! Where are you going to get enough to simulate the weight of the gold? You do know there are fifteen hundred bars?"

"Yes. Chairman Littleton told us. There are a couple of manufacturing plants near you."

"Mr. Parker, when was the decision made to transfer the gold?"

"About four months ago. Todd flew in for a meeting, and we set up a tentative schedule. I can get the exact date if you need it."

"No, that's sufficient. Please stay close to your phone. Either another agent or I will be in contact as we get the details set up."

"I'll wait in my office until I hear from you."

Scott disconnected the call and turned to the group whose faces reflected a variety of expressions. Larkin still had a grin, Vance a look of astonishment, and Paul had his usual stoic nothing-surprises-me demeanor. Frank was the surprise. He stared at Scott with a gleam of empathy, and Scott had the same sensation he felt earlier, an odd sense of knowing.

Mentally he shook his head and shifted his concentration to his plan. "This is what I propose. Send the trucks to the lead plant and load them with the ingots. If they are covered and banded, no one will be able to tell the difference. The trucks will arrive at the bank. Since no one can see inside, it will appear to any surveillance the trucks are there to pick up the gold. After a suitable amount of time, the trucks will leave and head to the air force base. From that point forward, there's no change in the routine.

Vance was the first to speak. "My god, it's so simple, it'll probably work."

"Paul, I want to send agents to the trucking company and commandeer the trucks. I don't want the company personnel to know where the trucks are headed, and I don't want to use their drivers."

Paul said, "I'll handle the substitution on this end and the coordination with the bank, so you can concentrate on what's happening in Texas."

Scott stepped to the table with the coffee pot and refilled his cup. He didn't doubt the plan would work, the difficulty was the human factor. It would only take one wrong word to destroy the illusion. The importance of his next request didn't diminish his concern it might alert someone the Trackers were snooping around the shipment. "I'd like to talk to Bracken."

Vance said, "I'll make the call." When Bracken answered, Vance explained an issue had arisen involving the gold shipment, then added, "Agent Scott Fleming will provide the details. Before I turn the call over to him, I need to stress this conversation cannot be shared with anyone in your organization or who is involved with the shipment."

Bracken's voice held a note of alarm, as he said, "All right."

"Mr. Bracken, I'm Agent Fleming. We've discovered a plot to hijack the convoy."

Bracken asked, "Has David Parker been notified to stop the shipment?"

"He's been apprised of the situation, but the shipment won't be cancelled," Scott said, and explained the plan to substitute lead for the gold, along with the reasons it was necessary. "Who has been involved on your end?"

"Several of my staff, the Fort Hood personnel, and the trucking company. I have a list if you need it."

"Yes, as soon as possible. I'd also like the route the convoy will take, personnel files for your security force, and any other documentation that concerns the shipment," Scott said. After relaying his email address, he asked, "How do you plan to secure the safety of the shipment."

"Two vans with security guards will escort the eighteen-wheeler."

"Only one?'

"Yes, the weight is within the truck's weight limit."

"When did you make the transportation arrangements?"

"I contacted the trucking company shortly after David and I set up the date. That would be close to four months ago. Two weeks ago, I provided the date."

"What about the security personnel? Are they hired, or do they work for you?"

"They work for the depository."

"How soon will I receive the information?"

"I'll have it to you in less than an hour."

"Mr. Bracken, I must reiterate Secretary Whitaker's comment regarding the confidentiality of this information. It cannot be shared with anyone. Lives depend on what happens tomorrow. We need you to continue as planned, as if this call never took place."

"Agent Fleming, I understand your reasons for wanting to continue with the shipment, but I disagree. My security force is at risk. That's not acceptable."

"I can't share any details, but I will say your fears are groundless. I'll have more information for you later."

Scott disconnected the call and stared at his notes. His thoughts whirled, he could see the pattern.

The President cleared his voice, and Scott's head snapped up.

"Scott, is there anything else you need?"

He thought for a moment, then quipped, "Yes, Mr. President. A check for twenty-one tons of lead."

Thirty

Texas

Adrian pulled the chair out, flipped it around and straddled it. His face grim, his eyes held a hard glint as they focused on Reynolds. Motionless, he continued to stare.

"Where's my phone?" the man growled.

"I like it when I learn someone has lied. It makes my job so much easier," Adrian said.

Reynolds snorted. "I don't give a fuck what you like or don't like."

"You whined about calling your lawyer, and all along you knew he was on the way. You contacted him when we arrived at the compound."

"What if I did, it doesn't matter. I'm still entitled to a phone call."

"Here you've been claiming your rights have been violated, just another lie to go along with all the rest of the garbage you spew. It'll be interesting when this comes out in the press. When your little group gets held up to the light of day, you'll look like cockroaches running to hide."

A tinge of red appeared on Reynolds' face as rage built. He snarled, "This is harassment. You won't get away with it." Hatred glittered in his eyes.

"Oh, I will, and you'll be left swinging in the wind, or I should say, on death row. Co-operate, and you might have a chance to live, albeit in prison."

Reynolds eased back, relaxed his hands, and a blank look appeared.

"Typical cop. You think all you have to do is play the bully. I'm innocent and not afraid of your empty threats."

A knock on the door, and it opened. A neatly dressed man in a business suit strode into the room.

"I'm Bentley Collier, Mr. Reynolds and Mr. Meyers' attorney. You are to desist in any further conversations with my clients and immediately release them." He laid a set of stapled papers in front of Adrian. "And that includes the return of all property removed from Mr. Reynolds' premises."

Adrian knew he had lost. His hope he'd get a lead on the whereabouts of Dyson and Harlowe vanished. He picked up the documents and scanned them. A judge had ordered the release of the men.

Reynolds sneered and held up his cuffed hands. "Looks like we're done here."

****

Adrian strode into the room and looked at the agents seated around the table. Reynolds' computer was open in front of Cat, and two piles of documents were between Blake and Lance.

"The attorney is here. Reynolds and Meyers will be out the door as soon as the paperwork is completed, along with everything we confiscated. Have you found anything?"

"Damn!" Cat replied.

Her phone was next to the computer, and Nicki's voice echoed in the background, "Amen, but it's not that bad. I'm in and starting to download his files. I only need two or three more minutes, but ..." followed by a short silence before she asked, "Can we keep the download?"

A smile of unholy glee crossed Adrian's face, and renewed hope surged on the faces of the other agents. "Yes. The only stipulation in the release forms was the items we removed from the compound. Not any copies we made. The attorney slipped up there. Probably thought we didn't have enough time or the distinction didn't occur to him."

He glanced at Blake and Lance who were examining documents and then tossing each back into a box. "Anything?"

"Nothing so far except ordinary business documents with a few catalogs and receipts," Blake answered. Motioning toward the stacks, he added, "This is all we have left."

"Wait a minute, I've found something," Lance exclaimed, flipping through a set of stapled documents. He handed them to Adrian. "Texas Department of Transportation registration forms. Reynolds owns the eighteen-wheeler."

"Get a copy fast before the attorney gets here."

Blake headed out the door.

"Cat, once the download is complete, wipe the inside to remove your fingerprints before you close it. May not be a problem, but I'd just as soon not give them any evidence we accessed the computer. Nicki, will there be any trace of the download?"

A snort sounded, then her indignant voice said, "You're kidding me, right? Steve Jobs himself wouldn't be able to find it."

"Sorry, Nicki. Don't know what I was thinking," Adrian replied, and heard her chuckle. "I asked Gabe to give me a call when they headed this way. Hand me those documents."

Cat finished with the computer, disconnected the call and grabbed a stack of papers. Blake had returned with the copies. With all four agents reviewing the remaining documents, it didn't take but a few minutes to finish.

With everything back in the boxes, Blake sealed each one, stacked them in two piles and pushed the boxes to the center of the table. Cat set the computer on top.

"It would probably be best if we weren't in here when the attorney arrives," Blake said.

"Hmm … good idea. I'd just as soon not be around to answer any questions," Adrian said, turning to look at the door. "We can lock the door from the inside. Gabe will have to unlock it. It will add to the illusion the boxes were left here and haven't been disturbed. There's a breakroom just down the hall, we can wait there."

****

Huddled in his car, Eddie watched the front entrance to the PD. He recognized several of the cars, including the one driven by the guy in the suit. It was getting late, and the temperature had dropped. He'd left the engine running, and the warm air blowing from the heater had a relaxing effect. When his face hit the side of the door, his head jerked upward, and he shut off the engine. It was better to be cold and awake.

The front door opened. Three men exited, the guy in the suit and the two who were arrested. The muscular one of the two carried several boxes, and the other had a computer. Grabbing the camera, he jumped out and ran. "Wait a minute," he shouted.

The men stopped and turned in his direction. He skidded to a stop and pulled his press card from his pocket. Holding it up, he gasped, "Eddie Owens, investigative reporter, Laredo Observer. Why were you arrested?"

"How did you know my clients were arrested?" the man in the suit asked.

Alarmed by the angry look in the eyes of the man who held the boxes, Eddie decided it was better if he didn't say he watched from across the road. Instead, he lied. "I talked to a detective."

The man holding the computer spoke up. "Our arrest was a miscarriage of justice. The Border Guards are innocent of any wrongdoing."

"Why did federal agents search your place?" Eddie asked,

"It's another example of how the federal government exceeds its authority by hassling innocent citizens. The Guards have no knowledge of the whereabouts of Agent Dyson or Detective Harlowe and were not involved in the thefts of any explosives or the murder of three men."

"Norm, that's enough, time for us to leave," the lawyer said.

236

Au79

The three men turned and walked to the attorney's car. The big man cast a hard look over his shoulder at Eddie. A shiver of fear rolled through him.

Washington D.C.

Scott walked into the office. The sound of the door brought Ryan out of his office.

"Conference, five minutes," Scott said.

Inside his office, he dropped his briefcase on the desk. He turned to stare out the window. His thoughts shifted to the meeting. Had he missed something, a detail that would come back to haunt him? He shrugged, nothing came to mind.

At the tap on his door, he glanced over his shoulder. Nicki stood in the doorway. "I ordered sandwiches from the deli."

He suddenly realized he was famished.

Ryan was already seated at the table with a sandwich and chips in front of him. On a tray, were several more.

Grabbing one, and unwrapping it, he said, "Vance Whitaker gave us the key to the puzzle. A shipment of gold bullion, valued at close to one billion dollars, is scheduled to leave New York City tomorrow. The destination is the new Texas Gold Depository."

Ryan whistled.

Nicki said, "It's located outside of Burnet, Texas, and that's why the map Tracy saw was significant."

Scott gazed at her as he chewed. She smirked. Nicki liked to stay one step ahead of him, and her mischievous grin told him she had scored another hit.

He swallowed. "And how long have you known that little detail?"

She laughed, as she relented. "Just a few minutes ago. Did you stop the shipment?"

"Yes and no." Interspersed with bites of the sandwich and an occasional chip, he explained the results of the meeting and the new plan.

A roar of laughter erupted from Ryan when Scott reached the part about the lead. "Lead ingots, I'll be damned. It's brilliant."

"What do you need from us, boss man?" Nicki asked.

He frowned, but ignored the nickname, "As soon as I get that list from Bracken, we'll have more names to research. I don't like the bit about the trucking company being informed four months ago. Where are you on a connection between the ATF or FBI personnel, the dead men and the Guards?"

"I haven't had a chance to review the results."

"I know there's a connection, just not who. I'll help search. Ryan, when we get the route from Bracken, start looking for a likely location to stop the convoy."

Waving a chip in the air, Nicki said, "We did get access to Reynolds' computer."

Scott's eyes flicked up with a look of anticipation on his face.

"Cat called from the PD. We linked it to my system, and I downloaded the contents. I just started to access the files when you arrived."

"I told Adrian to expect a conference call this evening." Scott glanced at his watch. "I'll set it up for an hour from now. It'll give us time to see what we can find." Tossing the wadded-up wrapper in the trash, he said, "Let's get started."

Texas

Rodriguez walked into the breakroom. A spark of humor gleamed as he looked at the four agents seated at the table. "Hmm … safe to come out now. They're gone, though Collier is mouthing lawsuits. To be expected."

Adrian scowled. "We didn't like to bail on you but thought it best if we weren't present to answer questions when they retrieved their property."

"Was there a reason for the subterfuge?"

Adrian answered, "Captain, I'm not certain you really want to hear the answer to that question."

Shaking his head in disbelief, Rodriguez said, "I want to know anything you can share."

Adrian stood. "Let's head back to the conference room. I'd like to have Gabe join us. Is Skip still here?"

"No, he's already gone home. I can get him back if you need him."

"No, it's okay."

His phone rang. He let the other agents follow Rodriguez as he answered the call.

"Scott, how did your meeting end?"

"Rather than to go into the details now, I'd like to have a conference call in about an hour. I need everybody on-board."

"We'll be ready."

"What happened with the two men from the compound?"

"Attorney showed up, and they're gone. But not before we got access to the computer, but you probably already know that. We also found out Reynolds owns the eighteen-wheeler."

When Adrian disconnected, he felt a surge of anticipation. They were getting close, he could almost smell it.

Inside, Adrian noted everyone was present. After closing the door, he said, "We have a conference call with our boss, Scott Fleming, in an hour. It should be more than sufficient time to get the two of you up to speed," directing his remarks to Rodriguez and Gabe.

"When the call comes in, we'll get out of your way," Rodriguez said.

"No, I'd like you both to stay. You have a vested interest in the outcome."

Adrian pulled out a chair and sat. "In a nutshell, here's what we've got. Three dead men all shot with Stuart Dyson's gun, and Dyson's fingerprint was on a circuit board we removed from Bardwell's garage."

Gabe, a look of anger on his face, said, "No! That can't be right. Something's wrong with this picture. I know Stuart. He's not the type of person who would be involved in criminal activity."

"We don't think so either, Gabe. It's our belief Stuart's been set up to be the scapegoat."

"My apologies then for interrupting," he said, and leaned back.

"None needed, we felt the same way. We have several missing detonators wired to cellphones and four thefts of explosives, Laredo, San Angelo, El Paso, and Carthage. We found three bridges that have collapsed over the last month."

Nodding toward Blake and Lance, he continued, "Blake is our resident explosives expert and Lance, as you know, is with TEDAC. They were sent to the locations to determine the cause and found explosive residue. Our theory is they were test runs. We identified the Border Guards as possible suspects, and Tracy did a midnight surveillance of their compound. When they spotted her, they tried to kill her."

Rodriguez groaned, then muttered to himself.

Adrian glanced at him, "Question?"

"Yes but keep going. I'll wait."

"There was another attempt last night at her house. I believe the assailant was Stan Meyers. She hit him in the head with her backpack that held her computer. He fits the description and has a bruise on the side of his face. We found evidence at the compound that Tracy was there. She knew we didn't have enough evidence for a search warrant. I'm certain she was looking for Stuart or something we could use."

Another groan erupted from Rodriguez.

His demeanor solemn, Adrian said, "Despite what's happened, Tracy's been a valuable asset. She spotted the eighteen-wheeler at the compound, and that expanded our investigation. The note she found in a box of evidence from Morris' house gave us a major break in the case.

Au79

It led to the identification of the target, a gold shipment headed to Texas."

"Holy hell," Gabe exclaimed.

"I don't have any details yet, which is why the conference call." Adrian shifted in his chair, uncomfortable with the next topic. "One other item. We believe someone in either the FBI or the ATF office here in Laredo is mixed up in this."

After dropping that bombshell, he was bombarded with questions from the two Laredo officers. Some he could answer, but others he had to defer.

When his phone rang, he said, "It's Scott."

Thirty-one

Reynolds loud voice echoed over the phone line. "Why the hell didn't you call to warn me about the search warrant?"

"What search warrant?" his contact asked.

His tone mocking, Reynolds said, "Give me a fucking break. You think I'm gonna believe you didn't know those D.C. feds showed up to search the place."

"I didn't know. What happened?"

"Meyers and I were arrested, and my computer and files confiscated."

"Goddammit! This can ruin everything. Was there any incriminating evidence?"

"It doesn't matter. When Dillard and crew showed up, I called my lawyer. He got us released along with everything they took."

"You're absolutely certain they didn't access the computer or look at the files?"

"Those bumbling idiots didn't have time to examine them. They were stacked in a locked room at the PD."

"I wouldn't underestimate those bumbling idiots. If you do, we're all going down."

Reynolds said, "Find out if there is any surveillance. I can't have anyone following us when we leave."

His contact said, "That might not be possible. You need to change your plans."

Reynolds snarled. "Seems to me, you haven't been much use to us lately. Maybe it's time for another type of change."

Rage vibrated in the contact's voice. "Don't you ever threaten me. You're not in charge of this operation. I am, and don't forget it. Whatever happened, no one in the ATF or the FBI office knew. There must be a reason, and I'll find out."

Reynolds said, "I don't give a damn about the reason. All I want to know is whether I've got some idiot watching the compound." He disconnected.

The contact's hands shook as he laid the phone back on the desk. He rued the day he decided to use the Border Guards.

****

Eddie sat at his desk and flipped through the pictures he had downloaded to his computer. Some of them were damn good. But he hadn't a clue what he could do with them. His research on the Border Guards hadn't provided any answers. They were just a group who occasionally protested something the government had done. Nothing overt that would get his story noticed. He needed more.

He thought about what the leader, Reynolds, had said. Was Harlowe missing? Then there was the bit about the explosives. All he'd found online was the break-in of a mining company here in Laredo. But he was certain Reynolds had said thefts, plural. He cursed his lack of foresight to purchase a recording device. That little item went to the top of his list. The three dead men, he already knew about. So, how did this all tie together?

The Guards were the key, but how could he go about finding the answers? All he could do was watch and take pictures. Wait a minute, that was something he could do. He could camp out in the same spot. If they left, he'd follow them, find out what they were up to, get his pictures and a story.

Elation spread through him as he considered his game plan. Then it dropped as reality set in. He didn't know the first damn thing about surveillance. Well, he'd learn as fingers pounded the keyboard.

****

When Adrian answered, Scott asked, "Where are you?"

"Still at the police department. We're in the conference room. I asked Captain Andy Rodriguez and SWAT Lieutenant Gabe Pearsall to sit in."

Once everyone listening had been identified, Scott said, "Tomorrow, a shipment of fifteen hundred gold bars belonging to Texas A&M University and the University of Texas is scheduled to be conveyed from a bank in New York City to McGuire Air Force Base. It will be loaded onto a transport plane and flown to Fort Hood. There the gold will be transferred to an eighteen-wheeler for transport to the Texas Gold Depository outside of Burnet. It's located northwest of Austin. The value of the gold is close to one billion dollars."

Gabe let out a soft whistle, and Rodriquez grunted.

"What's the plan?" Adrian asked.

"We're substituting lead ingots. The weight is about the same."

Adrian's gaze scanned the room as more sounds of surprise echoed. This time Blake whistled.

"Agent Fleming, this is Captain Andy Rodriguez. Why didn't you stop the shipment?"

"If we do, we lose any chance of finding Stuart and Tracy alive, as well as the recovery of the explosives."

"Ah," Rodriguez said, and leaned back with a look of satisfaction on his face.

"Do you have the security arrangements?" Adrian asked.

"Yes. I've received the route and other details from the director of the depository, Todd Bracken. I forwarded them to you. Two vans with armed personnel will escort the truck."

Adrian asked, "What time will the plane get to Fort Hood?"

"Two a.m., your time. Bracken and David Parker, CEO of the bank where the gold is stored, set up a night transfer. They thought it would minimize the risk. What we need to decide now is the game plan on your end and what resources you'll need."

Au79

"Scott, the four of us had a chance to bat this around earlier while we were waiting for the attorney and his clients to leave. Every bridge and overpass must be identified. Knowing the route will narrow the possibilities. We'll map out the locations tonight, then head to Austin early in the morning. I'm going to hire a helicopter to check the route."

"The FBI office in Austin has one," Ryan said, his voice distant in the background.

"We considered it, but if there are eyes on the ground, I don't want to use one that has FBI emblazoned on the side. I think it's best to low key our presence."

Scott said. "There's one other concern I need to pass on. The security on the bank side was tight. That's not the case on your end. Bracken notified the trucking company four months ago he would need a truck."

"It could be how the Border Guards found out about the shipment," Adrian said.

"Very possible. It's another lead we're running down."

Cat leaned toward Adrian's phone lying on the table. "Nicki, anything from Reynolds' computer?"

"Not as much as I would like. What I did find connects Reynolds to the thefts. He visited a number of websites for drilling and mining companies, including the ones that were hit."

"We found the vehicle registration forms for the eighteen-wheeler in the files we removed from the compound. I'll scan the documents when we're done and send them to you," Cat said.

Scott asked, "Adrian, what personnel do you need?"

"Enough to replace the depository personnel. I'll use the agents in the Austin office. I'd also like a helicopter and pilot to shadow the convoy. It would be best if we could borrow a unit from the base."

"I'll call the base commandant, Lieutenant General Farmington." Scott said. "I'll also contact Will Cooper and brief him on what's headed his way."

"Where do you want to make the substitution?" Scott asked.

245

"Fort Hood. Since we don't know who is involved, it would be better to let the convoy arrive as planned."

"Any news on Dyson or Harlowe?" Nicki asked.

Adrian sighed, then said, "No, nothing."

Scott said, "We'll probably be in the office most of the night. Nicki's program to find a local connection exploded with data. It's going to take a few hours to wade through it all. Ryan's also working on the map angle. We'll be in touch."

Disconnecting, Adrian's eyes shifted from Cat to Blake, then to the Laredo officers and Lance, who had tucked himself into a corner. "Questions or comments?"

Rodriguez eyed Adrian, his gaze glinted with respect and approval. "What can we do to help? If it's something above my paygrade, I'll take it to the Chief. As it is, I'm going to have to brief him in the morning on this mess."

"I'd like to continue using this conference room."

"Not a problem. What else?"

Adrian glanced at Gabe. He understood the look of anger mixed with frustration on the man's face. Gabe wanted to play a role in taking down the Guards, and figured he was going to be left sitting at home. Well, maybe not.

Adrian looked at Rodriguez. "I'd like Gabe's help. He knows the situation and who is involved. That's an asset."

Out of the corner of his eye, he caught the man's reaction. His body tensed, a look of shock was replaced with an avid eagerness.

"Gabe doesn't report to me, but I can assure you it won't be a problem." He glanced at Gabe. "As of now, you're on temporary assignment to the FBI. What about surveillance on the compound?"

Adrian leaned back in his chair, his head tilted upward as he stared at the ceiling. Blake had asked the same question while they waited in the breakroom. Adrian didn't have an answer but had been rolling the pros and cons in his head. He had to decide. Deep in his gut, he felt this was a crucial turning point in the investigation. If he called it wrong, two officers would be dead, but what was the right decision?

He glanced at each of the individuals seated around the table. They waited for his answer. For the first time in his law enforcement career, he felt the weight of command and the devastating consequences of his decisions.

"No surveillance. The terrain around the compound is wide open. Not much opportunity for concealment, and we don't know the extent of the cameras he has in place. If he spots someone, it might spook him, increasing the risk to Tracy and Stuart, who I believe are still alive. Reynolds walked out of here thinking he's in control, that we know nothing. Let's keep it that way."

Rodriguez stood. "If you change your mind, let Gabe know. He'll set it up," he said, and left the room.

Adrian said, "We need aerial maps and food, in that order."

"I'll help with the aerial maps. An oversized printer is in the crime scene unit," Gabe said.

"Is there someplace close we can pick up an order?" Blake asked.

"Better yet, we have a deli that delivers," Gabe said. "I'll call in an order."

Adrian accessed Scott's email on his computer and printed several copies of the extensive operational plan Bracken provided. It contained a list of all individuals involved in the gold shipment, their duties, and a personnel file on each. Bracken had kept a record of the dates and times of meetings, who attended and the topics of discussion, along with the contract and details of the arrangement with the trucking company. There were copies of the correspondence, letters and memorandums. The route assignment included a schedule of events, a map that outlined the route, and identity of the personnel assigned to the security team.

Gabe had pinned a large map to the chalkboard. The route the convoy would take was inked in red. Cat and Blake had the aerial map pulled up on their computers. When a possible site was found, they'd zoom in to get a closer view. Lance hung over Blake's shoulder as they studied the locations.

While the others discussed the route, Adrian examined each of the documents. Scott was right about the notification to the trucking company. The company had been notified weeks in advance.

"How are they going to get away with the gold?" he asked.

All eyes turned toward him.

Cat said, "The general consensus has been they'd steal the truck. They can't transfer the gold. Too heavy. The only option is to take the truck."

Adrian said, "I just found out that it's not that easy. I've been examining the details of the arrangement with the trucking company. Their trucks have a sophisticated monitoring and tracking system on board that connects to the company's dispatch center. With one touch of a button, the center will immediately know there is a problem. How are the Guards going to get past that?"

"Then what good will it do to blow a bridge if they can't get access to the cab of the truck?" Blake asked.

"That's my point. What about the security force? How do they plan to take them out?" Frustrated, Adrian tossed the report he'd been reading onto the table. "We're missing a piece of this puzzle. Somebody at the depository must be involved and will be on that security detail."

He'd laid his phone on the table. It rang. He glanced at the screen. "I hoped to avoid this until tomorrow."

He answered, and said, "Karl, sorry I didn't get back to you."

"Bill Goddard's in my office. Why didn't you tell us you planned to search the Border Guards' compound?"

"Extenuating circumstances. There really wasn't time. How did you find out about the search warrant?"

"Hell, you know how the rumor mill works around here. Bill and I both heard the news. What was the reason?"

Au79

"Detective Harlowe is missing, and we believed the Guards were involved in her disappearance."

Bill's voice echoed in the background. "I warned you about her. Harlowe's got a reputation for causing problems."

A flood of anger rolled over Adrian. He took a second to control it before he said, "That isn't an issue, but her disappearance is."

Karl asked, "Why did you arrest Reynolds and one of his men? What did you find?

"Circumstantial evidence, not enough to hold them."

Adrian heard Bill's snort of disgust.

"We heard you had to return the items you confiscated," Karl said. "Did you get a chance to examine them?"

"The attorney showed up with a court order before we had an opportunity."

"What's your next step?" Karl asked.

Bill's voice, harsh with anger, probably over the snub he'd just received, said, "If it's surveillance, I need to know. It takes time to get it set up."

The missed opportunity on the Morris surveillance flashed in his mind. Someone had dragged their heels on that one. The thought intensified his suspicions. "No surveillance, at least not yet. As we get deeper into the investigation, it might be warranted."

Bill's anger shifted to contempt. "Deeper! I can't see you're doing a damn thing except running around pestering people. What's stopping you from coming over to Karl's office? I don't like discussing this over the phone."

"At the moment, it's not possible. I'll contact you later."

Karl said, "I don't know what's going on here, but I don't like being kept out of the loop on the investigation. I know Bill feels the same way. This may be how things are done in Washington, but not on my watch. If I can't get your cooperation, then you leave me no choice but to lodge a formal complaint with Scott."

Bill said, "I'll add my name to that complaint."

"It's your call, but I can't alter my investigation to satisfy your wishes. I'll contact you when I'm able to discuss the details."

As he disconnected, he could hear Bill's curses in the background.

Laughter erupted from Blake and Cat.

Blake said, "I'd like to be in the room with Scott when that call comes in. Those two may not have much hide left by the time our boss is done."

Adrian said, his tone thoughtful, "Hmm … yes. I got the sense there was a hidden agenda behind the questions. Someone wants to know about our plans. But who? Is it Bill, Karl, or one of their personnel waiting to see what their boss finds out?"

Cat chuckled. "Are you going to call Scott and warn him?"

"What … and ruin his fun?"

Au79

Thirty-two

Eddie eyed the supplies he'd piled on the backseat of his truck. He'd swapped vehicles, and his sister was pissed. For what he planned, that rattletrap she drove wouldn't work. He didn't need to break down alongside the road somewhere.

Since he didn't know how long he'd have to camp out near the compound, his list of needs had grown. He'd added bottles of water, two sacks of groceries filled with snacks and small containers of food, a blanket, towels, a lined jacket with a black ski cap and gloves, a change of clothes, and another set of boots.

At a local sports store, he bought a lightweight rollup mat. After reading up on surveillance techniques, he learned it was important to blend into your surroundings. He couldn't do it standing. Sitting or lying on the rough ground would add to the discomfort. That was another tidbit of information he'd found in one article—stakeouts were usually uncomfortable. The mat should solve the problem.

His backpack contained a pack of wipes, paper towels, binoculars, camera, extra film, flashlight, extra batteries, a bottle of water, packages of cheese and crackers, and his mp3 player and earpiece. He figured if he was stuck out there all day, he could listen to music while he watched. Remembering the sharp barbs from his first trek, he even tossed in a first aid kit, along with hand and feet warmers that slid inside gloves and boots. When the package was opened, they'd get warm. He'd spotted them in the checkout lane when he bought the mat. At the last minute, he added his dad's gun and a box of ammunition.

He checked to be sure it was loaded. He'd never been interested in guns, but his dad had taught him how to shoot.

Even though he'd used his credit card to buy the stuff, cash was a problem. Jimmy kept money in the office for emergencies. He left a note that he'd taken the money. He'd pay him back out of his next check, and that he had to take a couple of days off. Jimmy wouldn't like it, him just up and leaving without notice, but not much he could do about it.

He glanced at his watch. Time to go. He wanted to reach the old farmhouse while it was still dark. He'd move into place just as the sun started to rise.

Washington D.C.

Blurry-eyed, Scott stared at the screen. They'd spent the night in the office, taking turns on the couch to grab an hour or two of sleep. He and Nicki had worked on the files from Reynolds' computer and the results of her search. File after file of documents, newspaper articles, genealogy charts, marriage and death certificates, city and state property taxes, driver's licenses, vehicle registrations, arrest and offense reports had been examined.

His frustration level ratcheted, though it did ease a bit when he got that damn call from Karl Chambers and Bill Goddard. The nerve of the two men was laughable. He'd listened, then informed them that since they weren't in charge of the investigation, they had no grounds for any complaint. His team would use whatever resources they deemed important. If Agent Dillard didn't believe the local ATF or FBI personnel could contribute anything of value, their only option was to stay out of the way. Of course, they sputtered in denial. Once this was over, he'd have some fence mending to do.

Ryan had been on the phone with the Texas team numerous times as the route was examined in painstaking detail. He'd commandeered Nicki's big screen to enlarge the aerial maps.

Au79

She grudgingly let Ryan use it, though she muttered and grumbled over having to use the desktop monitor. Scott anticipated he'd be getting a demand for another wall-mounted screen.

When Adrian raised the issue of how the Guards planned to pull this off, it started another round of phone calls and discussion. They hadn't come up with any answers.

He glanced at the cup on his desk. The coffee was cold, and a film covered the surface. Shoving his chair back, he grabbed the cup and headed to the breakroom.

Ryan was asleep on the couch. That must be why the mumbles from Nicki's office had stopped. She was back in possession of her latest toy. Hitting the button to start a pot, the hiss of water woke Ryan.

His head twisted as he looked up at his boss. With a grunt, he shifted and swung his feet to the floor. Rubbing his hand over his face, he felt the rough stubble of his beard. When was the last time he'd shaved? "Damn, what time is it?"

"Close to sunrise," Scott said.

"Anything new?"

"Not yet. I think if I have to look at one more genealogy chart, I might lose what little sanity I have left." He stepped to the sink, rinsed out his cup and refilled it with the hot brew. "You want a cup?"

"Oh, yeah. I need something to jumpstart my system."

"Scott! Ryan!" Nicki's voice echoed along the hallway. She stopped in the doorway. "I found a link." Turning, she headed back to her office. Scott and Ryan were close on her heels. The cups of coffee on the counter were forgotten.

She motioned to the image of a document on the wall monitor. It was a property tax form for Elsie Rutherford.

"This is Bing Morris' grandmother. When his mother died, the obituary listed her mother's name. It's how I found Elsie. I finally located a copy of Elsie's will in the county courthouse archives. It listed a piece of property northwest of Laredo she willed to her grandson—Bing Morris."

Her head swiveled as she stared up at the two men who stood next to her chair, their attention glued to the screen. Scott glanced down, his gaze met hers. Her eyes, though red-rimmed from the lack of sleep, glinted with excitement, and her face radiated the exhilaration that came from a major break in the case.

"We didn't find it because Morris never changed the name on the tax rolls," she said.

Ryan exhaled, "Nicki, you may have just found the holy grail."

Scott pulled his phone. "Pull up an aerial of the place, while I get Adrian on the phone. It may be where Stuart and Tracy are being held."

Texas

This time, Eddie parked his truck behind the old farmhouse so it couldn't be seen from the road. Through breaks in the brush, Eddie could see lights at the compound. What were they doing up this early? He itched to find out, but he couldn't pick his way through the brush without using a flashlight. It would give away his position. That was another one of the instructions in the article he'd read.

As the sky lightened, he stepped out of the truck. He zipped up his jacket, pulled on the ski cap, and stuffed his hair underneath. Then he grabbed his backpack and slid the straps over his shoulders. The mat lying on the backseat was tucked under his arm. The truck was left unlocked in case he needed to make a fast getaway.

Eddie eased his way along the driveway, and across the road. He dropped the mat on the other side of the fence but didn't give a thought to the backpack. He stepped on the bottom wire and tried to slide between the strands. The backpack caught on the wire. Muttering curses, he twisted until he could get the straps off. After he got through the fence, he untangled the pack.

Shouldering it, he picked up the mat and headed away from the fence, picking his way through the brush until he could angle and move to a position in front of the compound. Hunched over, he took slow steps to reach the spot where he'd taken the pictures. The mat slipped to the ground as he dropped to his knees and went flat. He stayed motionless for a few seconds and eyed the compound. It blazed with lights, inside and out. A half dozen pickups were parked in the driveway. What the hell was going on at this time of the morning? He'd counted on them being asleep while he got set up.

Slipping the straps from his shoulders, he slid the backpack to the ground. Unzipping the main compartment, he grabbed the binoculars and set them in front of him. Dirt settled around them. He'd better get the mat in place or there'd be dust in everything. He shot a quick glance at the compound before rolling onto his side. Pulling the straps apart, he unrolled the mat. Hell, it kept rolling back up. He finally put a foot on one corner to hold it in place until he was on top. He dusted off the binoculars before setting them on the mat, then reached for the camera case inside the pack. Under his heavy jacket, sweat rolled down his back, but he'd be damned if he was going to take it off. He'd just have to sweat.

Picking up the binoculars, he adjusted the focus until he had a clear view of the driveway and buildings. Even though the shades were drawn, silhouettes of a cluster of people inside were visible. Until someone came outside, there was nothing to see. He'd wait. That was another tip from the article. Stakeouts could be boring.

No one came in or out. He laid the binoculars on the mat and rested his chin on his crossed arms. He thought about the snacks in his pack. Should he eat something? No, then he'd get thirsty, and he didn't want to drink a lot of water. He scooted, trying to find a position where rocks didn't poke him.

Picking up a corner of the mat to remove a large rock, he didn't immediately realize the flood lights had been switched off. A man had stepped out of the door. Eddie grabbed the binoculars. The dim porch light cast shadows across the hard planes of Reynolds' face.

He changed to the camera. It was still too dark. He switched back. Reynolds stepped off the porch and walked toward one of the trucks. A line of men exited the house and followed him.

Eddie started counting. Twelve men got into the vehicles. One by one, the trucks turned and pulled out of the driveway and headed west.

He had to get to his truck. After shoving the binoculars and camera into the backpack, he glanced at the compound. It appeared to be deserted, and the gate had automatically closed.

He'd have to take a chance and hope there wasn't anyone watching. Standing, he grabbed the straps of the pack, looked at the mat, and said to hell with it. He turned and ran. This time he threw the backpack over the fence before he crawled through. Tossing it inside his vehicle, he got behind the wheel. His tires spun as he backed out and turned to follow. In the distance, he could see the tail lights of the last vehicle.

****

The phone rang. Adrian groaned as he came out of a deep sleep. Rolling over, he eyed the glow of the cell phone screen. Picking it up, he glanced at the time. Since the caller was Scott, his four hours of sleep would have to be enough. The team had stayed at the PD until late into the night.

"Scott, what did you find?"

"Morris owned a piece of property northwest of Laredo. I'm texting you the coordinates. Also, he's related to Jonah Grigsby, second or third cousin type thing."

Any traces of exhaustion vanished. The surge of anticipation was better than a jolt of caffeine. "I'll call you when I get to the PD." He hung up and started pushing buttons.

By the time Adrian and the other agents arrived at the PD, the sun had risen. Gabe was headed to the front door and stopped to wait for them. As they walked inside, Adrian said, "Let's head to the conference room. I'd prefer not to be overheard."

Inside, everyone grabbed a chair, and Adrian opened his laptop.

Au 79

Pulling up an aerial map, he pushed the computer to Cat, who was the closest.

"Scott called. They found a piece of property Morris owned. It's about fifty miles from here. It has a house and several outbuildings. Everybody, take a close look at the map. Gabe, we're headed there, but not with a search warrant. There isn't time. It's your choice whether or not you go with us."

"You heard the Captain. I'm on special assignment for the duration. Just try keeping me from going." he quipped.

Adrian glanced at Lance. "Same for you."

"Same answer as Gabe," he said, and grinned.

"I think we can all fit in the SUV," Adrian said.

Gabe held up a finger. "Let's take my truck as well. It has a roll-up bed cover if you need to stow any gear. Do you need any of our equipment, vests, weapons, ammo?"

"Appreciate the offer. When we arrived, we acquired some equipment, but it won't be sufficient." He looked at the three agents. "Grab what we need and load up the vehicles. We need to get on the road. I'll call Scott and let him know what's going down."

Gabe walked to the door. "This way, for all your shopping needs."

Cat chuckled as she followed him out of the room. She liked his attempt at light humor. It helped ease the tension everyone felt.

Thirty-three

Focused on keeping the vehicles in sight, Eddie's fingers curled around the wheel in a death grip. He'd turned off his lights and hoped they'd arrive at wherever they were going before the sun rose. In the flat landscape, they'd spot him for sure. One of the men was the big man he'd seen at the police department. The thought of another face-to-face meeting sent a ripple of panic through him.

As the sky lightened, he dropped further and further back. Another few miles and he would have to turn around. In the distance, brake lights flashed as the truck turned. He could see the faint outline of a house. He stopped on the side of the road. What the hell was he going to do? There had to be a way to get close to the place. His eyes scanned the rough terrain. Up ahead was a bridge that crossed a deep ravine. It appeared to be dry, but more importantly, it angled toward the house. If he could get into the ravine without being seen, he could use it to get closer.

But what about his truck? It would be too dangerous to leave it parked on the side of the road. He remembered passing a dirt road. Shifting into reverse, he backed until he lost sight of the house, then turned. Ahead was the gap in the brush. It was slow going as the truck bounced in the heavy ruts. Eddie followed the path until he reached a bend and was out of sight of the main highway. He turned the truck around just in case he had to get out fast.

There was no reason to take the backpack or binoculars. They'd just be in the way, but he did hang the camera around his neck. He hesitated, then reached inside the backpack and pulled out the gun. He stuck it in his waistband underneath his shirt.

****

The light streaming through the windows woke her. Cold and groggy, Tracy wondered why her body was contorted. What was she doing on the floor? Then she remembered, and the terror resurfaced. Her eyes darted toward Stuart. Slumped, his head had rolled to the side as he slept. It may have been her imagination or just wishful thinking, but his breathing seemed to have eased.

She was surprised she'd fallen asleep. It'd been nearly impossible to relax during the night. Apprehension about Stuart's injuries was intensified by the panic that raged inside her. She sensed time was running out for them.

Since Grigsby had walked in yesterday and taunted them, they'd only seen two other people. Not long after dark, two men had stepped inside and flipped on the light. One held a gun. The other removed Stuart's handcuff and told him to use the bathroom. He stumbled his way across the room. She heard a toilet flush and the sound of running water. She tried to talk to the men, asking questions. They ignored her.

When he came out, Stuart looked more alert. Once his hand was cuffed, it was her turn. After unlocking her cuff, the man jerked her upright. Her head spun as he shoved her toward the bathroom door.

Inside, as she used the facility, she examined everything. Was there something she could use as a weapon or to unlock the handcuffs? The room had been stripped bare, even the mirror had been removed. The only moveable items were the roll of toilet paper on the edge of the tub along with a filthy towel.

After splashing water on her face, she filled her cupped hands and swished out her mouth. Despite the unpleasant metallic taste, she drank two handfuls. Not about to touch the towel, she wiped her hands on her pants.

She checked all her pockets. They'd left her coat on, but everything, even a package of gum had been removed. Then a thought came to mind, maybe she did have something. The buttons on her long-sleeve shirt were held in place by a metal cotter pin. Unless the shirt was unbuttoned, they couldn't be seen. She might be able to use one to unlock the handcuffs.

She'd pulled the shirt from her pants, and removed the pin from the three bottom buttons, then shoved the shirt back inside her waistband. She tucked the buttons inside her boot, then stared at three small pieces of metal in the palm of her hand. A wave of hopelessness crashed over her. This was all she had to fight back.

The door crashed open, and the guard ordered her out of the bathroom. She curled her hand into a fist and stuck it in her coat pocket when she turned. The man had stepped back to let her exit, and by the time she walked through the door, the pins were in the pocket, and her hands swung free.

After cuffing her hand, they turned off the lights and left. She waited for the click of the lock but didn't hear it. Was it possible they'd left the door unlocked?

If she could get their cuffs off, they might be able to escape. During a defensive tactics training course, the instructor had demonstrated how to open handcuffs using a bobby pin. A cotter pin was a shorter version.

She pulled the pin apart and inserted one end into the lock, only to find it was too short. Stuart heard the shuffling sounds. Tracy explained what she had, and it was his suggestion to use two pins wired together. All night, she worked on them. When her fingers on the cuffed hand became numb, she used her teeth.

Interspersed between working on the metal and multiple attempts to open the cuff's lock, they talked about the twists and turns of the investigation. When Stuart said gold was involved, she hoped it might solve the puzzle, but it only added more questions, and they had no answers.

She'd done most of the talking. Stuart's lungs heaved in labored

Au79

gasps and talking exacerbated his condition. She suspected a rib had punctured his lung. The bitter cold added to his agony.

After dropping the pins several times and having to grope with her hand to find them, she stopped. All she had accomplished was to rub her fingertips raw. She put the pins in her pocket and slid her hand between her thighs. Once she got her fingers warm, she'd try again. She leaned her head against the wall and closed her eyes. The next thing she knew it was morning, and sunlight shone into the room.

She straightened to ease the pressure on the cuffed hand. Her entire arm was numb, and her head still ached, but her mind was clear and alert. What time was it? From the angle of the light, it must be early morning.

Fingers groped in her pocket to find the pins. She saw the bend in the metal that was the problem and used her teeth to flatten it. Poking the end in the lock, she twisted and turned it. Did she hear a faint click? She repeated the motion. Yes, there was definite contact with the locking mechanism. Encouraged, she kept trying.

Voices shouted outside. Her head snapped toward the door.

"Stuart," she whispered. "Stuart, wake up."

"Huh, what?" His eyes slowly opened.

"Something's going on outside."

More shouts, then the door opened. The man who assaulted her stepped through the doorway. His gaze locked onto her. His lips twisted into a smirk.

Fear sparked deep inside her and clawed its way into her mind.

He bent over Stuart and unlocked the cuff from the eye bolt. He grabbed him under the arms and hauled him to his feet. Stuart grunted in pain. The man grinned as he handcuffed both hands. Spinning him, Stuart was shoved out the door. Glancing over his shoulder at her, he said, "You're next."

A voice, it sounded like Reynolds, shouted, "Stan, get a move on."

When he walked back in, Stan unlocked the cuff, grabbed her other

261

hand and cuffed them together. Jerking her upright, he shoved her against the wall, his hand around her throat. "Seems like we did this once before." His breath, hot on her cold face, smelled like sour onions.

Behind him, Reynolds said, "Goddammit, Stan. We don't have time for your petty revenge. Get your ass in gear. Now!"

Her lungs gasped for air when he let go of her throat. He stepped back and said, "The boss doesn't want any bullet holes in you, but he didn't say I couldn't do this. Payback, bitch." His fist shot out and struck her face. Tracy slumped to the floor.

****

Eddie walked back to the road and crossed to the other side. The ravine was only a couple hundred yards away. After he slid down the side, he found he could walk upright. His pace was slow as he had to step over and around large rocks and debris. When he passed under the bridge, he could hear voices in the distance. As they got louder, he could distinguish the words. He eased his way up the side, careful to not dislodge any rocks.

Stunned, he ducked back down. In front of him, a big rig truck was parked along the edge of the driveway. Another semi was backed up to a metal barn. Men carried boxes out and loaded them into the trailer. The pickups that had left the compound were parked in front and around the house. A voice shouted, telling someone named Stan to get moving.

Eddie crawled up the side, just far enough to see over the edge. A door was open in a small building next to the big one. A man stumbled out. He was handcuffed. Holy shit, it looked like, it was—Stuart Dyson. Another man, the one he'd seen at the police department, stepped out, grabbed the agent's arm and dragged him to the rear of the trailer in front of Eddie.

Frightened, he watched Dyson fall to the ground. The man opened the trailer doors and pulled out a ramp. He hauled Dyson inside. Eddie heard the thud of the agent's body and a groan. The man climbed down and headed back to the building.

Cops, he had to call the cops. Eddie slid down and grabbed his phone from a pocket. Horrified, he stared at the screen—no service. His brain froze, all that circled in his head was he had to get help. But how? It suddenly dawned on him, he didn't even know where the hell he was. He'd been so busy following the trucks, he'd never even looked at a damn road sign. He was a fucking idiot.

Another shout got his attention. Scooting to the top, he saw the big man walk out of the building with a woman over his shoulder. Oh, no! It was the detective. When the man reached the back of the trailer, he easily tossed her body inside. He shoved the ramp back in place and walked to the house.

The bile rose in his throat. Was Harlowe dead? He could see her feet near the edge. They moved. She was alive.

His thoughts raced. He had to do something … but what? He was one against at least twelve men. If he went back to his truck, he could drive until he had phone service. But what if they left before the cops got here? It was obvious they were getting ready to leave.

Eddie's heart raced and sweat rolled down his back. In his entire life, he'd never been so scared. He'd probably get his ass shot, but he had a glimmer of an idea.

Moving further up the ravine, he could get to the side of the trailer. The men loading the boxes or anyone inside the house wouldn't see him. If he could get the detective and agent out of the trailer and into the ravine, they could get to his truck and get the hell out of here.

A short distance away, he spotted a large rock near the edge that was at about the right place. He eased down until his feet touched the bottom and crept toward the rock. Once he was under it, he crawled up and over the side. He wiggled his way forward until he reached the side of the trailer. He stood and inched toward the corner. Leaning forward, he looked inside. The agent lay on his back. Harlowe had scooted next to him and was jiggling his handcuffs.

He whispered, "Detective."

Her head shot up, and she stared at him. A look of disbelief crossed her face. "Eddie?"

"Can you move to the edge? I'll help you down."

A moan erupted from the agent. His voice weak, he asked, "Who is it?"

Tracy said, "An unlikely savior as you'd ever want to meet. We're getting out of here."

"No, you go. I'll just slow you down."

"Stuart, shut up and move your butt. Nobody's leaving you behind."

"Uh ... we need to go," Eddie said.

Tracy nodded and got to her knees. She slid her arms under Stuart's back and helped him scoot to the edge.

Panic coursed through Eddie at the sight of their injuries. Could they walk? The handcuffs would make it even worse.

As Stuart's legs came over the edge, Tracy was behind him and pushed. As he slid off, Eddie grabbed him to keep him from toppling over.

Once he was on the ground, Stuart limped to the side of the trailer. Tracy had scooted until she was on the edge. Eddie reached up and grabbed her when she shoved off.

When her feet hit the ground, he whispered, "We need to get into the ravine. My truck isn't far from here."

Tracy nodded. "Let's go."

Since she seemed to be in better shape than the agent, Eddie let her go first. With his arm around Dyson's shoulder, he braced him until they reached the ravine. Tracy slid down the side. Rocks clattered. Another surge of fear shot through him. Did anyone hear the sound? They had to move fast.

He eased Dyson to the ground and whispered for him to wait. Eddie went over the side and got in front of the man. Dyson scooted forward and as his body came down, Eddie grabbed him.

Au79

Once they were at the bottom, Eddie said, "Detective, you go ahead. I'll help Agent Dyson."

Tracy began to pick her way over the ruts and debris. Thankful that Stan was dumb enough to handcuff their hands in front, it was still difficult to keep her balance. Behind her, she could hear the footsteps of the men as they stumbled and slipped on the rocks.

Eddie's arm was around the agent's shoulders. He could feel the shudders in the man's body as his lungs heaved. God, this was bad. He wasn't strong enough to carry him. All he could do was support him, and it slowed them down.

Dyson must have sensed his thoughts. "I'm holding you and Tracy back."

Ignoring his comment, Eddie said, "If we can reach the bend up ahead, we'll be out of sight of anyone looking into the ravine."

They'd just made the turn when shouts rang out.

With a quick glance over her shoulder, Tracy asked, "How far to your truck?"

Eddie thought for a minute. It would take too long to go back the way he came. It was shorter if they got out of the ravine before they reached the bridge. The only problem was the men at the house would see them.

"About a half mile."

Tracy said, "We may not have enough time to reach it."

"I've got a gun if we need to use it."

Tracy stumbled, then stopped. Her head whipped around to stare at Eddie. "What! You've got a gun! My god, give it to me. You keep going. I'll bring up the rear."

Eddie pulled it out and handed it to her. As the ground began to level out, they were able to pick up the pace.

"Where is she?" Dyson asked.

Eddie glanced over his shoulder. "She's behind us but has slowed down." When he spotted the bridge up ahead, he said, "This'll be the hard part. We have to get up the side."

Dyson looked at the wall. His voice wheezed, as he said, "It doesn't look that steep. If you get on top, I think I can get far enough up to let you pull me over the edge."

Eddie looked back. Tracy had stopped behind them. She motioned for them to go ahead.

Eddie climbed up, then knelt on the edge.

Dyson leaned against the side and extended his arms. Despite the sharp stabs of pain that exploded in his chest, he grabbed a root protruding from the rocks. Finding a foothold, he pushed up with his legs and slowly inched his way to the top.

Above him, Eddie watched. When the agent stopped, he said, "Just a little bit closer, and I can grab your arms."

Dyson gasped. "Need a minute. Hard to breathe."

The terror inside Eddie intensified. The bruises on Dyson's face stood out in sharp contrast to his pasty, white face.

Someone shouted, "The ravine, check the ravine."

Tracy said, "They're coming."

Fear gave Dyson a surge of energy, and he pushed.

Eddie grabbed him under the arms and tugged.

The agent moaned in agony as he rolled over the edge. For a moment, he lay motionless.

Frantic, Eddie cried out. "What can I do? How can I help?"

The agent's voice was faint. "Help me up, then let's get to your truck. Where's Tracy?"

Eddie looked back. She rushed toward them, her feet slipping and sliding on the rocks.

"Behind us," he said.

Dyson's body slumped. It took all of Eddie's strength to keep the man upright and moving forward.

Gunfire erupted.

Eddie glanced over his shoulder. Tracy was lying near the edge of the ravine. Two men with guns were on the other side. She fired, and they dropped to the ground.

Eddie opened the back door of the truck and shoved everything onto the floor. He lifted and pushed until the agent was on the back seat.

He turned to look for Tracy. Running, she was a few yards away. Another shot rang out, and dust kicked up as the bullet hit the ground near her. He opened the passenger door and ran to the driver's side. He hopped in and started the engine.

Tossing the gun on the seat, she jumped in and her cuffed hands grabbed the door handle. "Let's get the hell out of here."

Thirty-four

Blake elected to ride with Gabe, and since he was more familiar with the roads, Gabe took the lead as they drove out of the parking lot. Once he passed the city limit sign, he punched it.

Cat drove the second vehicle with Adrian and Lance. Racked with doubt, Adrian stared out the window. There were only five of them. Should he have waited until he was able to get reinforcements? No, he'd already waged this battle. The answer had been, and still was, no time. Reynolds and his team would be on the move, headed to Austin, if they were indeed at the Morris property.

Cat must have sensed his internal conflict. "We didn't have time."

He shifted to look at her. "I wonder if we'll still be able to use that excuse at the end of the day."

From the backseat, Lance said, "If it's any help, I don't think there are any other options."

"That pickup coming at us just weaved into our lane. It may be a drunk driver." Cat tapped the brakes and pulled to the edge of the road.

Adrian's eyes flicked to the roadway. Gabe's pickup was on the shoulder. His gaze shifted to the approaching truck. He stiffened. "It looks like, good god, it is, that's Owens' truck. What the hell is he doing out here?"

As it passed, he caught a glimpse of Eddie hunched over the steering wheel with a look of desperation on his face. A woman was bent over the console.

He reached across and hit the horn. "Turn around."

Cat hit the brakes. The transmission rumbled when she shoved the gearshift into reverse. Turning, she headed after the pickup.

Eddie sped up.

"Cat, pull alongside."

She floorboarded the accelerator and swung into the opposite lane.

The two vehicles raced down the highway. Cat started to pull ahead.

Eddie swung across the center line forcing her to the left. "He's trying to ram us." This time she hit the horn.

Eddie looked at them. It took a second for recognition to register. When it did, he slammed on the brakes. The truck fishtailed and spun before coming to a stop in the middle of the road.

Tires squealed as Cat braked, and the SUV shuddered to a stop. Adrian and Lance shot out of the vehicle and raced to the truck.

Eddie stumbled out and screamed, "Ambulance, get an ambulance!"

The woman jumped out the other side. *My, god, it's Tracy.*

She shouted, "Stuart needs help."

Grabbing the rear door handle, Adrian opened the door. A man in handcuffs was stretched across the seat. Unconscious, his lungs wheezed, and his white face had a bluish tint.

When Tracy opened the door on the other side, he realized she was wearing handcuffs. Purple and black streaks marbled her face. She had a black eye.

Gabe stopped beside him. "Good lord!"

Adrian asked, "What's faster, call an ambulance or drive to the hospital?"

"Drive, and I'll do it." Gabe tossed his keys to Blake. He pushed Owens aside and got behind the wheel as Adrian slammed the back door, and Tracy hopped back inside. Weaving around the SUV, he raced down the highway.

Adrian looked at Eddie who shivered in the warm air. "Why didn't you call nine-one-one?"

Eddie gulped. "I lost my phone."

He grabbed his arm. "Come on, you can explain on the way to the hospital."

Seated in the car, Eddie leaned his head back and closed his eyes. Cat glanced at him in the rearview mirror. "Eddie, are you hurt?"

His eyes popped open. "I'm not sure what's wrong. I can't seem to stop shaking."

With a sympathetic look on his face, Adrian twisted to look into the backseat. "It'll pass. Tell us what happened."

Eddie began to talk and was still talking when Cat pulled into the emergency room parking lot. Amazement and incredulity had grown as the three agents listened.

Eddie's truck was parked in front of the glass doors. Cat parked nearby. Blake pulled alongside. He hopped out and opened Adrian's door. "What's the story?"

"You're not going to believe it. Let's get inside, and I'll fill you in."

Gabe was standing in the lobby when they entered.

"How is he?" Cat asked.

"I don't know. Tracy's with him. She wouldn't leave even though she's hurt. I've got a unit on the way. We'll keep an officer here until this is over."

They stepped to a corner of the room that afforded some privacy, and Adrian recapped Eddie's story for Blake and Gabe. He added, "We need to leave. There might be a chance they haven't left yet."

"I'll let the nurse know," Gabe said. "I'll meet you outside."

Turning, Adrian saw Eddie step back, his shoulders slumped.

"Eddie, you need to move your truck. You're going with us. I have several questions about what you saw."

"I ... uh, yes sir, uh, ... right away, Agent Dillard." His feet picked up speed as he headed to the door.

Blake stared at Owens as the door swung closed, then glanced at Adrian. "You're right. Damn hard to believe."

Outside, they waited for Gabe to join them. When he walked up, he asked, "What's the game plan when we get there?"

"I'm certain they'll recognize our vehicle, but not your truck. Cat, pull over before we get there, and let Gabe do a drive by. If they haven't hightailed it, he can size up the opposition, and we'll go from there."

During the drive, Eddie repeated the story. Alarmed by the discovery of another eighteen-wheeler, he asked about the details on the truck. Most of the questions, Eddie couldn't answer.

Cat's foot tapped the brakes, and she backed onto the same dirt road Eddie had used. They waited for Gabe to call.

It didn't take long. Adrian hit the speakerphone button and heard Gabe say the place was deserted.

"Damn, knew it wouldn't be this easy!" Adrian exclaimed.

Cat pulled into the driveway and parked behind Gabe's truck. Gabe had opened the rollup door on a large metal building behind the house. Blake stood in the doorway of a small building.

Exiting the car, Eddie pointed out where the two big rigs had parked and where he had crawled out of the ravine.

Blake shouted, "Back here."

As they approached, he motioned toward the doorway with his hand. "This is where Dyson and Tracy were kept prisoner. There are eye bolts, which is what they probably used for the handcuffs."

Adrian leaned through the doorway to examine the inside. "We need to have this processed for evidence." Then he walked to the large building. Inside were pieces of machinery, and not much else.

"Eddie," Gabe said. "Did you say you saw them hauling out boxes?"

"Yes, they put them inside the other trailer."

"Any idea how many?"

"Uh … no. They were loading them when I first saw them from the ravine and still at it when we escaped."

Adrian walked to the edge of the ravine. Cat and Lance stepped beside him. She said, "I can see how Tracy was able to climb down. But how the hell did Stuart manage it? What little I saw of him in the truck he appeared to have serious injuries. And the way he was breathing, he must have broken ribs. The pain would've been excruciating."

"I don't know. It'll be interesting to hear Tracy tell the tale."

He motioned for everyone to gather around. "We don't have time to waste here. Gabe, we need to lock this place down until we can get a unit out here to process for prints and any other evidence. Do you have a suggestion?"

"I'm friends with the patrol lieutenant for the sheriff's department. I'll get it set up."

"Before we go, let's look inside the house. Eddie, you wait out here."

"They left in a hurry. Nothing was locked up," Adrian said, as he opened the front door.

They split up and quickly walked through the rooms. The house had been occupied by more than one person. Beds were unmade, and towels hung over the curtain rods in both bathrooms. In the kitchen, an aroma of bacon hung in the air, and dirty dishes were piled in the sink.

Cat searched a small office but came out empty-handed. When Adrian glanced her way, she shook her head.

"Let's go. Lance, you go back with Gabe and Blake. Get whatever gear you need to take with you. We'll do the same after we drop Eddie off at the hospital and check on Stuart and Tracy. As soon as everyone is back at the PD, we're leaving for Austin," Adrian said.

All the way back, Eddie tried to convince Adrian to let him go along. Adrian was adamant it wasn't going to happen. As they drove into the parking lot, Eddie made another plea. "I'll do whatever you say, but I know what the trucks and these guys look like. I even counted them as I watched them walk out of the Guards' house."

"You didn't tell me you had a count!" Adrian exclaimed.

"Uh, I kinda forgot. There were twelve."

"Is there anything else, you … kinda forgot?"

"Uh, no sir, I don't think so." Then, with a sly look, he said, "But I can't be sure."

Au79

"No, Eddie. You're not going, and don't even think about following us."

Dejected, Eddie followed them into the emergency room.

Cat approached the desk and held up her badge. After a short conversation with the nurse, she stepped to where Adrian and Eddie still argued.

"Stuart is out of danger, though he'll be here for several days. He's badly dehydrated along with his injuries. Despite the objections from the doctor, they released Tracy. He wanted to keep her overnight. She threatened to walk out, so they didn't have much choice."

"That's just what I intend to do, walk out," Tracy said, as she walked up. She took a deep swig from a bottle of water as everyone looked at her.

At the expression on their faces, she grimaced, then said, "It looks worse than it is. I need a ride if you don't mind. My truck is probably still parked on the back-side of the Guards' property."

As they walked out the door, Adrian said, "No, it's at the station. We found it and the keys you conveniently left. We can take you home and have someone bring it to you."

"No, I'll get it."

Eddie had started for his truck when Tracy called out to him. He turned.

"I haven't had a chance to thank you. What you did was unbelievable. I want to talk to you later."

A blush spread across his face, and when she leaned forward to kiss him on the cheek, he turned bright red.

Cat and Adrian had stopped. She tilted her head toward him and whispered, "Just a thought, but it might not be a bad idea to take him with us."

In disbelief, he stared at her.

She threw up her hands. "I'm just saying, no telling what he's likely to do. Eddie's like an old hound dog that doesn't know when to go home. At least if he's with us, we know where he is and can control him. Besides, if we don't, he'll just follow us. He might remember something he hasn't told us."

"I hate it when you turn stupid into good sense. Eddie, come back here."

"Yes, sir."

"You're coming with us. Go home, get what you need and meet us at the station. If you aren't there in one hour, you'll get left."

Eddie came close to wiggling with excitement as he trotted to his truck.

Cat laughed. "Yep, just like a hound dog."

Tracy walked up. She chuckled as she watched Eddie climb in his truck. "Who'd ever believe there'd come a time that I'd be grateful to that little pissant for anything, let alone my life?" She shook her head in amazement before turning to look at Adrian and Cat. "So, what was that all about, and where are you going?"

"I'll tell you on the way," Adrian said.

As Cat parked in front of the PD to drop Tracy off, another argument resounded inside the SUV. When Tracy heard where they stood on the investigation, she was determined to go. Unlike Eddie, who pleaded, Tracy demanded, and she wasn't backing down.

Cat grinned to herself. Adrian wasn't going to win this one either. As Tracy got out of the car, she glared at Adrian. "I'll be back here in one hour, and you'd better not leave without me." She turned and marched inside to get her keys.

Adrian looked at Cat, hopeful he'd get her support. She shrugged. "Give it up, Dillard. She's going." She laughed at his look of irritation.

Washington D.C.

Scott rubbed his hand across his face. Uncertainty bubbled in him. Had they missed a detail in their intricate ruse?

Au 79

Earlier, his boss called to confirm the substitution of the lead ingots was a go. Agents had replaced the drivers of the security trucks, and they were at the lead plant. The plane would leave on time.

On the Texas end, the change in security personnel was set. He'd contacted the head of the Austin office, Will Cooper, to request a team of agents. The substitution would be made at Fort Hood. With agents inside the escort vans and the eighteen-wheeler, they weren't going in blind. The knowledge helped to ease some of the tension that had his neck and shoulder muscles tied in knots.

Nicki had sent out an alert to all Texas law enforcement agencies for Reynolds' eighteen-wheeler. They'd narrowed the locations where the Guards would make their move to nine sites. They still weren't any closer to figuring out the Guards' plan to gain access to the gold, let alone escape with it.

He glanced at the time on his computer. He should have heard from Adrian by now. He resisted the urge to call. Micro-managing wasn't his style. He trusted his team.

A rap on his door and Nicki stepped in with a self-satisfied look. "I found another connection."

"And," he prompted her when she paused.

Grinning, she said, "Reynolds is related to Jonah Grigsby. He's a distant cousin. Great-grandmothers were sisters, and, yes, there's more. Morris' grandmother, Elsie, is also related to one of the great-grandmothers. I can explain the connection,"

Scott held up a hand. "God, no! Please don't. I'll take your word for it. So Morris, Reynolds, and Grigsby are all related. Wonder who else in this nest of vipers is connected?"

His phone rang. Answering, he said, "Adrian, what happened?" He punched the speakerphone so Nicki could hear.

"Stuart and Tracy are alive. Stuart's at the hospital, and we just dropped Tracy off at the PD."

Nicki gasped, and when Scott glanced at her, tears shone in her eyes.

He nodded to her, before he said, "Then you found them at the Morris place?"

"Yes and no. Short version. They were at the Morris place, but were rescued by none other than our nosy reporter, Eddie Owens. It's a long story. Once we're on the road to Austin, I'll call and give you all the details."

"Owens!" Scott exclaimed.

"Yeah, and it's an amazing tale."

"Okay, one item you need to know. Jonah Grigsby is related to Reynolds."

"Grigsby, now why does that not surprise me. Here's something for you to chew on. There's a second eighteen-wheeler," Adrian said.

After disconnecting, he leaned back and laughed. "Unbelievable. Owens. This may be one for the record books." Then his thoughts turned to the reason for a second eighteen-wheeler.

Texas

When Reynolds answered, the caller exclaimed, "What the hell happened? I just found out Dyson and Harlowe are at the hospital, and that damn nerdy reporter you've been flirting with was responsible. As improbable as it sounds, it's evidently true."

"Owens! That's who helped them?" Reynolds said.

"You didn't know?"

"No. We never got a look at the guy. Owens. I'll be damned."

"This has gotten out of hand. We need to stop right now."

Reynolds' voice dropped. "Listen to me, we're not stopping anything. I'll send one of my men to the hospital. Dyson and Harlowe won't live to see another day. And, when this is done, I'll take care of Owens."

"Forget the hospital. Laredo PD has men staked out in front of Dyson's door. You won't get close, and Harlowe has already been released. I don't know where she is. All I got was she showed up at the station to get her truck keys and left."

"Where are the agents?"

"I don't know."

"Find out. That's all you have to do," Reynolds said, and disconnected the call.

Shit, how the hell was he supposed to do that? His pipeline into the investigation had been shut off.

****

Seated in the conference room in the Austin FBI office, they'd been at it for two hours. Will Cooper, the head of the Austin office and his agents, along with Adrian and his team, minus Eddie, were clustered around the large table. Frustrated by the lack of a consensus on a plan, Adrian pushed back his chair and said, "Let's take a break." He needed fresh air and a chance to think. They were running out of time, and he had to make a decision.

Outside, the light breeze cooled his skin and ruffled the hair that brushed his collar. He closed his eyes and let his thoughts drift over the last few hours.

For the trip to Austin, Adrian put Eddie in Gabe's vehicle. He wanted to talk to Tracy and didn't need Eddie absorbing every detail. Gabe's look of dismay when he found out Eddie was riding with him still brought a smile to his face.

When they arrived, Will had a helicopter on standby. Adrian and Blake, flew over the route. Cat, along with Lance and Gabe drove it. Each site was examined from the air and on the ground. Cat would stop to let Lance hop out and look for a bomb. It didn't take long to realize it would be impossible to identify which site could be the target. The numerous side roads the Guards could use to access the main route added another level of complication.

The one important piece of information was the route was free of explosives. Adrian expected the Guards would wait until after dark. But how would they know which site? Putting officers at each location was risky. If the Guards spotted them, it could ruin the whole plan.

What he needed was Ryan's profiling expertise to get inside the head of the leader of the gang, Jonah Grigsby. They'd reached that conclusion during the trip to Austin after hearing Tracy's story. Cat reminded him of their first attempt to gain access to the compound. They'd talked to Grigsby first. Cat had seen someone hiding in the shadows of the adjacent room. She believed it was Reynolds and that the man wasn't at the compound when they arrived. Meyers had been the driver of the truck who met them at the gate. He used a phone to contact Reynolds. The second time when they arrived, he contacted Reynolds by radio.

Then there was the disquieting phone call he'd received from Karl. Livid, he had demanded to know why Adrian didn't call about Stuart. He had to find out through the local grapevine his agent had been rescued. Bill was in Karl's office again and demanded to know the status of the investigation and what Adrian planned. Which one was on a fishing expedition?

At the sound of footsteps, he glanced over his shoulder. Tracy had followed him outside.

Anger stirred deep inside him at the sight of the hideous bruises on her face. Despite the fact she'd slept on the trip to Austin, she hadn't regained the vitality she normally exuded.

"Feeling any better?" he asked.

"Oh, yeah. I'm fine," she said.

She lied, and Adrian knew it. It didn't require a touch to tell him. Tracy's desire to take the bastards down was a deep-seated determination. She wasn't going to let her physical condition stop her.

"What are you going to do?" she asked.

Surprised she had sensed his dilemma, he said, "At the moment, I don't have a clue."

His hands in his pockets, he stared at the congested highway in front of the FBI office. Rush hour traffic, and it was stop and go. A glimmer of an idea registered in his head.

"Better get back inside. Where's Eddie?" he asked, realizing he hadn't seen the man since they arrived.

"Asleep on a couch in the breakroom. If I didn't know better, I'd say Cat put something in his coffee. He's really taken a shine to her. She can't get away from him. He follows her everywhere." Tracy laughed. "I caught her hiding out in the bathroom. It's driving her nuts."

Adrian chuckled, but as they walked back to the conference room, his thoughts shifted to the idea gaining momentum in his mind. In typical fashion, he examined it from all sides, looking for loopholes that would spell disaster. Not finding any, he grinned. He had a plan.

Thirty-five

Will Cooper, along with the base commandant, Lieutenant General George Farmington, and several of his soldiers mingled by the open door of the aircraft hangar.

The eighteen-wheeler and two vans had cleared the entrance gate and would arrive within minutes.

Adrian followed Cat, Tracy, and Gabe into a small office in the corner. He flipped off the lights as he entered. A large window overlooked the front of the hanger and the runway. With the room dark, no one would see them standing inside.

Adrian stepped to the window. The discussion from the previous evening about the Guards' plan dominated his thoughts. Whatever they were missing had to center around the depository personnel. He opted to let Will make the contact. He was a fresh face that wouldn't be associated with anyone in Laredo. With his cover story of being on the General's staff, his presence wouldn't be suspicious.

Will's team of agents waited behind the hanger. When they arrived at the base, they'd parked in the back. The SUVs would be out of sight.

Blake and Lance were in a military helicopter in a parking lot on the southside of the base.

Earlier, the rush hour traffic in Austin sparked an idea. When Adrian outlined it on paper, it was unbelievably simple. The route the convoy would take was sixty-eight miles from Fort Hood to the depository. Every fifteen minutes, a car would depart and travel the route, to and from Fort Hood. It was a trail of innocuous cars, driven by officers searching for suspicious vehicles parked along the route. The cycle of trips would continue throughout the evening and into the night. If an officer spotted suspicious activity, the pilot would fly Blake and Lance to the location to check for explosives.

On hearing the plan, Will contacted the Austin Police Chief and requested the loan of officers and undercover vehicles. Within an hour of the call, the first car headed out.

Now they waited, and he hated it. It left too much time to think, to question. The details cycled in his head. What had he missed or hadn't considered? How long would it take for the whole damn plan to come apart and end up on the dung heap?

Tracy stood next to him. She chuckled. "Do you think Eddie's still protesting?" The reporter had been left behind. This time his objections fell on deaf ears.

"Probably so. I'm just thankful he doesn't have transportation." On the other side of Tracy, he heard Cat's grunt of agreement.

Light from inside the hanger spilled onto the tarmac. Flood lights mounted along the roof added to the illumination. Will walked in front of the window and stopped at the edge of the building. He was waiting for the vans to arrive. Adrian wanted to keep the security personnel in their vehicles until they made the substitution. Will would inform the man in charge of the convoy, Larry Henning.

An escort jeep with two soldiers came into view, and behind it was the eighteen-wheeler and two vans. A soldier stepped from the front of the hanger with a light stick. He motioned for the truck driver to pull forward in front of the hanger. Then he directed the vans to the side of the building.

As the truck passed the window, the faces of the two men inside were clearly visible.

Tracy jabbed her elbow into Adrian's ribs and hissed. "Look at the driver. It's Joe Warden, and the passenger is Stan Meyers. How the hell did that happen?"

Stunned, he stared at the passing truck. Damn! The Guards didn't need to worry about getting into the cab—they were already inside. His plan started to slide toward the dung heap.

Gabe asked, "Tracy, is Meyers the one who did a number on you and Stuart?"

"He's the one." Anger vibrated in her voice. Then a memory pinged in her head. She looked at the truck. "Adrian, that eighteen-wheeler looks just like the one I saw at the compound and at the place where Stuart and I were held captive."

Cat exclaimed, "A duplicate! Are they going to switch trucks?"

"I'll be damned! That's exactly what they plan to do, steal the real one and leave the look-alike. Warden's probably learned how to disable the truck's security systems," Adrian said.

"What good would that do them?" Tracy asked.

"I haven't got it all put together yet. I need to look at those vans."

Will and another man came around the corner. Adrian recognized Henning's face from the personnel files he received from Bracken. He was head of the depository security force.

Adrian pulled out his phone and tapped it. When Will answered, Adrian said, "Don't react, listen. The driver and passenger in the eighteen-wheeler are Border Guards. Walk into the hanger."

Footsteps echoed, then Will said, "I'm inside. I'm out of earshot of anyone. This certainly didn't take long."

Adrian knew that Will was familiar with the dung heap theory, most cops were.

"What are you going to do about substituting Gabe for the driver?" Will asked.

"We can't. If Warden isn't driving that truck, Grigsby and his thugs will know it in a heartbeat." When Adrian found out Gabe had driven for a trucking company before becoming a cop, he was assigned to drive the eighteen-wheeler. One of Will's agents, Jack Davis, would take the place of the passenger.

Au79

"This is going to screw up our plan to make the switch with the guards," Will said.

"That may be the least of our problems. Tell Farmington to get the plane past the hanger and several hundred yards away from the entrance. When that eighteen-wheeler backs into position it has to be in front of the hanger. I don't want the driver or passenger to be able to see the vans on the side of the building. Make sure those two stay with the truck."

Will said, "I'll tell Farmington," and disconnected.

A few minutes later, a soldier approached the truck. Warden leaned out the window to hear what he said, then nodded his head. The escort jeep pulled in front. Warden followed the vehicle as they circled and moved further out onto the tarmac.

Adrian's phone rang.

Will said, "The plane is on final approach."

"I'm not waiting for the transfer to be finished to move the security guards into the hanger. I'm moving them as soon as that first pallet comes off the plane," Adrian told him.

The roar of an engine echoed as a plane dropped to the runway and turned. A soldier in the jeep waved the light stick as the plane taxied toward the hanger. The pilot followed the jeep until the soldier signaled for it to stop. Several men exited the hanger and trotted to the waiting plane, followed by a fork lift.

The plane's door opened, and the steps lowered. A man in an overcoat walked down the staircase.

"That's Harry Stenner, the bank representative sent to oversee the transfer," Adrian said. He wondered if the man was aware the plane was loaded with lead ingots.

Another jeep carrying the General, Will, and Henning stopped near the steps.

After greeting Stenner, the four men walked to the rear of the plane. The large ramp was lowered. Warden backed the eighteen-wheeler into position. Adrian grunted in satisfaction when he saw that it was in front of the hanger. The fork lift operator drove up the plane's ramp to pick up a pallet, backed until the wheels were on the concrete, then turned and rolled up the ramp into the trailer.

"Let's get the security force into the breakroom at the back of the hanger. Tracy, keep a lookout here. If anything changes, let me know."

The three headed to a door on the side of the hanger. Adrian said, "Cat, have them leave their weapons in the van. Once they're inside, collect their cell phones. Find out who has the keys to the vans."

Adrian approached the nearest vehicle. The driver's door opened, and a man in a security uniform stepped out.

Adrian pulled his badge. "I'm FBI Agent Adrian Dillard. Everyone, step out of the van. Leave your weapon on the seat. I'll explain inside."

Cat was at the other van. Gabe stood back and watched the men as they exited the vehicles.

The men grumbled, but followed his instructions. He waited until everyone was inside the building, then walked to a van. The parking lot lights were dim, but should be enough for what he needed to see. He dropped to one knee, looked underneath, then did the same with the second vehicle.

"Bastards," he muttered.

Inside, he motioned for Cat and Gabe to join him. "Explosives are wired to the undercarriage of both vehicles. Gabe, scrounge up some tools. At the very least, we'll need to cut wires. Cat, get Tracy over here to watch these guys, then come help."

Outside, he laid on his back and wiggled under a van. He pulled the small flashlight from the holder on his belt. The bomb was taped to a metal brace near the gas tank. While he wasn't an expert like Blake or Lance, he'd attended several bomb disposal courses at the academy. What he was looking at was a rudimentary device. A cell phone was wired to the detonator. Strips of tape wrapped around the device and a small block of C4 explosive. He heard the scrape of boots, and Gabe scooted next to him.

"I have wire cutters," Gabe told him.

Adrian said, "It's a simple device. Detach the phone, and we've neutralized the bomb." He pointed. "If we cut here ..." his finger moved, "and here, I think we can remove the cell phone."

Gabe quipped, "Think? I'd feel a lot better if that word was know."

Adrian held the flashlight as Gabe examined the wiring. Two snips and the phone's connection to the detonator was severed. Using his pocket knife, Gabe cut the tape that held the phone in place and slid it into his pocket.

Adrian reached with his free hand to hold the rest of the bomb in place as Gabe cut the tape around the metal brace. When it came free, Gabe laid it down and pushed it toward the edge of the vehicle.

Cat's hands reached down and picked it up.

Sliding out, they moved to the second vehicle and repeated the process.

As they stood by the two vans, Cat said, "Let me have the cell phones."

Gabe handed them to her with a questioning look.

She said, "Advance warning. When these phones ring, we'll know the Guards are about to make their move. What are we going to do with these?" She motioned toward the remains of the bombs on the ground.

Adrian looked around. A dumpster sat at the back of the lot. "Let's leave them behind that bin. We'll let Farmington dispose of them. Now, let's go talk to the security detail."

Twelve sets of eyes stared at him with varying degrees of anger and suspicion as he stopped in the doorway. "The FBI is taking over the convoy. You will remain here for the next several hours."

As he walked out, the mutters turned into a low roar of protest. He pulled his phone.

When Will answered, Adrian said, "The vans were wired with explosives. We removed them. An irate group of security guards are in the breakroom. I told them we're taking over the convoy. Ask Farmington to send a soldier to keep them there? No one would have seen them come into the hanger. I want to keep it that way. They've been disarmed, and their cell phones confiscated. How much longer on the transfer?"

"Ten pallets are left. Henning's been counting."

"Pull him to the side and tell him what's going on. Once the transfer is complete, have him walk to the vans. You come inside and exit out the side door. I'm moving your team to a van. Davis and Gabe will go with me."

A few minutes later a soldier walked up to Adrian. He explained what he needed. The soldier stepped to the side of the door. He ignored the angry looks the guards cast his way.

Adrian looked at Cat. "Get Will's team to clear out the equipment and weapons in the vans. Find a place to stash it. Then move our gear into them. Find out which vehicle will be following the trailer. Have the team wait in it."

She headed out the side door.

Adrian, Gabe, and Tracy walked to the office.

His phone rang. It was Blake. In the background, he could hear the thump of propellers.

Blake said, "We're in the air. Unit Ten called. A pickup is parked near bridge number four." The locations had been marked on a map and designated by a number. Distances between each had been added to the map. Everyone involved in the operation had a copy.

"Any sign of the Guards' two eighteen-wheelers?"

"Not yet."

When Cat walked in, she said, "We're ready to go."

As Adrian watched the slow progression of pallets being moved from the plane to the trailer, he was certain he knew the Guards' plan. "I figured out the reason for the duplicate truck. Once the security force was eliminated, they'd leave the duplicate and drive off with the real one. Then blow up a bridge to increase the confusion and hamper rescue efforts. It buys them time to escape with what they believe is a truck full of gold. The Mexican border is only a few hours away."

Puzzled, Tracy said, "That still doesn't make any sense. It would be obvious it wasn't the same truck."

"Not if they blow it up," Adrian said. "I bet it's wired with explosives just like the bombs on the two vans."

Gabe let out a whistle of amazement. "It would work. When the fire department and cops arrived, they'd be confronted with a horrific disaster. Just dealing with that would take hours. And it's doubtful any of the first responders would even know the reason for the convoy. By the time someone did arrive that knew, they'd see what they expected to see, a truck and two vans. I agree that Warden probably knows how to disable the tracking system. That means it would take even longer to figure out it was the wrong truck, and the real one would be long gone."

A bleak look in his eyes, Adrian stared at Tracy, and said, "Especially if there was a body behind the wheel and one in the passenger seat of the eighteen-wheeler."

"Oh, my, god!" The places on Tracy's face that didn't have a vivid display of colors turned white. "It's why they kept Stuart alive and planted all that evidence. Then I dropped into their lap like a gift from the gods." She gulped. "No wonder Meyers said the boss didn't want any bullet holes in us."

Adrian said, "Reynolds wanted to keep you alive until the last minute. Unless the bodies were totally destroyed, there was a chance the medical examiner would discover you'd been shot. That would destroy the illusion Dyson was the mastermind and you his accomplice."

Gabe asked, "Wouldn't their deaths be suspicious?"

Adrian paused again as he gathered his thoughts. "Not if someone suggested that the truck exploded before they could get out. It would look like Stuart and Tracy had inadvertently been caught in their own net of destruction. We're dealing with more than one sadistic son of a bitch."

Tracy wiped her sleeve across her face, and a look of grim determination pushed back the horror of what might have been.

Adrian gave her one last glance, needing to be reassured she was past the moment, then looked out the window.

The ramp on the plane slowly closed. Henning stepped to the back of the trailer and locked the doors. According to Bracken, Henning was the only member of the security team that knew the code to the lock.

Stenner handed a set of documents to Henning, then boarded the plane. The engines started, and the pilot pulled to the end of the runway. With a roar, it took off. The military jeep pulled in front of the truck and waited.

Henning and Will got back into the jeep with the General. It headed toward the hanger.

Adrian said, "Let's go."

Exiting the side door, he saw the agents were inside one of the vans, though with the tinted windows he couldn't distinguish any features. Behind him the door opened, and Will walked out and stepped next to him.

Henning came around the corner. His eyes glinted with suspicion.

"I'm Agent Adrian Dillard. There's no time for explanations beyond what you've been told. Were you going to handle the communications with the truck?"

"Yes."

"I need your help, but it's your choice. I'm hoping to avoid a fire fight, but it may not be possible."

Without hesitation, Henning said, "I'm in. Where's my rifle."

"I'm glad to hear you say that. The two men in the truck will expect to hear your voice."

Cat motioned toward the door. "All your equipment and weapons are in a mechanical room." She handed a set of the van keys to Adrian and the other to Will.

Adrian started to get behind the wheel, then paused. Considering the new complications, he might need to have the freedom to move.

Cat saw his hesitation. "Do you want me to drive."

She was a certified sniper and one of the top marksmen in the Bureau. He didn't want her tied up handling the wheel. He shook his head no. He turned to Gabe. "Mind driving?"

Gabe grinned and held out his hand for the key.

Adrian said, "Pull ahead of the escort jeep, then wait. Let the jeep pass us. I don't want to give the men inside the truck a chance to see our faces through the windshield."

He turned to Will. "Same for you. Once the truck is far enough ahead, swing in behind it. Hang back. I don't want you close enough that Warden can see you in his side mirror."

Henning ran out the door with a rifle in his hand and hopped into the back. Adrian slid into the front seat, and Gabe started the engine. Jack Davis and Tracy were already inside. Cat slid the side door shut.

Adrian said, "Henning, get it rolling." He slipped the headset in place that connected to the radio attached to his vest.

Henning, seated behind Gabe, said, "Hand me the portable radio on the dash." He keyed the mike, and said, "Move out."

Thirty-six

As they rumbled through the gate, the sound of Adrian's phone broke the silence. "Where ..."

Blake interrupted, "The target is bridge four. We've got a problem. We can't defuse the bomb. The pickup is still there. Unit Five passed the location and saw several men. We turned around and are heading back. Where are you?"

The dung heap moved closer. "Leaving Fort Hood. Make the call to the highway patrol office in Burnet. Get the troopers started toward us. It's possible when the Guard's plan doesn't work, they'll turn tail and run."

"Will do," Blake said.

Before leaving Austin, Adrian set up a backup plan. He contacted the Texas Highway Patrol office in Burnett. Officers would be on standby to help cut off any escape routes.

He tapped the mic key. "Will, it's going to be bridge four. Border Guards are hanging around the bridge. Blake couldn't land. I told him to contact the troopers."

Will acknowledged.

As the lights of the city vanished, only the headlights cut a swath in the total darkness of the landscape. He glanced over his shoulder at the truck that loomed behind them.

"Henning, what do you know about the driver and guard in the truck?"

"Not much. Everyone who works for the trucking company was

supposed to be vetted."

"Backgrounds can be faked." Adrian stared out at the black night. His mind raced. "Gabe, I expect Warden will try to run us off the road. He won't want a vehicle in front of him that's about to explode."

"I kinda had the same thought in my mind," Gabe said.

Henning leaned forward and interjected, "That probably explains the odd conversation I had with the driver. Before we left the depository, he tried to convince me it would be better if both vans were behind the eighteen-wheeler. It got a bit heated when I refused. I had to remind him who was in charge of the convoy."

When they passed another sign, Adrian checked his map, and said, "We're twenty-four miles from the bridge."

His earpiece crackled, then he heard Blake's voice. The helicopter must be close. "Adrian, Unit Seven reported an eighteen-wheeler and three pickups passed him. They're headed north and about three miles from the bridge."

Adrian repeated the information for Henning's benefit. He didn't have an extra communication set that linked the officers. He twisted to look over the seat. "Cat, call Unit One. Get the blockade in place on the north and south side of the bridge. Wait until we pass and are out of sight before they set up on the north side."

The route Bracken selected passed through a remote section of the county. At this time of night there was little traffic. The only cars he'd seen were probably one of the Austin officers driving the route.

The topic on how to stop traffic was another point that had been heavily debated during the initial meeting in Austin. When Adrian came up with his plan, they had a solution. Use the cars to block the highway. Each one was loaded with flares and small, portable barricades. It all hinged on whether the target location could be identified in time to get the cars in place.

After disconnecting, Cat tapped her mic. "Unit One said the three pickups headed north and the one at the bridge are now parked about a mile and a half south of the bridge. The eighteen-wheeler is on the shoulder about a mile south."

Adrian heard Will's acknowledgement, then said, "Will, when we reach the bridge, move as close to the rear of the semi as you can. They won't blow it until the truck is clear. I don't want you caught on the bridge. After we're on the other side, Warden may try to run us off the road, so be prepared."

Gabe watched the odometer. "Another mile."

Ahead the guardrails appeared. Then, they were across.

Gabe's eyes darted between the rearview mirror and the road. "The parked eighteen-wheeler is ahead. Truck just cleared the bridge." He steered to the right to pick up the trailing van in the side mirror. "Will's across."

As they passed the parked eighteen-wheeler, Gabe shouted, "He's coming!"

Adrian looked over his shoulder. The semi had moved to the inside lane and was pulling alongside. As Warden swung hard to the right, Gabe hit the brakes. The big rig raced by.

Behind them, the duplicate truck exploded. A ball of flames and smoke shot into the night sky. Pieces of metal, engine parts, and chunks of tires rained down.

Will's voice sounded through the earpiece. "Damn, that was close. I'd just passed the truck."

Cat hollered, "The bomb phones rang."

There was a second explosion. This time it was the bridge. Tremors buckled the highway. The crash of plummeting chunks of concrete reverberated in the air. A cloud of smoke and dirt rose above the gaping hole in the roadway.

Ahead, Warden attempted to recover from the abrupt move to strike the van and overcorrected. The truck fishtailed as it passed the parked pickups on the other side of the road.

Gabe shouted, "If those pallets shift, he's got a problem."

Au 79

Even as he spoke, the trailer rocked, then began to tilt to the right, pulling the cab over. The truck flipped onto its side. It slid along the road and across the shoulder.

When Gabe went by the pickups, Adrian caught a glimpse of the men beside the vehicles. Shocked, they stared at the plume of dirt and chunks of trees that flew into the air as the truck plowed into the field.

After passing the wrecked truck, Gabe hit the brakes, putting the van into a controlled skid. When the van shuddered to a stop, it was broadside near the edge of the road.

Adrian shoved the door open and jumped out. Gabe crawled over the console and slid across the seat to follow. Cat had the side door open. Tracy pitched a rifle to Adrian, then to Gabe.

As he reached for the bull horn, Adrian heard Cat tell Tracy to follow her. Hunched over, they disappeared into the brush and small trees. Henning followed the two women.

Will's van had stopped at an angle on the opposite side. The front tires were on the shoulder. Officers exited and ran into the adjacent field.

The eighteen-wheeler had rolled onto the passenger side. It was several hundred yards in front of Adrian. The driver's door swung open, and Warden crawled out. He dropped to the ground, followed by Meyers. The two disappeared around the front of the truck.

The Guards were trapped. Behind them was the deep hole in the road. In front was a semi-circle of officers who had the advantage. Backlighted by the blazing inferno that consumed the duplicate truck, the Guards were clearly visible.

Two pickups screeched to a stop in the middle of the road. Crossways, they formed a barricade. The other two were still on the shoulder. In a frenzy of movement, the men jostled each other to get to cover.

From behind the van, Adrian shouted through the bullhorn. "FBI! Throw down your weapons. Step in front of your vehicles with your hands in the air."

His answer was a hail of gunfire. Pings echoed as bullets struck the van. Gabe moved to the rear of the vehicle. Davis was by the front tire.

Adrian dropped the bullhorn. When a man leaned out from behind a pickup, Adrian fired over the hood. The Guard slumped to the ground. Gabe picked off one running toward the wrecked semi.

Another man made a dash to the field, shooting as he ran. Shots erupted from Will's agents, and he fell. Another started to follow, then stopped and ducked behind a vehicle.

Out of the corner of his eye, he glimpsed someone moving atop the trailer. Adrian's head swiveled. It was Warden. The man was inching his way to the edge where he'd be able to fire down on the agents in front of him. Before Adrian could get a bead on him, shots cracked near him. Warden rolled over the edge and plummeted to the ground.

Despite the two trucks in the middle of the roadway, the Guards had no room to maneuver. They clustered along the sides, trying not to be a target. A man got into one of the two remaining vehicles on the shoulder. Adrian shot, but missed. The Guard pulled the vehicle in line with the other pickups on the road. It was a fatal error. On the shoulder, the pickup protected the men in the middle of the roadway from Will's agents. When the truck moved, the Guards were exposed.

The officers' deadly accuracy began to take a toll. The intensity of the shots fired by the Guards rapidly diminished.

****

Tracy had taken up a position on the far side from Cat and Henning. Ignoring what was happening in the roadway, she watched the truck. Where were they? When Warden appeared atop the trailer, she fired. Other shots echoed. She didn't know if it was Cat or Henning. When Warden rolled over the edge, she went back to watching for Meyers. *You bastard, where are you?* He had to be behind the truck, unless he'd already turned tail and ran toward the bridge.

She had to get to another spot where she'd be able to see the other side of the semi. Moving away from the road, she slipped from tree to tree that dotted the landscape.

She saw Meyers dart out, a gun in his hand. He ran, weaving around trees.

Tracy slung the rifle over her back, pulled her gun from the holster and raced after him. She had to stop him before he escaped into the total darkness. The further they moved from the burning truck the darker it became and would make it easy for him to escape. If she had to follow him to hell and back, that wasn't going to happen.

She shouted, "Drop the gun! Hands in the air!" and ducked behind a tree.

He whipped around, firing wildly as his gun hand came up.

A round hit the trunk, and splinters of bark and wood flew. She stepped around the other side and doubled tapped two rounds into his body. He crumpled to the ground.

When she reached his side, she kicked the gun away that lay near his hand and holstered her weapon. She dropped to one knee. "Stan, ole' boy, lot of blood pumping out of your chest. You're already a dead man, your heart just hasn't caught up. It will. I'd give you another two or three minutes."

A gleam of recognition sparked in his eyes. "You!"

A sardonic laugh erupted from Tracy. "Yep. Payback is a bitch, and that's me."

She walked over and picked up his gun and stuck it in her waistband. As she walked by him, she looked down. The gleam in his eyes had dimmed. "I hope you burn in hell." She headed back to the road.

****

Suddenly, it was only the officers shooting. The remaining men piled into a pickup. The driver hit the gas to make a run between the two vans. Multiple shots echoed. Tires blew. The pickup skidded and flipped.

It was over. What seemed an eternity, had only been minutes.

Adrian's eyes scanned the roadway and fields. From the frantic activity on Will's side, agents must be down. Jack Davis leaned against the vehicle. Blood dripped from an arm that dangled. Adrian ran to his side and eased him to the pavement.

Gabe grabbed the first-aid kit from the van and pulled out several pressure pads. He looked at Adrian. "I'll handle this."

Adrian stood. Cat and Henning walked toward him. He didn't see Tracy. The adrenaline that still pumped through his system couldn't stop a jolt of panic. Where was she?

He shouted at Cat. "Where's Tracy?"

Cat looked behind her. "I don't know."

Adrian tapped his mic, "Tracy!"

Relief rushed through him at the sound of her voice. "Here."

He saw her emerge from the woods.

"How many on our side?" Cat asked.

Adrian said, "Jack took one in the arm. Will may have two men down."

Tracy stopped beside them.

Adrian exclaimed, "You're hurt! There's blood on your face."

She swiped at her face, and said, "Probably from a flying piece of wood. It's nothing. Meyers tried to escape. He's in the woods, probably dead by now."

Adrian knew there was more to the story, but it would have to wait.

Cat and Henning headed to the pickup to see if anyone inside was alive.

One by one, Tracy and Adrian checked the bodies on the roadway. All were dead. One was Reynolds.

****

Adrian stood alongside the road and watched the chaotic activity. Blake's helicopter sat in the middle of the roadway. Behind it was the Care Flight helicopter. The crater in the road had slowed the arrival of emergency vehicles. Some parked and the occupants walked across the deep ravine on each side of the road. Others had to detour and come in from the south. The officers who were part of the traveling parade of cars and the state troopers added to the confusion.

Only five Guards survived. Jonah Grigsby was one. All of them screamed for medical treatment and a lawyer, not necessarily in that order. By the time the medics reached Meyers, he was dead.

Three agents had been shot, and they were being loaded into the Care Flight helicopter. Will was headed to the hospital with them. The rest of Will's team was assigned to help with the collection of evidence.

Two troopers found the Guards' other eighteen-wheeler parked on a dirt road several miles away. It was filled with explosives.

His team walked up. Adrian looked at Gabe. "You were right. A remote location, vans and an eighteen-wheeler engulfed in flames with bodies inside, and a blocked highway to slow the emergency response. It could have worked."

He motioned with his hand toward the beehive of activity. "No telling how long it would have taken for someone in the know to arrive. Grigsby and crew would have had more than enough time to make their escape."

Blake said, "I'd like to see the expression on Grigsby's face when he finds out the truck was loaded with lead. He's probably wondering how his plan went awry."

"They weren't prepared for what happened," Adrian mused. "Instead of eliminating the resistance with two phone calls and waltzing off into the night with a truck full of gold, they found themselves in a shootout." He turned to stare at the truck that still smoldered and the bodies on the roadway. He muttered, "In the end it was their plan, not mine, that ended up on the dung heap."

Adrian made numerous calls, but the fruits of one showed up about an hour later. Eddie bounced from one side of the road to the other taking pictures. He had his story, an exclusive, and the photos to go with it. Adrian figured it was the least he could do.

When Cat saw him, she groaned. "Damn, we'll never get rid of him."

Adrian grinned, and said, "If I remember right, it was you who suggested we bring him along."

She glared at him.

Adrian added, "But I don't think you need to worry. We get to leave and go back to D.C."

Au79

Epilogue

A week later

Cat and Blake had returned to Washington. Lance was back in Alabama at TEDAC. Before Adrian could wrap up the investigation, he had one final task. They'd found the inside man. He and Tracy along with two patrol officers were on their way to arrest him.

As the four walked into his office, he looked up, his face tired and drawn. He appeared to have aged at least ten years since Adrian last saw him.

Seeing the gun in Tracy's hand, he said, "That's not necessary."

She ignored him.

His gaze shifted to Adrian. "As soon as I saw the news, I knew this was coming. I've been expecting you."

"Why?' Adrian asked.

His voice bitter, he said, "I've been stuck here for the last twenty-five years. Passed over for promotion time and time again. The last several months, I've been getting subtle hints it's time to retire. No rewards, just get the hell out."

He sighed and twisted slightly to look out the window behind him. "Well, they got what they wanted. I retired yesterday. The bureau won't be able to take away my pension. At least my wife will have that, for what it's worth."

His head turned to look at Adrian. "It was a foolproof plan. I could control the investigation." He grunted in disgust. "Then you showed up and it started going downhill. How'd you figure it out?"

"Too many connections, the bridges, three other thefts of explosives."

"Christ, you found those?"

Adrian nodded. "Then there was the homicides and the business with the reporter."

"That was Reynolds, the arrogant bastard. He couldn't stick to the plan, had to change it. Improvise as he called it. He leaked the planted evidence because he wanted to make a statement. How'd you snap on the gold shipment?"

"Tracy found a note in the stuff we removed from Morris' house. Written on it was a weight. Turned out it was the weight of a gold bar. Nicki and Scott put it together with the help of Vance Whitaker and the President."

Adrian glanced at Tracy. Her jaw was tight with anger, but her hands never wavered as she aimed her semi-automatic at the man behind the desk. "Tracy."

She said, "Cuff him." The officer standing next to her reached for his handcuffs. With a sense of grim satisfaction, she said, "Karl Chambers. Stand up and put your hands behind your back. You are under arrest. You have the right to remain silent …"

Karl's hand dropped to his lap and brought up a gun. Tracy pulled the trigger. The sound of the shot was deafening. The gun dropped to the floor as Karl fell forward onto the desk. Tracy holstered her weapon. The patrol officer stepped to the desk to check for a pulse. He shook his head no.

Adrian stared at the body sprawled across the desk. Karl Chambers had been liked and respected in the community he served. But it hadn't been enough.

Footsteps pounded down the hall. Matt and Randy stopped in the doorway, then turned and walked away.

Au79

Tracy ordered one of the patrol officers to wait in the hallway, then headed outside, followed by Adrian and the second officer. She reached for her phone and called the dispatcher.

While he waited for her to finish, Adrian leaned against the side of the car, thinking about what he'd discovered the last few days.

Grigsby rolled over in exchange for a reduced sentence. Karl had helped Grigsby with a couple of arms deals. Turned out to be the ones that alerted Stuart. Using Reynolds' group, Grigsby would supply the manpower.

Karl came up with the plan to use the planted truck and blow up the convoy. He'd found out about the shipment from the owner of the trucking company used by the depository. Several years back, he and the owner became friends during an investigation of the theft of two of the company's trucks. Occasionally, they'd meet to play a round of golf and have dinner. During one of the get-togethers, the owner mentioned the shipment of gold bullion headed to Texas. Karl set up the fake identification for Warden and Meyers. The owner was an innocent dupe, who hired the men on Karl's recommendation.

Adrian's supposition had been right. Plant the evidence pointing to Stuart as the ringleader, then kill him in the truck explosion. Tracy was an added bonus. Karl had counterfeit documents to get the truck across the Mexican border. The gold would have been sold on the black market.

Beside him, Tracy leaned against the car. "Doc Kennedy's on his way. This time, I called my Captain to let him know what happened."

Adrian chuckled. He knew Rodriguez had ripped her up one side and down the other for the idiocy of her actions, before he issued her a commendation. How could you fire or even suspend someone who received a letter of appreciation from the President of the United States?

"How's Stuart?"

"Physically, he's better. Mentally, not so much. He appreciated you stopping by and talking to him."

When Adrian realized it was Karl who was involved, he'd gone to the hospital. He didn't want Stuart to hear it on the news or from some idle chatter. When he learned his boss not only sanctioned his kidnapping but planned to kill him, Stuart was devastated. Adrian could see and hear Stuart's bitterness at the betrayal.

"Tracy, it's going to be difficult for him."

She looked at Adrian. Her eyes filled with tears. There was still a trace of bruises on her face. He wanted to reach out and smooth them away but knew he couldn't.

"I know. He's already talking about resigning and moving back to Ohio. I'm not sure where we're headed or even what it means for us." She sniffed and blinked, pushing back the tears.

"What about you? Are you doing okay," he asked.

"Me? Why wouldn't I be? All I got was a few bruises."

"That's not what I'm talking about, and you know it." He motioned with his head toward the ATF building.

Tracy sighed. "I didn't have a choice. We both know that. So, yes, I am. If he had won the day, a lot of good people would be dead. That's what I want to remember. He didn't win, we did. What's next for you?"

Satisfied with what he saw in her eyes, he said, "Back to Washington, and on to the next assignment."

"Hmm ..." she mused, her toe scuffed the ground. "I'm not much good at goodbyes. I had the same problem when your three cohorts in crime left. This is even harder. I'm glad you were assigned to the case."

He chuckled. "It sure didn't seem that way when we met."

"I guess I was a bit rough on you."

"Hell, you pointed a damn gun at me and threatened to throw me in jail."

"I did, didn't I?" Laughter erupted.

Police cars pulled into the parking lot. He eyed them, then said, "If you ever get to Washington, give me a call."

Au 79

A grin crossed her face. "Maybe I will. And if you ever get back this way, you call me. I'd better get this wrapped up. I still have to make one more rescue."

Mystified, he said, "Who?"

"Not who, but what. A dog. To be more precise, Morris' dog. When animal control picked him up, I told them to hang on to him. A friend has been telling me for some time I need a dog."

He laughed as he watched her walk away. She was an amazing woman, and deep in his gut, he knew there would be a day when their paths would cross again.

Washington D.C.

Scott tilted his chair back and propped his feet. A cup of hot coffee sat within easy reach of the hand resting on the arm of the chair. For the moment, he was content.

He'd finally finished the reports on the investigation. The agents injured in the shootout would recover. No innocent bystander was hurt or killed.

The gold owned by the University of Texas and Texas A&M University was safely in the vaults at the Texas Gold Depository. Yesterday, it shipped with nary a problem. Bracken hired a different trucking company.

Nicki tapped on his door. "You ready for this?" Her eyes twinkled with a look of glee.

"What?" His feet dropped to the floor.

"I subscribed to the Laredo Observer and didn't cancel it. This just came in." She handed him a copy she had printed.

The headline read, "Investigative Reporter, Eddie Owens, Saves Texas Gold." The article described how Eddie, at great risk to his own life, saved a local detective and ATF agent from certain death and foiled a plot to steal a billion dollars in gold bullion. In the picture, Owens held up a letter from President Larkin. The kid had a grin that went from ear to ear.

Scott roared with laughter.

Cat stepped into the doorway. "What's going on?"

Scott said, "Have you seen this?" He handed her the article.

As she scanned it, a look of horror crossed her face. "Oh, no! This must be why I got an email from Eddie. He wants to visit Washington and wanted to know if I had access to the White House?"

Nicki said, "Admirer?"

Cat sniffed in dismay. "More like a pain-in-the-ass."

Nicki and Scott's laughter erupted.

"You may think it's funny now, but you don't know this kid. If I don't figure out how to stop him, we may never get rid of him."

She tossed the article on the desk and rushed out of the room.

****

Thank you for taking the time to read *A u 7 9*. I hope you enjoyed the plot and characters.

Best Wishes

Anita Dickason

Au79

The Story Behind the Fiction

Texas Bullion Depository

In 2013, Texas State Representative Giovanni Capriglione proposed the development of a Texas gold depository. Texas lawmakers had evinced an interest in moving the gold assets of the University of Texas and Texas A&M University from New York City to Texas. The gold, managed by the University of Texas/Texas A&M Investment Management Company (UTIMCO), was valued at close to a billion dollars.

On June 12, 2015, Texas Governor Greg Abbott signed into law, the Texas Bullion Depository Bill.

"Today I signed HB 483 to provide a secure facility for the State of Texas, state agencies and Texas citizens to store gold bullion and other precious metals. With the passage of this bill, the Texas Bullion Depository will become the first state-level facility of its kind in the nation, increasing the security and stability of our gold reserves and keeping taxpayer funds from leaving Texas to pay for fees to store gold in facilities outside our state." - Texas Governor Greg Abbott

The location of the Texas Bullion Depository is in Leander, a city northwest of Austin, Texas. Construction is expected to be completed in 2018.

https://www.texasbulliondepository.gov/

For information on the Author, please turn the page.

305

About the Author

Anita Dickason is a retired Dallas Police Officer with a total of twenty-seven years of law enforcement experience, twenty-two with Dallas PD. She served as a patrol officer, undercover narcotics officer, advanced accident investigator, tactical officer and first female sniper on the Dallas SWAT team.

Awards

Law Enforcement Professional Achievement Award—State of Texas, House of Representatives

Officer of the Year—Texas Women in Law Enforcement

Officer of the Year—International Association of Women in Police

Runner-up Officer of the Year—Dallas Police Department

Officer of the Month—Dallas Police Department

Multiple Police Commendations, Certificates of Merit and citizen/business commendations from the Dallas Police Department and the Dallas community.

Instructor Certifications

Texas Commission on Law Enforcement
National Highway Traffic Safety Administration.
Defensive Tactics
Batons
Spontaneous Knife Defense
Field Sobriety Procedures
Drug Recognition Expert program
Advanced Accident Investigation.

Au79

She is a Past President of Texas Women in Law Enforcement, and Past Treasurer for the International Association of Women in Police.

Anita's first book, *JFK Assassination Eyewitness: Rush to Conspiracy*, is non-fiction and details her reconstruction of a 1966 vehicle accident near Midlothian, Texas that killed a key witness to the Kennedy assassination. The project opened the door to a new career, Author and Publisher. She owns Mystic Circle Books & Designs, LLC and provides manuscript and design services, helping other authors turn their manuscripts into a published book.

Her fictional works are suspense/thrillers, and her plots are drawn from her extensive law enforcement knowledge and experience. Characters with unexpected skills, that extra edge for overcoming danger and adversity, have always intrigued her. Her infatuation with ancient myths and legends of Native American Indians, and Scottish and Irish folklore creates the backdrop for her characters.

www.anitadickason.com

25336678R00172

Made in the USA
Columbia, SC
30 August 2018